The Moon In the cards

Lisa J. Hogan

The Moon in the Cards

Zelda Harcrow Series, Volume 2

Lisa Hogan

Published by Lisa Hogan, 2024.

THE MOON IN THE CARDS

First edition. March 29, 2024.

ISBN: 978-1732471740

Written by Lisa Hogan.

To my husband Dan

To my readers

and to my writing companion Kiki

Prologue

In a lab lit only by the outside hall, a body lies on the floor, its features unremarkable in the gloom. Moving swiftly, a figure rummages through the poor soul's pockets, ripping fabric in their haste.

No luck.

Glancing at a ticking clock, the sneak thief dashes to the nearby table and rifles through stacks of folders without care, their neck throbbing with tension. They leap for the file cabinets along the side of the room, tearing out file after file in a frenzy.

All too aware of the passage of time, their desperation mounts as the search continues to yield nothing. Their breathing grows shallower, and they cast a panicked eye over the room.

Their breath hitches when their eye catches on a satchel tossed carelessly under the table.

In nothing flat, the distressed sneak snatches up the bag and searches through it, only to stop and stare at a single piece of paper. Folding the paper with care, the figure places the prize in their pocket, looks at the ticking clock one last time, and leaves, making sure the door locks behind them.

"I WANT TO KNOW WHERE all those credits went!" a woman screams in anger. "You cannot keep things from me. No more secrets."

"It's nothing to concern yourself with!" snaps the subject of her ire. "The credits, plus more, will be back in the accounts by next turn."

Before she can retort, an enormous boom rocks them. Alarms blare from the back building that houses the factory and laboratories.

Arguments forgotten, the two rush out of the office, down the hall and stairs, and out the back door, just in time to witness the collapse of the outside brick wall on the second floor of the laboratories building. Fire shoots through the hole, flames licking the outer brick wall as tears of dread run down the woman's cheeks.

The man rubs his face and shakes his head as the Safety Council's Fire Brigade arrives on the scene. He leaves one hand covering his mouth as his other dangles at his side, clenched around a piece of parchment.

Wiping the burning smoke and mascara from her eyes, the woman pulls her wireless from the pocket of her lab coat and dials.

A woman answers. "Hello, dah-ling."

"I need help. Now. Find Zelda."

Chapter One

In an instant, I swing my forearm up, blocking the punch of my muscular opponent. As it makes contact, I let my fist fly toward his nose.

I hit air. "Dang. You ducked."

My back hits the hot, gritty sand as a firm hand pulls my ankle out from under me, knocking the air from my lungs.

"Ow."

Struggling to catch my breath, I stare up at the big orange-yellow ball in the sky, squinting against its fierce light. When a shadow looms over me, I switch my gaze to my opponent's face and stick out my tongue.

"That's not pretty," he says.

"Thbbtt." I give him the raspberries.

"You should use this opportunity to throw sand in my face." He holds out his hand wiggling his fingers to encourage me to get up off my butt.

"Well, that would be rude, first off. Secondly, I don't want to get up." Despite my complaint, I take his hand, grateful for the boost back to my feet.

"When defending yourself, you must use everything at your disposal. Sand, a chair, a vase—anything that's handy. You must disable your opponent and get to safety."

"I know, I know, I know. You must've said it a hundred times."

My large, handsome companion crosses his arms and eyes me expectantly. "Then why don't you listen, Zelda?"

"I need a drink." Turning, I walk up the beach, leaving my—not exactly sure what to call him, honestly—to catch up.

My name is Dr. Zelda Harcrow. It's important to note that I am on a self-imposed sabbatical. I'm an alchemist, a scientist . . . and a little broken. My mother thinks I need a husband, or at least she used to. Meanwhile, my father, Titus Harcrow, president of Harcrow Alchemy Inc., thinks I'm the very link between the imaginable and the unbelievable.

However, I'm a little angry at my father right now.

3

Okay, scratch that; I'm downright pissed off. He put me in loads of danger and almost got me killed or kidnapped—I'm not even sure which would have been worse. So I decided to take a break from him, HA, my lab, my work, and my life.

I've needed time to heal.

"Wait up."

Stopping, I turn, hands on my hips, and watch Jean jog toward me. I met Jean during the first part of my sabbatical while skiing on the slopes of Mount Hutton. One night, while six sheets to the wind, I blabbed to him all the sordid details of my life and jumped in the sack with him. We've been hanging out ever since.

"Hurry up. It's getting hotter out here."

The sun glistens off the perspiration of the shaved head, creases and dimples present themselves on his face as he smiles at me. "You drink too much. You really should stop."

"I'll do anything you say," I tease. "In fact, I'll stop right now. But I must be going to get that drink now." Turning, I continue trudging up the beach toward the bar and libations.

"Zelda, I don't think Marta will be happy to see you, especially after the mess you made behind her bar with that exploding drink."

I chuckle to myself, pretty sure it's not the exploding drink. Instead, I think she has a thing for Jean and doesn't like that he stuck to me like glue. And who could blame her? His bronze body is muscular and robust, his eyes a smoky quartz, and his teeth as white as pearls straight from an oyster.

Marta's pub sits right on the edge of the red sand beach, its back deck facing the ocean and the enclosed area fronting the road. Coming up from the beach, we hop up on the raised deck, only to find all the chairs sitting upside down on the little wooden tables. It appears the bar has not yet opened.

No problem.

I make my way behind the bar, which is built from bamboo and dried palm fronds. "What's your poison?" I ask Jean.

"Too early for me."

I shrug. "Fine. Be that way." Picking up bottle after bottle, I pour different liquors into a clean cocktail shaker. Jean narrows his eyes. "Don't give me that look. I have this now." Shaking my head, I scoop ice into the shaker and put on the lid. "Jeepers, it was a fluke. How many times can one particular drink combination explode on someone?"

Jean leans his head to one side. "Zelda, I think you should get out from behind the bar."

"What? Why?"

The sound of a clearing throat interrupts my attempt to create a fabulous new cocktail. "What are you doing?" demands a gravelly voice.

Futz. Startled, I swing around to face the pub owner Marta and raise my hands placatingly, ready to apologize. Without warning, the cocktail shaker in my left hand explodes, the lid flying off to hit Marta between the eyes. As Marta's expression morphs into disbelief, the sugary, sticky contents of the cocktail I was making quickly follow, and she's left standing there in a daze, soaked and dripping syrupy liquor.

"Jeepers creepers, Marta. I am so sorry."

Marta's face turns a shade of red I would have thought impossible with her dark skin tone, and the veins in her forehead and neck begin to pop out. "You . . . you . . . bit—"

Dropping the cocktail shaker, I make a mad dash up and over the bar, landing in Jean's perfect, bulging arms. "We better make a run for it."

He drops me to my feet, and we skedaddle out through the front of the pub and onto the street.

Jean glances back at the pub. "I don't think we should visit there for a while. I don't think we would be too welcome."

I take his hand, and we trot down the street. "I don't think she would mind seeing you." Jean is picture perfect. No one would turn down time with him. "Let's head back to the house."

The house is a sweet little cottage we're renting that sits on stilts across the road from the beach. It's weatherworn, but it has a beautiful view of the ocean.

Jean is the first to break the silence on the short walk home. "Have you returned her call yet?"

"Whose call?" I ask, despite knowing darn well who he's talking about.

"Your friend Mae. Have you returned her call yet?"

"No," I answer curtly.

"She's called several times. She's said it's important."

I refuse to return Mae's calls. I'm sure she'd just try to convince me to go back to Fulcrum, back to HA. I'm not ready to forgive my father just yet, and I never want to set eyes on Inspector Greyson again. Jean keeps telling me I need to face my demons, but I still wake up in a panic sometimes—hence why I drink a little too much.

"I'll think about it," I lie, having no intention of calling her right now.

Suddenly, a whistling scream barrels toward us. Diving out of the way, we tumble over each other, and the object embeds itself in the sand in front of us.

"What in the stars is that?" yells Jean.

I climb to my feet and approach the mysterious object. "Definitely a close call."

Chapter Two

As we stare at the burning object, Jean joins me. "Is that—"

"Our dinner."

"Zelda, what have I told you about trying to cook?"

I shrug. "Not to?"

We move a little farther down the street and stop. My mouth hangs open. There is a gaping hole in the roof about the size of the pressure cooker that nearly killed us.

"I am so sorry."

"I thought we agreed that I would do the cooking. We can't keep fixing the roof every time you try to make something."

"It was supposed to be a surprise."

Jean closes his eyes, obviously trying to stay calm. "I may not survive your surprises."

"What can I do to make it up to you?" I bat my lashes in his direction.

"Call Mae." He stamps off toward the house.

I kick a stone in frustration. "Futz!" I forgot I was barefoot. After a few more expletives, I limp back to the cottage.

Jean is already inside, trying to clean cicen stew off the walls.

"Let me help. It's my fault."

Jean just gives me a dirty look.

The wireless begins to ring. "Jean, could you—" I glance at him; he's still pretty angry. "Never mind. I got it." I pick up the receiver. "Hello."

"Dah-ling, it's about time!"

"Hi, Mae." I try to act nonchalant. "How are you?"

"How am I? I've been trying to get a hold of you all string!"

"Mae, I'm not coming back. I'm just not ready." I take a breath. "Please don't ask me to."

"That's not why I'm calling, darling."

That piques my curiosity. "What's wrong?"

"Coco is in dire need of your help." Excitedly, she adds, "There was an explosion at the cosmetics lab. She thinks it might have been sabotage."

"I'm not sure how I could help. The local Legere Legalis should be able to handle it."

"Except they aren't treating it as a sabotage. They're treating it as a possible accident or worse. And there's more." Mae dramatically drops the *r*, stretching out the vowel sound.

"Well, I'm intrigued now."

"The Legere aren't treating it as sabotage from the outside, my sources tell me. They suspect someone, possibly Coco, set the explosion. And there's a victim."

"A victim?"

"Unidentified at this time. Zelda, Coco is one of our oldest and dearest friends. She needs you to prove who set the explosion, find out who the victim was, and clear Coco Cosmetics of any wrongdoing."

"Why me? What about her husband, what's his face?"

"I don't think I ever met him myself. It certainly was a surprise when she married him, but I think it's a marriage of convenience. You know Coco is the creative one. She's the one who formulates all the cosmetics and develops all the fragrances, and she's the face of the company, but running turn-to-turn operations just isn't her thing."

"Go on."

"From what I understand, her hubby is a financial genius and runs the turn-to-turn operations. I have my doubts that she is actually happy."

"I don't know, Mae." I begin giving her my excuses, but for every excuse I come up with, Mae provides a logical counter. "Okay, okay, okay," I finally say. "I'll help."

"Attagirl! I knew we could count on you. I've shipped trunks of clothes for you to your sister's house. You can pick them up there."

"W-wait, what?" I stutter in disbelief. "You already knew I would say yes?"

"Zelda, you are a darb of a friend. I know you would never let down anyone you hold dear."

As I hang up, I consider Mae's final words. Besides being my best friend, Mae has an uncanny gift for knowing what people want and sometimes need.

Spying my very sturdy Jean wearing a frilly apron as he cleans up the kitchen, I wonder if I'm ready to face being out on my own without my muscle. Even knowing Alexander Textrix is gone, I still wake up in cold sweats from nightmares of him pulling me through the portal to who knows where.

Looking up, Jean catches me staring. "You will be fine," he reassures me gently. "Your self-defense skills are improving every turn." Walking up to me, he puts his hands on my shoulders. "Zelda, all the training on Gaia will not heal what's in here"—he taps my temple—"or in here." He taps my chest, where my two hearts beat heavily.

"You'll miss me," I tell him.

"Yes, I will." He looks around the room. "Have you seen the broom?"

I glance aside and shrug. "Don't know. Haven't a clue." I give him a peck on the cheek. "I'm going to take a shower and pack."

I head to the bedroom, hoping Jean won't notice my deception. Technically, I wasn't lying about the broom. I'm not exactly sure where I sent it—or the tea kettle or Jean's right sandal. Never again do I want to be unprepared for facing and dealing with portals, so I've been practicing. I can create a tesseract, and I can put something through the portal, but I'm unsure if the items I've sent through arrived in one piece. Since space-time travel is illegal and even bending time is frowned upon, I haven't involved anyone else.

Eventually, if I ever make it home to my apartment, there may possibly be a few random items sitting in my living room.

I don't have much to put in my saddlebags. When I left Fulcrum and my life, I didn't have much time to pack; in fact, I didn't pack at all. I left everything behind when I drove away on my Zenith motorcycle, taking only the clothes on my back.

Once I'm set and ready to go, I call Coco to let her know I've agreed to help, much to her elation. I give her my itinerary before we end our conversation.

Next, I ring my older sister Ava. She and I don't really get along. Like all big-sister–little-sister relationships, Ava is critical and thinks I'm spoiled. I'm not even the youngest sister.

The call, however, seems friendly enough.

"Why don't you stay here in our guest room?" Ava offers.

"That's very kind of you," I respond politely.

"The kids would love to see you," Ava remarks.

Ava may be a pain, but my niece and nephew are little dolls. "I can't wait to see them. Tell them I'll bring them something sweet."

"Don't go overboard. I don't want them spoiled."

"As their aunt, it's my job to spoil them."

"Fine," she relents. "See you in a couple of turns. Be careful driving."

"Will do." Hanging up, I move to join Jean in the kitchen. "What will you do when I'm gone?"

He leads me out the door. "I'm thinking about starting a project having to do with self-defense and fitness. With the skills I learned in the Tesla Defense Division of the National Security Council, I thought I could work at some sort of spa."

"Attaboy!" I respond with enthusiasm, before growing solemn. "Jean." I tear up. "Thank you for your friendship and your companionship. Especially for giving me some tools to help me cope and feel safe again."

Jean hands me a packed lunch that he prepared. "I love you, Zelda Harcrow."

"I know."

Once I've tightened the saddlebags on the Zenith motorcycle, I straddle the cycle and drop my tinted goggles down over my peepers. There are no more words to be said between us, so I start up the Zenith and begin my two-turn journey to Capital City.

Chapter Three

S o far, the journey to Capital City has been easy enough, the weather fair and warm. The Weather Council must be working magic overtime today.

The Weather Council controls the weather in conjunction with Gaia's other countries—all except Hyde. Without the weather-working regulations we have in place, bad storms would develop; one such hurricane robbed me of my fiancé over three rotations ago. After a Hyde agent attempted to kidnap me, Hyde was expelled from the Trade Council. Ever since, Hyde has tried to work the weather to its own advantage, which undoubtedly makes our council's job harder.

Checking my mirrors, I note only a few autos keeping pace with me. Since my stomach has begun to growl, I click on my blinker and pull over to the side of the highway. "Looks like a good spot."

As the tins whiz past, I walk my iron onto the wide, grassy berm between the road and the edge of a wooded park, where I plant it and myself. The moisture of the lawn seeps into my pants. "Jeepers." Noting the time I dig into the food I brought with me. "Best make this quick." This stretch of highway has no lamps so as not to disturb the local wildlife, visibility worsens and becomes dangerous to drive. If I'm to make it to the Palms Court Motel before nightfall, I better get a wiggle on. Putting on the steam I speed toward my first destination, The Palms Court Motel.

Arriving right at dusk just as the sun star disappears over the horizon, revealing the crescent of Biota and the bare sliver of the larger moon. The Palms Court Motel is a single-story U-shaped structure centered around a dot of a building that acts as both check-in and owner's residence. I glide to a stop in front of the sign that reads *Main Office* and eye my surroundings, attempting to get a lay of the land before I dismount.

I'd like to think I'm not paranoid, but who are we kidding? I get suspicious if the wind changes directions.

Towering palm trees line the entrance and backside of the motel, which I guess is the source of the name Palms Court. The motel itself is white stucco, and each numbered deep-green door is separated from the next by a large, square window. Posts support the wide overhang that travels the length of the building. Small bright-yellow metal sling chairs decorate the spaces between the doors and windows. Tidy narrow garden beds filled with short brightly colored plants line the sidewalk separating the rooms from the graveled parking lot.

Smacking road dust off my leather duster and dungarees, I stride into the motel office to check in. A bell tinkles as I open the wood-and-glass door.

"Hello?"

The small reception area consists of a wooden reception desk, a brochure stand sparsely filled with leaflets on local attractions, and a couple of round-backed leather-upholstered chairs the same deep green as the lodging's doors. Approaching the counter, I ring the tiny bell that occupies the otherwise-empty counter.

"Hello?" I call again. "Anybody about?"

The other side of the counter holds a paneled door with a small plaque labeled *PRIVATE* and a few cheaply framed photos that I can only guess display the owners and their family. Squeaking on its hinges, the door opens inward to reveal a wrinkly old egg.

"Checking into the inn, aye?" The old man laughs.

I examine the elderly face that inches toward me, my eyes travel to the photos on the wall. Jeepers these photos must be ancient; I say to myself. I belly up to the counter. "Yes, I'd like to register for the night."

The thin gray hair on his head stands up in every direction as if he'd just been hit by a bolt of electricity. He shakes as he walks, and he places an equally shaky hand to his ear. "What?" he says loudly.

I raise my voice as he makes his slow final approach. "I'd like to register for a room."

He squints and purses his lips. "Well, you don't have to holler. I can hear you."

The comment takes me aback. "What?"

"Are you hard of hearing? I can talk louder," the old bird yells.

I smack my forehead with my palm. Ugh. This dope's a regular cuckoo. "I can hear fine. Can I sign in?"

"Why didn't you say so?" He lifts a large ledger onto the counter for me to sign. "That'll be five credits. None of that old papery stuff—hard credits only."

Tesla is in the process of transitioning away from paper currency, adopting a credit-debit-based economy instead. For some, this has taken a bit of getting used to, but apparently, that's not the case for this old codger.

"Yes, I have my card." I hand him the paper-thin square of metal.

"Here's your key. No smoking in the rooms."

Smiling, I head out the door and hop on the Zenith. I ride it across the short distance to my room, where I park and plug it into the provided charging outlet. The Zenith has a cyclone engine, which means I can pile on the kilometers without having to recharge the battery every turn, but I'd rather not take any chances.

Grabbing my gear, I walk up to the dark-green door labeled with a gold *20*. Examining the simplistic key, I realize the motel's locks use a standard tumbler system.

One of my many talents is the ability of telekinesis. Telekinesis is a very misunderstood gift. A person cannot go around moving and lifting things all willy-nilly. It takes diligent practice, knowledge of the subject, patience, and tons of time. When I unlock a door, I move a physical system of tumblers and mechanisms. Having memorized several of the standard tumbler locks, I wave my hand to unlock the door and let it swing open.

Suddenly, a noise erupts from my stomach, and I rub it. "Yes, I hear you. I saw a diner across the road."

Chapter Four

I survey my tiny accommodations for the night. The walls are a blue so opaque it could almost pass for white. The furniture is undusted white wicker, which easily shows its age and wear with bits of broken and jagged sticks.

I toss my saddlebags on the double-wide bed as I venture farther into the room. Opposite the bed is a small glass-topped wicker desk, which is home to a chair, motel notepaper, an inked pen, and a glass ashtray. The latter is useless because, as the creaky old goat pointed out, there is "no smoking in the rooms."

Next to the desk is a narrow wooden door that can only lead one place. Turning the brass knob, I push open the door. "Guessed it right: a miniature bathroom." At least it has a tub and not just a shower stall.

Closing the door, I look toward the large picture window that faces the parking lot. "That won't do." I take the few steps over and close the drapes, plunging the room into darkness.

I immediately feel foolish for not turning on a lamp or two first. Searching for a light switch, I plow into the small wicker table and chair that live under the window.

"Ow."

Opening the drapes enough to let in the dim yellow glow of the porch lanterns, I flip on the wall switch. Then I pull the drapes fully closed once more and I feel a little more relaxed. Okay, so maybe only one muscle in my body relaxes, but it's nothing a good soak won't cure.

I open the small solid door to the bathroom again and step in. Not much can fit in such a cramped space, just a pedestal sink, a mirror, a toilet, and the shallow tub sitting under a calcium-covered showerhead sticking out of the tile wall. It's so tight in here, I would have to leave the room just to change my mind.

I shrug. It's only for one night.

Eyeing myself in the oval mirror above the sink, I pull my dusty leather skullcap and goggles off my head. I shake free my matted in need of trim bobbed hair. Usually a golden bob, it's dingy and dirty and in need of a good wash and comb. Lifting an arm, I smell my armpit – not so good – *Pee-yew!* I am in desperate need of a scrub.

My stomach angrily disagrees. A bath will have to wait. Food first.

Shoving the worn brown leather skullcap back on my head, I grab my goggles and head out the door, locking it behind me.

The bright neon lights of the diner glow pink against the night. The stars are numerous but dulled by the parking lot lights and the neon decorating the diner. The script letters of the sign read *Joe's & Moe's Diner* and travels the length of the restaurant. Long windows cover the front and are surprisingly clean for being located so close to the road.

Entering the joint, I notice the servers wear the same eye-popping pink as the neon sign and the customers are just as road grungy as me. I fit right in.

"Take a seat anywhere, doll," says a gum-cracking server.

I nod at her and sit in a booth, choosing the side facing the door. The two-sided menu I grab from the table is filled with a variety of greasy foods. I have a choice between fried this and fried that; even the vegetables are battered and fried. Normally, I would pass on this much grease, but my hunger is excruciating, so ish kabibble.

Raising my hand, I call the server over. "I'm ready."

The server wears a frilly starched white cloth headband around her wavy steel-gray bob. Her uniform is a bit baggy, and a starched white apron covers the front, toning down the bright neon pink. "What have you decided?"

The door of the diner opens, and a few weary travelers enter. Looking up briefly, I notice a couple of joes and a smarty I assume are touring together. The server, whose name tag says *Flo*, clears her throat, bringing me back to the menu.

"I'll have the patty melt with a side of batter-fried tubers, please," I say without looking up from the menu.

Flo taps her pen on her order ticket pad. "You want something to drink with that?"

"Um." I turn the menu over and glance over the choices of teas, fermented beverages, and fruit drinks. "I'll take a mug of birch beer." I place the menu across from me.

"You are expecting somebody?" She points to the menu. "I can hold your order till they get here."

"Oh, no. I'm alone." I pick up the menu and hand it to her.

"Okay, sweetie. I'll bring your drink over." Flo walks away to place my order with the fry cook.

I eye the smarty and one of the joes, who sit in a booth near the door, but their companion isn't anywhere in the diner. The smarty and her guy start having a row about something or other.

My entertainment for the evening. I chuckle.

My birch beer arrives in a nice frosty mug. "Thank you."

"You wanna bet she plows him one in the kisser any minute?" Flo jerks her head in the general direction of tonight's floor show.

"Do you know what they're arguing about?"

Flo scratches her head with the end of her pen. "Probably the same old: she thinks he's not spending enough credits on her; he thinks she's a cheating vamp."

"You really think it'll come to blows?"

"Easy-peasy. Just watch." Flo leans on the edge of my booth.

The argument escalates quickly. The gal is quite the bear cat. She's standing up to walk out of the restaurant when her guy grabs her by the wrist to pull her back. This is getting good. The dumbo starts to rise out of the booth.

Whammo! The fiery girl hauls off and belts him in the kisser. The bimbo loses his grip on his girlfriend and lands on his ass.

A bell rings a few times as the boxing match finishes, quickly followed by "Order up" from the fry cook.

"Told you," Flo says. "That'll be yours. I'll be right back." She's tortoise-like as she walks back to the kitchen.

I watch the play go on for a few more seconds as the smarty walks out of the diner, her bloody-lipped and apologetic boyfriend bringing up the rear.

Once my food arrives, I scarf down the contents of the plate as if I haven't eaten in turns. With no more excitement to witness, I notice how tired I really am. I wave Flo over for my ticket.

"Anything else, doll?"

I smile. "No, thank you. I'm good."

Flo adds up the bill and hands me the ticket. "You can pay at the register up front."

Nodding, I take the small piece of paper up to the register to pay. As I do, I notice the man I thought had come in with the bear cat and bimbo sitting at the counter, sipping at a mug of beer. Where had he gone, and when did he come back in? I give him a once-over; he doesn't look in my direction.

"Here's your receipt," says the cashier.

"Thank you," I mumble. Turning, I look at the suspicious-looking man one more time. Nondescript, dark car coat, black felt fedora, black slacks, and black wing tips. Nothing to make him stand out. He's just sitting there, nursing his beer and staring straight ahead.

My stomach grows queasy. Either my imagination is running over time, or it's just the food.

Chapter Five

What I really need for my bone-tired road-weary self is a hot bath and some shut-eye. Luckily, it's a quick hop back to my lodgings for the night.

I wave my hand across the door, but there is no click of the lock releasing. A shiver runs up and down my spine, raising an alarm in my brain. I swear I locked the door as I left.

Pivoting back to my bike, I begin to unplug it, then remember I left my saddlebags on the bed. *Dang.* I turn back to the green door. *Sigh.* Maybe I'm being silly and just overly tired.

Playing it safe, I decide to use a newly acquired, if unreliable magical ability. Magic is an interesting thing; it can be described as a vibrational intention. Magic isn't really manipulation, as many may believe. What you put your attention to, you attract. Everyone has the ability; some of us are just so connected to the universe that we can create or manifest what others cannot. Some believe it's because we have two hearts; others believe our brains are wired differently. Whatever the reason, some can wield magic, while others cannot. Magic allows me to move energy in a positive way.

Thrusting my hand forward, I push the molecules of air in front of me, forcing the door to swing open. No sound emerges from the room. Nothing. I stand still and listen for few more moments. Still quiet.

Jeepers, I must not have locked the door. I'll have to be more careful.

Cautiously, I step inside the blackened room. I immediately regret not leaving at least the floor lamp on.

I feel the grummy wall near the door. *Diddly, crappa, where is the switch?* I creep farther in, the only light available shining through the doorway from the parking lot and porch lanterns.

I begin to sweat. My chest tightens around my hearts and lungs. My breathing is labored. The trauma from less than a rotation ago haunts me. I freeze. I'm stuck like a bee-fly on flypaper.

This won't do.

"Get hold of yourself," I chastise myself out loud. Tremors of fear shake my hand. Once, I could count on my gut to let me know things. Now, a bit of nausea, and I'm in a panic.

I try to visualize calm. Not working.

Try a deep breath. Nope.

I pull a spell out of my pocket that I learned during my sabbatical to ease such situations. I whisper the spell just loud enough for me to hear.

"Locked in my body, full of fear.

My panic is static, more than I can bear.

I'm in need of reprieve so I can breathe.

Take away my fear; make it leave."

I repeat the spell. By the third time, I feel free from the panic of past trauma. Still, something gnaws at my insides like a mousacorn at a piece of cheese in a trap.

Guardedly, I move forward. I'm just beginning to make out the floor lamp next to the table and chair under the window. As my eyes grow more accustomed to the darkness, I head straight to the lamp.

I scream as two arms engulf my waist, pinning one arm against my side, and begin to lift me from the floor.

"REALLY?"

A grunt is the only response from my assailant.

My mind races. Having only one hand free is making it difficult to grab for my assailant's groin. And what if it's a woman? Sure, they're muscular, but have you seen some of the women from North Tesla? Built like brick houses.

So I need another soft, painful place, like an eye or a nose. Reaching my free arm behind me, I quickly find a very squishy eye socket.

I dig my thumb in. A scream follows, and the grip around my waist relaxes. Whipping around, I face my attacker. The dark figure is bent over, holding a gloved hand over their very sore eye. Taking the opportunity, I knee them in the face, sending them to the floor.

Wanting to leave little time for my assailant to collect their composure, I remember what Jean taught me. *Use everything at your disposal.*

I grab the floor lamp. As I try to lift it, though, I fall forward, landing on the floor with a thud, and my hand slips off the long, thin body of the fixture.

"Who the fuck bolts a lamp to the floor?"

Now upright and looming over me, my attacker shrugs. "Lamp thieves?"

Okay, they're definitely a guy—or maybe a doll with a deep baritone voice.

"A lamp thief?" I exclaim. "That's stupid."

I pop my foot out and nail him in the kneecap. He stumbles.

"That hurt!" He lunges at me.

Shuffling backward along the floor, I right myself before he can grab me again, but his hand catches the corner of my coat. Stretching to reach the desk, I fumble for anything I can use as a weapon. With a *r-rip rip*, the hem of my duster tears in the grasp of my crasher.

My hand finds the ashtray, which I bring down to meet my attacker's head, and a crack echoes through the room. *Thrack!* I guess having an ashtray in a nonsmoking joint isn't nuts after all.

Stumbling back, my opponent clutches his head and staggers out of my motel room.

I wait a moment in the small dark room, ready to defend. Hearing the hum of an electric motor and the crunch and rustle of gravel, I hesitantly follow the rushed noise outside. I watch as my injured attacker flees.

Other motel residents open doors to take a gander at the commotion. Just as quickly as they open, they close. Except for one, my next-door neighbor.

"Hey, keep it down, will ya? Some of us are trying to get some shut-eye!"

I give her the stink eye. "Aw, go chase yourself!"

She responds by slamming her door shut.

I lean up against the door jamb and rub my side, hoping I didn't bruise a rib or worse. Why would someone try to hurt me? Was it an agent of Hyde? Did it have something to do with Coco? My breath is shortening; the calming spell is fading prematurely. How am I going to sleep? With one eye open?

Going back into the room, I turn on the worthless floor lamp and gather my saddlebags in a panic. "Jeepers, this is stupid. Where am I to go?" I throw up my hands. "Being out on a dark highway would just make me an easier target." I drop onto the bed, feeling slightly more grummy than earlier.

Deciding, I run to the door and open it wide. Looking first to the right and then to the left, I make sure the parking lot is clear and I won't get jumped. Pulling the Zenith into the room, I close and bolt the door. Maneuvering my bike between the table and the bed, I park her. Then I drag one of the chairs over and prop it under the door handle.

Tossing my saddlebags, a pillow, and a blanket into the bathroom, I yank the desk chair in behind me. The click of the lock on the bathroom door isn't enough; I wedge the chair under the bathroom door handle as well. Then I proceed to make myself a bed in the tub.

Tucked in with my flask, I drink till I am quite warm and numb.

———— ◉ ————

OPENING ONE EYE, I groan. A drum is banging out a very loud rhythm in my head, and I have a painful crick in my neck from spending the night in a cold porcelain tub.

I stretch out, only to bang my foot on the spigot. "Ouch!" A gurgling in the pipes is my only warning before freezing water sprays down on me from the showerhead. *Futz!*. I leap from the tub, but my foot hooks the edge of the tub. *Thud!*

Lying on the cold white penny-tile floor, I look up at the ceiling and wonder how my life got so discombobulated. I was once the most sought-after alchemist on Gaia. I had my own apartment, friends, work I loved, and the pain of loss that I could escape. Now, I'm lying fortified in a tiny bathroom, hungover, bruised, wet, and sad. No lab, no work. Sure, it was my choice to leave, but I'm no longer sure if I am running toward something or away from what happened.

Chapter Six

I down a few feverfew-and-white-willow-bark capsules with a glass of tepid water from the sink. At least the glass is clean. Stripping out of my wet clothes, I dump them on the bedding I removed from the tub. The *sritch* sound as I open up the spigot gives me hope for more of a warm experience this time.

The water hits like hot needles on my scalp and shoulders; its violent showerhead spits out searing water. It seems the shower only likes to expel freezing or scalding water. Showering as fast as my aching body and head allow, I towel off and put on the only dry clothes I have available.

Or rather, the only other clothes I have, period.

I pull up the rust-colored dungarees and button up the thick cotton long-sleeve shirt. Less than a rotation ago, I dressed with such purpose and panache. An outfit and accessory for every occasion. Sure, most occasions were spent in my lab, but dang, I was a fashionable alchemist. I even dyed my hair color to match my outfits.

Looking in the mirror, I stare at the dull pasty-golden face it reflects, surrounded by hair that no longer shimmers and shines but has the appearance of dried-out hay. I have maintained my eyebrows, though, so there is that.

I gather my things and strap my saddlebags onto my dear Zenith. After removing the barricade from the door, I back my cycle out into the parking lot to continue my journey north to Capital City.

I was supposed to stop one more evening, but after last night, I'm thinking better of it. I would rather drive straight through.

My Zenith is a beaut. Steel, black, and chrome. Clean lines and enclosed bodywork, pressed-steel bridge frame sleek and beautiful. The chrome top houses a cyclone engine, solar and electric power heating water to create the steam that powers the bike. With the help of the tinkers at HA, I refurbished and rebuilt this iron. I also have a breezer, a yellow electric roadster, but it sits back home in Fulcrum. The Zenith, with her graceful, elegant, flowing lines and curves, is my favorite mode of transportation.

The change in itinerary will put me in Capital City in the evening. Originally, I was to meet with Coco tomorrow morning and have her take me to the scene of the explosion. Instead, I'll drive to the factory tonight and call her when I arrive.

If her predicament was caused by sabotage and not a horrific accident, then the attack on me might possibly have been someone trying to stop my arrival. I don't want anyone tipping off any notorious individuals about my travel plans.

Keeping a keen lookout for any torpedoes, I hop on the highway. I've been chased down on a freeway before, almost laying down my iron on the Industria 2 at high speeds. Not something I plan on reliving.

I arrive on the outskirts of Capital City in the early evening, driving past pastures and agricultural farmland that help feed Capital City and parts of Tesla. Spotted cattle graze in the long purple grasses. Ochre grains flow and wave like rivers as I speed past.

Almost five hundred kilometers wide and just as long, Capital City occupies a valley of rolling hill country around the Forel River. Surrounding the bustling city are farms and suburbs. Driving through from the south, I pass the lavish country estates around Lake Evelyn to the east; this is where my sister Ava and her family reside. Farther north are additional suburbs, where the more modest-income folk live.

I turn toward the western outskirts of the capital. The entire area, northwest to southwest, is industrial. Coco gave me decent directions when I started out little more than a turn ago.

I pull up to Coco Cosmetics. Glass panels front the building from ground to roof line. Entering through the brass-framed glass doors, I look around and up; it's dazzling. The lobby ceiling is an oval dome capped with a stained-glass oculus to let in the light and add greater dimension to the lobby's ceiling. From the ceiling hang large posters of faces from every walk of life wearing the array of cosmetics Coco's company manufactures. The evening light misses the stained glass, giving the lobby a quiet, eerie, empty feel.

It appears that personnel are gone for the turn. The lobby is empty except for a lone security guard behind a small circular stand in the middle of the hall. My dusty riding boots make a *clappity-clap* sound on the speckled terrazzo floor as I approach.

"Hello, I'm here to see Coco."

The security guard peers up from a crossword puzzle he's working on. "I'm sorry. Dr. Charden is gone for the turn. You can call and make an appointment with her assistant tomorrow."

"I'm Dr. Harcrow. Coco asked me to come look at the damage in the factory."

"Sorry, but it's now after hours; the staff are gone. As I said, you'll have to call tomorrow to make an appointment." His head dips back down, and he continues his puzzle.

Crap. Well, I don't need a guided tour. I've been on the road all turn, and cranky is a generous way to describe my demeanor. I lean on the counter. "Do you think I could pop back to the factory and take a gander at the mess?"

"I am sorry, Dr. Harcrow, but that area is off limits to all but employees and now the Legere Legalis." He doesn't even look up from his paper this time.

I sigh a very long drawn-out breath. "Well, can I at least use the facilities?"

"Well—"

"I've been on the road a long time without stopping." I shift from foot to foot to help get the point across. I mean, who doesn't know the potty dance?

He sighs in surrender. "Fine. Behind me down the corridor, past the lifts, and to your left."

"Thank you. You are a darb of a joe for helping a lady out."

He just nods.

I make my way down the short hall past the two sets of lifts to the back of the building. At the very end of the hall is a glass double door that leads out to an open breezeway connecting the office building to the factory building.

I make a left, as if heading to the toilets, and glance back to see if the security guard is watching. He isn't. Aren't I a lucky gal? Veering back to my previous path, I exit out the double door.

The breezeway opens onto a courtyard. Picnic benches dot the weed-filled lawn. Litter around the benches proves that the courtyard's primary use is for employees to take smoke breaks to puff away on their gaspers.

Shadowed by the breezeway's canopy, I walk straight ahead toward the single glass door that leads into the back of the factory. The cosmetic factory and office building are set on the same land, only connected by the open breezeway. Separately, each building maintains its own main entrances. I'm hoping this side of the building doesn't have any security.

Chapter Seven

I haven't been to the factory since it opened about three rotations ago, but as I recall, each of its three floors houses the manufacturing of cosmetics on one side of the building and laboratories on the other. The offices were originally also in this building, but with the newly built office building, the entire first, second, and third floors of this half of the factory became exclusively laboratories.

Back then, I came in the front entrance. Now, I'm sneaking in the back.

I enter a small vestibule, clean but worn; the factory is a bit older than the fancy modern office building.

On one side of the vestibule are metal doors and a large metal sign with large reflective neon-red letters that read *Caution: Please Wear Safety Gear upon Entering the Manufacturing Area.* Obviously, that's the manufacturing entrance. To the left of the metal doors is a set of wide stairs that I assume lead to the other manufacturing floors.

On the right side of the vestibule is a set of solid wood doors that indicate a laboratory setting. To the right of the doors is another stairwell that leads up. I try the wooden doors.

Locked.

I decide to climb the stairs on the laboratory side of the building, hoping I'll find my way to the damaged laboratory, the location of which is the one thing I didn't ask Coco about.

The second floor is an open corridor lined on either side with closed frosted-glass doors. I could continue up the next set of stairs to the third floor or investigate here. Choosing to get a lay of the land and make sure no one else is lurking, I scan the hall. No movement. It seems everyone has gone for the turn.

I climb the stairs to the third floor. Again, not a peep; I am alone.

Galloping back down to the second floor, I begin my search, trying each door I come to as I walk down the empty hall. The hall is dimly lit with small recess lighting in the ceiling, a big contrast to what I was used to at my family's company in Fulcrum. Harcrow Alchemy was so brightly lit everywhere, it always seemed like a cheery place to be. A shiver creeps up from my tailbone as I remember my last turn there and my close call with the big sleep—or perhaps something even more gruesome.

The dim lighting and lack of people noise—the sounds of people bustling about, conversations held between colleagues, the tinkling of glass test tubes—lends the building a sense that, at any moment, something's going to jump out.

Gives me the heebie-jeebies.

The only sound I do hear is a creepy flappy noise, like a ripped flag waving in the wind. Cautiously, I follow the sound down the hall.

In the very back corner, I find it—a lab lit only by the hall lamps. Most of the debris appears to have been removed, but some burnt paper and broken and melted glass still litter the floor. The outer wall is marked by a large hole covered by a blue tarp that waves in the slight breeze.

I visually take in the room. A wall clock hangs above the door behind me, its gears still moving, ticking away, unharmed by the explosion. The inside wall is scarred and covered in soot. My eyes follow the adjoining wall, which slowly transitions from soot smudged to charred black, and ends abruptly in blue. The tarp-covered hole encompasses the corner where the two outside walls meet and part of the wood-planked floor. The point of origin I determine as I continue to follow the walls around the room.

It's dark outside, and the hall lights are anemic. Pulling out a thin cylinder a few centimeters long, I shake it for a few seconds and then push the little rubber-covered button on the bottom. A clean white light shines out the other end, illuminating any area I choose. Slowly, starting at the edge of the blast site, I move my light over the scene, looking for anything the investigators may have missed. Squatting down, I swipe my fingers across the burnt flooring and bring them to my nose. Sniffing, I try to determine what I'm smelling. It smells a little musty, but without a COORS machine, I can't be sure what combination of chemicals could have blown a hole in this lab. I'll need to know what was being developed here before I can draw any conclusions.

Standing back up, I continue my investigation, slowly moving my light back and forth and up and down the floor.

A flash of reflection catches my eye. Backtracking with my light, I spy a bluish-white material no more than a centimeter in diameter lying partially covered by a splinter of wood. Bending down, I carefully dust away the splinter and take a closer look at the small fragment. No bigger than a fingernail, it looks like smoke frozen in time.

Fascinating.

Reaching into the inside breast pocket of my duster, I pull out a hinged wooden case. I fumble with the latch, and as the case easily opens, I smile at my treasure.

Inside lies a set of magnifying glasses that I created based on a terrific pair of goggles owned by Tick Croft, Head Tinker at HA. Tinkers are some of the most ingenious people you will ever meet when it comes to machinery and gadgets, and Tick is the best in Tesla. I've known Tick for most of my life; he's a bit short and a bit pudgy, and he smells of grease and acetone, but I can always count on him to bring a smile to my face. He wouldn't have wanted me to set my creative and curious nature on the back burner just because I'm on sabbatical.

Hence, my treasure.

The first lens is about 1.5x magnification. Flip the next lens over, and it increases the magnification to 3x. Another set of lenses flip over to increase another 2x magnification, with two more lenses increasing it up to 10x magnification. This works better than my old fuddy-duddy handheld magnifying glass, which only goes up to 5x magnification and requires the use of at least one hand. I still carry it in my coat pocket, though; old habits die hard.

Placing the spectacles on my face, I peer at the piece of debris. I flip the next lens over to get a better view. The springs click as I continue flipping over lenses, till I'm at full magnification. The substance is solid yet extremely porous; the density must be incredibly low.

"I've never seen anything like this." I poke at it with a thin splinter of wood. "I wonder if this was accidentally created during the explosion." I poke at it again. "A solid cloud."

"A solid what?" says someone behind me.

A little yelp escapes my throat, and I collapse onto my behind. "Oof." Lifting my head, I see a large blurry figure with huge eyes come at me. I squeal.

"You may want to take off the glasses, Dr. Harcrow," says the blob.

I reach up to my face. "Oh," I say with some embarrassment. "I forgot I had them on." I remove my fancy goggles.

"Dr. Harcrow, what are you doing here?"

I stare, unable to believe my eyes. Constable Ethan Hodge holds out a hand to help me up.

Glancing at my discovery, I shift from my butt to my hands and knees, palming the frozen smoke. Giving him my free hand, I pocket my prize with my other.

"What are you doing here?" Releasing my hand, he wipes the grime that transferred from my paws onto his slacks. "I thought you were on sabbatical?"

"I was." I brush the ash off my hands as well. "I mean, I am. I'm helping my friend Coco. But what are you doing here? Did you transfer here?"

"Sort of. I'm now FCI Ethan Hodge." He puffs out his chest in pride.

I raise an eyebrow. "FCI?"

His chest puffs out further. "Forensic Criminal Investigator."

I smile. "Really?"

"All thanks to you and your family."

Astonished, I put a hand to my chest. "Me?"

"If you hadn't introduced me to your father, I wouldn't have received the necessary training, and there would be no Forensics Unit."

At least my father got one thing right out of that whole fiasco.

Hodge's expression becomes more serious. "How are you doing?"

"Fine."

"Really?"

I just stare at him. I can barely handle how I'm coping. How am I supposed to share that with a virtual stranger?

Hodge cocks his head. His once-blond hair is now an intense white, which makes the green in his playful blue-green eyes stand out. I can't tell if he thinks I'm full of it, but he smiles softly and nods, accepting my answer.

"So, Doctor, how do you know Dr. Coco Charden?"

"University. Are you investigating this as a crime?"

"Why do you say that?"

"I hear they found a body."

"Yes, there was a victim."

He doesn't expound any further, so I decide to prod him.

"What have you found so far?"

"Doctor—"

"And who are you?" demands an authoritative yet shrill voice. A tall woman walks in. Her short slicked-back bob is black as onyx, her eyes almost as dark. Her skin is the color of paste, which makes the red lipstick on her lips look like blood.

"Inspector Zex, let me introduce you to Dr. Zelda Harcrow." Hodge extends his palm toward me in a sweeping motion.

I give her a once-over. She wears a white long-sleeve dress shirt with a thin black tie, black suspenders, skinny black trousers, and shiny black rubber-soled wing tips. Her finger hooks a black blazer over her shoulder.

"I don't care who she is," says the imposing woman.

"Dr. Charden asked her here."

"I said I don't care." She looks at me and thumbs toward the door. "Beat it."

"Coco asked me to look into the accident," I say, addressing the inspector. "No offense to Hodge here, but I have much more experience in matters such as these."

She thumbs to the door more violently. "Are you deaf? Beat it. I don't care who you are."

Hodge starts to say something in my defense, but I put my hand up to silence him, narrowing my eyes at Zex. "I'm going. I'm going."

Pausing in front of Hodge, I slip him a card from my pocket and mouth, "Call me."

He nods.

Walking past the inspector, and I purposely bump her shoulder with mine. I don't excuse myself; I just keep walking.

I leave the way I came. The security guard is nowhere to be seen. I don't think he even looked for me. Then again, maybe he did; I don't know. All I can say is, anyone could get in or out without issue. Someone could've set the explosion and gone without being noticed.

Hopping on my bike, I start her up and take off toward the house of my elder sister, Ava. I take a deep breath. This should be fun.

I have three siblings. My younger sister, Phrennie, is at the university on Trade Island. My elder brother, Ephron, is the CEO of Harcrow Alchemy Inc., our family company. The eldest in our family is Ava.

Ava used to work at HA, as all our family has. She trained as an alchemist, but Father said she lacked the necessary imagination to be an alchemist, which didn't go over well with her. When I joined HA as an alchemist and was hitting it out of the park with almost every idea I came up with, it sent her over the edge. She married the first joe she became attached to and moved to Capital City, leaving HA and the company in Fulcrum behind her. Strangely, she blames me, and not Father, for her demotion.

She isn't my biggest fan, to say the least. Now, since she thinks I've turned on good old Father and split the family, I'm tops on her shit list. So it came as quite the surprise that she invited me to stay at her home.

This is going to be one awkward visit.

I motor across Capital City. Unlike Fulcrum, which is set up in circles and curves—mathematical perfection—Capital City is set up in a weird grid, with uneven diagonal roads intersecting here and there. I guess it's supposed to help people get from one corner of the city to the other easily. But I see no symmetry in it, and it feels full of disarray—kind of like how my life is right now.

My journey eventually takes me out of the city and into the countryside around Lake Evelyn. Long drives line the avenue, each leading to its own gated-off mansion. The funny part is, while the idea of a gate is to keep others out, there is no fencing or walls around the properties. Magical protection barriers would be time-consuming, so it's not like those are being employed either.

Must be for aesthetics. Though, really, you never know with the well-to-do.

Finding Ava's drive, I turn up it. Thankfully, my sister is not a dumb dora and doesn't bother with a gate; however, she does have an iron fence around the property. I pull up to the modern-built joint, which is surprisingly modest for the area. I slow to a stop in front of a well-lit red stone pathway that leads to matching red stone stairs. The home itself is white stone and stucco, with the lower three meters covered in large rough gray brick.

The lawn and garden surrounding the home appear meticulously kept. Lush grasses, perfectly sheared hedges, and sternly pruned rosebushes—nothing out of place.

The round covered porch is partially walled. Standing before the door, I take a deep breath. I haven't seen my sister in over two rotations. My niece and nephew, yes, when they came to stay with my parents on occasion, but not my sister, nor her milquetoast hubby.

A pull cord hangs next to the large wooden door. The door itself is rounded at the top and has roses and vines carved vertically down the door. A sign above the pull cord reads, *Ring bell only once.*

Well, that's specific and a bit weird. So of course, I pull the cord twice.

The door yanks open. I expect to see a butler or a maid. Instead, I get my sister.

"Hello."

"Can't you read?" my sister snaps.

I grin mischievously. "Ab-so-lute-ly."

Her eyes narrow. "Then why did you pull the cord twice?"

"Why were you waiting for me to pull the cord when you were standing on the other side of the door?"

She doesn't answer.

"Nice to see you," I say.

She stands aside and ushers me in. "You're early."

I walk past her into the foyer.

The foyer is small but seems large due to the minimalist approach with the furnishings, or lack thereof. There isn't a stick but a telephone table with no telephone. An archway to my left leads into a front room of sorts and an asymmetrical fireplace that sits off-center on the opposing wall. At a glance, I can tell it's filled with furniture: oversize sofas and chairs, with large planters scattered throughout the room and filled with fresh flowers. The furnishings are placed in such a way I doubt anyone could have a conversation unless it was through one of those monstrosities.

It dawns on me that I've never been to Ava's home before. What a sad commentary on our relationship.

I'll have to wait to see the rest of the downstairs or upstairs. We pass the stairs that lie ahead and toward a nearby archway that leads into another area of the home.

As Ava leads me through her house, she speaks to me over her shoulder. "Mae sent trunks for you."

"I heard."

"Why?"

"Because I have no clothing."

"That's a poor excuse."

"I drive a motorcycle," I defend. "There isn't much room for trunks of clothing."

"Ha."

"What's that supposed to mean?"

I follow her past the stairs, through the arch, and around a sharp corner to the front of the house.

"Here is your room. You have your own water closet and wardrobe. There is a built-in dressing table." She points straight ahead to a half-circle bench and table of white stucco concrete that are attached to a full-length mirror on the wall.

"Nice."

"Thank you." She motions with an outstretched arm. "Your trunks."

I nod.

"The door next to your room is the bathing room and an additional water closet." She walks down the short hall, opens the door, and closes it again before I can get a gander. "Continue ahead down the hall to find the kitchen. Dinner is promptly at eight in the evening, which you missed. Breakfast is between seven and eight in the morning, then Hazel cleans up. Hazel doesn't live here and has lots to do, so please don't get underfoot or in her way."

"Okay, got it. Leave maid alone." I have got to get out of here, into a hotel or something. Geez Louise.

"The kids are sleeping. You can see them in the morning," she adds.

"Terrific. Looking forward to seeing them. I bet they've done some growing since I've seen them last." I try on the loving-aunty cap.

My sister's expression doesn't change; she just sighs, turns, and walks away. I stand there, mouth open catching bee-flies. I hear her feet hit the stairs. Suddenly, all the lights in the house go out. Now, not only am I standing with my mouth wide open in disbelief, I'm also doing it in the dark.

Okey dokey, I guess it's bedtime. Reaching out to the wall, I drag my fingers as I try to sense my way back to the guest room. I pat my coat, feeling for my small light, as I turn around and head to the room. "Which pocket did I put you?" I check the front two pockets, first one, then the other. I shuffle my feet as I continue toward the guest room.

Must be an inside pocket.

I explore my left inside breast pocket. "Aha! There you are!" As I fumble with the promising gadget, I bump my knee. *Ow!* Dropping the light, I grab my knee and hop forward, only to stub my toe into something immovable. "Oh, crap!" I fall forward, landing on my shoulder with such momentum that I flip over flat on my back.

I stare up at the dark ceiling. "I need a drink."

Flopping onto my hands and my one good knee, I gingerly crawl toward what I hope is the bed. I keep moving forward until—*thunk*, I find the bed with my head. Using the bed as a lifeline to avoid more bruises, I locate the nightstand and turn on the light.

Turning, I find that my demise was the trunks Mae had delivered, which couldn't have been placed any more centrally between the door and the bed. I give the raspberries. "Thbpt."

I grab my tiny light from the floor where I dropped it, and set it on my nightstand. Peeling off my clothes, I drop them to the floor, though not before retrieving my flask. With flask in hand, I snuggle under the covers and drink my way to dreamland.

———— ◉ ————

I WAKE UP TO THE SAVORY smells of cooked meat, sage, and marjoram. My lips widen into a smile as my peepers open. Sparkling sunlight peeks through the shades. I stretch my arms overhead and point my toes, only to jerk in pain. Grabbing my calf, I attempt to massage the cramp as my eyes water and I fight back the groans of pain trying to escape my voice box. When I finally work out the cramp, I stumble out of bed.

I reach for the ceiling and then bend at the waist, attempting to touch my unvarnished tootsies. "I really have neglected you, haven't I?" I say to my toes as I wiggle them.

Reaching up again, I put my hands on my waist and twist one way and then the other a few times. I wiggle my hips to loosen up so I can practice my self-defense kicks. Jean drummed it into my head: *Practice, practice, practice. Make it automatic, and it will save your skin one turn.*

I do practice my punches, but punching a bimbo in the chin would only give me broken knuckles, so I double up on the kicks. Moving toward the dressing table, I use the vanity mirror to keep an eye on my form. Digging my feet into the plush woolen carpet to center myself, I get into the stance Jean taught me. Bending my knees, I kick one leg out to the side, then the other, alternating. Not bad. I could possibly take out a kneecap or two.

Moving to my next stance, I practice my front kicks. I always have trouble getting them high enough and keeping my balance. Dang. I can't seem to get this. Maybe if I move over, I could see what's wrong in the mirror.

Shuffling to the side, I let my leg fly.

Too late, I realize I'm too close to the vanity, and my neglected toes hit the crystal vase full of flowers. Helplessly, I watch as the vase teeters for a millisecond, before crashing to the floor, shattering into millions of little chunks of lead glass. Among them, the flowers lie like torn corpses as the water soaks into the carpet.

With the tip of a towel from the water closet, I attempt to dry the sopping-wet spot of carpet. Gingerly, I pick up the pieces of the vase that I can find and place them on the vanity. The flowers are goners, just as I'm going to be when my sister sees this, so I chuck them in the trash.

Maybe I'll try those kicks later.

A sharp ding comes from the silver, red, and black enamel box on the nightstand, reminding me of the time. I only have an hour before breakfast will be lost to me.

I unfasten the buckles that help keep the upright trunks closed. Releasing the locks and latches, I open the steel-framed luggage. One side holds hangers full of different garments; the other side, drawers full of lingerie, scarves, and stockings. There is a separate trunk that holds shoes and another for hats, as well as a case for toiletries.

I grab the dressing case, a panty and bra set, socks, and a flannel pants outfit appropriate for the cool spring equinox weather and for motoring on my Zenith. From what I can garner, Mae did a stellar job choosing the garments I may need. I am sure there are a few standouts, but I expect that from her.

Hurrying down the hall to the bathing room, I set the dressing case on the counter and hang the clothes on the hook. Then I look at the deep porcelain tub and hum. There is no way I can resist a long hot soak in that.

I open the deep-emerald enamel dressing case. The top section carries a variety of crystal jars. I open one at a time to determine their contents: facial lotions, creams, an atomizer with perfume, talc, and just what I need—bathing bubbles.

Opening the tap to fill the tub, I pour an aromatic capful into the stream of steaming water rushing from the chrome spigot. The scent of lavender fills the room as soapy bubbles fill the bath. Stepping in, I slowly lower myself into the rising bubbles and lavender water.

I try to clear my mind to prepare myself, not only to deal with my *I have an opinion about everything* sister but mostly to help solve Coco's predicament.

Realizing I have no idea of the scope of Coco's dilemma, I sink down until the warm soapy water is up to my neck and close my eyes. I'm just pushing all thought from my mind and relaxing when my eyes pop open. Unfortunately, not from a brilliant idea but from a growled reminder from my stomach that Ava mentioned breakfast was served only till eight.

Finishing quickly, I try to dry off with a fluffy oversize salmon-pink towel. The towel looks and feels nice and plush. Sadly, it doesn't really draw the water off a gal.

Moving to the counter, I remove the front tray of the dressing case, which is full of decorative hair jewelry, clasps, and combs. From it, I retrieve a gold-plated comb and boar-hair brush, but I struggle just to comb my damn tangled hair.

I pull the soft slacks on over my undergarments and slip the matching boat-neck long-sleeve sweater blouse over my head. The deep-burnt-sienna outfit is pure comfort.

Getting the socks on is a bit of a challenge. With the pretty but crappy towel, my feet are still a bit damp, making woolen socks almost impossible to pull on. I can't seem to get the heels and toes in the right place. Ish kabibble.

Giving up on the socks and the comb, I run the brush over my locks and spritz some flowery perfume on my neck. I look at the dressing case and then at my reflection in the mirror; I really should do my face. At least lip rouge.

I shake my head. No time. Food first, war paint later.

I leave the case behind in the bathing room with all intention of returning. I ankle down the hall, past the door to the formal dining room, and through the archway into the kitchen. The kitchen is spacious and open, only a long buffet countertop separating it from a casual private dining room. The onyx granite countertop holds a few silver chafing trays.

I look up at the wall clock. Not quite eight.

Good.

I'm alone; everyone else must have already eaten. Grabbing a plain white porcelain-like plate and silverware, I open the first warming tray to reveal billowy green Gallus eggs, scrambled. Forgetting all about the broken vase and my tired, stretched face, I pile several spoonfuls onto my plate. The next one reveals a few hamon sausages, their savory aroma of sage and marjoram wafting to my nose. I inhale, taking in the pungent and sweet smells. I fork all that's left onto my plate. What can I say? I'm starving. The last covered dish is a cold serving tray filled with mixed fruits. Of course, there's room on my plate. The more, the merrier.

No one seems about, so I sit down in one of the eight lonely chairs at the table, ready to dig in and enjoy the real, fresh home-cooked food. I'm just wondering if there's any fresh-squeezed juice of any kind when a flash of an arm and a hand swipes the delicious dish from me.

"Hey!"

A brusque, pinched-face matron scowls at me. "Breakfast is over. I'm cleaning. You, out."

"I was eating."

"It's eight o'clock. Breakfast is over." She scrapes the perfectly tasty food from my plate into the waste bucket.

"But I wasn't finished."

"Well, then you should have gotten here early." She never looks at me, just continues with her mission to destroy any hopes I had of filling my insides.

I stand up and open my mouth to protest once again, when my sister enters. "Zelda, please do not make a fuss. I told you what time breakfast was last night."

"You said *served*, not *finished and digested*!" I throw my napkin on the floor and stamp back toward my temporary digs to retrieve my boots and coat.

"Zelda, you're acting like a spoiled child," she yells at my back.

"I'm acting like a hungry guest in your home, you ninny," I holler back.

The yelling brings back sweet memories of growing up with her. Sweet as wild elderberries or rhubarb leaves. Toxic and deadly.

Chapter Eight

Coco's digs, albeit in the same countryside neighborhood as my sister's, but they're double, maybe even triple, the size. Coco's house sits closer to the avenue than Ava's and has no fencing or gates, just a tree-lined property and small, immaculately kept gardens scattered throughout the turquoise-green lawn.

Turning the Zenith up the circular white stone drive, I park off to the side of the wide white marble stairs and look up at the mansion and its curved white lines. The home, the stairs, and the drive—that's quite a bit of stark white, and contrasting against the turquoise lawn, it could blind a person.

I take the marble stairs two at a time. The white ornately carved double door is almost three meters tall. Flanking it are turquoise stone planters in which grow matching turquoise roses.

I ring the bell; a symphony of chimes plays a faint, familiar tune I just can't put my finger on. A tidy young doll answers the door. Not a hair out of place on her finger-waved do and framberry-colored bow lips, she is waterproof. "May I ask who is calling?" she softly requests.

"I'm Dr. Zelda Harcrow. I'm here to see Coco Charden," I answer with an equally soft expression.

"Miss Coco is expecting you. Please follow me." She steps aside, allowing me to enter. Closing the door, she turns away and indicates for me to follow. "This way."

I follow her out of the huge vestibule into the entrance hall. The curved lines outside give way to clean, straight lines inside and all-white walls. We turn toward the open expanse of the parlor but are stopped by a shriek, a laugh, and an echoing clap.

"Zelda Harcrow! As I live and breathe," a smooth soprano voice calls out.

I look across the entrance hall to the sweeping curve of stairs that flows down from the second floor in the stair hall. "Coco!"

"Zelda."

We run into each other's arms and embrace. "Oh, Coco, it's been ages."

Coco rocks me back and forth in our friendly embrace. "And whose fault is that?"

"I know, I know. You don't have to tell me." I place a peck on her lightly rouged cheek. "I'm sorry, but I'm here now." I release my embrace and step back.

Coco's hand flies to her cheek, her face filling with terror. "Zelda . . ."

I begin to panic as a lump finds its way into my throat. Am I too late? Have I let my friend down? "Coco, I'm so sorry. I should've gotten here sooner." I lay my hand on her shoulder. "Has there been a new development?"

"Zelda . . ." Her eyes gather a little mist. She moves her hand from her cheek to the bits of mop hanging from my cap. "Your hair!"

"My hair?"

She grabs my chin and whips my face from side to side. "Your skin!"

"My skin?"

"Oh, Zelda, what have you done?"

"Wait, what?"

"Look at yourself." She shakes her head in dismay. "You are a mess."

"Jeepers creepers. A bit harsh, don't you think?"

"I'm being kind."

"This is kind?"

"Sally," she says to the young doll. "Call Harry and tell him to get here pronto. It's an emergency."

I'm speechless. And who is Harry?

Coco turns back to me. "Zelda, upstairs now. We must rectify"—she waves her hands frantically to indicate all of me—"this."

My hands find my hips in defiance. "Coco, I'm not here for a makeover." Grabbing my wrist, she pulls me toward the stairs, and I follow hesitantly. "Dear, for me to help you, I need you to answer some questions."

"I'll answer anything you want," she agrees, "as long as I can rescue you first."

Unwillingly, I begin to climb the stairs. Halfway up, I stop and pull on Coco. "We really need to go over why I'm here."

"And I can't concentrate with you looking like *that*." She points at me violently, both hands open and fingers spread.

"Fine." I trudge up the stairs.

We enter a suite of rooms near the end of the hall at the top of the stairs.

Behind the white double door is a room that holds a chaise lounge, a couch, and a quilted ottoman, all in a plush, deep violet. The floor lamps that accompany the chaise and the couch are transparent glass bases with sparkly white shades. The drapes are a strange violet-on-white geometric pattern. Looking at the deep plush carpet, I can't help imagining that a purple monster vomited violent violet splotches all over the pristine white carpet.

Coco leads me to a vanity table with the largest round vanity mirror I have ever seen. Bright large round bulbs encircle the mirror every few centimeters. I can only imagine how hot it must get in here once they are all lit.

I stand aghast, staring at the setup. Every imaginable fragrance covers the tabletop, drawers down each side are most likely filled with cosmetics, and tall, wheeled shelving units on either side are filled with an array of pretty bottles, tubes, and boxes.

"Sit down." Coco pushes me into the swivel chair before the vanity and stands poised before me, puzzling over my appearance. "How you've let yourself go!" Coco smooths back her fiery-red hair and presses her hands against her forehead.

"Coco, where exactly were you during the explosion?" I might as well just start asking my questions now.

"In Piers's office. We had a little tiff." Her eyes widen, shining like peridot, and she thrusts her hand in the air. "We will start with exfoliants, which will get the glow back in your skin."

"Fine." I remove my leather cap. "What were you fighting about?"

Coco's face falls.

"Was the fight that bad?"

"Your hair!" she screams.

I scratch my head. "You argued about hair?"

"No, your hair. What did you do to it?"

"Nothing," I answer meekly.

"Well, this won't do."

"Coco," I try again. "What was the argument about?"

"Nothing to do with the explosion, I'm sure." Coco opens her perfectly drawn coral-colored lips and yells, "Sally, Sally, come quick."

The slip of an assistant comes running—sprinting, even. "Yes, miss?"

"Call Harry back and tell him to move quickly and bring everything. We are dealing with a disaster." Coco takes my hand. "Sally, tell him hands and feet as well."

Deciding to leave her alone about the tiff with Piers, her husband and the CEO of Coco Cosmetics, I move on to the next question. "What do you remember?"

She turns toward the table and begins to open several jars she retrieves from the shelves. "I remember a large boom. Everything shook."

"Which building were you in?"

"The office building. We evacuated. Once outside, we could see it was the factory building that was on fire."

"What was being developed—" Having clipped back my hair, Coco rubs a cool cream on my skin. I try again to ask the question as she turns to retrieve something else. "Coco, in the lab that exploded—"

She turns to face me with a steaming towel in her hands. *Where did that come from?* I crane my neck to see, but she walks around behind me. Before I can ask the question again, the hot towel covers my face, and she begins to remove the cream with the towel.

Now's my chance. "Was anything being created that would cause an explosion?"

She swivels around with another jar. "This one has a coarse exfoliant. Your pores are so clogged." She begins scrubbing away at my face.

"Coco—"

Too late. Another hot towel magically appears on my face. "Jeepers." The terry-cloth towel muffles my voice.

Once she finishes wiping the gritty cleanser from my chin, I speak up again. "Coco, you really need to answer the question."

"Which one was that?"

I close my eyes to gather all the patience I can muster. "What was being developed in that lab?"

"Why didn't you ask?"

I squeeze my eyes tight and let out a deep sigh.

"Nothing," she answers.

My eyes pop open. "Nothing?"

She nods.

Just as I'm ready to ask another question, Sally walks in. "Harry has arrived."

Coco claps her hands together. I swing my head around to get a gander as a very well-dressed, flamboyant, and perfectly coiffed gentleman prances into the room.

"Coco, dahling," he squeals.

"Harry, my dear."

Once the cheek kissing is over, she introduces Harry Wonderkind. *That just cannot be his real name.*

"My dear, what has she done to her hair?" He is flanked by two assistants on each, all in black with the same black finger-waved do and all wearing black horn-rimmed glasses over their peepers.

"Harry, I'm perplexed indeed." Coco crosses her arms over her chest. The two consult each other about my supposed predicament, while I just sit there, totally ignored and almost glad of it.

"Then it is decided?" asks Harry.

"It's decided," agrees Coco.

I butt in. "I'm not sure what's been decided. Coco, dear, we really need to finish our conversation."

"I promise, Zelda, as soon as you're looking like you again, I will give you my undivided attention."

"Fine." I cave. "Okay, Harry, go for it."

A very wide, toothy grin creeps over Harry's mug, and his yellow eyes sparkle.

Harry spreads goop on my hair. Coco spreads goop on my face. Harry's silent, nondescript assistants spread goop on my hands and feet. I decide to use my time wisely; after all, nothing good can come from a cluttered, hurried mind. I use this seemingly chaotic situation to meditate. From quieting the mind, great ideas, clarity, and solutions can arise.

Unfortunately, I get nothing.

Coco shook my shoulders. "Zelda, Zelda, you're not sleeping, are you?"

"I am not sleeping," I snap. "I'm just deep in thought."

"Harry needs to rinse."

"Okay." I twist my neck to see a portable sink behind me. "Do you have this stuff just sitting around in a closet somewhere?"

"Don't be silly. It's stored in the bathing room."

I really need to learn not to ask questions for which I don't really want answers.

Harry produces scissors and combs. *Snip, snip*—wet hair falls to the carpet. *Whir, whir*—one of the assistants vacuums it up as it lands. *Buzz, biz, buzz*—the clippers scrape the back of my neck. Coco stands directly in front of me, casting a judicious eye over me and blocking my view of my reflection. Once Harry's done, another of his assistants snaps a gathered cap over my head. The cap connects to a hose, which in turn connects to some type of contraption that blows heat, drying my covered locks.

I should have invented this.

"Your nails should be dry now," Harry says, before barking orders at his entourage to begin cleanup.

"Is she done?" Coco eyes the worker bee-flies, making sure nothing is left behind, not even a single speck to disturb her bold violet-blotched carpet.

Harry removes the cap. "Yes."

Coco steps away from me, and I finally see my reflection. The damaged, neglected hair that once reflected my life is completely changed, replaced by an angled cropped bob with short, straight bangs, all the most beautiful, brilliant sapphire blue I have ever seen.

I begin to tear up. "Coco . . ." I sniff.

Coco holds up her hand. "I understand."

Harry and the gals pack up and move out, escorted by Sally.

"Thank you, Coco," I say. "However, we really have got to finish answering these questions."

"As long as I get to finish up." She circles my face with her fingers. I nod in agreement.

I return to my original question. "What were you and your hubby arguing about?"

"Money."

"What money?"

"Money went missing."

"A lot?"

She nods. "But now it has been replaced."

"Do you know what it was used for?"

"No. I don't see what this has to do with the accident."

"It could be nothing; it could be something. I don't know yet." I move on. "What was being developed in the lab."

"Nothing."

I think of the piece of porous substance I found. "That's not possible."

"That lab wasn't used. It was just storage."

"What did it store?"

"File cabinets, a desk, and some equipment."

"Any chemicals?"

"Not that I'm aware of. We gave the list to that horrid Inspector Zex."

"Could you get me a copy?"

"Yes."

As we go back and forth, Coco keeps busy. Working quickly and with a deft hand, she places cold cream on my face and wipes it off. She pats a big powdered puff all over my face. Using a wet cotton ball, she applies rouge in small crescents high on my cheekbones. She cleans up and pencils my brows, then smudges pencil into my lashes and places mascara on my lashes. Finally, she smudges dark eyeshadow on my lids.

"Have there been any visiting chemists or alchemists?" I push on.

"No."

"Any missing employees?"

"Not sure. Some were on holiday. We're still waiting for everyone to check in."

"Is there anything missing?"

"Not that we're aware of." She continues to blot and brush colors onto my golden skin.

"What's being developed in the other labs?"

"The norm: perfumes, lotions, creams, eyeshadows, mascaras, liner, and so forth."

"Any unexplained visitors?"

She pauses in the process of drawing the bow on my lips. "We have been working on a new lip rouge—an all-turn-wear stick that won't smudge or wipe off. It's revolutionary and will change the whole market."

"How do you get it off?" I stupidly ask.

She holds up a container of cold cream.

I flush, embarrassed. "Oh, yeah, that."

Chapter Nine

Turning her wrist, Coco looks at the time.

I don't have to. My tummy is grumbling, and my head is aching for a snort.

"Sally," Coco calls. The doll appears as if out of thin air. "Sally, tell Cook to whip up some yummy delectables."

"Yes, miss."

Coco glances at me. "Zelda, do you like raw blue thunna?"

"Over rice?" My mouth waters.

"Sally, tell Cook thunna on rice, coconut aminos, pickled ginger root, some fresh fruits, and some bubbly."

"Yes, miss." With a figurative poof, Sally is gone.

I lean into the enormous mirror and study my reflection. I see me—the me I've always known, the confident alchemist. I wish I could feel on the inside as I look on the outside. Like they say, though, fake it till you make it. "Thank you again, Coco, for the pampering."

She gives me a squeeze. "My pleasure. Now, let's stroll down to the solarium. We will enjoy our fare there." When I look around for my boots, she shakes her head. "Sorry, you'll have to barefoot it. I had Sally take your things to be cleaned and polished."

I nod. "Aren't you going to change for lunch?" Coco is wearing cream-colored spider-silk lounging PJs and a dressing gown hemmed with feathers.

"Why? I'm not going out today."

"What about visitors?"

"You are my visitor." She twirls. "Do you mind my garb?"

"No."

"Ducky." She links arms with me, and we stroll down the curved staircase, through the stair hall to the mirror-walled dining room, and straight out to the solarium.

Surprisingly, the room is not white. It's topped with a dome that is partially made up of stained glass. The floor is paved with rough deep-red brick. Walls of windows overlook a lovely flower garden, complete with a white marble fountain carved in the shape of male and female figures in an intimate embrace. A lead-glass door leads out to the garden. Small floor fans scattered about the solarium move the humid air, keeping the room at a comfortable temperature.

"This is one of my favorite rooms during this time of year," Coco says.

I can see why. Within a curve of the outside wall, a smaller version of the fountain outside sits among ferns, trickling water. A brown wicker chaise and a small book table lie in front of the fountain. I imagine daydreaming or reading in the crisp mornings here in the countryside.

Chandeliers designed to look like stems with bulbous flowers hang throughout the room, some above couches and chairs that are surrounded by palm trees and floor lamps that look like palm trees. One of the steel-and-frosted-glass chandeliers hovers over a little wooden table that seats four.

Covering the table is a lovely embroidered green-gold table runner. The table is set for two. A silver standing bucket of ice sits to one side of the table. A bit of cork peeks out from beneath the towel that covers a bottle. Bubbly. True paradise is kept in this tiny room.

The moment we sit, our lunch is served. Once the help leaves the room, I begin to ask more questions. This time about Piers.

"I'm surprised I've never met him. Doubly surprised you got shackled to him; he's not quite your type." I think of baby-doll Sally; now that's more up Coco's lane.

"You've met Piers," she states.

"When?" I pop a piece of fish in my mouth.

"The rotation after we launched the company."

I wash the mouthful down with the bubbly vinum. "Don't remember."

She scrunches her mouth, clearly irritated. "We'd just rolled out the new line of lip color."

"Still don't recall."

"The lip rouge color is named after you." She pours herself another glass.

I grab the bottle from her and top off my flute. "I remember the party. That lip color—which I adore, by the way—is always on hand. I just don't remember Piers." I raise my glass and take a long drink of sweet, bubbling alcohol. "So why did you get hitched?"

She shrugs. "We became friends. We spent all our time together. He's a genius with marketing, money, and management."

I raise my brow.

"Zelda, without him, this company would not be as big and prosperous as it is."

"Coco, you are the company."

"I want to create, and Piers can get it to the people. Since I handed the reins over to him, we've built the office building out front, increased production, and gone Gaia-wide. It helped build this house." She waves her arms to encompass the room and beyond.

I'm still a little perplexed. "But why did you marry him?"

"I don't know, Zelda. It seemed like a promising idea at the time. As a team, we were unstoppable."

"And now?"

Her bright-gold face darkens. "What has this got to do with the explosion?"

"You said you argued about money." I can see she's getting in a lather.

"Enough! None of this has to do with our current predicament!" She jumps up, almost knocking her chair back. "We're almost at a standstill. Until this investigation is over and that horrid woman, Inspector Sex—"

"Zex," I correct.

"What?"

"Inspector Zex."

"Well, whatever her name is, she's dragging her feet." Coco is steaming up.

"Sit down, Coco," I insist, deciding to drop the subject of Piers for now.

Coco is still standing, hands on her hips. "Zelda, the authorities think we have something to do with the explosion."

"Calm down and sit down. Why would they think either of you have something to do with it?"

Coco reluctantly takes her seat. "Something about how the explosion was contained in one small area of the building."

Thinking that over, I take a sip of bubbly and shove a berry into my mouth. I can see the Legere Legalis's point. The damage pattern would indicate that something was set to explode only in one spot and directed in such a way that there was minimal damage. Sure, the outside wall was compromised, but the floor above is intact. There's some damage to the ceiling on the lab below, but basically it was greatly contained to the one room.

I slouch back in the rattan chair. "Tell me about this new lipstick you're developing."

"Do you think it has something to do with the espionage?" Coco at least seems to be calming down.

I shrug.

"It's creamy, it's long-lasting, and it doesn't smudge. No more lipstick stains on glassware or handkerchiefs."

"Sounds amazing."

"We still have a few kinks to work out in the formulation, but it should be ready by the Autumn Equinox."

"Who is working on it?" I try to pour myself another glass of bubbly, but nothing comes out. Frowning, I shake the bottle; it appears I've already finished it off.

Coco fiddles with her napkin. "Me and several in-house chemists and assistants."

"Everyone who works on it has been fully vetted?"

She stops and looks up. "I think so."

I cock my head, raise my eyebrows, and stare at her.

"Piers's assistant, Juju, takes care of that, I think."

"Juju?" I lean forward. "The gal that used to be your assistant when you first started?"

"This, you remember?" Coco laughs.

"She followed you around and acted like Gaia revolved around you. How could I not?"

"I must admit, it was getting to be a bit much. I hated to fire her—she is such a good worker—so Piers gave her a promotion instead." She smiles. "I now have Sally." She wiggles her eyebrows. "I'm one lucky gal."

"You are one bad girl."

Smirking, she finishes her glass of bubbly.

"Doesn't Piers mind?"

She makes a funny face and shrugs.

I look at my empty glass, wishing for some more bubbly vinum. "A few more questions, and then I better skedaddle. I want to see my niece and nephew, and I think I'm expected for dinner. One minute late and you don't get fed."

"Seriously?"

"Cross my hearts." I relay to her my tragically horrid breakfast story.

"Poor thing." Coco stands. "Let us take a turn around the back gardens."

"Works for me."

We ankle out the glass doors and walk out into the beautiful flower garden. The fountain is much larger than I first thought. Beautiful flowers float on the water's surface, and blue and yellow fish swim around within. I admire the paths laid out throughout the garden. In silence, I take in all the beauty around me.

I finally break the quietude. "Were any records kept in the lab that could have been worth stealing?"

"Most of the records kept there were of past employees, receipts, and old shipping orders. Destroying them or stealing them would mean nothing. Everything is on crystal discs; those were just hard copies."

"Do you think someone could have been using the room for something else?"

"You mean like a liaison?"

"Or maybe an experiment. You did say old equipment was kept there."

She shakes her head. "No, with people always moving about, I think one of us would have noticed."

"True." I think for a moment. "Could someone be storing something they shouldn't?"

"Possibly, Zelda. Yes, I guess they could." She stops and smells one of her turquoise roses. "What about the body?"

"I won't know anything until I find out who the victim was."

"How are you to do that?"

"Not sure, but I know a guy who might help." I think of Hodge.

We spend the rest of our walk catching up on what's going on in our lives and talking about my near-death adventure. She gives me a hug. "I'm so glad you're in one piece."

My voice cracks as I respond. "Me too." We walk back to the house.

"I was hoping for you to meet Piers before you left."

"Maybe I could see Piers at your office and take another gander at the damaged lab."

"I'll make the arrangements." Coco walks me to the entrance hall, where we meet up with Sally.

"I have your things." Sally hands over my boots, coat, and skullcap.

"Thanks."

"There is an upholstered bench near the vestibule you can use to put your things on." Coco gives me one more hug and a kiss on the cheek. "Drive carefully." Turning, she disappears up the stairs.

I ankle on over to the mirror bench with silver-gray tufted cushions. Slipping on my socks and boots, I ask Sally, "You fixed the hem on my coat?"

She smiles and nods.

"What about the items in my jacket?"

"Oh, yes, here you are." She hands me a clear bag containing my magnifying lens, my magnifying goggles case, my tiny light cylinder, my driving gloves, and most importantly, my flask.

I have the odd sensation that I'm forgetting something. "Was that all there was?"

"Oh, silly me, no." Sally hands me my motorcycle goggles.

"Thank you."

Once out the front doors, I bop down the steps and ankle over to the Zenith. Only as I begin emptying the little bag does it dawn on me: my card case and wireless are missing!

I rub my chin. Maybe I left them at my sister's? I can't imagine why Sally would nick them.

Deciding that must be it, I drop my goggles over my eyes—only for another realization to hit me.

"Unicornfeathers!" I'm casting kittens right and left.

The small blue clue is missing!

I begin floating ideas. Did Sally know what it was and decided to toss it? What if she thought it was a bit of nothing, just unimportant garbage, and chucked it?

I stamp my foot. "How could I have been so careless?" I look back at the stark-white mansion and contemplate what to do for a few seconds. Deciding there's probably nothing I can do about it now, I climb on the Zenith to begin the drive back to my sister's.

Chapter Ten

I putter along toward my sister's. I had forgotten to plug the Zenith in last night, and she's losing power fast. Without electricity, there's no steam, and without steam, she has no power. Luckily, the streets have been quiet so far.

It really is beautiful out here in the country. Tiny new leaves burst from the small limbs of the trees, and the different color grasses are still thin but oh so full of life. Going slow allows me to see the tiny white flowers peeking their petals up among the new grasses.

I glimpse something in my handlebar side mirror as I crest a small, curved hill, but it quickly disappears as I descend the other side. I'll have to wait till I climb the next hill to get a gander. I stop enjoying the scenery. My hearts begin to pound in my chest, trying to break free in my panic. As I start the next climb up a slight incline, I keep my peepers peeled for the object.

As I hit the top, I spot a dark tin behind me.

I attempt to put on more steam. The pedal hits the metal, and the Zenith sputters.

Tears gather in my eyes.

My breath shortens.

I look for the vehicle again.

Nothing.

I continue to drive, waiting for the next hill, the next opportunity to see it.

Waiting.

My muscles stiffen.

Waiting.

Nothing.

I grip the handlebars, my knuckles surely white within my driving gloves.

The iron putters toward the next incline. "Come on, baby. You can do it." I caress the Zenith with my words of encouragement.

It appears in my mirrors again. "There you are!" I clench my jaw; the dark vehicle appears to be closer now.

My stomach churns. I'm being followed.

I try a deep breath. It's a labor to even get my lungs to expand.

I'm getting lightheaded.

Can't stop.

Shit, shit, shit—crap, I'm swearing a lot.

A quick look in the mirror confirms the carriage is getting closer.

"What are they playing at?"

My speed slows.

"No, no, no. Come on, baby. Hang in there."

The iron jerks from lack of fuel. Tears sting my eyes and fog my goggles.

I rip the goggles from my head, screaming in frustration—or fear. It could be fear. Lately, they've begun to feel the same.

Last hill and then it's straight and even from there.

"Go . . . go . . . please!" I yell.

I'm up the hill! The road levels. I take an easier breath.

I eye both mirrors. It's no longer following me.

It's on top of me!

My hearts leap into my throat. I feel as if I'm choking.

I must say my spell to calm myself! But I can't. I have to get away.

The dark motor swerves back and forth behind me.

I'm losing control.

The Zenith falters.

I pull to the side of the street, out of power.

I close my eyes.

I wait.

A whoosh of warm air whizzes past me.

I open one eye, then the other.

I'm still standing.

Looking down the road, I watch my imagined threat continue driving along the avenue.

They weren't following me. I was just losing power, and they were trying to pass.

What a fool I am!

I prop the iron up on her kickstand, step off and back, and squat down, hugging my knees. It doesn't take long for the dam to break and release a flood of tears. I rock back and forth, exhaustion washing over me like a violent saltwater wave.

I'm not sure how long I've been curled up on the side of the road when I finally wipe snot from my nose and chin. I'm sure my mascara and liner are long gone. Straightening up, I release the kickstand, take a breath, and embark on the long push back to my sister's.

I'm not exactly sure how many kilometers away Ava's is. I don't have my wireless and not one vehicle has yet to pass me.

Too bad magic can't start my dead battery. Instead, I'll have to wait till I can plug her in. Now, had I realized her charge was low before I started her up, I may have been able to prolong the charge with magic. Now, I'll never know.

Hours pass. A few cars race by, but no one stops. Which is fine; I'm way too paranoid at this moment to trust the kindness of strangers.

Finally, I arrive. Somehow, Ava's drive seems so much longer than before.

The journey exhausts me. I am too tired to feel anything. Upside, I can breathe again. Downside, I'm out of breath from pushing an iron up and down all those hills.

Pushing the Zenith to the rear of the house, I find the outside solar plug by the garage and attach my baby.

I stumble to the side door that leads into the kitchen and private family area of the house. Inside is the indomitable housekeeper—the Iron Maiden—chopping and sautéing. By the stars, I didn't miss dinner!

"Zelda." My sister walks into the dining area from the family room, catching me before I can skedaddle down the hall.

Stopping, I hang my head. "Ava."

"You missed the kids again. They have eaten, are already tucked in, and are sleeping."

I turn around to face her. "I know. I'm sorry."

She screws her face up. "What happened to you?"

"I ran out of power and had to push the bike back."

"Your face is all mushy. Did you get caught in a freak rainstorm?"

"It's my latest look. Like it?" I curtly sneer, turn around, and head toward the boudoir.

"Zelda," she calls after me.

"Yes?" I call back, still walking away.

"Mae called."

Entering my room, I plop face down on the bed. "Okay."

Ava follows me in and stands in the doorway. "You may want this." The wireless she tosses onto the bed bounces next to me.

"Thanks. Where did you find it?"

"On the floor while I was busy cleaning up the mess you left from the broken vase."

"Sorry. I didn't mean to break it." My voice is muffled by the mattress.

"I didn't think you did. May I ask how you managed it?"

"I was practicing."

"Practicing what?"

"Self-defense kicks."

"Why do you need to practice kicking?"

I lift my head just a little. "Really?" I bury my face back in the bed.

"Well, can you do it outside?"

"Okay." I roll over onto my back. "Ava?"

I'm met with silence, so I push on. "Thanks for finding my phone, and I'm sorry about the vase."

"Supper is in less than one hour." I hear the click of the latch as my sister leaves, closing the door behind her.

Picking up my wireless, I ring Mae.

"Dah-ling," Mae answers, drawing the word out.

"How are you, Mae?"

"Fabulous, darling. I recently opened a lovely little shop right in downtown Fulcrum."

"Really? Well, I'll be honest, I can't see you as a shopgirl." I kick off my boots.

"Darling, I was a smash at it!" she purrs.

I sit up. "Was?"

"Closed it up."

That piques my curiosity. "Why?"

"There was this truly little man, a very large box, and nylons. I decided retail really wasn't for me." She speaks very matter-of-factly.

"How long was your shop open?"

"It doesn't matter, darling. The retail industry is just too boring, boring, blah, blah, blech for me."

"So, what, a turn?" I tease.

I'm met with silence.

Mae has been my best friend since we were toddlers growing up in the very upper-class Seaside Village outside Fulcrum. Mae is bronze, Mae is beautiful, and Mae is a bit eccentric; she changes careers like anyone else would change clothes. She never has to worry about funds. Her family is very well off and connected to councils and businesses here in Tesla and abroad. Batty as she can be, she is the most loyal, loving, and kind person I know, she will do anything for me, and I am lucky to have her as my Best Friend.

I break the silence. "Ava said you rang."

"Yes, darling, I tried you several times."

"I must have dropped my wireless in the room. Sorry you couldn't reach me."

"For crying out loud, Zelda, I was worried. I haven't heard from you for two turns."

"I should have called. I'm sorry." I seem to be apologizing quite a bit lately.

"I forgive you, darling. Now, give me the scoop-boo-poop-a-doop."

I leave out my adventure at the hotel and my almost nervous breakdown on the side of the road—no reason to worry her. "I saw Coco. Other than her giving me a complete makeover, I really didn't get anywhere."

"You must have needed one, then."

"How would you know? I haven't seen you for almost half a rotation."

She sighs. "Because, darling, I know you. I'm sure that other than your eyebrows, you haven't lifted a finger to take care of yourself since you rode off into the starset."

"Thbpt!" I give her raspberries through the mouthpiece, leaving a little spit. I wipe the spray off with my hand. "It wasn't starset, so there." I give her another raspberry; this time, I try not to spray all over the place. It's impossible, let me tell you.

"Ish kabibble," Mae says. "So what do you know?"

"I know that she and Piers had a fight over money missing from the company . . . and has since been replaced. Also, the lab that was damaged was supposed to—"

"Who is Piers?" Mae demands.

"Her husband."

"What's his face is named Piers?"

"Yes. As I was saying—"

"Did we meet him?"

"Supposedly I did way back when he was just an employee. Didn't you go to the binding ceremony when they got hitched?"

"I went." She pauses. "I guess I just didn't notice him."

I scratch my head. "He was the groom."

"If you say so, darling."

"I say, I say." I smack my forehead.

"Well?" Mae prompts.

I've lost my place. "What was I saying?"

"Something about a lab."

"The lab," I start again. "The lab supposedly was used just for storage."

"Go on."

"But I found a strange substance that makes that impossible."

"What is it?"

"I don't know?"

"Isn't there some way to test it?"

I blow out a breath. "I lost it."

"You lost it."

"Or it was stolen." I tell her about Sally.

"Well, that's balled up."

"Pretty much."

"What else?"

"The explosion was set so there was minimal damage."

Mae changes direction., "What about the body?"

"I've no info on him or her, and I'm trying to figure out a way to see it."

"Darling, do you have a plan?"

"Sort of."

"What is 'sort of'?"

"Remember Hodge?"

"No, darling."

"The constable that you took over the driving for on our way to see if we could catch up with my assistant, Clover," I offer in an attempt to remind her.

"Hmmm . . . possibly. Darling, how will he help?"

"He's on a forensics team."

"So?"

"He's got the remains."

"Aha."

"I just have to get past the hard-ass Inspector Zex. She's a real doozy. I seem to have gotten off on the wrong foot with her."

"What did you do?"

"How come you think I did something to make her hate me?"

"How should I know?" she asks, irritated.

I sigh, and a yawn escapes.

"Tired?"

I answer through another yawn. "Exhausted."

"Take a nap."

"No time. My sister's a stickler for mealtime."

"She gets that from your mother." Mae understands.

"I better get ready." I yawn again.

We disconnect after goodbyes and my promise to call her with an update in a couple of turns.

Maybe I could just rest my eyes for a moment.

Chapter Eleven

My peepers fly open. *Crud.* Looking at the nightstand clock, I can't believe my eyes. I seize the silver, black, and red enamel box. Holding it, I stare in disbelief.

It's after eight.

I groan. Dinner has already been served, I'm not dressed, and my face still looks like some strange inkblot sheet. Setting the timepiece back down, I scamper around looking for my dressing case. Just as I'm about to look under the bed, I remember I left it in the bathing room. I may not have time to change, but I can at least have a clean face.

I race down the hall and into the bathing room. "Worse than I thought," I say to my reflection. At least my hair is still the chat's meow.

The jars rattle against each other as I locate the cold cream. The cool oily cream feels soft on my skin, and I spread it liberally over my face. Swiping tissues from a box on the counter, I use the thin cottony sheets to wipe the cream and makeup off, leaving my skin soft, very satisfying, and smelling like baby talc.

The icy bite of the water as I splash it over my face revives me just a little. I attempt to pat my face dry with the useless bath towel's matching useless face towel. I end up leaving the bathing room with damp skin, but at least it's clean.

I'm all set. Off to the kitchen I go. I take a deep breath, preparing myself to be chastised for being tardy, but the clamminess under my arms distracts me. Lifting one arm, I find my shirt is soaked and stained from sweat. Great, I'll have to be a few more minutes late.

Stepping back inside my room, I find a tray on the bed.

As I pull the flannel shirt over my head, I walk over to the bed to check it out. Lying on the covered dish is a small note.

You look tired, so I let you sleep. The teapot contains an energizing tea to detox and energize your organs. I made a plate for you; hopefully you still like air-fried cicen breast. I also included a spell for you, if you think you need it.

—Ava

My sister may not have the most creative imagination, but her spells are top-notch.

Sitting carefully in front of the tray, I lift off the stainless-steel cover. I am met with a waft of steam carrying appetizing, mouthwatering flavors.

I waste no time digging in. "Oh, my stars! So yummy! I guess I don't completely annoy my sister. Good to know."

As I pour my tea, I read the spell.

A spell for bravery. Use this sparingly when you need to be courageous, the instructions read.

> "Gaia grant me courage
> and lend me strength.
> Give to me true grit,
> so that I may be brave."

As I repeat the spell, I start to feel rather good. I decide to repeat it again for good measure. Finishing the tea, I stand up and stretch. I suddenly feel centered, something I haven't felt all turn.

The Zenith should be almost charged. With my newfound strength, I decide to take an evening drive through the countryside. The fresh air will do me good and will help me get a good night's sleep without the need for spirits.

Swiftly, I change into corduroy riding pants, a fresh shirt, a clean pair of socks, my newly polished riding boots, and my duster. I grab my white spider-silk scarf, wrapping it around my neck, and take a quick peek in the mirror. I'm ready to go.

Jeepers, I almost forgot. I turn back and grab my wireless off the nightstand.

Bouncing down the hall, through the kitchen, and into the dining area, I peek my head around into the family room. Ava sits there working on some papers.

"Thank you for the scrumptious dinner. The tea was just what I needed." I tap my forehead. "And I placed your spell up here."

"You're welcome. You look much better."

"Thanks. What are you working on?"

"I'm teaching a class at the university on binding spells."

"Attagirl, you are the darb at spells. University is lucky to have you, and that's on the level."

"I know. Are you going somewhere?" Ava never looks up from her work.

"Just for a small drive."

"Do you think that's a good idea?"

She's acting like Mother; I'm getting a little heated. "I'm feeling decidedly better, and surprisingly, your roads out here in the countryside are pretty well lit. It'll be easy to motor along in the evening. The fresh night air will do me good." I puff out my chest.

"If you say so." She looks up. "Just don't be gone too long, and be careful."

I give her the okay sign and scan the room. "Where's the old ball and chain?"

"Working late. He'll be home soon."

I feel a tinge of guilt. "You ate by yourself?"

"Don't worry about it, Zelda. You needed to rest."

Saying nothing, I turn and make my way out the kitchen door by the garage.

The sky is a black-and-indigo backdrop for the trillions of stars that light up the night. The small moon, Biota, is waxing, a little more than a quarter now, and the larger moon, Desero, is just a sliver. When the moon is waxing is the best time to do spells to promote things as it's the time of creation. Thinking of the spell my sister gave me, I decide to speak it out loud again. A little extra bravery while I'm on the road won't hurt.

Ava really gifted me a great spell. It really has a nice ring to it.

I zip up and down the hills under the bright night sky, until I find myself near Coco's neighborhood. Maybe I'll swing by to see if she's up knocking about.

I pull up in front of her well-lit drive entrance. The lamps flanking the drive top white stucco pillars that allow the light to shine out onto the entrance as well as the drive leading to the house. Pulling up quietly, I look for signs of life. The house itself is dark except for the porch light.

A fluttering movement catches my eye. Dangling from the roof to the ground is a rope. "What the stars?" I mutter under my breath.

My boots crunch on the white stone drive. Stopping, I sidestep onto the grass. Something tells me to be as stealthy as possible.

I move a little closer across the soft, damp turquoise lawn, my boots no longer making sound. As I do, I spy a dark figure pulling himself over the roof ledge.

I cannot seem to stop myself. "This is foolish," I tell myself, but I keep making my way to the rope. Surprisingly, I find my hand holding the rope. I look up toward the roof, back down to the rope in my hand, and then back up to the roof.

"I should call the Legere Legalis," I whisper, even as I begin to climb the rope.

Not even halfway up, my forearms are burning, and my muscles want to give out. Yet something keeps pushing me to put one hand over the other. I continue till I reach the roof.

Pulling myself up, I straddle and hug the ledge. I feel the cool, rough white stucco on my stomach. Panting like a dogacorn, my attempt to get up fails, and I roll onto the roof, falling flat on my back. *Oof!* Dazed, I gaze up at the clear night sky and all the twinkly little balls of firelight that are rotations away. What the stars am I doing?

Struggling to sit up—the climb really did me in—I reach into my pocket, pull out my wireless, and begin dialing the Safety Council's emergency number. Before I can connect, the door from the attic to the roof flies open with the clang of metal on metal.

A figure rushes toward me. The man, dressed all in black, has a stocking pulled over his face. He stops suddenly when he sees me. "Who are you? What are you doing here?"

Still panting, I struggle to my feet. Holding up a finger, I lean my other hand on my knee as I try to catch my breath. "I . . . I . . . I could ask the same of you."

"Just move out of the way, and you won't get hurt!"

I straighten up. "I'm not moving." I notice then that he's empty-handed. "Tell me why you broke in here."

He makes a dash for the rope.

Pocketing my wireless, I attempt to block the sneak thief's escape. Instinctively, my body moves into a fighting stance. The warm breath from my lungs flows out through my nostrils. As I twist to the side, my leg flies with purpose, targeting his midsection.

He pulls up his leg and covers his ribs with his arms, trying to protect his body.

Too late. The sole of my boot contacts his rib cage.

He stumbles back, almost falling.

Good thing I've been practicing my kicks.

I gallop between him and the rope and point at him. "You're not leaving."

"Move." Rushing me, he brings his arm and hand to my opposing shoulder.

Lifting my arms, I plant the heel of one hand on his upper arm and the heel of the other on the inside of his forearm. I push his arm down and back, just like Jean taught me, successfully blocking him.

He throws a compliment at me. "You move very gracefully."

"You should see me tango," I successfully block his pretty words.

Our scuffle seems to have garnered a little attention. I can hear sirens far in the distance.

"I'm sorry." He rushes me one more time.

His shoulder and broad chest hit me squarely in the face, neck, shoulder, and breast, sending me reeling backward.

I scream.

My calf slams into the ledge of the flat roof, and I tumble over the side.

I'm still screaming.

A viselike grip clamps down on my ankle.

Still screaming.

"I've got you!" yells my opponent.

My back hits the stucco with a thud, and air rushes out of my lungs. I am now hanging upside down from the roof. Not good!

"Don't look down," he orders.

My arms flail as I panic. "That might prove a little difficult considering that's where my head is facing."

"Stop wiggling!"

"Are you kidding me?"

"Hold still."

"I'm trying!" I scream.

"You know you're beautiful?"

"What?"

"You're quite a looker," he repeats.

I grit my teeth. "Lift me up."

"I can't do that."

"Why not?"

"Because I have to escape."

"At least swing me toward the rope so I can save myself."

"I need that rope."

"I'm the one hanging precariously from the roof. I think I need it more."

"I can't get caught. Wish we'd met under different circumstances."

"Me too! Then I wouldn't be hanging upside down, waiting to die!" This guy was really getting my lather up.

"Why did you follow me up here?"

"It's my sister's fault."

"Your sister?"

"She made me tea."

"I don't understand."

"Please help me up. I don't want to die tonight."

"I've got an idea."

"Better be a good one—and one that doesn't require me plummeting to my death."

"Do you have a rope on you?"

"Let me check my pockets," I answer sarcastically. "Why would I have a rope?"

"It was just a question."

"I don't want to die." I start flailing my arms again.

"I have extra rope."

"If you have extra rope, why did you ask if I had rope?"

"Because I don't know if I might need it."

"How many houses were you planning on climbing?" The sarcasm oozes from my mouth.

"Just this one."

I can hear him fumbling around. Suddenly, I start to slip.

I start screaming again. "Hey!"

His head pops over the ledge. "It's not easy doing this one-handed, you know."

"Yeah, well, it's a lot easier than what I'm doing." I can feel his hand shifting away from my boot. "What are you doing up there?"

"Saving your life."

"It's your fault I'm in this predicament."

"I'm not the one who followed me up here."

"Are you insisting this is my fault?"

"You drank the tea."

I cross my arms over my chest and tightly purse my lips.

"Are you ready?" he calls down.

"For what?"

He doesn't answer. Instead, I fall.

I scream.

Something yanks on my ankle, and a sharp pain runs from my ankle straight to my hip.

There's a rope tied around my ankle. I am still dangling from the rooftop.

The sirens are getting closer, and I can hear commotion from the roof.

"Baby, may I say, you're one of the most beautiful dolls I've ever seen. Maybe if we bump into each other again, we could get dinner. What do you think?"

"Did you just ask me on a date?"

"Well?" Hanging from his own rope, he swings closer, pulling up the stocking nylon to reveal a set of pearly whites. Wrenching my neck with his strong grip, he plants one right on my kisser. I just dangle there in shock and disgust.

The door up to the roof bursts open, and suddenly, there's a lot of shouting.

My newfound nemesis—of sorts—slides down, landing safely and running off into the darkness of the tree-lined road.

The coppers pull up in their conservative blue sedans topped with flashing, spinning red lights. A dozen coppers begin to swarm property; I can hear one banging on the door below.

"I'll get that," says one of the voices from the roof.

Struggling to look up, I see Sally staring down at me, one hand covering her mouth, as well as several men and women I don't recognize. "Would you mind giving a girl a lift?" I ask.

I drop my head back down, and the blood rushes to the top of my noggin. I struggle to lift my pounding head back up.

Then I hear a little scream and see Coco's face.

"Zelda, what are you doing upside down?"

"Just hanging about."

Even through the pounding in my head, I hear Coco barking orders to her staff to pull me up.

By the time they get me up, all the blood has successfully rushed to the top of my head.

"Zelda, let's have healers take a look at you."

"Did they get the guy who broke in?"

"I don't know." She turns to her help. "Let's get her downstairs."

The staff help prop me up and get me to my feet. I stagger toward the door. The stairs from the roof through the attic is a metal spiral staircase and only one person can descend at a time. One of the men—I assume a gardener based on his strong torso—tosses me over his shoulder.

By the time we exit the stairs into the upstairs hallway, I'm feeling a bit better. "You can put me down now."

The gardener gently lowers me.

"Attaboy. Thank you."

As I wobble down the hall, I notice something interesting through one of the open doors, in what I think must be Piers's office. Inside, I spy above a credenza, a painting on hinges open to reveal a wall safe that's now visible.

Interesting.

My ankle is throbbing, so I use it as an excuse to sit down right there in front of the open office door.

A gentleman in a silky quilted garnet dressing gown comes running up the sweeping staircase ahead of the coppers, closing and locking the office door as soon as he reaches us. This must be Piers.

Piers is older than I expected. Kind of an odd bird. He's short in stature, has a bald spot on the crown of his head, and has a neatly trimmed mustache and beard. His ruddy complexion makes me wonder if he has two hearts or just one.

"Was anything taken?" Coco asks Piers.

"I don't think they got into the safe."

I butt in. "How do you know? He could have closed it back up."

Piers glares at me through narrowed eyes, then slips back into his office and closes the door behind him.

"Secretive, isn't he?" I study Coco.

She doesn't answer.

Touchy subject.

Coco bends down to check my ankle while the staff is being questioned by the coppers. "Why did you come here?"

"Ava made me tea."

"Tea?"

"And a spell."

"I see. Let's get you into my sitting room and attend to that ankle."

"Okey dokey."

The strong man picks me up like a baby and sets me up in the purple chaise lounge in Coco's sitting room. At least this time, there are no makeovers.

Once we've all given statements and Piers has assured the coppers that nothing was stolen, the crowd of badges retreat, and we all are free to go about our business.

Standing up, I gingerly ankle over to the door. "Coco."

"Yes, Zelda?"

"You would tell me if something was missing? Right?"

"Ab-so-lute-ly," she assures me.

"Tell Piers I'll see him tomorrow." I make my way downstairs with great care so as not to injure my ankle any further. Wobbling over to the Zenith, I start her up and head back to my sister's.

The drive back is easy. I pull into my sister's drive, park, plug the Zenith back in, and limp into the kitchen.

"Zelda."

My stomach leaps into my throat.

"What were you thinking?" Ava sits at the kitchen table with cup of judgmental tea in her hand. Okay, maybe it's not the tea, just her. Her eyes dig into me all criticizey.

"How do you know?"

"Coco called."

"What a snitch."

"You drank the tea and said the spell, didn't you?"

I look around for an escape route.

The chair scrapes the floor as she pushes herself away from the table, leaving behind her steaming cup of tea. Shaking her head, she walks past me toward the stairs.

Hoping not to wake the kids, I whisper-yell, "It's not my fault you're a super-duper-pooper spell maker."

The lights go out, and I am left standing in the dark again.

Chapter Twelve

Rolling over, I open one eye and peer at the clock. Futz! It's eight. If I'm lucky, there may be a cup of tea left.

My muscles thwart any attempts to sit up, abs, thighs, and arms burning like they've been dipped in acid. I guess climbing and then hanging off the side of a house upside down is a workout.

Giving up on the direct approach, I roll to my side. Propping myself up on my very tired arms, I'm able to sit. I maneuver to the edge of the bed and drop my legs over the side. Taking a deep breath, I stand up.

Ow! What the stars?

I fall back on the bed and grab my ankle, pulling up the leg of my pajama bottoms. I inspect it. My poor skin has a nasty red, black, and deep-blue bruising circling my ankle.

Well, that's a nice how-do-you-do. Pushing myself upright, I put all my weight on my healthy appendage, keeping the weight off my sore ankle, and hop over to my saddlebags. I dig through them and pull out white willow bark, holy basil, and a turmeric-ginger blend I created for myself.

The turmeric-ginger blend is great for inflammation. I created it after all the bumps and bruises and other injuries I sustained during my self-defense training with Jean.

Limping over to the trunks, which I have yet to unpack, I pull out a light silky tweed getup. My face contorting as I wince in pain, I struggle to the door and down the hall to the bathing room. I grab a drinking glass from the counter and fill it with water, the cold-water lever squeaking a little as I turn it. In one quick motion, I toss the pills in my mouth, flinging my head back, and take a large gulp of water. The water feels good; the coolness on my throat refreshes my insides.

The fasteners of my dressing case clap as I open it and rummage through the jars within, which clink against each other as I search. Aha! I lift out a squat transparent glass jar filled with egg-white cream. Unscrewing the lid,

I inhale the contents. Perfect. The light medicinal scent of sage and pine confirms what the label claims: arnica cream.

The chilly morning floor makes it easy to be quick about getting across to the water closet. Sitting on the commode, I lift my leg and survey the damage once more. It looks worse than it is, and I suspect there's no actual damage. Once I get the inflammation down, it should cause me no further problems.

It isn't an easy task dressing on my own with a bum leg. Bearing up, I use the wall to get back to my room.

The bed envelopes me as I flop on my back. Looking up at the darted texture of the ceiling, I plan out my turn. Sort of.

First, I shall scrounge and beg for food.

Second, I'll find my niece and nephew and lay their presents upon them. I smile at the thought of their cute-as-a-button faces when they open their goodie bags. And the sour face of my sister when she gets a load of what I bought them. A small snicker escapes.

Next, I'll get these stiff muscles working again with a little easy exercise. Stretching my neck, I look at the dressing table; I'll do those outside, I think.

Then, off to Coco Cosmetics.

I have no idea what I'll be able to find out. I want to investigate Piers just a little further. I just don't trust him. He's obviously secretive about something in his home office. It concerns me that Coco is oblivious to it all.

I rummage through one of the trunks, opening and closing each drawer, and I manage to find low-heeled open-lace shoes. Limping into the kitchen, I make my entrance. Expecting an empty kitchen, I'm instead surprised to see the Iron Maiden finishing the dishes. She flashes me a look of disapproval—or more like I'm an inconvenience.

"Good morning."

"Hmph," is her reply. "Well, I hope you're happy."

Looking behind me and then back at the Iron Maiden, I place a hand on my chest. "Me?"

Flattening her lips till they disappear, she narrows her eyes at me.

I put my palms up in self-defense. "Okay, I give. Don't keep me wound in the sheets."

"Don't just stand there," she snaps. "I don't have all turn. Go sit down and eat your food so I can finish the kitchen."

I raise my brows, and my lips curl upward. "Food?"

"On the table. Hurry up."

Glancing up, I thank the stars. Then I hurry to the table and begin devouring my breakfast.

As I eat, I wonder where my brother-in-law Harvey is. Looking out to the side patio, my peepers zero in on Ava lying on a lounge chair. The kids run back and forth with a ball.

A rustle pulls my attention away from my meal and my niece and nephew. Glancing to the side, I see an upright newspaper and a cup of hot tea leaking steam into the dining room air. I could have sworn I was alone at the table.

The paper crinkles as it bends down, and my brother-in-law smiles at me from behind it. "Good morning, Zelda."

"I didn't see you there, Harvey."

"I get that a lot."

"Bet you do."

"How has your stay been?"

"Eventful." I'm not sure how much Ava has told him.

"That's nice." With that, the paper slides back up.

I gulp down my juice. Before I can replace the glass on the table, Hazel yanks it from my hand. Looking down, I realize my plate has already disappeared too.

The paper at the end of the table crinkles, and Harvey reappears. "She's quick."

I glance at him. "How come she doesn't take your drink?"

"I gave her an advance on her salary."

"Oh?"

"Hazel bets on the bangtails and loses. She had to pay off her bookie."

My eyes widen in disbelief. "She has a bookie?"

The Iron Maiden pipes up. "Ricardo is a crook!"

My brother-in-law grins softly. "He's her nephew."

"He wanted to juice me!" she snaps. "His own aunt!"

I gulp, and Harvey's paper goes back up.

Pulling her apron off violently, Hazel hangs it on the hook near the electric icebox and charges off to the family room.

I'm beginning to get up when the VER turns on and some overacting floats in from the other room.

"What—"

"Her stories," Harvey answers, still hidden behind the paper. "She never misses them."

"Okay, this is just wacky."

"Try living here."

I sweep up the two fabric drawstring bags I brought with me. Sliding open the glass-panel door, I step out of the dining area and onto a cement patio.

My sister looks up from the thick novel she's reading. "Good morning."

"Good morning. Thank you for saving breakfast for me."

"You're welcome." She eyes me up and down. "How are you feeling after your foolish escapade last night?" She drops her head, already returning to her book.

I don't bother answering the question. "I just saw the kids. Where'd they run off to?"

"Eggs," Ava calls. "Flo."

The little ragamuffins pop out from behind the line of cypress trees that separates the front garden from the back.

"Auntie Zelda!" cry my niece and nephew in their squeaky baby voices. "Auntie Zelda!" they shout in unison as they break into a run. Their little legs carry them as fast as they can move.

"Flo!" I squat down and catch her as she plows into my arms, my mouth twisting in discomfort as my ankle complains. Egbert—or Eggs, as he's called—hangs back just a bit. "Come here." I hold out my arm to bring him into the hug.

Eggs, who is a little small for five rotations, shyly steps in and hugs me tightly. "Where have you been?"

"Traveling, silly," Flo says matter-of-factly.

"Yes, I was traveling," I confirm.

Ava chimes in. "Is that what you call it?"

Flo puts her tiny seven-rotation-old hands on my cheeks and whispers, "Momsy is worried about you."

"Aren't you sweet?" I kiss her little golden cheek.

Eggs cups his hand over my ear and whispers, "Did you bring us a present?"

I let them out of my embrace and hand them each a small sack. "Well, open them up."

Squeals erupt from their small mouths. "Momsy!" Flo skips over to my sister with her open bag. Eggs follows closely behind.

My sister peeks in the bags. "Terrific," she mumbles sarcastically.

I stand, trying to keep the weight off my sore ankle. "They are flavored rock-candy lollies."

Ava's mouth tightens. "Pure sugar."

I grin from ear to ear. "Flavored sugar."

"You may each have one now, then they go up in the cupboard," Ava instructs Flo and Eggs.

"Thank you, Momsy!" Flo pulls out one of the flavored lollies.

Eggs pulls at Ava's sleeve.

"What is it, Eggs?"

"Hazel will find them." He starts to cry. "She'll eat them all." He buries his head in her chest.

Placing her book on her lap, Ava hugs him and kisses the top of his head. "How about we hide them in Momsy's room, then?"

Eggs looks up at his mother and nods. His tears miraculously evaporate as he chooses a sugar treat.

"Thank your Auntie Zelda." Ava raises her book and buries herself within the pages.

In unison, Flo and Eggs politely chime, "Thank you, Auntie Zelda." Eggs meekly shuffles over and hugs my legs.

As the kids sit down to suck on their treats, I move behind the cypress trees to stretch and practice a few moves that won't bother my sore and bruised ankle. Swinging my fist out and around, I think fondly of Jean. I haven't spoken to him since I left. Maybe I should give him a call. Although I don't want to encourage him to get stuck. I have no intention of being shackled right now, especially after being dealt betrayal by Nickolas and Chance. I'm going to fly solo from now on.

Throwing another punch at the air, I can't keep my mind from wandering to Inspector Chance Greyson and his sexy good looks. I shake my head violently, trying to free myself from him and the past.

"What are you doing?"

I jump, startled by the tiny voice. "Flo, I didn't see you there."

She skips forward. "What are you doing?"

"I'm practicing."

"Practicing what?"

Flo—whose full name is Florence—has a short bob the color of corn silk and is a curious little girl full of energy and spirit. Her bright mustard-yellow eyes pry for an answer. "Well?" Flo stands with her hands on her hips.

"I'm practicing self-defense."

"What for?"

I think carefully on how to answer. "To protect myself from bullies."

"Show me!"

"Oh, I don't know, Flo."

"What if a bully tries to get me or Eggs?"

"You're seven. I doubt you have many bullies."

"How do you know?"

"W-well . . ."

"Show me!" her babyish voice insists.

"Fine," I reluctantly agree. "Just a few moves."

She jumps up and down, clapping excitedly.

"Auntie Zelda's ankle hurts, so I'm just going to show you how to block a kick and do a punch sequence—just enough to run away and find an adult.

Flo nods violently in agreement and excitement. I proceed to show her a few moves that won't get me in much trouble with my sister.

At one point, Eggs pops his head around the tree. Then he just stands with his shoulders up, watching silently.

"Eggs, do you want to learn?" I ask.

He shakes his head. "No."

"Don't worry, Eggs," says Flo. "I'll protect you."

Eggs smiles, and his shoulders relax. "Momsy said, time for school."

Chapter Thirteen

Standing outside Coco Cosmetics, I look up at the shiny, stocky four-story office building. Turning, I bend down to pass my credit to the taxi driver through the passenger window. "Thanks," I say as the driver hands me my card back. No motorcycle for me today; with my sore ankle, I've found that I can't manage the Zenith. I'll be hiring drivers until it recovers.

Limping up the steps, I pass through the main entrance. Unlike my first night here, the lobby is busy with all sorts of people coming and going, each with some sort of purpose. The stained glass of the dome decorates the terrazzo flooring with multicolored geometric shapes. It lends the space an otherworldly feel.

I hobble to the security desk. The guard on duty isn't the same, either. This one plays solitaire, not word puzzles. What do these guys actually guard? It seems anyone can just come and go at their leisure.

"Hello," I say to the disinterested guard.

"How can I help you?" He can't be very old. His fresh face is full and shows no sign of razor stubble.

"I'm here to see Coco and Piers, please. I am Dr. Harcrow."

He blinks a couple of times, his expression blank. "Okay."

I watch, stupefied, as the guard goes back to his solitaire. "Excuse me." My voice is firm as I lean over the counter aggressively.

He looks up at me. "What?"

I take a deep breath and slip a lock of hair behind my ear. "Where can I find Coco and Piers?"

"Oh. Fourth-floor offices." His eyes fall back to the cards.

I shake my head in disbelief. I must speak with Coco about her security. Pushing the lift button, I wait for the car to arrive.

THE FOURTH FLOOR IS an open-concept design with an office for Coco on one end and for Piers on the other. A desk guards the door to each office, and several rows of typists fill the space between. Sally sits at the desk guarding Coco's office, while the desk at the opposite end is manned by Juju.

The differences between the two women couldn't be more startling. Where Sally is waterproof, Juju is just average. She is neither a raving beauty nor ugly; she's just dull. In stature, Juju is heartily built, while Sally happens to be petite.

The stark differences don't end with their appearances but extend to their desktops as well. Sally's desk is clear; there's the normal desk stuff used in secretarial work, but no actual files or papers. Behind the desk, Sally sits reading a book. Meanwhile, Juju sits typing away on a crystal-reader desktop, surrounded by stacks of files.

I decide to reintroduce myself to Juju. She's been around since the inception of the company, so if anyone knows the dirt, it'll be her.

As I approach the almost-middle-aged woman, I take in her appearance. Her hair is neatly slicked back and wrapped in a tight bun at the nape of her neck. Her already-pale skin is made even more pallid by the heavy amounts of powder she's applied. She wears no eye makeup, but she does have a rosy blush applied a little too heavily. Her red-stained lips are set and hard as she types, deep in concentration.

"Excuse me," I interrupt. "Not sure if you remember me, Juju. I'm Dr. Zelda Harcrow, a friend of Coco's. We met ages ago."

Juju immediately springs to her feet and shoves her hand out. "Yes, Dr. Harcrow. Wonderful to see you again."

Taking her hand, I shake it. "Wow, you have quite a number of files going on here. You must be quite busy."

"Yes, yes." She looks around at the mountain of work.

"Can I ask what you're working on?"

"Nothing important, so sure, I can tell you." She shuffles a few of the papers around her desk. "I'm inputting these old files onto crystal-reader discs."

"Old files? Like the ones kept in that old lab that blew up?"

"Exactly. It's a good thing I've been transcribing these."

"Yes, what luck." I change the subject. "How do you like working for Piers?"

"Mr. Astuce is somewhat demanding. But the work I do here is important. Coco relies on me to keep an eye on things."

"She's a very lucky person to have someone as loyal as you."

"I would do anything for Coco; she is very special."

"Special?" I repeat. Juju's word choice seems odd.

"I mean, she's a really good boss." Juju stumbles over her words. "I really need to get back to work." She abruptly sits down and begins clicking away on the keys of the crystal reader.

Not sure how to react to that, I back away. "Nice to see you again." Pivoting, I walk to the other end of the fourth floor, to Coco's office.

"Hi, Sally," I say, greeting the young nymph.

"Dr. Harcrow. Coco is waiting for you inside." She gestures toward the double door behind her.

Giving her a quick salute, I walk over and open the door. "Coco," I say as I pop my head in her office.

Coco is looking over some papers with a pencil hanging out of her mouth. She waves me over to join her at her desk.

Like her home, Coco's office is pure white with splashes of color. Her oval desk is white laminate, polished to a shine, while the high-back desk chair is the brightest orange one could imagine, almost neon in its vibrancy. The carpet, the walls, and the desk are all white. The chairs for her guests, however, are a light blue, a nice contrast to the orange of her chair. The wall behind her desk is all windows, which look out at the factory so she can survey her domain. The art on her wall consists of different renditions of her portrait. There's one done all in blues, another in oranges, another in hues of green, and still another in every pigment of red.

I limp over to Coco's desk. "How's it going?"

"How's it going?" She looks up from her paper. "How are you feeling after last night?"

"A bit sore, but I'm just fine."

Coco eyes me favoring my ankle. "Are you sure?"

"Yes, and don't nag."

"Fine . . ." She sighs and pushes back her throne, grabbing a paper from her desk as she stands. "Come on, we have to go over to the labs. I'm working on this new fragrance, and I'm just about finished with the formula."

"Jeepers, it would be nifty to watch you work for a bit before I go snooping around in the damaged lab."

"Not sure what else you can find there, but you're welcome to look."

"Sounds like a plan," I agree. "So, when do I get to interrogate Piers?"

"Zelda, I'm sure Piers had nothing to do with the explosion. He was with me when it happened."

"But—"

"Zelda, let it go!"

"Coco, I can tell he's hiding something."

"Zelda, I know you've been hurt by several men in your life, but Piers isn't like that. Don't project your insecurities onto my relationship."

I stop dead. That really stings. "Maybe that's true, Coco, or maybe, because of my experience, I can see when someone's up to something."

"I'm sorry, Zelda. I don't mean to be so harsh. I know you went through the wringer, and I'm grateful you're okay."

"I promise." I cross my hearts. "I won't let my sad adventure color my judgment."

Coco wraps her arms around me and gives me a quick squeeze. Then she motions toward the door with her head. "Let's go."

We walk out of her office, grabbing Sally on the way downstairs and out to the factory.

Our trip to the factory is accomplished in silence. Coco has opened a wound in me that hasn't quite healed yet. She apologized, sure, but what was said was said, and it's out there like a run in a fine pair of stockings. The damage has been done.

We enter the rear of the building and, without hesitation, ankle through the now-open doors of the first-floor laboratories. Alchemists, chemists, and their assistants come and go through the variously colored frosted doors that line the hall.

"Busy," I observe.

"We are on a time crunch." Coco flows with grace to one of the steel tables. "We lost so much having to be closed for almost a string."

"Tell me, what is this perfume you're working on."

"It's a new fragrance I'm going to call Mabon."

"Sounds intriguing," I say as we enter one of the labs.

Coco introduces me to the fragrance team. "Dr. Zelda Harcrow, please meet Dr. Yves and his assistant, Lauren. Dr. Yves is our lead alchemist and Nose on this project."

I shake his hand. "Nice to meet you."

"Dr. Harcrow, I've heard quite a lot about you." He shakes my hand with violent enthusiasm. "An honor to meet you."

I thank him with a nod and turn to greet the other professionals in the room.

"Dr. Malle is one of our leading chemists, and this is Dr. Trudon, another chemist. Rounding out the team are their assistants, Chloe and Gabe."

We exchange pleasantries, and I shake everyone's hand. Then I turn my attention to all the wonderful bubbly beakers, tubes, funnels, and distillers that are steaming, percolating, and whistling away on the tables. "This looks so fascinating." I look closely at all the distinctly colored liquids fizzing, burping, and swirling. "What kind of scent are you going for?"

"I would like Mabon to remind everyone of the cool crisp air that falls after the Autumn Equinox. Yet also the warmth that still emanates from Gaia during that time." She studies the codes marking the different vials. "The woodsy scent of cedar, cinnamon, clove, frankincense, possibly myrrh." She glances up at me. "I'm thinking of adding a hint of floral fragrance too."

Noticing that the laser under one of the bulbous glass containers seems low, I reach out to adjust it.

Coco's hand comes down on mine. "Don't touch!"

I pull my hand back and rub away the sting of the slap. "I was just going to turn it up."

"I've already had one explosion, Zelda; I don't need another."

"What are you saying?" I walk over to a contraption consisting of copper tubing, glass tubing, a large canister on one end, and a small vial on the other.

"I'm saying, when you're in a lab, things explode."

"Not always."

Coco scoffs. "I went through most of university with no eyebrows and very short bangs because every time you were in a lab, there was an explosion."

"Fine, I won't touch it." As I glance back at the low laser, my palms itch. It really needs to be higher.

Trying to distract myself, I motion to the entire room. "Tell me how this works."

"We decide what scents we want to go with. We use flowers, spices, fruit, grasses, leaves—almost anything you can think of."

"Is everything done through an extraction process? And which one do you use?"

"Depending on the substance, we extract using either distillation, maceration, expression, enfleurage, or in some cases, solvent extraction."

"Fascinating. Then what happens?"

"Once the different oils are collected, we decide which ones go together well to create a particular scent. It can take rotations to come up with the perfect combination."

"That long?"

"Yes, and now we're trying to bring something totally new to the market."

"Oh? Do tell."

"Most perfumes have a high oil content, which makes them extremely expensive. What we're trying to do is see how much we can dilute the oils. Still get the fragrance, but cut the cost."

"You are really branching out." Out of curiosity, I ask, "Who came up with this business plan?"

"I did, of course," responds Coco.

"It wasn't Piers?"

"No, I came up with this on my own. This may allow me to cut down on the aging process and get the product on the market faster as well."

"Attagirl. Remind me, what is Piers's job?"

Everyone in the room stops and looks at Coco. She narrows her eyes at me. "Did you want to see the lab upstairs?"

I take the hint to shut up. "I'm going to do that now." I skedaddle out and up.

Climbing the stairs, I ankle on to the back of the building. Stepping across the threshold of the bombed-out lab, I stop.

"Crappa, crap, crap."

Everything's been swept away. The burned-up debris has all been removed. The walls and the floor have been brushed and mopped clean. Nothing is left except the charred remains of the floor, the walls, and the big hole in the corner, which is still covered with a blue tarp.

Reaching into the breast pocket of my tweed jacket, I pull out my magnifying goggles case. The hinges squeak as I open it. Removing the glasses, I hook the temples over my ears, adjust the lenses, and scour the floor and walls for anything that could possibly have been missed.

I come up empty. No funny solid blue clouds. No little pieces of this or that. I had nothing. "Dang."

I spy a figure standing in the doorway out of the corner of my eye. Remembering to remove my goggles this time, I look up to see Piers standing there, glaring at me.

"Can I help you?" His face holds a flat smile.

"When did everything get cleaned up?"

The flattened corners of his mouth curl up. "I made sure we took care of it last night."

My blood begins to boil. He purposely had someone come in and scrub the room so I wouldn't find anything.

"Is that a problem?" he sneers.

I don't want him to think he's won anything, no prize of any sort. "It's okay. Thankfully, I got in here the night I rode in." The corner of my mouth slides up into a smirk. "I think I have everything I need. I was just double-checking." I glare back at him.

His face becomes almost crimson, the curl of his lips disappearing. "You know, you should be careful investigating on your own. Wouldn't want to hear about any accidents."

"Excuse me?" Did he just lob a veiled threat my way?

He opens his mouth to speak again but is quickly interrupted by the appearance of Juju.

"Mr. Astuce."

"What is it, Juju?" he asks, aggravated.

"I just received a call from Inspector Zex."

"What did that fascist copper want?"

"She's on her way over. She has news on the information you had passed on to her."

"What information?" I blurt out.

The corners are back up on his mug. "I'm sure you'll find out in good time. And Dr. Harcrow . . ."

"Yes?"

"Do try to be careful." He pivots on his heel and struts out.

Juju starts to join him, but I call her back.

"Juju, what is he talking about?"

"Two of the employees haven't returned from holiday, and one of the current formulas is missing."

"The formula that is missing—where was it kept?"

"I think a sample went missing from one of the labs. That's all I know."

I give her a deep look as I straighten up.

She hurriedly responds in a lowered voice so as not to be overheard. "I would do nothing—I would never do anything to hurt Coco. I'm just telling you what I know." She sounds sincere.

"Thank you, Juju."

I wait till she exits before running down to speak with Coco.

Slowly, I turn the knob, open the lab door, and peek my head in. Coco spots me and waves me over with a flap of her hand. I remain as quiet as a mousacorn walking over so as not to disturb them working. I watch the Nose very closely. The entire team all stand in a little huddle, passing around a test tube.

"Come over here," Coco says, calling me to enter the seemingly sacred circle. "I want your opinion."

Really, it feels good to be back in a lab again, being part of something like what I'm witnessing in front of me. I eagerly join the group.

Coco's eyes brighten as she hands me a long slender test tube. "Here. What do you think?"

Being an alchemist, I know the rules: you never smell directly from any container. Many combinations of anything can be volatile. And How! Holding the test tube away from my face in one hand, I slowly wave my other over the opening. Wafting the fragrance into my nostrils allows the smells to meet my olfactory nerves.

"Yowza!" I exclaim.

"Do you like it?" There's excitement in her voice. "What do you smell?"

I take my time wafting and thinking. Also attempting not to embarrass myself in front of my peers. "I smell a fruity opening of bergamot. I can smell the myrrh." I waft again. "Jasmine."

"Anything else?"

"Hmmm . . ." I close my eyes, allowing my mind to work. "Spices, earthy yet sweet." I open my eyes. "Poppies."

Coco brushes the side of her nose with her finger.

"I love it." I hand back the test tube.

"Attagirl. There are a few more wonders in there, but you nailed the basics."

Chapter Fourteen

A series of knocks has everyone in the circle turning their heads toward the door. "Come in," Coco shouts in response to the repeated knocking.

The door creaks open, and Piers shoves his head in. "Coco, dear, Inspector Zex is here with some information on the investigation. You have a moment?"

"Ab-so-lute-ly." She puts a cork in the vial with the new concoction and moves toward the door, just as it swings open to reveal the strict-looking Inspector Zex.

Myself, I slowly fade to the back of the group, not wanting to be in Zex's line of sight. I want to hear what is being said and not thrown out on my keister. Moving a little farther back to the counter, I stand quietly, listening while I fiddle with one of the laser burners.

Inspector Zex is very up front. "Dr. Charden, I have some information."

"Give me the goods," Coco says sweetly.

Coco's smile and higher-octave response seem to irk Zex. The inspector lets out a heavy sigh, clears her throat, and gets to her point. "With the additional information that Mr. Astuce supplied us with . . ." Zex folds her hands behind her back, stands even more erect, and tilts her chin up. "It has come to our attention that a formula has shown up on Trade Island that may be the one you were working on for lip rouge." Her blood-red mouth tightens. "We suspect any of the employees that have not been accounted for may be the culprit."

Coco's hand flies to her open mouth. "Yowza."

Moving from behind Zex, Piers stands next to Coco and puts a hand in the middle of her back. He isn't looking at Zex, instead studying Coco's reaction.

"Please fill us in, Inspector," he says.

Zex nods. "The formula has been retrieved on Trade Island. Since the theft involves espionage and the delivery of stolen goods across Tesla's borders, this has become a national security issue; everything will be handled by the National Security Council. If you have any further questions, you may refer them to the NSC."

I close my eyes for a moment to take in what she is saying. Screwing up my lips, I take a deep breath and raise my hand from the back of the room. "Ahem."

Everyone turns, their eyes centering on me. Coco cocks her head. Piers's face reddens. Zex removes her hands from behind her back and crosses them in front of her chest, narrowing her eyes at me.

I lower my hand and smile. "What about the body?"

"Excuse me?" asks Inspector Zex.

"The burned-up body—who was it?"

Inspector Zex does not answer right away. Instead, she stands there with daggers coming straight from her eyes. I think she is mustering up the patience to answer me. The room becomes deathly quiet, and all eyes shift to Zex.

"At this time, we still do not have any information on the identity of said corpse. It is believed to be an accomplice of the employees who stole the formula."

I can't let it go. "How do you know?"

Steam is emanating from her collar. A finger rises to adjust her collar. "That will be for the NSC to determine. This is no longer my case." She nods to Piers and Coco, turns on her heel, and exits the lab.

"Well, that seems to wrap everything up," exclaims Piers.

I move toward Coco and Piers. "How?"

"You heard the inspector; it was espionage. We have our formula back, and the NSC will have a manhunt out for the culprit."

"How did the employee get the formula? I thought it wasn't finished."

Coco looks up, breaking her silence. "It's not finished. The formula isn't worth anything yet."

"Then why would they steal it now?" I ask. "Why wouldn't they wait for you to finish it?"

Coco eyes Piers. "Good question."

"Well, maybe—" Piers stumbles over his words. "Well—well, maybe—he didn't know it wasn't finished." Piers shifts back and forth on his feet. "Maybe he thought he could finish it."

"Did they tell you which employee it was?" I ask.

"No," he says. "I just gave her all the files of the employees who had not called in since the explosion."

"Maybe I need to look at the list."

"Applesauce!" Piers protests. "I don't think that's necessary."

Coco's face has become ashen. I can see she has come to a realization. "I think Zelda needs to see the list."

"Unicornfeathers!" exclaims Piers. "The NSC can handle this, not some washed-up alchemist."

Washed up! I pull back my arm, ready to haul off and deck him. Maybe a little chin music will put this guy in order.

Coco grabs my arm to hold me back, so I content myself with words. "I'm anything but washed up, and unless you have something to hide, I expect a full list by the end of the turn."

Piers appears to be having a stroke, his face contorting. "I'll make sure Juju has it for you." He walks to the door. Pausing with his hand on the knob, he turns back to me. "By the end of the turn."

The door slams shut behind him.

"I think you made him mad," Coco says to me gently.

"Ish kabibble. Coco, I understand you have a lot of respect for him, and I can't even begin to comprehend your relationship. But please listen to me when I say that something's not right."

I look back at the chemists, alchemists, and their assistants, and they quickly pull their attention away from us and scatter to do busy work so as not to disturb us.

I lower my voice. "Coco, this may have nothing to do with what's currently going on. I could be totally off base on this. But he's hiding something; I just feel it."

Coco covers her face with her hands and sniffs. "Zelda." Removing her hands from her face, Coco puts her hands over her hearts. "Until now, I didn't want to believe it. But you're right; he's not on the level with me."

I put both my hands on her shoulders. With my voice still lowered, I ask an exceedingly difficult question. "What do you want me to do?"

"Do?" She raises her eyes to meet mine.

"I can drop this right now. I can go and spend time with my niece and nephew and then go back to Jean."

"Or?" She sniffs again.

"Or I can stay and find out what's going on."

"What should I do, Zelda?"

"I can't answer that for you. Coco, this is your decision, but I will honor your choice."

"Can you?"

"You are my friend. Of course I can."

"Zelda—" Coco stops. She swallows hard, and her voice cracks as she continues. "Zelda, please stay."

"I'm here for you."

Just as I give her a kiss on the cheek, a pop echoes through the room. The crack of shattering glass follows, before we are all thrown back hard against the wall.

The assistants are on their feet in a jiffy, pulling out the fire-foam canisters and getting to work smothering the fires started by the explosion.

Coco, up against the wall next to me, turns her head. "Zelda, you just had to mess with the burner."

"Whoops?"

Chapter Fifteen

I leave behind the mess I caused and wait outside for the hired car to take me to downtown Capital City. The green-and-yellow taxi pulls up.

"Where to, lady?"

I slide into the cab. "The main Legere Legalis downtown, please."

The lever gives a metallic click as the meter starts. Sitting back, I settle in for the drive into the city. This could give me some time to think about the few puzzle pieces I have.

"Been here long?"

Terrific, a chatty cabbie. Just what I don't need. "Just a few turns," I answer, because I'm polite.

"Business or pleasure?"

"A little of both." Hoping this satisfies him, I look out the window and watch as the factories turn into empty landscape.

"So, how do you like our city?"

"It's been a while since I visited. It surely has expanded."

"Can't stop progress."

"No, you can't. It's part of nature to constantly move forward and expand."

"Don't get me wrong. I'm not complaining."

I continue to gaze out the window as the landscape changes into shiny, sleek skyscrapers and streetcars and pedestrians.

Cabbie can't take a hint; he is still talking away. "Business is booming. We have more and more companies starting up, which means more cab fare for me."

"Nice." I nod and smile.

"Yep, prosperous times."

I don't respond.

"Here we are," informs my driver. "Be five credits. You want me to open the door for you?"

"No, thank you, I have it." I exit the vehicle and wave as I hobble to the stone steps of the Safety Council's Legere Legalis.

The building looks like a new construction. The structure is at least twenty floors tall, comprising steel, white stone, and mirrored glass. Entering the first set of doors into the vestibule, I stand there for a moment, collecting my thoughts, before I pass through the second set of doors. The lobby contains tulip-shaped pink fiberglass chairs that attach to one another. Lined up in rows facing one another, the chairs are provided for citizens of every shape and size.

"Busy place," I comment to myself.

I ankle on over to the main desk at the far end of the lobby. The long shoulder-high desk that guards the working area of the station is attended by an elderly gentleman in a blue constable's uniform with shiny brass buttons. The white-haired constable looks down at me from his perch.

"How can I help you, miss?" he asks politely.

"I'm looking for your forensics unit and one of your investigators, Ethan Hodge."

"What you need him for, young lady?"

I raise my eyebrows. "Really need to see him."

His voice becomes a little gruff as he starts talking down to me. "What is your business?"

"My business?"

"Yes, young lady. What would be your business with the investigator Ethan Hodge?" The old man is condescending.

I slip a little blue hair behind my ear, and my fists tighten up.

"Are you having a little trouble?"

He may not realize it, but he's pushing me. I smile, trying to keep back the venom. Quaintly, I say, "It's personal." Then I bat my eyelashes.

"Aha." The old codger chuckles and winks.

It takes everything in me to hold my tongue.

"Well, you won't find them here."

"No?"

"No."

I slip more hair behind my ear. "Where can I find him?"

"In the old building."

"The old building?"

"The old building."

Patience, Zelda, patience, I tell myself. "I'm not from Capital City; I'm visiting from out of town. Could you direct me to the 'old building'?" I make quotation marks in the air with my fingers.

"Well, why didn't you say so?" the old man comments. "Just exit through these doors, make a right, and walk down three blocks. There's an old stone-and-brick building only about three floors tall. You'll see a good-sized engraved stone that says City Building. Just go through them doors and down to the basement, and you'll most likely find him there."

"Most likely?"

"Most likely."

"Thank you?"

"Now be on your way, and have a good turn." He shoos me away with the back of his hand.

As I walk the several blocks, my ankle starts bothering me. Terrific. I'm hoping I'll come to the building soon. I really need to get off my leg.

I find the building exactly as the old codger described. It's a deep-rust-colored brick building with arched windows. The covered entrance only has one set of doors leading in. No vestibule, no desk, no officer who can give me directions, no secretary—just a small front waiting room and a long hall.

I pass several wooden doors painted with gold lettering. Opening the door marked stairs, I look up and then down. I close the door and peer down the hall. What, no lift? Now my ankle is throbbing in pain. "Unicornfeathers," I swear under my breath. I open doors to the stairs once more and begin the descent.

The first set are pretty easy. I get to the landing and check my ankle; it's swelling up. I gimp down the second set and am greeted by a door labeled *Basement.*

I've arrived.

Opening the door reveals a small hall. I don't know if the space is considered a hall; it's more like an area with no purpose. Corridors of older structures built during the Steam Age were often designed this way: lots of rooms, lots of doors, lots of corners. Not the open spacing we see in modern buildings, with their clean, sweeping lines and rounded edges.

There are only two doors to choose from, so I knock on the first.

A voice calls out, "Come in."

Clutching the knob, I push the door open to reveal an exceptionally large room with lots of waist-high steel tables, microscopes, shelves full of different beakers and containers filled with different colored liquids, sandy solids, cotton balls, and such. There are wooden racks that hold the flat pieces of glass that are used when examining items under a microscope. Shallow cylindrical glass dishes are stacked neatly. I can see some contain agar, which is used when they need some sort of setting agent.

"Hello?" I call as I search for the owner of the voice that invited me in. I make my way to the back of the room, to a steel cabinet that appears to be a laminar flow cabinet. Sitting in front of it is Ethan.

He swivels around on a stool and winks. "To what do I owe the pleasure of your visit, Dr. Harcrow?"

"I came to see your new digs."

"Aha. And?"

"And what?"

"I know I don't know you all that well, but I doubt you came just to see me."

"I could use a seat. My ankle is a bit swollen."

Standing up, Ethan escorts me over to a messy desk and a round leather swivel chair.

I take a seat. "Thanks. You're a darb of a guy."

Leaning against the desk, he crosses his arms. "What can I do you for?"

"You see right through me," I confess.

"Not really, it's just a guess."

"Well, then, you guess correctly. Although it is nice to see you and your setup here. It's stellar, except you're in the basement. Windows?"

Ethan points to either end of the room, where half-moon block glass windows let in light.

"That's depressing."

"It can be. Luckily, the work is interesting."

I open my mouth to speak, but instead, a screechy voice calls from behind me, "You're a looker, you're a looker—awk. You're a looker, hot-tot-tot-tot—awk." A long whistle follows.

I almost break my neck turning around. "What is that?"

"That . . ." Ethan moves behind me. Lifting a sheet, he reveals a cage housing a green horned parrot.

"What the stars?" I get up and hobble over for a better look.

"He's a witness in a crime."

"A witness."

"I am a witness, I'm a witness," repeats the bird.

Ethan continues. "Here in forensics, we are the low man on the totem pole. The inspector feels the parrot is evidence and put it down here with me."

"Evidence? I thought you said it was a witness."

"He talks too much, and he is annoying."

I point at him and click my tongue. "Gotcha." I gimp back to my seat and put my leg up.

"You want a wrap for that?"

"I think it'll be fine. I just need to get off it for a little while." I adjust myself in the chair. "Spill. When you were going through the stuff from the exploded lab, did you come across something that seemed bluish and cloudy in nature?"

"I'm not sure exactly what you're talking about," he says. "I really haven't had a chance to go through all the debris." He points to a notably large barrel sitting next to one of the steel tables. "That's just one of them."

"Oh, boy."

"Inspector Zex didn't want me to go through those just yet. She insists I go through all the burnt papers first."

"She didn't want you to go through the charred remains to find the accelerant?"

"Zex is kind of particular about how she likes to do things." Hodge is being polite.

"Personally, I think Zex needs some sex, because she seems a little uptight to me."

"I don't know about—"

"Zex needs sex, Zex needs sex, hot-hot-hot."

Hodge and I laugh at the bird's repetition.

"Attaboy, pretty bird." I coo at the green horned parrot.

"I'm a pretty bird, I'm a pretty bird—awk. I'm a witness, I'm a witness—awk. You're a looker, you're a looker, hot-hot-hot, Zex needs sex, Zex needs sex, hot-hot-hot—awk."

Ethan's face suddenly goes ashen.

"What's wrong?"

"I hope he doesn't say that when Zex picks him up for court in a few turns. She'll crucify me."

"We just have to teach it to say something else."

He slid me a look.

I shrug and change the subject. "I found blue stuff."

"You are more than welcome to sift through the debris." He thumbs over his shoulder to the barrels.

I frown. "Tell me about the body."

"What's to tell? It was burned beyond recognition, so there were no fingerprints. Nothing left to tell us who he was."

"You know it was born male?"

"By the facial bone structure."

"Was he Homo sapiens or Homo illuminati?"

"Many of the organs were completely destroyed, almost melted. It'll be difficult to tell if he has one heart or two at this time. I'm trying to carefully restore it through a hydration technique so the cutter can examine his internal organs, but this may go as an unsolved case."

"Jeepers, that's terrible."

"That's terrible—awk. Zex needs sex, the sexy sex on the pretty bird—awk-hot-hot-hot."

"Shut up!" Ethan roughly says as he walks over and puts the sheet back over the cage, completely covering it this time. "That should make him quiet."

"It's worth a try."

"Listen, I'm about to head out for lunch. Would you like to join me? It's right down the street; you won't have to walk far."

"Love to."

"Afterward, we can come back here, and if you wish, you can start going through the barrels."

"Sounds like a plan."

A rapid knocking at the door has me jumping out of my seat. A determined and familiar shrill voice pushes through the door. "Hodge!"

Ethan's eyes pop, and he mouths to me, "It's Inspector Zex."

"Zex needs sex—awk. Zex needs sex, pretty bird," comes from the covered cage.

"This isn't good," I mouth back.

Ethan shouts at the door, "One moment, sir, I mean ma'am."

The rapping at the door becomes louder, and her voice becomes shriller. "Hodge."

A sudden yank on my arm, and Hodge pulls me over to another door. He jerks it open. "A broom closet?" I put my hands out. "Oh no, I'm not getting in there."

"Please, Dr. Harcrow." With both hands, he shoves me into the closet and closes the door.

"Zex needs sex, Zex needs sex—awk. I am a witness, I'm a witness, hot-hot-hot-hot—awk."

The closet door opens again, and Ethan pushes the large cage into my arms. "Here. Keep it quiet." He slams the door shut.

"Well, this is surprising," I say.

Placing the cage on the floor as quietly and gently as I can, I put my ear to the door.

"I'm a witness, I'm a witness."

"Shut your trap, you goofy bird."

"What was that?" demands the strict voice of the inspector.

"Um," Ethan begins. "It's that bird."

"You mean the annoying horned parrot?"

"Yes, ma'am. I put it in the closet because it was being very noisy and breaking my concentration."

"Well, that's fine, I guess. Just make sure it stays alive."

"Yes, ma'am. May I ask why you came down? You never come down here."

"I came to tell you we're off the Coco Cosmetics case."

"I don't understand, Inspector. I'm not even nearly done with my work."

"Not my call, Hodge."

"May I ask why?"

"It seems the case extends beyond our borders and has now become an NSC case."

"I see," Ethan replies. "What do I do with the evidence we've collected and the body?"

"Put it aside. NSC will come for it."

"Yes, ma'am."

"Between you and me, Hodge,"—I can hear the door opening, its hinges squeaking—"something about this case stinks."

There's a long pause. Pressing my ear harder against the door, I hear her say, "And stay away from that Dr. Harcrow. She's dangerous." I hear the click of the door closing.

I wait for a few moments. When nothing happens, I feel for the door handle—only I can't find one. Jeepers! I can't get out.

"Hodge! Hodge! Let me out." Leaning on the door, I try to push it open. I begin to feel panicky, my hearts racing. "Hodge?" My voice shakes.

A bright light abruptly pierces my eyes, and I fall flat on my face.

"Why were you leaning against the door?"

I look up at Hodge's rosy face. "I panicked."

"Jeepers, I'd never leave you trapped in there." He holds out his hand, which I grasp and pull myself up with.

"Sorry, it's been kind of rough since I left Fulcrum."

Ethan grabs the cage out of the closet. "I'm sure. Have you been talking to someone about it?"

"Don't worry. I'm dealing." I sit down and lean back in the swivel chair.

He ignores my response. "I'm not sure if you heard what Inspectors Zex said."

I lift the sheet from the cage and look at the bird. The horned fowl is moving back and forth from foot to foot on his little perch. "I heard about it earlier when I was at Coco's. Although I didn't realize she thought something was hinky about it too."

"Zex needs sex, Zex needs sex—awk. I'm a pretty boy, hot-hot-hot—awk."

I pull the sheet back down. "What about lunch?"

"She thinks you're dangerous."

"Doesn't matter what she thinks. It matters what you think."

He grabs the top of the cage and heads toward the door. "The café's only a few doors down. Are you coming?"

"You're bringing the bird?"

"I am a witness, I'm a witness, Zex needs sex—awk. Zex needs sex, pretty bird, pretty bird, hot-hot-hot."

Chapter Sixteen

Ethan and I step out into the warm sun and onto the sidewalk. "Which way?" I ask.

Ethan points. "Down that way, just a block or so."

"How do you like it here in Capital City?"

"It has a vibrant nightlife, people are pretty nice, and the apartments are reasonable."

"Do you miss your family?"

"That may be the upside of having moved to the Capital." He snickers.

"I'm on that trolley with you," I say, thinking about my own family. "Streets are pretty quiet here. Not a lot of traffic."

"Not too many people own a motor. Most folks who live within the city get around by trolley, foot, scooter, or bicycle."

"How do you leave the city?"

"You can hire a dimbox or take the trolley to the train station. Or"—he points to the sky—"we do have dirigibles, you know."

Following his finger with my gaze, I smile. "I guess I just can't imagine not being able to zip around on my Zenith whenever I choose and go wherever I want."

"We're not all as lucky as you are, Doctor. Some of us have to stay put."

"Pshaw. Look at you."

"Me?"

"Yes, you." I laugh. "You were a constable in Fulcrum. Now you're working forensics in Capital City. You didn't stay put."

"Ha! You are right, I guess. I didn't see it that way."

"Perception is everything."

"What does that mean?"

"Well . . ."

"Here we are." He waves to the door of a little café.

A tinkle rings out, announcing our arrival, as I open the door for Ethan and the crazy horned parrot.

"Where would you like to sit?" he asks as we scan the room for an available table.

"I—" My peepers abruptly stop on a very intriguing and hostile conversation. Eyeing an available booth to the right, I grab Ethan by the shirt sleeve and drag him toward the booth.

"Okey dokey, I guess this will do." Placing the birdcage on the table, Ethan settles on the bench across from me and tries to smooth the wrinkles out of his sleeve.

"Shush," I whisper, dipping my head. I thumb over my shoulder. "That's Piers. It looks like they're arguing."

"Piers is?"

"Piers Astuce. He's my friend Coco's husband. I thought you knew that."

"Not really. I'm just a bag-'em-and-tag-'em guy. I'm the one who gets to sift through the mess; I don't get to talk to people."

"Can you tell what they're discussing?" I sat with my back toward Piers, not wanting to be recognized, so Ethan has a better view

"Looks pretty intense, from what I can tell."

"Can you get close to their booth?" I ask. "I'd like to know what they're arguing about."

"How am I supposed to do that?"

Ducking down, I peer around the back side of the booth. Piers and his companion sit at the far end of the restaurant, near the restrooms. I catch an idea. "Go to the bathroom."

"I don't have to go."

"Go to the men's room and listen at the door so you can eavesdrop on the conversation."

"What if someone comes in?"

"Wash your hands."

"Wash my hands?"

"So you don't look conspicuous."

"This is your plan?"

"You have a better one?"

"Excuse me while I go to the restroom." Ethan gets up and walks toward the back of the restaurant.

I'm itching to watch them and find out what they're saying. Instead, since we're here for lunch and I'm hungry, I pick up a menu and cruise the lunch specials.

Making my decision, I toss aside the menu and rummage through my purse for my compact. I'm not concerned that my nose is shiny; I just want to see what Piers and his mysterious luncheon companion are doing. Peering into the mirror as I angle it toward the back of the café, I smooth out my hair to make what I'm doing less obvious. The young man sitting with Piers leans aggressively over the table, his face centimeters from Piers's anger-red countenance. It must be some lulu of a conversation.

Suddenly, the young man sits back confidently. He must think he has the upper hand.

Maneuvering my mirror a little, I pick up the soft, flat puff from the powder and dab my nose ever so lightly. Not that I can see where exactly I'm dabbing; I'm much more interested in what's happening behind me. Their mouths move with zealous intention, as if each word is a matter of life and death.

An elderly gentleman scrapes his chair against the floor at the table next to me. In my mirror, I watch him slowly hobble his way to the back. Anticipating his intended destination, I angle my compact to focus on the gentlemen's room. As I expect, the old man goes in. Only a moment passes before I spy Ethan popping out. I watch him hustle back, keeping his head down till he slides back into the booth.

"Spill," I whisper excitedly.

Ethan places the strangely quiet birdcage on the bench beside him. "The two men were arguing. The young one said, 'I'm alive. I know you're disappointed.'"

"You don't say?"

"The older gentleman—"

"Piers."

"Piers said, 'What do you want?'"

"Really?"

"The younger man answered, 'I wanted my formula back.'"

"Ha!" I'm now extremely intrigued. "I wonder if he means the formula for the new lipstick."

"Piers said, 'You already received payment for it.'" Ethan picks up the menu and starts looking for something to order.

"Is that it?"

"Jeepers, no. The young man informed Piers that it wasn't his problem." Ethan sets the menu down. "Then Piers begged the kid: 'If I don't give them the formula, they'll kill me.'"

"Did he spill who wants to rub him out?" I'm sitting on the edge of my seat. This is getting good.

"He told him to just give them the cabbage back."

"What did Piers say to that?"

"Told him he needed the paper."

"Piers is rich; he's got credits."

"That's what the young guy sneered at him, that he had plenty. But Piers said, 'Damn the new currency credits, they're traceable.'"

"Hmm . . . so he needs untraceable funds. Jeepers, what else?"

"The kid told him again that it wasn't his problem. Piers came back and claimed, 'If it weren't for me, you'd never have been able to develop it.'"

"Did he spill what he was developing?" This is a real nail biter.

Ethan shakes his head. "He didn't, but he did say he didn't expect Piers to try to cheat him."

"Dang."

"There's more." Ethan shifts a little in his seat. "Piers offered him half the kale."

"Did the kid bite?"

"Nope, he said he wanted his formula and that if Piers refused to back off, he'd go to the NSC."

I lean over the table. "Seriously?"

"Piers tried to call his bluff."

"And . . . ?"

"The kid laughed and said, 'Watch me.'"

"Anything else?"

"Piers said, 'What's to prevent me from copying it and selling it anyway?'"

"Coco already has the lipstick formula. It's not even completed yet. I'm confused."

"I don't know. Just then, some old guy needed to use the restroom. I had to exit so as not to draw attention. I missed what formula they were referring to."

"Can't be the lipstick. I must find out who this guy is," I say, just as a nondescript waiter appears.

"Can I take your drink order?"

"Yes, please," I say. "I'll take an iced white tea."

"I would like an orange fizzy." As the waiter moves away, Ethan adds, "If the guy Piers is talking to heads out, should we follow him?"

"Hot stuff, hot-hot-hot." squawks the previously silent horned parrot.

I try to quiet the annoying bird.

"Maybe it's hungry?" Ethan lifts the sheet up a little higher over the cage.

I shrug. "What do they eat?"

"Your guess is as good as mine."

"Seeds, nuts, and insects," answers an uninvited voice.

I glance up. The interloper, who has a cute, boyish face, flashes me a smile and a wink before I can utter a word. Then he vanishes out the door.

"That's the guy Piers was arguing with," Ethan comments. "Do you know him?"

"Not that I remember." I cock my head and furrow my brows; he seemed familiar.

Ethan taps my hand to bring me out of my search of the gray cells. He subtly points at a man heading toward the door. Dressed all in black, the man swiftly pulls a black cap from his overcoat and places it over his thick, wavy dark hair. A shiver runs up and down my spine. The man surveys the street from the glass door before stepping outside.

"Did he just follow the guy you said met with Piers?" I ask Ethan.

"Can't tell from my angle."

"Was he with Piers?"

Ethan lifts his shoulders and tilts his head. "I think he was at one of the other tables. I can't be sure."

The waiter clears his throat as he sets glasses on the table., "Your drinks. And may I take your order?"

"Thanks," says Ethan.

I nod in agreement and proceed to place my order.

"Do birds eat tuna fish sandwiches?" I ask once I've finished.

Ethan raises his eyebrows. "You want to feed a horned parrot a sandwich?"

"I`m trying to think outside the box." I take a swig of my tea. The cool refreshing liquid slides down my throat. "Do birds drink tea?"

Ethan puts a hand gently on the birdcage as if to protect it. "Are you trying to kill the bird?"

"Why are you following me?"

The angry demand gives me a jolt, and I turn to find Piers standing at the end of our booth.

"I'm not trailing you." I respond in a very snotty voice.

"Then why are you here?" His voice is a growl now.

"Lunch." I take a gulp of my tea, grinning as wide as I can, I set my glass down with purpose on the table. I cannot stand this guy.

"Why don't I believe you?"

"Guilty conscience?"

"You heard the inspector; they have a suspect."

I just stare at him, letting my eyes sear right into him.

"Let it go and blow. You're not wanted here."

"I'll leave when I'm good and ready. You're not the boss of me." I stick my tongue at him. A childish move, but oh, so satisfying.

"I hope you don't regret your decision," Piers responds in a threatening tone.

Ethan pipes in. "Sir—"

"I'm a witness, I'm a witness, I'm witness," the loud parrot squawks.

Piers's face reddens as he looks around the café. All customer attention zeroes in on him. Behind him, our waiter is trying to get past him with our lunch plates. "Excuse me."

Like an angry, petulant child, Piers stamps out of the café.

Chapter Seventeen

"Thanks for lunch, Doctor," Ethan says.

"My pleasure." We head out to the sidewalk. "And please, it's Zelda."

He blushes. "Zelda."

"Attaboy." I take a deep breath and pat my tummy. "I think I ate way too much."

"Their food is always great."

"Hodge—"

"Ethan."

I nod. "Ethan, can I have a look at the debris from the lab? I'm hoping somewhere in those barrels is another piece of the blue cloud substance." I could kick myself for losing a possible clue.

"Ab-so-lute-ly," he answers. "First, I'm going to take birdbrain to my place."

A shrill whistle accosts my ears. "Hot-hot-hot, what a looker," the bird squawks as an airtight skirt struts by.

"Watch it, mister," she squeaks at Ethan.

"I-I-I-I'm sorry." Ethan's face deepens to crimson in utter embarrassment. He promptly adjusts the sheet over the cage to make sure it's completely covered.

"I see the dilemma."

"I can meet you back here in a half?"

I move my ankle back and forth. Time off my feet at the restaurant made an impact. "I can check a few stores out and meet you at your lab."

He gives me a thumbs-up and crosses the road, heading for the streetcar stop.

The annoying squawking continues. "I'm a witness, I'm witness, hot stuff, hot stuff."

I watch as Ethan struggles to get on the trolley car with the oversize cage. "That bird is going to get himself axed."

Now, which way to go?

My eye catches on the man in black, who stands in the middle of the walk staring in my direction. My gut lurches, and the deafening bells and whistles of warning blare in my head. Swiftly, I turn my head in the other direction, acting as if I don't notice him, and check my bag for my compact.

Where is it?

My hands shake. I thought he was following the dreamboat, the kid with the bright smile.

Futz!

My fumbling fingers clasp the flat, circular compact. The bumps of colored glass stones that decorate the front of the smooth Bakelite compact give me a little reassurance. Lifting it out of my bag, hands still trembling, I open it at eye level. I pretend to touch up the munitions, checking my lipstick, even as I get the angle right to view my voyeur.

The man in black has moved to the brick front of the store. He's terrible at nonchalance, posing himself with his back against the wall and the sole of one wing tip flat against the brick. Problem is, he doesn't know what to do with his hands. First he puts them in his pockets, then he crosses his arms over his chest, and then his paws are pushed back in his coat pockets.

Jeez, he sticks out like a sore thumb. Really, he needs a different line of work. I close the compact and begin walking slowly down the sidewalk, keeping the compact in my hand just in case. Halting in front of a store window, I slip a glance to the side. I'm still being followed.

The store window is filled with toys.

Well, if I'm going to pretend to shop, I might as well make it look good. I pop into the toy store and shop for a few things for Flo and Eggs.

"Could you please have these delivered?" I ask the salesperson.

"Yes, miss."

I proceed to give her Ava's address and hand her my card to pay. I slyly check the street as I exit the store. The man in black stands in front of the store window. Holding my breath, I walk past him, trying not to make eye contact. As I continue down the block, my ankle begins to throb a bit. Stopping, I raise the green jeweled colored Bakelite compact and pretend to powder my nose. My stalker is still in front of the toy store, staring in the window, fidgeting back and forth, and occasionally looking my way.

He is giving me the heebie-jeebies. I need to lose this goober, and fast.

Closing my compact once more, I stroll farther down the block. Crossing an alleyway, I come across a modern ladies' clothier. I pretend to window-shop to see if my shadow is still behind me. There he is, just in front of the alley, stooping down as he pretends to tie the laces on his black wing tips. At least this time, he actually looks normal.

I duck into the store while his head is down.

The quaint shop has the latest high fashions. Cascading racks of suits greet me as I enter. Waterfalls of dresses hang on one side of the shop, while the other bears shelves of shoes and accessories. Farther into the store are plaster mannequins dressed to the nines, modeling the latest Spring Equinox couture.

One particular coat draws my attention. The deep-forest-green velvet coat drapes down to mid-shin. The thick brown faux fur asymmetrical collar is realistic in color and texture. The wide cuffs match the cowl, and three simple velvet-covered buttons close the full overcoat, giving it a seamless appearance. Classy.

I forget my dilemma momentarily and decide a shopping spree is in order. I must be feeling better. I'm sober and thinking about clothes.

What's next? Hats?

Yes, hats!

I garner the attention of the saleslady and have her show me complementary hats. The hat Mae chose for me isn't corny, but it just doesn't match the fabulous new coat I decide I must have.

"I love your ensemble," the salesclerk gushes. "What style!"

I think she's laying it on a bit thick, but I can accept a compliment. "Thanks."

She continues to shower me with compliments, till I am practically drowning. I try on a myriad of distinctive styles of millinery.

The bell announcing the front door opening makes me jump and brings me back to reality: I am being stalked by a man in black who may or may not work for Piers. Who may or may not have attacked me at the motel on my journey to Capital City. My head spins toward the door as my hearts jump into my throat.

"Are you okay?" questions the salesclerk.

I sigh a breath of relief at the sight of a young woman sheepishly walking in.

"I'm fine," I assure the salesclerk. "Just a bit stressed today, that's all. Thank you."

"Let shopping be your key to relaxation," the salesclerk happily touts.

I throw on a fake smile.

The young woman begins to browse the hats, flipping the tags and sighing at each turn. I notice her suit is almost the duplicate of the tweed I am wearing.

The salesclerk notices as well and looks down her nose at the gal. "I don't think you can afford the things we carry."

I adjust the velvet cap on my head, minding my own business.

The salesclerk, who is impeccably dressed and perfectly coiffed, adjusts the pin cushion secured around her wrist with an elastic band and leans toward me. In a thinly veiled whisper, she comments, "These cheap suits nowadays, copying the higher fashions. What a shame. Why can't they just get clothes that are more appropriate to their station?"

I raise my brow and look at the young girl. She clearly overheard the salesclerk's comment; I can see tears brimming her eyes.

Ignoring the salesclerk, I speak directly to the girl. "Where did you get your lovely suit?"

She seems shocked that I'm conversing with her. "I picked this up last week on the other side of town near my home. It's made of some new man-made fabric." Looking me up and down, her eyes widen. "It looks like yours."

The saleslady hops in. "Not at all the same!"

Before she can make another remark, I interject, "Well, it's very becoming on you."

"Do you think so?" The girl blushes. "I have an interview today. I want to make a good impression."

"You will."

"Thanks. I need a hat. I only have a couple of hats, nothing that goes with this suit."

"What," the salesclerk says snottily, "don't they make cheap hats to match your cheap suit?"

I am really trying not to haul off and smack this snooty saleslady.

Dropping her head, the girl begins to make her way to the door.

"Wait!" I call her back. "I'm buying a new hat to go with my new coat. I have no use for my current hat."

"Miss, that's exceedingly kind and charitable of you, but no thank you. I'm sure I can find a hat elsewhere."

"You misunderstand. It's a gift from me to you."

"Why?"

"Anyone smart enough to buy a suit made out of a fabric I created deserves a big thank-you from me."

The young girl's eyes bug out. "Created?"

I believe I hear the salesclerk make a funny, surprised squeak, but I completely ignore her. "Yes, I'm the alchemist who created the imitation spider silk. I'm grateful to see it on the market so quickly."

"Still," the girl responds, "I can't take your hat."

"When is your interview?"

"In an hour."

I hand her the hat. "You don't have time to shop. Take it. If you don't want to keep it, just bring it back to the shop, and they'll forward it to me."

"Jeepers, miss, you're the darb!" She puts on the hat.

"It's a perfect fit! Good luck on your interview."

She waves as she leaves the store, and I turn back to the salesclerk with a smug smile. "Now, let me see some more hats."

I make my final choices, and the salesclerk begins to wrap my purchases for delivery. "I think I'll wear my new coat out." Taking off my jacket, I hand it over the counter. "Have this sent with my purchases, please."

"Certainly, miss," she says in a subdued tone.

I eye the clock behind the sales counter. Time to hustle back to the crime lab. Slipping on the coat and hat, I head out the door, keeping my peepers peeled for any sign of the man in black.

He is nowhere to be seen.

Chapter Eighteen

The frosted glass in the lab door rattles as I knock.

"Enter," Ethan calls.

I slip in and begin slipping off my coat and hat. "Hey."

Ethan's head is hovering over a microscope. "I put some screens and a bucket over by the steel table near the door. Should be a good place for you to work."

"Gee, you're swell." I hang my coat and hat in the closet I which I hid earlier. Then I roll up my sleeves and get busy.

I stick the screen form trays on top of each other, placing the finest mesh on the bottom and the coarsest mesh on the top. Laying out a square white cotton linen on the stainless-steel table, I settle the tiered trays on top of it. Then I begin dumping a small amount of debris into the top square.

Lifting the top tray, I shake it back and forth, rattling the larger pieces of debris and allowing the smaller pieces to fall through to the next tray. The first lens of my magnifying goggles clicks into place, and I begin to pick up each piece with tweezers and examine them.

Nothing.

Removing the top tray, I continue with each subsequent tray till I reach the white linen square.

Nothing

Blowing out a frustrated sigh, I pull my magnifying goggles roughly off my face. Then I start over with another bucket.

Nothing.

Pushing my goggles onto my forehead, I turn my head to look at the barrels of debris sitting to the side. I am never going to find what I'm looking for before the NSC goons come out and take away the evidence.

"You okay over there?" Ethan inquires.

"Just frustrated. Taking longer than I thought."

"Need help?"

"Maybe I'm barking up the wrong tree."

"How so?"

"If the piece of evidence I'm looking for is important, why haven't I come across any other pieces, large or small?" I complain.

Ethan stares at me, then looks at the barrels. "Well, there's a lot of debris." He pauses. "And you don't know the original size of the item before the explosion."

"True. I agree, plus since I'm unable to determine what the object is, I don't know how it reacts to high heat."

"What if the piece you had was broken off a larger piece that was removed before the explosion?"

"So many possibilities!" I pound the heel of my hands against my forehead. "Too many possibilities."

"I'm going to grab myself a cup of joe. You want to come with me?"

Pushing my stool back from the waist-high table, I say, "Ab-so-lute-ly."

Grabbing our coats, we ankle on out of the building and into the dimming sunlight and cooling temperatures.

"There's this great little shop that sells a variety of pastries and hot or cold beverages," Ethan suggests.

"Didn't we pass it on the way to the café?"

"It's just past the cafe."

"I must have seen it when I went shopping after lunch, then."

"It's pretty popular. Great for a late afternoon pick-me-up."

"Sounds delish." We continue our way to the shop.

As we pass the café we ate at for lunch, I notice a large crowd gathering a block or so away. "What's going on?" We ankle up farther to get a gander. I lift myself up on my tippy-toes. "I can't see over all these people."

Ethan cranes his neck back and forth like a cicen rooster.

I choose a broad shoulder to tap. "Excuse me."

The broad-shouldered joe in a three-piece suit swivels around. "Yes?"

"Do you know what the hubbub is all about?"

"Some dame got herself wrung dead. Some hobo found the body in the alley."

"Jeez Louise, that's terrible," I say as the man turns back around toward the commotion.

Ethan shakes his head. "And in broad sunlight."

"You get a lot of crime in Capital City?" I ask.

"More than Fulcrum, yes. Murder, though, is—"

The beep of Ethan's wireless cuts him off, and he answers it. "This is Hodge. Talk." He rubs his five-o'clock stubble. "Yes, ma'am, be right over."

"Everything copacetic?"

"I've been called in to a crime scene." He thumbs toward the blocked alley.

"Really?"

"Sorry about the bakery."

"Can I tag along? I'd love to watch you work on the scene for a bit."

"Normally, I'd say yes, but the inspector in charge is Zex. And she isn't a fan of anyone outside the Legere Legalis in her crime scenes. Especially you."

"Yeah, yeah, yeah. Jeepers, that stinks." Then another thought hits me. "I'm not going to be able to finish sifting through the debris, am I?"

"Sorry."

"Can't you just leave me there?"

"No can do. I could get in deep trouble just having you there when I'm working."

"Futz!"

We ankle back to the lab in silence.

"Do you think the barrels will still be there tomorrow?" I inquire as we step outside the building to part ways.

"Not sure. Cross your fingers."

I hold up both hands, fingers crossed double for luck.

Ethan smiles. "Stop by tomorrow to see if they're still here."

"I can't call?"

"Maybe we could do l-l-lunch again?" he stutters.

I wink at him, and a blush rises to his cheeks.

Letting out a shrill whistle, I wave my hand toward the street, hailing a taxi.

Chapter Nineteen

As the white-and-silver blur of the city melts into the blue green of the countryside, I punch my knee. "What a disappointing turn," I mutter under my breath.

"Enjoying your stay in our fabulous city?" The cabbie clocks from the front.

Great, another yapper. "Yes." Pulling my silver-and-enamel flask from my bag, I take a swig. The cabbie eyes me through the rearview mirror with a disappointing look. "Mind your own beeswax," I snap, taking another hard swig from the flask.

His eyes move back to the road. The rest of the drive happens in silence—just the way I like it. I slouch into the seat, feeling grummy. Taking another swig, I let the warm liquor race down my throat. The numbing effect should begin soon. My lips touch the cool silver, and I pour the last bit of giggle juice down my throat.

The more I try to clear my brain, the more I seem to muddle it up with booze. Jeepers, I'm supposed to be helping Tesla be the first country on Gaia to land a ship on our smaller moon, Biota. Instead, I've lost all creativity and can barely sleep at night.

I cap the flask and shove it deep into my bag. The weight of my depression sits on me, squishing my body into the back seat of the dimbox. I cross my arms over my slouching chest and squeeze my eyes shut against the darkness of my mood and the effects of the alcohol.

When the dimbox comes to an abrupt stop, my eyelids open just as quickly. The driver nudges his head in the direction of the nearby building. Wiping the drool from my mouth, I answer sleepily, "Yes, please." I just hope I wasn't snoring too.

I give the driver a salute and wobble up the steps to Coco Cosmetics' shiny office building.

As usual, the security is lacking, and I go straight to the lifts and to the top-floor offices of Coco and Piers.

I don't see Sally at her desk. Most of the typing pool is absent as well. "Must be after hours," I say quietly, eyeing the gears of the copper wall clock.

Spying Juju, I wave and walk toward her. "Hey, Juju," I say as I hobble up to her desk.

Juju peers over the stack of files filling her desk. "Dr. Harcrow, to what do I owe the pleasure of your visit?"

"I'm wondering if Coco or Piers left a list of employees for me."

Juju's fingers continually fly over the keyboard of the large desk-sized crystal reader. "Yes, Coco had me put a list of names together for you." Without missing a beat, she pulls a faceted quartz crystal out of the port of the reader, replaces it with another one, and continues typing.

"Coco had you put it together?"

"Mr. Astuce and Sally both left early." Juju moves the file she's been working on to one of the stacks and chooses a new file from a different stack.

"Where is Coco?"

Opening the file, Juju continues hammering away at the keyboard. "She's in one of the labs." Juju swivels around in her chair and pushes off the desk, allowing the wheels of her chair to carry her to a file credenza behind her. Pulling the wide drawer open, Juju pulls out a file, closes the drawer, and catapults herself back to the desk. Then she holds up the file. "Here you go."

I flip open the manila file folder to reveal a single sheet of parchment with a list of half a dozen names. "This is it?"

"No." She offers her hand to take back the folder.

Good. Six names doesn't give me much to go on. I roll my eyes.

Picking up a fountain pen from the blotter on her desk, Juju cruises the list and proceeds to make some markings on the paper. Closing the file, she shoves it back in my direction.

I smile. "Thanks." My smile quickly fades to a frown as I open the file and glare at the list. She scratched three names off the list. "Jeepers." I sigh.

"The names won't mean much to you without the files."

"Where are the files?"

"Most I have transferred to a quartz drive." Juju stands and walks around the desk to one of the empty typist desks, indicating its crystal reader. "You can use this one."

"Thanks." I make my way over with the anemic file.

"Do you know how to use this?" Juju asks.

"Yes, I use a crystal reader."

"Excellent." She hands me a crystal.

Sloppily, I look for the port to plug it in.

"Let me." Juju snatches the drive from my fingers and easily inserts it near the back of the reader.

"Sorry."

She smirks. "No problem."

I'm one of Tesla's greatest alchemists, yet at this moment, I feel like a dingbat.

"Now, let me show you how to locate the information."

I nod.

"After each name, you'll note I put their title and department."

I nod again.

She moves the keyboard so she can type. I don't know why she just doesn't do all this for me.

"Now, type in the department. We'll do the secretarial department first." Her fingers move like lightning over the keypad, and up pops a list of personnel.

Maybe I can con her into doing the rest of these for me.

"Then scroll to a name and push enter." She flips the keyboard back to me.

There goes my plan to get her to pull up the info for me. Dang. I begin scrolling, looking for the first name, when a familiar name catches my eye. Sally Renis, Coco's assistant. I push the enter key.

Sally Renis

120 Marcus Ave. #90, Capital City, Tesla.

Date of employment: . . .

I glance up at Juju. "Sally has been here for over two rotations?"

"Yes, she started in the typing pool." She narrows her eyes as she peers over my shoulder at the screen. "Pretty swanky digs on her salary."

I continue to read the screen. "Piers hired her?"

"One of the secretaries who sat there . . ." She lifts her arm with great purpose and points to the front corner desk near Coco's office. "He was fired and replaced the next turn with Sally."

"Oh. I see."

Her arm moves to point across the room at what is now Sally's desk outside Coco's office. "Piers ran me ragged. He refused to get his own assistant."

Maybe I didn't see so clearly after all.

"Every turn, Sally maneuvered her way into Coco's good graces." Juju sounds jealous. "Soon, she was spending time behind closed doors with Coco and following her everywhere."

I look back at the screen and take a look at the dates. She was here less than fifty strings before she replaced Juju.

Interesting.

I study Juju's face. A dull-faced woman with over-rouged cheeks, her eyes seem lit with resentment. "What else can you tell me about her?"

"I don't like to gossip. Besides, I thought you were interested in the names on the list?"

"Sorry. I am interested in the list. Thank you for showing me the files."

"Sure." She spins toward her desk and marches back. "Let me know if you need any more help." With that statement, she's back to work.

Letting out a huge groan, I begin to scroll through the names again.

The first one, Anne Sheridan, was in the secretarial pool. She quit two turns before the explosion. Supposedly, she left to join the family business in Portafaran Fisc. That's easy enough to check. Portafaran Fisc is on the barrier island on the other side of where I grew up, Seaside Village. I'll put a call in to Mae for her to check it out. She would love to help.

I move on to the next name.

Albert Slack, accounting, took time off a string before the explosion. He never returned to work. Address: 1878 Gilbreath, Bunkertown, Tesla.

I call over to Juju, who is up to her elbows in files, typing away. "Juju, I hate to be a bother, but where is Bunkertown?"

Juju lifts her head and stares at me as if I just spoke in a foreign tongue. "I'm sorry. What was the question?"

"Bunkertown. Where is it?"

"It's one of the river suburbs of Capital City." Swiveling her chair around to face me, she pushes aside files on her desk to see me. "It's northeast of us. East side of the Forel River, just north of the city."

"How long would it take me to get there?"

"Not long if you catch the rapid."

"The rapid?"

"It's what the pedestrian transport outside the city is called. The rapid between the suburbs and the city and industrial areas. It's faster than our regular train."

"Electric railway versus electric train?"

"Yes."

"In Fulcrum, we call it the LRT. Is it faster to take the rapid or hire a tin?"

Juju eyes the wall clock. "I'd say the rapid at this time of turn. There is only one road leading in and out to that 'burb, so it might be backed up."

The last name on my list is Ruth Cotter, assembly line. Ms. Cotter works in the manufacturing area of the plant. I really cannot see how she could have gotten access to the labs or the formulas that were still works in progress. Although, since I've been able to walk right in, maybe she could have too.

I jot down Ruth Cotter's information and turn to Juju to ask how far Birdtown is from Bunkertown. "Juju?" She's nowhere to be seen. With a heavy sigh, I turn off the reader and place the file back on Juju's desk. A bit nosy, I push a few files around to see exactly what she's working on. It appears to be exactly what I was told, though: transferring hard copies onto crystals.

One file catches my eye. Opening it and pushing it around, I begin to read it. Inside is a spreadsheet, a few lines of which have been highlighted, possibly by Juju.

"What are you doing?" yells a voice from across the room. I quickly close the file and grab a pen from her desk. Lifting the fountain pen, I turn with a fake smile plastered across my face. "There you are. I was just leaving you a note."

She squints at me. "A note?"

I really need to sell this. "Yes, but I couldn't find a pad of paper among the mountain of files." I swing my arm out as if presenting a stage act.

Juju walks quickly to her desk.

I continue to blab. "I just moved a few files so I could just jot my note on your blotter."

I turn to face her as she rounds her desk. Her eyes dart from file to file.

"I hope I didn't mess up your system," I say in an exceptionally soft voice, hoping to appear innocent.

Juju frantically gathers the files I uncovered. "Why didn't you use the pad at the desk you were at?" she demands.

Think fast, think fast.

Just as I'm opening my mouth with a lame excuse, a security guard strolls into the offices.

"Are you going to work late?" he asks.

"No, John, I was just finishing up."

John the security guard looks at me.

I raise my hands. "Nope, on my way out now." Silently thanking John's timely appearance, I begin to follow the security guard out.

"Dr. Harcrow," Juju calls.

Crap. I turn slightly. "Yes?"

"My fountain pen."

"Fountain pen?"

"You still have my fountain pen."

I glance down at my hand. "Oh, yes. Sorry." Walking back, I hand her the writing instrument.

"Thank you."

I give her a quick salute and hightail it out of there. Closely following the security guard onto the lift, I clear my throat. "I didn't catch your name."

"John," he answers, keeping his eyes front and center on the lift gates.

"John." I decide to ask some questions. "Do you work here in the main building only?"

"Naw, I do rounds on both buildings a few times a night."

"Where are you when you're not doing rounds?"

"On duty at the old entrance."

"Old entrance?" I furrow my brows for a moment. "You mean the factory entrance?"

"Yes." He shifts his weight back and forth, as if my presence made him uncomfortable.

"You were here before the new building?"

"Yes."

When the lift lands firmly on the ground floor, the guard efficiently unlatches the gate, pulls it back, and opens the door for me. "Here you are."

Futz. I want to ask him about the employees on my list.

"Miss?" He extends his hand toward the hall.

Nodding, I move out slowly. Abruptly, I stop and twist my head in his direction. "Do you know . . . ?" I pull the parchment out of my pocket. "Do you know a Ruth Cotter?" I dip my chin and study his face.

He raises his brows. Clearly, he knows who she is.

"She works on the assembly line."

"I know who she is. Why?" He narrows his eyes. He must be suspicious of my motives.

"I notice she hasn't been here at work, according to her file."

"You should mind your own business." He closes the gate, and the door slides shut as the lift travels up to another floor.

Crud. I scared him off, and I still have to check her out. I sure was hoping for something to be easy-peasy for once.

I follow the line of employees out the door and onto a rickety-looking bus. The ugly green wood-paneled double-decker bus definitely does not appear reliable, but the stiffs boarding it don't seem to mind. I pile on with the rest of the maroons. The thinly tired spoked wheels make the ride uncomfortable on the tush; I don't need any more bruises. Hopefully the ride to the rapid is short.

Would it be less bumpy had I sat on the upper deck?

The noisy old hack of a bus slogs along. Fidgeting on the wooden bench, I attempt to find some sort of comfortable position. I can't imagine what it would be like if I were one of those stick-thin flapper-style gals. The discomfort they must feel! At least I have some padding on my rear for cushioning. I used to complain about my fuller hips and bust, envying those with thinner frames and flatter chests. Not today, and certainly not on this monstrous green torture vehicle.

Just as I think I've found a sitting position that will minimize the unpleasantness of the ride, the bus screeches to a halt, rocking me forward with a jolt. We have arrived at the rapid-transit station.

Like cattle, we disembark from the rickety bus and funnel through the turnstiles toward the trains. I ankle over to the ticket window and purchase a token. I rub the small flat, circular token between my thumb and forefinger. The Tesla tower emblem is on one side, and I can feel the wreath of wealth on the other.

I continue to fidget with the token as I search for the correct transit car to board. The screech of metal wheels on steel track sends a shiver up my spine. It reminds me of nails scratching a slate board. One of my professors at the university would do that when trying to get her students' attention. I shiver again.

Oh, shit! The train I need is getting ready to depart, and I'm not sure when the next one is due. I am so out of my element. My feet start running before my brain does.

"Oh, boy!" I exclaim as I leap onto the train, the closing doors narrowly missing the back of my coat as I land inside the car.

"Drop the token and find a seat," the conductor instructs without turning to look at me.

I find myself a seat on a molded-fiberglass bench next to a very ripe, extremely large woman. Her hair is wrapped in a red-and-white handkerchief, from which wisps of jet-black hair escape. Her ruddy complexion is moist with perspiration. I shift in my seat, scooching closer to the aisle. The oversize woman wears gray and white pinstripe overalls with pockets on the pant legs and loops for holding tools. I wonder where she works. Maybe somewhere putting together something or other that we use every turn.

Narrowing my eyes against her heavy body odor, I turn my shoulder to face her. "Excuse me—"

I stop as I realize the woman's chin is almost resting on her chest. With her eyes closed, her chest softly rises and falls in an even rhythm. The large woman is sleeping, obviously tired from her turn.

Facing forward, I surrender to the rhythm of the transit, using the time to plot out my next step toward finding out what happened to Albert Slack.

Chapter Twenty

The train screeches to a stop. The high-pitched scream of metal against metal jogs me back to the present.

"Move," says the sizable woman next to me.

"Yeah, yeah, I hear you," I mutter as I shuffle off the train, spilling out onto the platform with my fellow passengers. I move with the small sea of people down the steps to the exit. As I do, I rummage through my bag for my wireless; I must ring Mae and get her on Miss Sheridan.

The polished black wireless fits in the palm of my hand—such a handy device. I swivel back the cover to reveal the keypad, receiver, and three small colored lights: green for charge and signal, yellow for no signal, and red for no signal and no battery. Unfortunately, the yellow is lit.

I seek out one of the station attendants. "Excuse me. Where can I get a hookup?" I tap the yellow light with my finger.

The stiff lady in a starched and pressed uniform points toward the exit. In an equally stiff voice, she directs, "Through the depot exit and across the street. Can't miss the tower; just head straight."

"Thanks."

"You should be careful, though."

"Why?"

"Not a neighborhood you may want to be walking around by yourself."

I tilt my head, furrow my brow, and stare at her.

"You stick out like a sore thumb. Fancy clothes." She wags her finger up and down at my attire.

I wave away her concern. "I'll be fine, thanks." I head toward the exit.

The tower is easy enough to spot from a distance, looming over the suburban square. As I make my way toward it, I study my surroundings. The streets seem neat and tidy. I see no sign of housing near the depot or in the town square. Shops sit around the square and the tower, set up like a continuous chain, with the depot and one road leading out of the square as breaks in the chain.

I cross the street to the green sheltered booths that encircle the tower. A few of the dozen or so booths are in use. The stations are made up of waist-high counters attached to slightly angled roofs. The steel pedestal counter contains wires that are connected to the tower. Not much in Tesla is hardwired any longer, but older areas such as these are some of the few exceptions.

On the counter are several receptacles that hold different retractable cords for different devices. Upon locating the one I want, I attach the charging communication cord to my wireless. It only takes a moment for the small brilliant green light to pop on, replacing the yellow. I punch in the exchange number to connect to Fulcrum.

"Hello?" answers Mae.

"It's me."

"Darling, how are you?"

"Good."

"Have you found the saboteur yet?"

"That's why I'm calling."

"You found the perpetrator?" There is excitement in her voice.

"No, not yet."

"Then why did you say you did?"

"I didn't."

"You didn't what?"

"Tell you that I found the saboteur."

"But you just did." I can hear her getting irritated with me.

"Did what?"

"Find the person with the bomb."

I grumble. "I didn't."

"No, you didn't find them?"

"Yes."

"So you did find them."

"No, I mean . . . I . . ." My head is spinning from the conversation. "I need your help."

I'm greeted with silence.

"Mae?"

"I don't know who it is! I'm not there, Zelda. Are you getting enough sleep?" Mae sounds confused.

"Mae, I just need you to track someone down for me."

"I'm not in Capital City." Her voice has become shrill.

"In Fulcrum! I need you to track down someone who's supposed to be in Fulcrum."

"Why didn't you just say you're needing my help?"

I blow out a sigh of frustration. "I did."

"When?"

"In the—" I stop. No way am I going to get caught up in the whirlpool of that conversation again. "Can you just find an Anne Sheridan for me?"

"Sure," she answers. "Why?"

"Supposedly, she quit to work at her family's shop. I need you to confirm that."

"She's a suspect?"

"Now you're on the trolley." I give her Anne Sheridan's details. "I just need to confirm the circumstances of her departure."

"Gotcha."

"Thanks, Mae."

"No problem, darling. Just be careful and take care of yourself. I'll ring you as soon as I have the info."

With a click, the connection is lost. Scanning the area, I start toward the road out of the square. I need to find the street Albert Slack lives on.

A Wallworth store stands on the corner of Main Street, the exit out of the square. The dispensary is more than just a place to pick up medicines and supplements. It now carries everyturn items, such as cheap cosmetics, toiletries, toys, and candies. Some even have drink counters that serve fizzes and frozen treats. Ankling in, I survey the store. A young pimply-faced teen is wiping down the counter near the candies.

"What can I do you for? Would you like a fizzy or sweets?"

"No, thanks. I'll pass. Can you give me directions to Gilbreath Street?" I hand him the slip of paper with the address.

"Sure. You go straight on Main and cross over Moller Avenue; the next street is Gilbreath. If you see Taylor Street, you've gone too far. That street number is most likely between the Blix and Martha Street. Are you sure I can't get you something?" He hands me back the address.

"I'll take a few lemon drops. There for my niece and nephew."

"You know, they're cheaper by the dozen."

"A dozen it is."

I check my ankle for swelling, then start my journey down Main Street. I stop at the first block. The tree lawns hold only singular lampposts, no trees, not even solar fake trees like those that line my street back in Fulcrum.

The houses appear to be older two-story doubles, each containing two apartments. Some of the doubles appear to have a top apartment and a bottom one, while others appear to be side-by-side apartments. Despite the age of the homes, everything is tidy and quaint. The front porches with their swings and their planters filled with multicolored plants and flowers lend the area a small-town appeal.

The sidewalks, on the other hand, leave much to be desired. The slabs of concrete are uneven and, in some places, cracked. One such crack catches the toe of my shoe, and I trip. Luckily, I catch my balance and stay upright.

No more bruises.

I continue up Main till I come to Gilbreath.

Standing on the corner, I take a gander to double-check which way the addresses run. Then I ankle down the street. The houses are similar to those on Main, except for a few that appear to be single-family dwellings.

I end my journey in front of a large two-story brick-and-wood home. The large covered porch wraps around from the front to the sides of the house. A line of dirty red paint-chipped rocking chairs neatly line the wooden porch. The whitewashed porch steps lie off-center from the front glass doors, on which is displayed a sign: *Rooms for Rent.*

Albert Slack is a boarder here. Taking out one of my cards, I grab a deep breath and rap my knuckles on the front door.

Chapter Twenty-One

The hinges squeak on the lead-glass-and-wood door as it opens, revealing a sight that leaves me flabbergasted. The garish woman I assume is the landlady has a head of frizzy orange hair the likes I have never seen.

"What you want?" the clownish woman yells.

"Ah . . ." I'm at a loss for words. I'm muted not just by that hair but the makeup as well. Eye shadow in neon blue, blush as red as cherries, and the lips! There are no words to describe the orangey-red lip rouge. None, not one adjective. In fact, I don't believe I've ever seen a color like that in my entire life. Definitely can't be a Coco Cosmetic product.

"What you want?" the garish woman repeats.

"Yes. Hello. My name is"—I hand her my card of introduction—"Dr. Zelda Harcrow."

"I got no rooms to let," she states, staring at my card. She begins to hand it back to me.

I hold up my hand in refusal. "I'm looking for one of your tenants."

The landlady squints her eyes at me, the neon blue still prominent from lid to brow.

"I'm looking for Albert Slack."

She squints at the card and then at me. "What you want Albert for?"

"He hasn't shown up for work."

"What's that got to do with me?"

"Nothing. I just want to talk with him."

She waves my card back and forth, judging me with her narrowed eyes and ugly pursed lips.

"Is he here?"

"Haven't seen him." She begins to close the door on me.

Not putting much thought into it, I shove my foot forward, stopping the door from closing. Ow! That was painful. I raise my voice and push on the door. "Wait."

"What are you up to, lady?" she screeches.

"I'm sorry. Please I need your help." I talk faster. "Albert was due back at work." I push the door farther open. "He hasn't shown up. From his attendance record, I know he's never been late and is an exemplary employee." I step over the threshold. "We at Coco Cosmetics are concerned," I lie. I walk into the entry as the landlady steps back, no longer barring my entrance. "I really must see his rooms to make sure nothing untoward has occurred." I'm swimming in the deep end now; I better not drown in the falsehoods. "He could be upstairs dying or, worse yet, never made it back and is lying on the side of the road, wondering if the end is near." I'm laying it on thick as peanut butter.

I stop.

She stares.

I open my mouth to try another story.

She shakes her head. "Bullshit."

My face falls.

"Albert hasn't returned from out of town. He's paid up for three more strings." She starts up the wooden steps to the second floor.

To my right, I notice a front room with chairs and couches. The room is occupied by a couple of slouches reading the paper, while a third is just weirdly staring into space. A hall to the right of the stairs ends with a door that most likely leads to the kitchen. To the left of the stairs appears to be the dining room, with a variety of sundry chairs crowded around a long oblong table.

"If he doesn't come back, stuff goes out on the lawn." Holding on to the chipped-paint railing, she twists around to look back at me. "Are you coming?"

I turn my head toward her. "Yes! Thank you."

I follow the landlady up the chipped-paint wood stairs to the first landing. The wallpaper is an odd pink floral pattern that has faded and yellowed with age. I continue to tag along behind the proprietor of the rooming house to the second floor. There are four aged dark wooden doors on the second floor. There are no numbers or names to distinguish one door from another.

The overly painted landlady fumbles in the pocket of her housedress. I can hear the jangle of keys. Holding the ring of keys in one hand, she counts each key with the other. I'm guessing the keys aren't marked either.

"Here we are." She holds up the desired key, rattling the ring of keys in the air. She proceeds to unlock the door and wave me in. I enter the surprisingly large room. The landlady stays in the doorway, leaning against the jamb.

The room is a simple layout and sparsely furnished. An empty coat and hat rack is set next to the door. No hat, no coat, no shoes.

Slowly, I stroll counterclockwise around the room, taking in as many details as I can.

An old wardrobe sits next to the coat and hat rack. The doors are carved with a leaf pattern. Opening the doors, I study the interior. The wardrobe contains suits neatly hung up and shirts folded. I glide my hands across and up and down the suit jackets, looking for any hidden items.

Nothing.

Closing the doors, I peer at the top of the wardrobe. No suitcase.

I open the lower drawers one at a time. Just neatly folded clothing.

Moving on to the adjoining wall, I examine an old-fashion washbasin that sits on a stand with a tarnished mirror. A shaving kit is shoved behind the porcelain washbasin, indicating one of two things: either Albert Slack has a travel case or he did return from his vacation.

The next wall is lined with the bed and a nightstand. A dusty unsigned painting of an angry seascape hangs above the full-size bed. To the right of the bed stands the small single-drawer nightstand. It holds a lamp with a yellowed lampshade that was once white and a green glass ashtray. Two stubbed-out gaspers dirty the ashtray.

"When was the last time these rooms were cleaned?" I ask.

"Once a string, I have a lady who comes in and vacuums, dusts, and washes the floors." She eyes the ashtray I'm now holding up. "There ain't no smoking in these rooms."

I nod and replace the ashtray. I run my hand along the side of the neatly made bed and drop to my knees, lifting the bedspread. I expect only dust bunnies but am greeted by two pairs of shoes and a suitcase. Pulling the suitcase out, I click open the clasps, swing the top open, and . . .

"Nothing," I say out loud.

"What were you expecting?" the landlady asks.

"Not sure."

Replacing the suitcase, I move along to the other side of the bed. A few books lie on the floor. I pick them up, shaking each, hoping for something to fall out. More nothing. I continue to the next wall, which holds a large bay window that looks out over the street and a window bench. I look under the cushions, pull back the curtains, and zilch.

My search continues as I make my way back toward the door. A decent-size writing desk with a sturdy ancient wooden chair is planted next to the door.

A buzzing sound creeps in from the hall.

"That'll be my pies," says the landlady, now standing inside the room. "I have to pull them out of the oven to cool. You'll need to be moving on now."

"I just need to go through this desk," I beg. "I promise I'll be quick."

"I should not be leaving you alone in one of my tenant's rooms," she informs me. "What if you steal something?"

I hold up one hand, crossing my hearts with my other. "I promise I'll be good. Plus, by the time you go down, get pies, and come back up, I should be done. Then you can lock up, and I won't have to come back."

"Come back?"

"Well, if I can't look through the desk now, I'd have to come back to look at it."

"Fine. Look through the desk, and be quick about it." She disappears through the doorway and down the stairs.

The desktop of the writing desk is occupied by a blotter, ink pens and pencils, some stamps, and a few envelopes. There is also a picture on the corner of the desk of a woman, a man, and another, younger man—Albert and his parents, I'm guessing.

Picking up the frame, I look closer. Brownish hair, ruddy complexion, glasses, not too tall, not too short. Homo sapiens. I set the picture back down and contemplate whether the body in the morgue might be Albert's.

Pushing the thought aside for a moment, I go through the drawers. The middle drawer has blank sheets of paper, a few more pens, and a few more envelopes. I open the drawer to the right of me to find a few takeout menus and other brochures. The next drawer yields a few books and a couple of file folders. The books are on accounting, which makes sense since Albert is an accountant. The first file I open is empty. I open the second to find a single piece of paper lying inside. The paper has a list of names, none of which I recognize.

Conveniently forgetting the promise I made to the landlady, I shove the paper into my bag. Then I replace the files and books and close the drawer. Grabbing a couple of envelopes from the desk, I take a couple of hairs from his brush by the washbasin and place them inside one envelope. Over at the nightstand, I retrieve one of the cigarette butts, sealing it in another envelope. I survey the room one more time to make sure I'm not missing anything. I notice that other than the picture on the desk, there are no personal pictures or items.

The clown of a landlady arrives at the door. "You all done?"

"Do you know anything about Albert's parents?"

"Not really. I know that the mother died a few rotations back."

"And the father?"

"From what I remember, Albert told me his father died sometime before his mom."

"Thank you." I leave the way I came, thinking how no one would be missing Albert.

As I walk back toward the square, contemplating Albert's possible demise and lonely life, I'm confronted by three hoodlums.

Simply great.

Chapter Twenty-Two

"Hey, lady!" one of the scruffy roughs says.

Ignoring him, I try to pass.

Another of the delinquents steps directly into my path. "Where you going?"

"Through you, if you don't move out of my way."

The rowdy bullies all laugh.

"I'd like to see that!" the shorter of the group guffs.

"Gimme your bag," demands the taller boy blocking my route.

"Nope. Now get out of my way before I hurt you." I'm a bit nervous, but luckily I'm more irritated at the three punks than anything else.

They laugh at me again.

My fist shoots out, aiming right under the taller kid's chin. I catch him right in the pipes.

The hooligan's hands fly to his throat, holding it as he gasps for air. He stumbles back into his friends, who prop him up.

"What did you do to him?" demands the red-headed punk standing next to the short one.

"He will be fine, possibly, maybe." Crossing the street, I call back to the ruffians, "Next time a lady tells you to move, move!" Jeepers, the station gal wasn't kidding about it being a rough neighborhood.

The rapid back to Capital City is almost empty. The working stiffs are all home for dinner or hanging out at their local speakeasies.

Back at the old Legere Legalis building, my achy ankle and I descend to the basement. I rap on the frosted glass with a bit of force, till it shakes slightly in its frame. Ethan opens the door, coat and hat in hand.

"I was just leaving for the evening, Doctor—I mean, Zelda."

I hand him the envelopes. "I took these from Albert Slack's room."

"Who is Albert Slack?"

"Sorry, it's been a long turn." I bring him up to speed on my investigation.

Nodding, Ethan takes the envelopes. "I can test these against the remains tomorrow. NSC hasn't collected the samples yet, just the body."

"Jeepers, that's good news." I take in air and sigh out a warm breath of relief, then follow Ethan back into the lab. "How long do you think it will take?"

"The test?" He scrunches up his face and cups his chin with his hand. "Probably a few turns, maybe more."

I groan. "That long?" Something familiar catches my eye, and I point toward one of the long stainless-steel tables. "Where did you get that hat?"

"Unfortunately, I can't discuss it. Don't worry, it has nothing to do with the Coco Cosmetics case."

Tears brim my gold-and-amethyst eyes. "Ethan, is that a clothing evidence bag?"

"What's wrong, Zelda?"

"Jeepers," I breath out, placing my hand over my mouth.

"Looks like you've seen a ghost."

"Worse," I reply. "I see my hat."

"I don't understand."

"Ethan, why do you have my hat?"

"Aren't you wearing a hat?"

"Yes, but I just bought this hat and coat."

"Oh." He tilts his head and scrunches up his brow.

"You didn't notice I had on a different hat and coat?" I would be insulted had my old hat not been sitting on top of evidence bags.

"I noticed, it just . . ." His face turns a bright crimson.

"Forgiven." I gather my thoughts. "Tell me about the hat."

"It was found in the alley with a victim."

"I was afraid you would say that."

"What's going on, Zelda? Why would my victim have your hat?"

"Remember the Bruno in black we saw following that fella out of the diner?"

"Yeah, he was a bit of a creeper."

"I think he's some type of hatchet man. He followed me for a while after we split."

Shifting back, Ethan leans on his desk, propping himself up with his hands behind him, preparing for my account of the bimbo tailing me. I present the play-by-play of my chat-and-mousacorn game with the man in black.

"He's a boob. He must have thought the gal was me and followed her into the alley."

"He bumped off the wrong person." Ethan's eyes move to the evidence bags from the crime scene. "Zelda, we have to tell Inspector Zex."

"Bushwa! No way, don't be goofy. Knowing Inspector Zex, she'd haul me off to the hoosegow."

"If the fella was trying to fit you with a wooden kimono, then that changes everything," Ethan says sharply.

Well, this really puts a wrench in me nosing around. "Is there some way we can leave me out of it?"

"How the stars am I to do that?"

I cross my arms in defense. "You have a very judgmental look on your face."

He stands, fists at his sides. "This is not my judgmental face."

Closing my eyes, I drop my arms in surrender.

"I don't want to fight with you," Ethan says. "I'm worried someone is going to succeed in knocking you off. Inspector Zex may be harsh, but deep down, she's a good egg and swell at finding the bad guys."

"If you say so."

"I say, I say."

"Fine." A heavy sigh of resignation leaves my lungs. "How can we minimize my role, then?"

"I don't know. All I do know is it is getting late and I have a rude parrot to take care of." Taking up his hat and coat, Ethan ushers me toward the door.

"Sorry, I am being selfish. You're the darb of a fella, a good egg, and I'm taking advantage."

"Don't be silly." He closes and locks the door behind us. Pocketing his keys, he turns to me. "You could come back to mine."

"Excuse me?" I raise both eyebrows at his invitation.

His face hits the top charts of reds. "Jeepers, I just meant we could get takeout and brainstorm how to reduce or play down your involvement with the evidence collected."

I try not to chuckle at his small gaffe. "Well, then let's get a wiggle on. I'm starving."

Chapter Twenty-Three

E than Hodge's apartment is situated in a building that seems to be its own neighborhood within a neighborhood encapsulated by the ever-growing Capital City. The old white granite thirteen-story building was built during a bygone era. As I step off the last streetcar and onto the brick-paved street, I am seemingly transported back to a time before a gal could show a knee. The building boasts an impressive archway that leads into a notable courtyard with an equally remarkable granite fountain. The fountain's Larimar-blue water softly trickles in the background among the buzz of tenants enjoying the evening air.

Our shoes crunch on the red crushed-granite walkway as we stroll through the courtyard, and I am struck by the modern improvements made to the old building that blend so well with the architecture. The first-floor shops that line the interior courtyard are all fitted with solar-powered downward-facing lighting in the shape of inverted tulips above each sign. The shops advertise different wares. There's a deli, a floral boutique, a shop dedicated to cheese, a shop that sells sundry liquor, and specialty clothing shops.

"You wouldn't have to leave here," I remark. "Everything you could want is basically right at your fingertips here."

"Almost." Ethan glances at me. "Sometimes, you have to leave to find something truly special."

"It must have been scary leaving Fulcrum and your job to come here and embark on a whole new career path."

"Not quite what I meant, but yes."

"Then what did—"

"Right through these doors," Ethan interrupts.

The brass-and-metal double door is a pair of ornate peafowl facing each other. Each peafowl has cascading brass and copper feathers that melt into the bottom framing of its door. Ethan opens one of the doors, allowing me to pass over the threshold and into the lobby.

Another modern update is an newer caged elevator lift in the center flanked by stairs leading up. The dark paneling along the walls tell that they are original to the complex, as it's warped and faded due to age and water damage. The ceiling is painted with scenes of city life, and it, too, could use a refresher. Many of the faces and landscapes have long chipped away or peeled off. The floors, however, appear to have been recently buffed and polished. There are a few unremarkable chairs scattered about against the walls; the lobby is less inviting than the courtyard by far.

Ethan pulls back the accordion gate of the elevator. "I'm on the fourth floor."

The elevator rises slowly with lots of jolts and jumps. I latch on to Ethan's arm with a viselike grip. "Sorry," I say as he flinches.

"Just startled me, that's all." He places a hand over mine. "The elevator always does this. I usually take the stairs."

Hanging my head, I look down at my ankle. "Oh."

"I noticed you were still limping and thought it best to take this unmaintained contraption."

"Jeepers. Thank you, I think." I chuckle.

We step off the lift and onto the fourth floor. The hall, unlike the lobby, is floored wall-to-wall with a low-pile wool carpet with geometric shapes in rouge and black on a beige background. Taking a sharp left, we head down the hall. The hall is dimly lit with electric wall sconces patterned with leaves, which hides the age of the faded, dingy grass-cloth wallpaper. Everything looks younger and prettier in low light. Throw in some booze, and the carpet will even look new.

Sadly, my flask is empty, and I could use a libation or two. Maybe three.

Ethan's apartment is small. The choice of white paint on the walls, baseboards, and ceiling makes it appear brighter and larger than it is.

He closes the plain solid white door behind us. "I know it isn't much, but make yourself comfortable." He gestures to a couch that sits against a plain wall next to a curtain that appears to hide glass doors leading to a balcony. "In its heyday, this building was quite the place. Not top-of-the-line luxury like you're used to, but still not too shabby. The apartments actually used to be seven to nine rooms each; however, as time moved on without this old girl, they chopped the apartments up into smaller units." He hangs his hat and coat up next to mine on the hall coat-tree and sits on one of the simplistic metal-and-leather chairs across from the couch.

"Kind of sparse," I comment, observing that all but one of the walls is empty. "Where is the annoying bird?" I ask as I examine two island masks that hang above a tiki-style bar, the only adornments of the otherwise bare walls. The whimsical bamboo bar seems out of place among the minimalistic modern decor. I wonder how much this seemingly reserved joe entertains. My eyes roll upward as I imagine Ethan Hodge in a conga line. Shaking my head, I rattle my eyes and my attention into the present.

"In my bedroom." Ethan points his thumb over his shoulder at the closed door behind him.

I note the small kitchenette behind me. A small icebox, stovetop, sink, and cupboards line the back wall across from the entrance to the apartment. Making my way over to the low silhouetted sofa, I take my assigned seat.

Ethan places his wireless on the black laminate cocktail table between us. "The food should be here soon." He nods toward his kitchenette. "I don't really do much cooking up here, even when I have the time."

"Oh?"

"For the convenience of tenants with smaller places like me and those who just don't wish to cook in their own apartments, there are large kitchens in the basement for us to use.

"I can see why you wouldn't be able to cook a decent meal here. Although, I've never cooked a decent meal anywhere."

"The complex has a lot of amenities, many dating back to when it was first built." Rising, Ethan steps over to the bar. "Would you like a drink?"

"Would I!" I clap my hands together several times. "Ab-so-lute-ly."

Ethan pulls a shaker from under the bar. "Besides the courtyard with stores and eateries, each building has its own elevator, green spaces, and telecoms for ringing an attendant. Sadly, we still have coal-powered steam heat, as you can see." He motions toward the radiator outside the bedroom door, even as he shakes an assortment of liquors with ice. Straining the yellow-green mixture into two coupe glasses, he garnishes them with orange peels.

"Looks yummy."

"It's called the Corpse Reviver." He hands me the libation.

"What's in it?" I take a sip. "Hot socks!" I drain the glass before Ethan can even sit down. I wiggle the glass up at him.

"Best be careful. These things can be powerful."

"I'll take my chances. Hit me again." I hand over my glass.

"All it is, is gin,"—he splashes the clear liquid into the shaker—"as well as Kina Lillet, lemon juice, and Cointreau, which give it its citrusy sour flavor."

He uncaps a bottle of bright-green liquor, and my eyes brighten. Absinthe!

"I know what that is."

"Splash of absinthe and some ice." The liquor dances to the beat of the ice hitting the metal of the shaker, creating music worthy of gyrating my hips to.

Soon, another coupe glass full of sweet-and-sour licorice giggle juice is safely in my hand and heading for my lips. I quietly promise myself to resist the urge to knock this one back.

Ethan leans back into his chair. "What have you found out so far?"

"You already know most of it." I set my drink down in front of me and lean forward, clasping my hands together, fingers intertwined. "I have Mae following up on a lead in Fulcrum—a gal who's on the list of missing employees."

"How many are missing?"

"Three are unaccounted for. One I checked up on today myself in Bunkertown."

"Are you crazy? That isn't the safest place for a swell like you." Ethan gulps down his drink.

"It was fine," I lie. "I'm here, aren't I, and in one piece?"

"Please don't do something like that again. Next time, let me know."

I raise my eyebrows at him.

Ethan attempts to two-step around his misstep. "I mean, it's safer in numbers, that's all. Who is in Bunkertown?"

"Albert Slack, an accountant at Coco Cosmetics." I give him a play-by-play of my trip to the more economically challenged side of town.

"You're thinking this Slack fella might be our burnt-up corpse."

"Yes siree." I pick up the coupe glass of motivation and take a few generous sips.

"Couldn't he be the dope on the lam on Trade Island?"

"I don't think that story is real."

"You think it was used to throw us off the case."

I touch the tip of my nose. "Now you're on the trolley."

"Then why would Albert Slack have been in the room when it blew up?"

"I don't know. I'm not sure if he has something to do with this or if he was simply in the wrong place at the wrong time."

Ethan blows out a long breath. "So you still don't have a clue about what's going on over there."

A loud rapping interrupts our conversation and awakens Ethan's annoying new roommate.

"I'm a witness, I'm a witness—awk, awk, awk," comes the screeching from beyond the closed bedroom door.

"Somebody is up."

"Unfortunately." Ethan answers the apartment door. "Looks like our dinner has arrived."

The green horned parrot continues to make a racket while Ethan retrieves our dinner. "Here, let me." I take the warmish delivery from him and set it on the cocktail table. "Maybe you should get the mouthy bird. I don't think he's going to stop yammering until you do." I raise my voice to be heard over the foul fowl.

"I'm a witness, I'm a witness—awk, awk, awk." The bird's vocals carry through the closed door.

"I'm on it." Ethan enters his room. "Come on, you. It's dinnertime, and if you're a good boy, you won't be the main course."

Bobbing his slightly off-center horn, the bird nervously rocks back and forth on his perch, muttering and cackling. Ethan sets the cage down on the end of the tiki bar.

"I need to feed him and get him fresh water. Why don't you go ahead and dig in?"

I give him a thumbs-up and unpack the two white sacks that contain our dinner.

A rapid pounding on the door makes us both jump out of our skins, and Ethan spills the tiny tray of water he was bringing to the green monster of a bird.

"Are you expecting company?"

"Not that I'm aware of. Did they forget something in our order?"

"It doesn't appear so."

The knocking gets louder.

Ethan yells through the door, "Who is it?"

"It's Inspector Zex. Open up."

Ethan looks at me in a panic. Palms to the air, I shrug.

"Just a moment, Inspector." Ethan grabs the cage off the tiki bar. "I'm just going to put the horned parrot away."

Grabbing my wrist, he wrenches me up from the sofa and shoves the cage into my arms. "What . . . ?" My voice trails off as he pushes me into his bedroom and closes the door behind me.

I place my ear to the door to listen to the conversation.

"Sorry about that, Inspector. The bird is a bit crude and inappropriate at times. I thought it best to put him in the bedroom."

"I appreciate the thought, Ethan. I can call you Ethan, right? FCI Hodge feels a bit formal after hours."

Is she making a move on Ethan? I put my hand over my mouth to stifle a snicker. This is getting good.

"Um . . . yes, sir—I mean, ma'am—I mean, Inspector Zex."

"Ethan, you can call me Matilda." She stretches out the first *a* in her name uncomfortably.

"What can I do for you, Inspector—I mean, Matilda?"

I press my ear firmly against the door, hoping to get some information about the case.

"Are you expecting guests?"

Ethan's voice shook. "No. It's just little old me. Here by myself. On my own. No one else."

"Oh, you're not little at all. I just noticed all that wonderful-smelling food. Seems like a lot for just you."

"I'm really hungry?" Ethan's voice goes up an octave.

She better be eyeing just Ethan and not my food, I think as my stomach grumbles.

"Nice place you have here," Zex says, complimenting Ethan. "Is this your bedroom?" Her voice is getting louder. She's heading my way! I give Ethan's room a once over. Bed—I could hide under there, maybe. Bathing room—but what if she needs to use it? There is a chair—no good. I could go out on the balcony, though she may hear the door slide open and closed.

"Thank you, ah . . . Matilda." Ethan coaxes the inspector away from the door. "What was it you stopped by for?"

"Mmm . . . ? Yes, I was wondering if you've seen that annoying alchemist of yours?"

Annoying! That flat tire is a bore. I am not annoying. In fact, I'm quite charming.

"Zelda—er, Dr. Harcrow?" Ethan inquires. "Not recently. What's this about?"

"She was in a store with that young victim today. The one found in the alley."

"Oh?"

"Seems Dr. Harcrow gave her a hat."

"I believe she's visiting her sister. Have you tried her there?"

"You aren't dizzy with that deb, are you?"

"Inspector Zex, Matilda—"

"Zex needs sex—awk, awk," the horned parrot squawks, interrupting Ethan. "Zex needs sex—awk, awk."

The inspector's voice becomes hard. "What did that parrot say?"

"Shhh. You stupid bird." I attempt to quiet the squawking birdbrain. I take a step back from the door, just in time for Ethan to slip into the room and slam the door behind him.

Ethan shouts at the door, "I'm just going to quiet the bird. I'll be right out."

The green monster of a bird continues its rant. "I'm a witness, I'm a witness, Zex needs sex—hot-hot-hot."

"You need to hide, now!" Ethan whispers to me. "And try to quiet that bird before I lose my job."

"Where? How?"

Ethan shoves me and the caged troublemaker toward a mirrored door catty-corner from the bed. "In here."

"Oh, no!" I protest. "Not another closet."

"Sorry." He shoves me into the garments hanging haphazardly from the clothing rod. Slamming the door on me and the confined witness, Ethan rejoins his unwanted visitor.

Great. I am back in a closet with this lousy thing.

"I'm a pretty bird, I'm a pretty bird."

"Shut up, stupid bird."

"Shut up, stupid; shut up, stupid—awk, awk," repeats the annoying feathered fiend. The parrot sings out a gravelly whistle as one last insult.

The closet isn't very wide. Backing into the door, I lean over and press my ear to the wall, hoping to listen in on the conversation once more.

Just a garble of muffled voices.

I smell something rancid. Jeepers, my closetmate just farted. Pinching my nose closed, I whisper, "What is he feeding you?"

The parrot squawks at me. "Shut up, stupid; shut up, stupid—awk, awk."

"When I get out of this closet, I'm leaving your stinky feathered butt in here." I place the cage on the floor, leaving no space for myself. The closet door handle digs into my back.

"You're a looker—awk, hot-hot-hot—awk."

"Don't try to butter me up now. It's too late to—"

A sudden rush of air interrupts me as the closet door swings open and I fall backward.

Chapter Twenty-Four

Déjà vu strikes me as I lie on my back, staring at yet another ceiling. Ethan's face slides into view, hovering above me.

"She's gone." Ethan reaches into the closet and grabs the cage inside which my new nemesis squawks. "Do you need a hand?"

"Naw, I'm good. Just contemplating my life choices."

"Okay?" Ethan sounds a bit confused by my answer.

I right myself. "Hopefully our food isn't cold."

"I could heat it up if you want."

"No, I'll just suffer. As long as you make me another of those Corpse Revivers."

"My pleasure."

"I couldn't hear everything. What did Inspector Zex want with you, besides the obvious?"

Ethan hands me another glass. "What do you mean by 'obvious'?"

"She was coming on to you. Zex is interested in more than a working relationship."

The parrot puts in his unneeded two cents. "Zex needs sex, Zex needs sex—awk, awk."

"Pshaw." Ethan waves his hands back and forth. "There is no way on Gaia."

"I'm just making an observation; don't shoot the messenger."

Ethan ignores my comment, moving on. "One good thing came from her visit: we don't have to bring up the story about your hat. However, you should give your sister a heads-up. I told her you were staying with Ava."

"I need to call her anyhow to let her know I won't be back for dinner." I grab my bag from the side of the sofa and rummage for my wireless. Pulling it out, I punch in Ava's digits and wait for the connection.

"Hello," Ava answers.

"It's me. I wanted to let you know I'm having supper with a friend."

"With Coco?" she asks.

"Someone else."

"I see."

"What do you see?"

"Nothing."

"What are you implying?"

"I'm not implying anything. You can have dinner with whomever you choose."

"Ish kabibble." I sigh loudly, making sure my sister can hear it.

"Is there anything else?"

"As a matter of fact, there is."

"Well?"

"An Inspector Zex may be coming around to ask me some questions."

"Does this have something to do with Coco?"

"Yes and no."

"I don't understand."

"I'll explain it all to you when I get back to your place. In the meantime, if she should come by or call, just tell her I'm laid up in bed and will be happy to speak with her tomorrow."

"Why am I lying to an inspector?"

"It's complicated."

"If you want me to do this, explain."

"She stopped by Ethan Hodge's apartment looking for me."

"Let me guess: Ethan told her you weren't there, but you are."

"Now you're on the trolley."

"Why didn't you just tell me you were having dinner with Ethan?"

"I don't know."

"Zelda, he's a decent joe; don't lead him on or ruin his career."

"I would never do that."

"Maybe not on purpose. We'll talk more about it later."

"Is there something I should know?"

"Just enjoy your dinner, and I'll see you here at the house later."

"Okay, thanks." I hang up without worry. My sister and I can annoy each other and get on each other's nerves, but I believe she has my back.

"Is everything copacetic?"

"Yes, she's willing to cover for me."

"What will you say when Zex interviews you tomorrow?"

"The truth."

"The truth?"

"Yes. I went shopping and bought a new hat and coat and gave the gal my hat to go with her outfit for her big interview."

"Don't you think Zex will wonder why you gave your hat to a stranger?"

"The saleslady was being a complete snob to the girl because she had a knockoff suit that looked like mine. Hers was made of the imitation spider silk I created. So I gave her my hat."

"Hope the inspector buys it."

"I'm just leaving out the bit about the man in black following me. I'm just being selective in what truths I tell her."

Our food isn't ice cold, but it isn't warm either. I have to get something in me to start soaking up all the absinthe I've been drinking.

I take a bite of lukewarm noodles, then gesture at my dinner companion. "Ethan, a question."

"Shoot."

"What was it like being a student of my sister's?"

"Ava is a really good professor. She knows how to work with facts and science without using any magical assistance."

"I don't think I understand."

"Ava, you, and many others on this planet have magical abilities that assist them not just in your personal lives but also your professional lives. When you don't have those skills, you must be able to perform the same tasks using other methods. Your sister knows how to teach both those with magic and those without."

"Huh. I never really thought about science without magic. Are you enjoying your work?"

"Yes, I love it. One turn, I hope there are forensic units in every major city in Tesla."

"Have you ever thought about moving back to Fulcrum?"

"I have. Especially if I have something to move back for."

I consider asking him what that something might be, but my gut twists with suspicion that I may not appreciate the answer. So I change the subject.

"Where is Birdtown?"

"Why?"

"The last name on the list of missing employees lives there; she hasn't been seen at the plant in quite a while."

"I thought you decided that the body was Albert's."

"If the body is male, then yes, it's Albert. But Ruth Cotter could still be an actor in the explosion."

"Birdtown is on the other side of the Forel River on the north side of Capital City."

"Is that next to Bunkertown?"

"Opposite of Bunkertown, and near the more affluent neighborhood of Countryside."

"Is it like Bunkertown?"

"Do you mean, is it as crime filled?"

"Yes, I guess that's what I mean."

"No, it is not. It is closer to a middle-class allotment than a lower-class allotment."

"I think I would like to head up there."

"May I accompany you?"

"I don't need protection."

"I'm not saying that. I just want to help." Ethan glances at me several times, looking as if he wants to say something. I avert my eyes from his gaze, and he eventually continues eating, without uttering a word. We finish the rest of our room-temperature meal in silence.

I finally break the spell of awkwardness. "I should call a cab. It's getting late, and you have to work in the morning."

"I can call down and have the concierge order a taxicab to get you to your sisters."

"I would so appreciate that. Thank you."

Ethan rises from the chair opposite me, his shoulders down and his head drooping like that of a lost puppycorn as he walks toward the front of his flat. I watch as he opens a tiny cabinet door that lies flush with the wall and pulls out a handset with a transmitter and receiver.

"Hello. I'd like to order a taxi." He pauses for a moment. "Yes. Ethan Hodge. A friend. Countryside. Thank you." Ethan places the handset back in its cradle and closes the small cabinet. "It won't take long for the cab to arrive."

"Thank you so much for having me over for dinner."

"You're welcome. It's my pleasure. I enjoy your company."

"Thank you for helping me out with this case."

"I'm not sure how much help I've been."

"You've been a lot of help. I just don't want you to get in trouble by assisting me."

"Don't worry about that. I promise to be careful." He crosses his heart, then raises his hand palm out, signaling his oath.

"We may have to come up with the story if we start hanging out together more."

"I'm sure if we leave it up to people's imagination, they'll come up with a story all on their own."

I tilt my head and scrunch my brows, not quite understanding what he's insinuating.

"People can come up with some crazy stories when they're not let in on the truth."

I must be tired or fried from too many Corpse Revivers, because I still don't understand what he's getting at. So I change the subject. "The bird is awfully quiet."

"He always is when he's eating. It's the only time I can truly get any peace."

"I never asked, but what is its name?"

"I have no idea."

"Shouldn't you give it a name?"

"He's a witness. Once the court date comes in, I won't have him anymore."

"I'm a witness, I'm a witness—awk, awk," the bird squawks.

"Seems kind of strange to just keep calling him 'the bird' or the countless derogatory names you secretly say under your breath." I laugh.

"You have a point. I'll think about it." His mouth widens into an ear-to-ear smile.

"Not sure I like that expression. What are you up to?"

"Maybe we'll name him after you."

"What are you saying? That I'm annoying, or that I have a mouth on me?"

"Neither. You are an original, Zelda Harcrow."

"Uh-huh." I cross my arms in front of me and nod. Then I shake my finger at him. "Better not name him after me, if you know what's good for you."

Ethan laughs.

"I'm a pretty bird, I'm a pretty bird—awk, awk," the bird adds.

"You're not that pretty," I mutter.

"Shut up, stupid; shut up, stupid," the horned bird squawks at me.

Ethan's mouth drops open, and he cocks his head. "You taught it another saying?"

"It was neither my intention nor my fault. The bird just chooses what it wants to say, mostly to irritate me."

"I don't think it goes out of its way to irritate you."

"I'm sure it does." I walk past the cage on the tiki bar and grab my coat and hat from the coat-tree.

Ethan plucks them from me. "Let me help you with that." Ethan holds out my new stylish overcoat as I slide in one arm, then the next.

I fix my hat over my shiny sapphire hair and turn around to face my host. "I know I've said this before, but please let me say it again. Thank you so much, Ethan."

"I enjoy your company, Zelda. I wouldn't rather be anywhere else."

Ethan's eyes are hooded as he leans in. Without hesitation, I turn my head slightly to offer up my cheek. His soft lips briefly brush my cheek before he quickly backs off, his face flush with either embarrassment or uncertainty at me spurning a kiss on the lips.

The slightly awkward moment passes quickly. I thank him once more and make my speedy exit out of his apartment, down to the ground floor, out the brass peacock doors, through the courtyard, and out to the front, where my cab waits.

Chapter Twenty-Five

I make sure I am up, dressed, and in the kitchen before seven the next morning. My sister feigns fainting, and Hazel stands frozen in place, her mouth hanging open.

"Seriously?" I demand.

Ava straightens herself up. "Just shocked by your timely appearance."

"And you?" I cast my gaze upon the Iron Maiden of the kitchen.

Slamming her mouth shut, she narrows her eyes and huffs as she pivots to the sizzling pan on the stove.

Ava lifts a teacup to her lips. "What is on your agenda today?"

"Other than dealing with Inspector Zex?"

She places the cup on the table and takes a seat. "Other than the inspector."

"I need to talk to Mae to see what she's been able to dig up on one of Coco's past employees in Portafaran Fisc. Then I have one more current employee to track down and chat with." I take a bite of fruit from my plate. "Hopefully I'll have more to go on after that. As it stands, I'm no closer to figuring out why someone would blow a hole in Coco Cosmetics than when I started."

Just as I'm about to put another piece of juicy fruit in my mouth, the doorbell rings and angry knocking follows.

Ava slowly rises from her seat. "Most likely your Inspector Zex."

"So early?"

"You might want to skedaddle to your room," she advises.

Before I can pop the piece of fruit in my mouth, Hazel snatches the fork from my hand and the plate from the table.

"Hey!" I protest.

The Iron Maiden smirks as she empties my plate into the trash.

Grunting at my bad luck, I ankle down to my room and hop into bed, placing a pillow under my afflicted leg.

Ava and Inspector Zex enter the open door of my room. "Inspector Zex, to what do I owe the pleasure of your visit?"

"Good turn, Dr. Harcrow." Inspector Zex's thin blood-red mouth is set firm, and her eyes narrow as if she were judging whether my injury was a facade. "I'm sure you already know why I'm here."

"Actually, I don't." I keep a straight face, trying to hide my lie.

"You have been sticking your nose into things that don't concern you."

"I have no clue what you are referring to."

"What's wrong with the dogs?" Zex nods toward my afflicted leg.

"Just the one. It's wrenched; too much shopping yesterturn, I guess."

"What is your connection to Lucy Marsh?"

"Who is Lucy Marsh?"

Zex looks unimpressed. "Were you at Gabriel Boutique yesterturn?"

"Yes, why do you ask?"

My sister pipes in. "Inspector, what is this all about?"

Ignoring Ava's question, Zex snaps, "Did you, Dr. Harcrow, give a hat to Lucy Marsh?"

The girl had a name. Hearing her name for the first time almost made my hearts skip beats. The poor, innocent thing. No, not a thing—Lucy. Lucy Marsh. I swallow hard, struggling not to give myself away. If Zex finds out I'm aware of the murder, it could put Ethan's job in danger and me one step further away from figuring out the why of the explosion at Coco Cosmetics.

Zex raises her voice. "Dr. Harcrow?"

"Yes," I answer. "I mean, I gave my hat to a young girl, but I never got her name. She was going to a job interview."

"You gave your hat to a stranger, why?" Zex reaches into her suit jacket and pulls out a slim notepad from the besom pocket. A small stub of hard-graphite pencil is tucked into the elastic-banded notepad. "Ahem." Zex clears her throat as she prepares to scribble down notes from our impromptu interview.

"I don't understand," I say. "What is going on?"

Ava repeats my question, but more forcefully. "Inspector, I insist you tell us what is going on."

"You insist?" Zex's eyes never leave me, even as she replies to my sister in an even yet harsh tone.

"Inspector," I say, "is the girl in some sort of trouble?"

"She found trouble, all right."

"What does that mean?" Ava demands.

"Miss Lucy Marsh's body was found in an alley near the boutique," Zex answers very matter-of-factly.

Ava's hand rushes to cover her mouth. My eyes brim with tears. "That's terrible," I whisper.

"You still haven't told us why you are here or what this has to do with Zelda," remarks Ava.

Zex continues her questioning. "Where did you go after you left the shop?"

"Why?"

"Just answer the question." Zex starts poking the paper in her little book with the pointed end of the pencil.

I can see Zex is getting frustrated. "Which question?"

Her voice becomes sharper. "The question I just asked."

"Which is?" I stall, hoping to aggravate her enough to throw off her line of inquiry.

"Don't play games with me, Doctor. I'll ask again: what did you do after you left the shop?"

"Just ran a few errands, then I came back here."

"What were those errands?"

"Inspector, my sister answered your question," Ava snaps.

"How about this? Why would you give the victim your hat?" Vex's pencil hovers over the paper, ready to jot down my answer.

I keep it simple. "Because she needed it."

"Excuse me?" Her pencil is still hovering, waiting for some worthy information.

"She was headed to an interview and the sales lady was being unkind, so I gave her my hat."

"What are we missing here?" Ava asks.

Zex ignores my sister and continues her interrogation. "Did any of your enemies follow you here?"

"Enemies? As far as I know, I don't have any."

"I understand there was an incident involving you in Fulcrum that led to several deaths."

"That is over, and the parties involved are no longer around. I don't have enemies."

"Are you saying the fact that the victim was dressed just like you is a coincidence?"

Ava has had enough. "That is what the council pays you to figure out, not my sister."

"Inspector Zex, I'm petered out, and I really must rest." I point to my ankle.

Zex closes her notepad, slipping the stumpy writing utensil inside. "Dr. Harcrow, enjoy the turn with your family. Then I expect you to leave Capital City. Keep your nose out of Legere Legalis business. Am I clear?" *Snap!* The elastic band vibrates over the pad violently. Letting out a huff, Zex returns the notepad to its home in her jacket.

"She understands." Ava extends her hand. "Let me show you the door, Inspector Zex."

Once they're out of the room, I let out a loud, exaggerated sigh of relief. Then my sister stamps back through the doorway.

"Spill."

"Huh?"

"What actually happened? Inspector Zex isn't stupid; she can see you know more than you're telling."

"I can't be certain."

Ava crosses her arms over her chest. "Tell me anyhow. Let me be the judge of whether it's important."

I recount to her the afternoon and the man in black. Ava stands silent for a bit.

"Ava?"

She holds up her hand to shush me. "Zelda, are my kids in danger?"

"I don't think so. I mean, no, they are not."

Ava's brow knits in worry. "You don't think so, or you don't know?"

I shrug.

"Zelda, I love you, but I have to protect my kids."

"I understand. Give me just a little more time."

"Fine. Only, spend some of that time with your niece and nephew, will you? They rarely see you."

I nod my thanks. "How about I watch them after school? You and Harvey could go out for dinner."

Ava lowers her eyelids and purses her lips. "Are you sure?"

"Yes." I attempt to sound enthusiastic.

"What about your investigation into Coco Cosmetics?"

"I have a couple of calls to make and a possible visit this afternoon. Then I'm all yours, so to speak."

"Okay. I'll give Harvey a ring and let him know. But if things escalate, you have to let me know, okay? Deal?"

"Deal. Cross my hearts, hope to die, stick a gin and tonic in my eye."

The guest-room door clicks softly as Ava closes it behind her.

I pick up the enamel bedside clock from the nightstand. "I know Mae will not be awake at this time of morning." I set the timepiece back down. My stomach grumbles at the missed breakfast opportunity, and I contemplate my next move. Should I go out for breakfast or sneak food from the icebox while Hazel watches her stories on the VER? I already have the Man in Black wanting me out of the way; I don't need a hostile maid chasing me as well. So I opt for eating breakfast out.

A buzzing reverberates from inside the nightstand drawer. Sliding open the drawer to retrieve my wireless, I take a deep breath and answer. "Hello?"

Chapter Twenty-Six

A familiar voice floats through the receiver. "Doc?"

A lump forms in my throat. It has been about half a rotation since I last heard his deep penetrating voice. "Inspector Greyson." My voice shakes.

"How are you?" he asks.

I don't answer the question. The audacity to ask me how I am doing! He is one of the reasons I left Fulcrum. I don't trust him or this phone call. "What do you want?"

His voice becomes deeper, soft, and comforting. "I was worried about you."

I'm still angry at him for helping my father keep secrets from me and putting my very existence in jeopardy. "You're worried about me?" I exclaim. "Why are you calling?"

"I know I hurt you, and for that, I am sorry. I really thought I was doing the right thing." There is a long pause.

I finally break the silence. "I-I-I realize you acted in good faith, b-but—jeepers, Inspector! Chance." I take a deep breath. "Why are you calling now?"

"An inquiry came across my desk."

"Inquiry?" Sitting up, I swing my legs off the side of the bed.

"An inquiry about you and our trouble with Hyde."

"Let me guess, Inspector Matilda Zex." It nettles me that Zex called the Fulcrum Legere, and it seeps from my voice. There is no mistaking my irritation.

"What have you gotten yourself into, Doc?"

"Nothing I can't handle," I counter. "I'm helping a friend, if you must know."

"I can catch an airship and be there today."

"NO!" I yell at him. I know I could use his help; I just don't want it.

"You're still angry."

"Yes. No. I don't know how I feel right now." I let out a long-held breath. "I'm fine, and I don't need your help."

"Don't need or don't want?" His voice cracks.

I stay silent. This conversation is going nowhere and is becoming uncomfortable.

"Doc?"

I stay quiet.

"Doc, are you still there?" His voice is low.

I can hear the hurt in Chance's voice. I answer in a whisper, "I'm still here."

"Listen." He clears his throat before continuing as if he has been crushed. Slowly, he forges ahead. "If you need me—or need anything, for that matter—please don't hesitate to call."

"How do I know I can count on you?" I feel I have the right to ask after what I went through and still have nightmares about.

"You can. I'd like to be friends, Doc. I do care about you."

"Fine," I say. "If I need help, I'll give you a holler."

"Doc, be careful."

"Goodbye, Inspector." I disconnect the line and plop back onto the bed.

My eyes shift to the nightstand and the clock resting on it. It is well past breakfast, and I am positive Hazel has removed every scrap of food from the table. No chance of subduing my grumbling stomach here. Playing slave to my hunger, I pop open my wireless and hire a car.

The Grand Café sits inside the border of Countryside where it butts up against Birdtown. The first thing I notice when entering the small but quaint café is not just the fragrance of fresh baked bread but the large windows that run from the ceiling to the waist-high wainscoting. It's a mild turn, so many of the windows are open, allowing the gentle breezes the Weather Council creates to waft through the establishment, carrying all the yummy smells out to the stone patio.

I find a seat at one of the bistro tables. The chair is high backed and made of thick mahogany wood, as are the rest of the café's furnishings in the café. The chair's seat is covered in a two-toned green vertically striped sateen material, which matches the material on all the booth benches, the cafe curtains, and the luminaire shades of the brass chandeliers. The menu is one sheet and very minimal. I decide on a bit of toasted bread, a bowl of mixed fruit, and a large black tea. Once my order is in, I lean on the cold granite tabletop while I wait to be served.

Seeing as my time for getting answers is limited today due to volunteering to watch Eggs and Flo this afternoon, I call Ethan.

"Good morning," I say when he answers the phone.

"Good morning to you."

"You sound chipper."

"Will I see you today?"

"Depends."

"On what?"

"Do you still want to accompany me to Birdtown to locate the missing factory worker?"

"When?"

"Now." As I wait for his answer, I take a sip of tea, hoping the caffeine will start to kick in.

"Ab-so-lute-ly!" he reacts with enthusiasm.

"I'm at the Grand Café in Countryside. Do you know where it is?"

"I believe so. I'll grab an auto and pick you up."

"Terrific." I hang up and dig into my toast and tea.

The meal might not be much, but it is delicious. I'm in the middle of taking another bite when I see a flash of black out of the corner of my eye. Trying not to panic, I take a deep breath and slowly scan the café. The toast is now a square peg trying to fit in a round hole as my throat closes up in intense fear. I grip the sides of the cool granite tabletop to anchor myself. My hearts feel as though they may leap out of my chest at any moment. My mind blanks on the spell to keep me calm as creeping tendrils of doom crawl up my neck to my jaw and cheeks.

What are the first words of the spell? I scream in my head.

"Ma'am . . . ma'am . . . ma'am!" A voice cuts through the static in my brain.

Looking up, I see the young server who delivered my food earlier. "Yes?" My voice comes out small and weak.

His eyes are wide and expressive. "Are you okay?"

I nod.

"Are you having an allergic reaction?" He raises his hand and waves, and another server races over. "Get her a glass of water now," he tells the other server.

My eyes blur as they tear up. "Thank you."

A glass of water is placed in front of me. The tremors in my hand make picking up the glass difficult. Letting go of the table, I hold the glass with both hands and take a few small sips. Placing the glass on the table, I repeat, "Thank you."

"Should we call someone for you?"

"No, no, I, uh . . . have someone coming. I'm fine, really."

"Are you sure you're okay?"

"Yes, I'm sure." I wave the back of my hand to shoo them away. With my mind a little clearer, I whisper the calming spell under my breath three times.

"Locked in my body.
Full of fear.
My panic is static,
More than I can bear.
I am in need of reprieve,
So I can breathe.
Take away my fear.
Make it leave.

Once more free of panic and fear, I look around the café once more. There's barely a customer in the joint. An older couple sits at one of the booths with what appears to be their grandkids, a young couple hold hands across the table at which they sit, and an older lady sips tea while reading a book. Besides the servers, there isn't anyone else present. No one from Hyde, no murderous man dressed in black, nothing but my overactive imagination.

At least, I hope that's all it was.

Not wanting to overthink my current panic attack, I ring up Mae. She should be awake by now. I need to see if she has any information on Anne Sheridan, our missing typist.

"Hello," Mae answers.

"It's me," I announce.

"Me who?" Mae yawns.

"Zelda me, that's who!" My voice rises an octave.

"Darling, you sound positively depressing."

"Jeepers, I don't sound that bad."

"Keep telling yourself that, darling. What can I do you for?" She yawns into the receiver.

"I was wondering if you had information on Anne Sheridan yet."

She yawns again. "Who?"

"Mae!"

"Refresh my memory. I was out late last night, at this new hot spot I found. I was cutting the rug with this sap who had a mug like a rodent. Beady eyes and frayed whiskers, the whole shebang. I swear, he was going to start squealing any minute."

"Why were you hot-footing it with him?"

"He's a big cheese over at the Weather Council, and I'm trying to secure a nice turn for Poppy's celebration." Mae always refers to her father as Poppy, something to do with him traveling around Gaia so much as she was growing up.

"What is A.P. celebrating?" I just call Mae's father by his initials like everyone else.

"He is not."

"You just announced it was a celebration."

"Uh-huh."

"Mae, spill. What are you up to?"

"Poppy sort of cut me off from any new ventures after the last snafu," she says as if it were an unimportant detail.

"So you're trying to butter him up."

"Now you're on the trolley."

"Let me guess: something to do with a little man and nylons?," I tease. Mae always has a new scheme of some sort that never quite works out. I wonder if one turn, she'll find her calling.

She is very matter-of-fact in her response. "I was completely left holding the bag. I was stiffed. In a jam."

"Are you going to get good weather?"

"He is a boob. I got dolled up for nothing. A regular flat tire, the rat. I hightailed it out of there. The night was a complete bust." She blows a raspberry for extra effect.

"Sorry to hear. Nothing on the secretary from Coco Cosmetics either?"

"Oh, that? I talked to her in the afternoon."

"Why didn't you say so?"

"You didn't ask."

"Yes, I did!" I am a bit perturbed.

"When?" she says in a bit of a babyish voice.

My frustration has my voice shaking. "When I first called you."

"I wasn't awake then."

I roll my eyes. "Are you awake now?"

"Smarty." She huffs.

"Just lucky I love you." My irritation subsides.

"I know."

"Well?"

"Well, what?"

I am beginning to get irritated again. "The goods, give me the goods on Anne Sheridan."

"I hiked over to the fishmonger shop her family owns to talk to her directly."

"Why did she leave?" I inquire.

"It's all on the up and up. Her family needs her to help run the trawler and the shop."

"Go on."

"Her younger brother took a job underwater mining with Fischers and Sons Inc. Silas—you remember him—has been very proactive with the Ocean Exploratory Council that he developed with A.P. and obtaining the rights for mining."

"I'm impressed," I say.

"He's very ambitious, Silas is."

"I'll say."

"With Anne's brother leaving, this left their parents shorthanded."

"All copacetic, then."

"No corn, completely straight," Mae confirms.

"Well, that was a dead end." I rub my forehead with my thumb and forefinger, struggling to relieve the knot of stress I'm feeling.

After a brief silence, Mae adds, "Possibly."

I drop my hand and sit up straight. "I'm not following."

"She has more to say about the goings-on over at Coco Cosmetics that she didn't want to say in front of her folks."

"Dry up!" I am astonished by this hopeful revelation.

"I'm serious, darling. Sounds like she's got the goods."

"Tell me more."

"I'm taking her out for a little dinner tonight. I'll give you the scoop-de-do-poop next turn."

"Mae, you are the cat's meow," I say, granting her the best of compliments.

She accepts in her usual manner. "And don't you forget it, darling!"

"Thank you."

"Tata and kisses." A smoochy sound comes loudly through the speaker, then a click and dead air.

I shut my wireless. "Phew." I can cross Anne Sheridan off the list. That still leaves me with the mysterious Ruth Cotter and possibly fried-up Albert Slack. I just have to sit tight and wait for Ethan to come scoop me up for our adventure into Birdtown.

The high-backed mahogany chairs make it difficult to remain comfortable sitting down. I wiggle in the seat with the scant hope of allaying the ache in my sit bones. Rhythmically, my fingers tap the cold granite in an impatient melody as I wait for Ethan to arrive. The ticking of the copper gears in the mounted wall clock above the service counter seems to slow. The click of the minute hand moving to its next mark seems a little louder than before. My expectancy is of low quality, and I crane my neck, looking out the open windows to see if I can spot my friend.

I spot a hint of a shadowy figure peeking out from behind a tree beyond the attached patio. With my spell still in place, my heart rates stay steady and my breathing calm. Did I pick up a tail? Does the Man in Black know where my sister lives? Was it him I caught a glimpse of earlier when I started to relive my trauma?

My next question is interrupted by a tap on my shoulder. I jump from my chair, taking my eyes off the figure. "Jeepers!" Balling up my fist, I raise it shoulder level, preparing to lay any opponent flat.

Ethan holds his arms up to protect his face. "Sorry, Zelda."

He's lucky I didn't take a swing. "Don't sneak up on me like that. I could have hurt you." Truth is, it's a toss-up whether I would fight or ball up and hide under a table. I just never know these turns.

"Geez, I'm sorry. I didn't mean to scare you." He drops his arms. "Would you have really decked me?"

I unclench my fist and brush back my hair. Then I cover my mouth as I remember what I was doing before Ethan scared me. "Oh!" I scramble over one of the booth benches to an open window and peer out. "Darn it!"

Ethan comes up next to me. "What are you looking for?"

"I think I saw the man in the black getup spying on me from behind that tree." I point across the patio.

"I don't see anything, Zelda. Are you sure?"

"Yes—no—maybe." I'm not sure what I saw, especially after my near meltdown earlier. "It might just have been my imagination; I've been on edge."

He gently places a hand on my shoulder. "Understandably so."

I slide out of the booth. "We should get going."

As we head out, I keep my peepers open to spy any unwanted mugs.

Chapter Twenty-Seven

"So, where are we headed, exactly?" Ethan inquires.

I pull the address out of my small beaded purse. "She lives at 1920 Parker Street, Birdtown." Today, I chose a small bag to complement the shift dress I am wearing. Since the weather seems to be warming up, I decided on a light-red-orange sweater and matching knitted beret that complement my blue hair and golden skin. I hope I didn't make a mistake bringing such a delicate bag. It isn't big enough to hold a weapon, let alone act as one.

"Map is in the glove box."

I retrieve the thick, compact, neatly folded rectangular paper map. Trying to open it is like trying to unravel a puzzle box. *Crinkle, crinkle, crunch.* I punch and turn the blasted map.

"Okay, I think I've located Birdtown. I thought it was to the north of town?"

"You have the map upside down." Ethan reaches over, and the borrowed tin swerves slightly.

My elbow bangs against the door as he corrects our course. "Ouch! Hands on the wheel! I got this." *Crinkle, crinkle, crunch, rip, slap, crinkle, crinkle.* I let out a few choice words. "Futz, crap, jeepers, futz." Finally, I let out a small howl. "Got it. Water Street."

"I saw that street on my way to pick you up. What's after that?"

"Hold on, I'm trying to see." I wish I had brought my magnifying goggles; this is ridiculous. "We need an automated device that gives a topographical description of an area and delivers directions to your destination."

Ethan screws up his face and looks at me. "Huh?"

"Tesla Positioning or Directional Navigation." I point out the windshield. "Keep your eyes on the road."

"You can invent that after you tell me where I'm going."

Rip, crinkle, crunch, crinkle, rip. "Futz, crap, yikes." A few more obscenities flow easily from my kisser. "Ah-ha! Turn right on Ory Avenue."

"We just passed that," he grumbles.

"Well, turn around. Why did you pass it?" I punch the map and try to stretch it out.

Ethan pushes the wrinkled behemoth of a map out of his field of vision. "You told me too late."

"Did not," I protest.

"Hold on." He cuts the wheel and swerves, making a U-turn onto the opposite side of the street, angering the other drivers. Horns blare and echoes of curse words fill the air as the tin straightens out and we head back toward our missed turn. "Turn right?"

"No. It's left now."

"Right."

"No, left."

"Yes," he confirms.

"Right," I acknowledge.

His eyes widen as confusion washes over his face. He frowns. "You said left."

"Left! Here!" I shout, pointing at the street sign.

The car veers left, the tires screeching around the corner.

"Look out now for Cornet Drive," I say.

Ethan nods. "Which way?"

"Left." I turn the map again.

"Are you sure?"

"Left," I reiterate.

Upon the turn, he asks, "Now what?"

"Let me see . . ." I scrunch up my nose and eyes, trying to make heads or tails of the infernal piece of paper. Give me a formula, and I can create anything; a math equation, and I can calculate in my head; but a map, and I am completely lost. "Crap, futz, jeepers, futz," continues my swearing. *Rip, rip, crinkle, crunch, crunch, crinkle.* I fold and unfold, turn, and attempt to straighten the map.

Ethan slows the car. "Zelda?"

"Morton."

He throws up his hands. "Morton what?"

"Morton, the street name. It's another left." I point straight ahead.

We continue passing streets, none with the name Morton.

"We are getting close to the Forel River. Are you sure we haven't gone too far?"

Birdtown sits across the Forel River from Bunkertown, next to Countryside and north of downtown Capital City. The tidy suburb is full of middle- and upper-middle-class folk. It's a diverse collection of hominids. Like all suburban sprawls, Birdtown started with a Main Street that led directly from the city and along the train tracks to a Main Square. Streets then shot off the square like spokes on a wagon wheel, spreading out in every direction. As more and more people flooded into the suburb, new streets and tiny box houses cropped up betwixt and between, creating more of a web. And not a mathematically perfect silk web like that of a spider, which totally befuddles my alchemist mind.

"I'm sure," I say.

"I see it." Ethan nods toward the sign, not taking a hand off the wheel this time.

"Turn left, then left again onto Parker." I crumple the blasted map into a ball and toss it behind me into the back seat. "Look for 1920."

"You know we may need that map to make it out of this maze?" Ethan asks.

I look at the back seat. "The map didn't survive the trip. We'll have to fend for ourselves."

"Too bad your GDS isn't a thing yet."

I squint at him. "Huh?"

He gets ready to make the turn. "Gaia Directional System."

"Hmm . . ." I tilt my head. "I never thought about going all the way, just Tesla. Global, interesting. Although I'm not quite thrilled with the initials. Maybe GP—"

"Found it." Ethan slowly passes the target before slamming on the brakes.

The all-white house, identical in build to every other house we've driven past, sits on a small square lot. The one-story home has a front stoop and a bright-red wooden door flanked by a picture window on one side and a double group of windows on the other. Black decorative shutters frame all the windows, and an auto-port attaches to the house and partially covers the driveway. No tin is parked there.

Backing up, Ethan parks along the curb in front of the house. A single black electric lamppost sits at the end of the drive next to a small black iron sign with the address printed in gold-colored enamel paint. It reads *1920*.

Ethan puts the motor in park. "So, what's the plan?"

I scratch the back of my neck. "The plan?"

"You have a plan, right?"

I slide a piece of hair behind my ear. "Sure . . ." The long tail of the *r* trails off revealing, I have no plan.

Ethan shuts off the motor and turns sideways to face me. "What were you thinking of saying? Hello, we came to see if your daughter blew up a building and murdered someone in the process? Is she home?"

I shake my head. "That would be a terrible idea."

Ethan washes his hands over his face. "You better come up with something."

"I'll just wing it."

"Dry up, Zelda. Do you really think that's a good strategy?"

Turning to face him, I toss up my hands. "Don't get your lather up. Do you have something better?'

I look out the window at the little white home. I can see someone takes considerable pride in the place. The turquoise grass is neatly cut; the garden hedges running along the front of the house are uniformly trimmed. Nothing is out of place. Even the small live tree at the side of the house is precisely pruned.

Ethan sighs. "Well, I know we can't let on who I am, just in case this lead pans out and we need to inform the authorities. I'd lose my job for going off on my own."

"The nice part of being an alchemist is that it's my job to explore things off on my own. I cannot imagine having to be confined to too many rules and regulations."

"And you get to blow things up," Ethan remarks.

I chuckle. "There is that too." I must admit, I miss my lab, my assistant Clover, and the opportunity to create new and interesting potions and inventions. Maybe when this mystery is solved for Coco, I'll finally head home. For now, though, I need to focus on the task at hand: getting the goods on where our mysterious Ruth Cotter has absconded to.

"Shall we?" Ethan opens his door and slides out.

Opening mine, I step out onto the curb. "Ready or not."

We travel up the driveway to the front walk and follow it to the front stoop and door.

I rap loudly on the bright-red door. "No tin in the drive. I wonder if anyone is home."

"Someone is in," Ethan notes, pointing to the front window sheers. "The curtains just moved."

The solid door creaks open a pinch, and a soprano voice speaks softly. "Can I help you?"

"I hope so." I cock my head to the side, trying to get a look at our greeter. "Are you Ruth?"

"No!" The soprano voice hops a couple of octaves higher, and the volume increases so much that I think her voice can be heard across Birdtown. The door slams shut. We both jump back somewhat in surprise.

"That could have gone better," Ethan says.

"Jeepers, you think?" I tuck a piece of hair behind my ear and knock again.

"Go away," the voice calls from inside.

I raise my voice so as to be heard through the door. "My name is Dr. Zelda Harcrow. I'm helping out over at Coco Cosmetics, and I've been tasked with locating missing employees after the accident. We're just trying to make sure Ruth is okay and wondered when she would return to work."

"Who's the goof with you?" replies the female voice.

"This is—"

"Her driver," Ethan pipes in.

"Oh." The door slowly opens to reveal a middle-aged woman.

The woman, whom I guess to be Ruth's mother, has dark wavy hair tied back and pinned in a chignon at the nape of her neck. Two small pin curls are plastered to either side of her forehead. She wears no makeup, nor does she need any. Her long lashes are the color of coal, and her eyes are a bright green. Her freckles dotting her face are only a shade or two darker than her skin color. She's a handsome woman of average height and build.

"Ruth is fine," she says.

"May I speak with her?"

"She is not available right now." The woman begins to close the door.

I place my hand on the door, preventing it from blocking my agenda. "Ma'am, please, this is very important and urgent."

"I don't see how." She pushes the door back against me.

Ethan clears his throat. "Ma'am, as you may know, Coco Cosmetics has been accosted, and we have several employees still unaccounted for with a possibility of a victim. We need to know Ruth's whereabouts to eliminate her from our inquiries."

"You sound like a copper," Ruth's mother quips.

I throw Ethan the side-eye with a mental nudge to take a powder. Before I can utter another word, the door swings completely open, and standing there is an exceptionally large man. His hair is an angry orangey red, and his pale face is covered in an explosion of freckles. That pale face begins to turn a shade of crimson I don't think I've ever witnessed on a person before.

"Ruth ain't coming back to that loony bin," the man bellows. "Now get off my property!"

"Sir, we are just trying to help," I assure. "The NSC has been tasked with the investigation into the probable accident; we just don't want any of the employees being wrongly accused." Realizing how that might sound, I add, "What I'm trying to say—"

"Not our circus, kid. If you were really concerned about your employees, then you would have taken better care of Ruth when she was there."

With that last statement, the large man slams the door in our faces.

"That didn't go well," Ethan says, stating the obvious.

"Oh, dry up." I step down from the stoop and head back toward the vehicle. "What do you think he meant by 'you would have taken better care of Ruth'? Did something happen at Coco's before all this?"

"He called Coco Cosmetics a loony bin." Ethan makes his way around to the driver's side. "Wonder what he means."

I've just grabbed the handle on the tin's passenger-side door when someone calls my name.

"Dr. Harcrow." A young woman runs toward us, her hand waving frantically through the air. She looks like an amalgamation of the elder Cotters, with Mr. Cotter's hair color and skin and Mrs. Cotter's eyes. She's either Ruth or another relation.

"Yes?" I greet the young woman.

"I'm Ruth's sister, Nettie. Are you really Zelda Harcrow?"

"Yes, I am. You know who I am?"

"Jeepers, of course I do. I read about you. You're an alchemist in Fulcrum who fought agents of Hyde." Her voice is as filled with excitement as her eyes.

"Jeepers, I don't really think I fought them. More like escaped." A small chill runs through my bones as my mind flashes back to that harrowing experience with Dr. Textrix. I reach out to steady myself and find Ethan at my side, his strong arm ready for me to hang on to.

"You were so brave. Maybe you can help my sister Ruth."

Ethan says, "You'd better explain."

"Drive me around the block. If my folks see me yapping to you, I will never hear the end of it."

"Hop in," I say.

Ethan starts the sedan's engine. I'm in the front passenger seat, and Nettie is perched in the middle of the back seat. Nettie scooches forward to sit on the edge of the bench, leaning forward and propping her elbows on the back of our seats.

"You're tooting the wrong ringer if you think my sister is wrapped up in that explosion. If anything, she is a victim."

Chapter Twenty-Eight

My eyes practically pop out of my head at Nettie's statement. Do I have it all wrong? Is our victim not Albert Slack? Is the truth that Albert absconded with a formula and did Ruth and some nameless joe in? My mind splinters off in different directions with numerous questions.

While my mind spins, Ethan asks, "Is she okay?" He pulls away from the curb and slowly makes his way toward the end of the street. "You may need to give us directions back to your house, by the way; this place is a maze."

Nettie reaches down and picks up the crumbled map I threw to the back.

"We may also need directions on how to get out of Birdtown and back to downtown Capital City," Ethan adds.

I finally get my brain onto one wave and attempt to ride it with the right questions. "Nettie, first, tell me a little about Ruth."

"Well . . ." She gives a big sigh. "Ruth is so pretty. And I don't mean just pretty. I mean knockout gorgeous."

"Go on."

"Ruth has skin that almost looks unreal, no visible imperfections. Rosy cheeks, auburn hair, eyes of jade. Unlike me, who takes after my pa. I can't go without a hat, or I turn a special color of red that is extremely painful. I tried bleaching my freckles once, but I ended up with a rash redder than my freckles. Ma says I should embrace myself and love my freckles, but she doesn't have to live with the sea of them all over."

I admit, her hair and freckles practically match my beret. More orange than redhead, but I think she's adorable. Full of energy and wit. Her personality matches her looks: unique and vibrant. "Your mother is correct. You should embrace your looks. You are cute, a regular darling. Don't forget that."

Her cheeks fly from a pinky undertone to more of a scarlet. "Oh, jeez, Dr. Harcrow, thank you." She lets out a sweet giggle.

"Now, tell me more about Ruth. You said she's beautiful. Is that a problem?"

"Yes."

Ethan pipes up as he makes a turn. "How can being attractive be a bad thing?"

"I want to tell you about Ruth's looks, so you'll understand."

"Understand what?" I ask.

We are back on Cornet, heading toward the square, and Nettie addresses Ethan. "You're going to want to turn left here; otherwise, we'll dead-end into the main square, and it isn't very auto friendly."

Ethan nods, and Nettie continues her story. "Ruth has never wanted attention from others. Boys line up for a chance to ask her on a date. Girls want to be her best friend. This makes Ruth very shy, and well, that just adds to her mystique, if you know what I mean."

"I think so," I say. "How does her being demure relate to her missing work and everyone being so cagey about it?"

"Sometimes, some of the stiffs don't know how to take no for an answer."

Ethan frowns, completely nonplussed.

"Ethan is a gentleman," I explain to Nettie. "A good egg. He wouldn't understand how some people just don't understand the word *no*. You're going to need to explain further."

Nettie nods. "Ruth stepped out with this fella from work once or twice." She shifts her body on the seat to lean in closer to us. "She really didn't like him, but he was just so persistent. Pretty soon, he was telling everyone she was his girl."

"Go on."

"Ruth did everything she could do to dissuade him. My father even tried to set the bum straight." She wiggles her eyebrows. "Ya follow?"

Ethan and I nod in unison.

"Ruth finally reported him to management at Coco Cosmetics because he began harassing her at work." Nettie takes a breath. "Sadly, management then took it up with security."

"I don't follow," Ethan says, then adds, "Which way?"

"Right."

I decide to steer the conversation while Ethan steers the auto. "Why would there be a problem with security?"

"The bozo is on the security payroll at Coco's. That gang sticks together like white rice on a roll. They did nothing."

"Nothing?" I'm flabbergasted that no one would have stuck up for a vulnerable young woman.

"He stopped outwardly pursuing her when she changed shifts so as not to be working at the same times he did."

"That helped?"

"For a while." Nettie instructs Ethan to circle back to her house.

"So why didn't Ruth quit?" Ethan stupidly asks.

I volunteer to answer that one. "Why should she have to leave her well-paying job? First, he should have just left her alone. Secondly, when he didn't, the company should have stepped in." My lather is up. "I wonder how he would feel if someone decided it was okay to act like that toward his mother or sister."

"Don't tighten the screws on me," Ethan protests. "I'm innocent."

"Sorry, I got carried away." I shift in my seat and ask Ruth's sister to continue her tale.

"Everything seemed to be going well, and because she changed shifts, Ruth met one of the office employees. A nice boy. My folks just love him."

"And . . . ?"

"They became engaged. They even applied for permission to marry with the Tesla Family Council."

"That sounds like a perfect ending."

"That's not the end." Nettie's eyes well up, and she wipes them with the back of her freckled hand.

"Jeepers."

"The masher found out and began making aggressive remarks toward them both. My folks thought they should go visit some relatives, get away and let things cool down. But Ruth's fiancé was working on something at the cosmetics firm and needed to head back for a meeting. He never arrived, and he hasn't been heard from since."

"When did all this happen?"

Looking up, Nettie places her thumb and forefinger on her chin. "Before the explosion. The explosion happened after Albert left to return to Capital City."

Albert!

My brain reels again with revelations and more questions. "Albert Slack was Ruth's fiancé?"

Nettie just nods, sighs, and slides back to slouch on the rear seat.

"Where is Ruth now?"

"In Aladar City, at my auntie's house."

"Do you know the name of the masher who was harassing them?"

"Naw."

"I'd like to talk with your sister; it's important. I think I might know what happened to Albert."

"You think he's the joe from the explosion, dontcha?"

I close my eyes and nod.

"I'll give you the address. Just don't let anyone know where she is."

"I won't."

"You promise?" She scooches up behind me.

"Cross my hearts and hope to die, stick a gin and tonic in my eye!" I draw an X over my hearts with my forefinger and middle finger, then give her a small salute.

Ethan pulls up to the curb in front of the Cotter's well-kept home and drops off the young gal.

"What next?" Ethan asks as he pulls away from the curb to begin our journey back into the city.

"I'd like to see if the results on the body have come back yet and if we're right and it is Albert Slack."

"If it is?"

"Then it begs the question of who and why?"

"Who and why?" Ethan glances at the directions Nettie provided to get us out of the labyrinth called Birdtown.

"Was Albert done in by the masher because of Ruth? Maybe Albert came back and was just in the wrong place at the wrong time. Possibly his meeting had something to do with the sabotage, and he was silenced." I vomit out ideas as if I had the screamin' meemies.

"Not to add to the list of annoyances, but I think we just picked up a hanger-on."

"A hanger-on?"

"A tail." Ethan cuts the wheel. "Hang on tight." The tires of the tin behind us screech as it follows us into the turn.

The well-used coupe speedster behind us is gaining fast and easily keeps pace with the Legere nondescript sedan. We're pushing our wheels to the limit, dodging and weaving through traffic. Ethan makes a few more calculated turns, each failing to shake our pursuer.

I hang onto the dash as this turns into a white-knuckle ride. The sedan leans hard, the tires gripping the pavement for dear life, and the world blurs as we speed around the tight turn. Every nerve in my body is on the fritz.

Dead end.

"Futz!" Ethan swiftly countersteers while slamming the brakes, causing the car to spin out and screech to a halt facing the opposite direction, just inches from the weathered steel guardrails that stand between us and the drop-off into Forel River. We are now face to face with our tracker.

The time-worn tin is too far away for me to get a look at the driver.

Ethan revs the engine. "Hold on to your hat. Here we go!"

The two automobiles speed toward each other on the suburban road. Ethan grips the steering wheel with fierce determination. The tins race toward their inevitable collision, and the thought of the crunch of metal and shattering of glass spreads through my imagination like wildfire.

I can do nothing but watch in panic as the cars close in on each other at breakneck speed. Suddenly, at the last possible moment, our hunter swerves, barely avoiding catastrophe and leaving us the winner in this game of cicen.

We speed away without looking back.

"That was too close!" I shout at Ethan. My hearts are racing, and my hands are shaking, I am overcome with a sense of hypervigilance. Memories of the past flood my mind, and I'm reliving the events in Fulcrum.

Ethan briefly glances at me. "I've trained for this, Zelda; you're safe. I would never put you in harm's way. Please trust me."

"It's just whenever I've driven with you before,"—my voice cracks like lead glass—"you were always following all the rules."

Ethan places a hand over mine. "Just breathe."

I more than just breathe. I close my eyes and repeat my spell to calm down and keep a level head. I swear, one turn, I will face my demons.

We continue our drive back into the city, avoiding any mention of the car chase.

As we pull into the city, I can't shake the feeling that something isn't right. I tell myself it's just the aftermath of the car chase, but I can't shake the feeling of unease. We arrive at Ethan's forensic lab, and he shows me the file report on the charred body, but my mind is elsewhere. As we leave the lab, Ethan turns to me.

"Now what?"

When I answer, my voice is steady. "I'll need an overnight case and an airship ticket to Aladar City."

Chapter Twenty-Nine

F aster than a train, a luxurious airship is designed for long-distance passenger transportation. On the Empress airship, passengers climb a grand staircase to access the main passenger deck, which features plush seating, polished wood paneling, and large windows that offer panoramic views of the surrounding landscape. This trip isn't long enough to require a private cabin, so I settle in on the main passenger deck, placing my travel case under my seat. My overnight bag is in the hold.

Before leaving, I made sure to change into comfortable travel clothes for the trip. Airship travel is a privilege, usually reserved for the high hats and fashionable elite, so I donned a floor-length shift of natural spider silk, its bodice adorned with intricate beading and sequins that sparkle. Mae really has great taste in clothes, and I'm thrilled she sent this along in the trunks she had delivered to my sister's. The dress flows around me like a gentle breeze, allowing me to move with ease and comfort.

A sumptuous fur stole encircles my shoulders, a luxurious piece of mustel fur that will keep me warm during the flight. The cloche on my head completes my elegant yet functional look, along with long gloves of soft leather and a small handbag, the perfect accessories to keep my hands warm and my essentials close at hand. My essentials being my munitions and my flask. A girl should never leave home without a compact, lipstick, and hooch.

"What can I get for you?" a steward asks with a charming smile.

I give him a little shake of my head and a twinkle in my eye. "I think I'll just have the good stuff." I pull my trusty flask out of my purse.

He can't help but chuckle and grin. "Well, in that case, I'll leave you to it, but please let me know if you need anything else."

Taking a sip from my flask, I lean back in my seat with a content sigh.

The hum of the engines and the gentle sway of the ship make for one smooth ride. State-of-the-art propellers and engines power the airship, allowing for smooth and efficient travel.

The other passengers are all dolled up in their glad rags, punching the bag and laughing like it's the chat's pajamas.

I'm seated in one of the plush armchairs, taking in the breathtaking views through the large windows. The clouds look like fluffy cotton candy, and the starsun is shining bright like a bright yellow diamond. The stewards are on point, always at the ready to fetch me a drink or a snack. They're dressed sharp as a tack and move with the grace of a chat.

My mind moves to more pressing matters. A trick I use when trying to invent something new is to close my eyes and meditate with paper and pen nearby. When inspiration hits, I write it down. Here's hoping it works when trying to solve a mixed-up mystery.

Closing my eyes, I breathe softly. A picture begins to form—

"Excuse me," says a voice, snagging me away from my solution.

I open an eye to see a flour-loving face stretcher leaning over me.

"Excuse me, doll," says a dame with a face like a bulldogacorn's behind, "I couldn't help but notice you're sitting in the chatbird of seats. I demand you switch with me so I can catch a gander at the view."

Opening both my peepers, I give her a once over, trying to hide my annoyance. "Jeepers, I'm sorry, but I paid for this seat, and I plan on enjoying the view."

The old dame lets out a huff. "Well, I demand you scram. I've got seniority and deserve the best seat. Plus, you had your eyes closed."

I can't help but let out a little giggle. "I'm sorry, but just because you've got a few hundred rotations under your belt doesn't give you the right to boss people around and snatch their seats."

The dame lets out an indignant huff before storming off in search of another victim. I close my eyes again, ready to pick up where I left off in my meditation and possibly even solve the mystery I was trying to figure out before I was so rudely interrupted.

I take a deep breath. I can almost see the thread.

"Excuse me," says a tenor voice, pulling me from my moment.

"You have got to be kidding me!" I open a lid to see a weasel-looking steward leaning over me, his face centimeters from mine.

"Miss?"

"Beat it," I warn and close my eye.

"Miss?" His voice is whiny, like a mosquito in your ear that you just can't swat away. The type of voice that inflames your nerves and makes you want to put cotton in your ears—a regular yodeler.

I keep my eyes shut this time. "Put a sock in it, would ya?"

"Mrs. Gateson insists you change seats with her immediately." His voice grates against my ears.

"Beat the bricks. I'm busy." Using my pointer finger, I touch the tip of his nose and press, moving his face out of my personal space.

"Miss, she insists," he persists.

I stand, my lather up and my manners forgotten. I ankle over to the entitled old fart, place my hand on her face, shove her, and reply flatly to her ridiculous demand. "Aw, dry up will ya!"

The steward's voice goes from tenor to alto in a split second. "Miss, we do not tolerate—"

I interrupt him. "First, I paid for this seat. Secondly, it isn't Miss, it's Doctor." I stand nose to nose with him. "Dr. Harcrow." I retake my seat. "Now take a powder and remove that nuisance from my sight."

"I'm so sorry, Dr. Harcrow. I didn't know. I didn't realize it was you. My apologies." His voice is still an octave higher than normal.

"Attaboy. Now be a good sport and get me a sandwich. I've worked up an appetite." I settle into my seat and stare out the window. The steward nods and proceeds to step over the vexatious face stretcher, who happens to still be seated on the floor, mouth wide open and cheeks red from embarrassment.

I have given up hope of any type of meditative revelation. What was once within my grasp is now kilometers away, just like my life, my home, and my family.

I pick up the paper and my writing utensil from the table in front of me and begin to make a list.

Number one: explosion. Number two: burnt-to-a crisp-victim. possibly Albert Slack. Number three: strange blue cloud like substance. Number four: mysterious break-in at Coco's.

I place the end of the pen to my lips. "Hmm, what else?" Number five—

The yodeler is back. "Your sandwich, Dr. Harcrow."

"Thank you . . ."

"Jimmy," he finishes.

I nod. "Thank you, Jimmy."

"I added some fried root-vegetable chips."

"I appreciate that, Jimmy. Thank you." Taking a bite of my sandwich, I place it on the table and return to my list.

Five: supposedly nothing was taken. Number six: Piers spotted arguing with a young man about money and possibly a formula. Number seven: a man dressed in black followed me and killed Lucy Marsh, mistaking her for me. Number eight . . .

I slump back in my chair with a heavy exhalation. Number eight: nothing. I have nothing. A bunch of random facts that add up to squat.

I stare out the large tinted window of the airship. We are still a ways from my destination, Aldar City. The city of Aldar is a sprawling young metropolis; gleaming perpendicular skyscrapers reach for the sky, their facades adorned with intricate patterns and sparkling neon lights powered by the city's advanced solar-energy system.

The city is a melting pot of cultures and styles, with influences from all over Gaia. The city is split into several districts. The financial district is home to the towering silver skyscrapers, while the industrial district is a maze of flat-top factories and warehouses. The garden district is a collection of elegant apartment buildings and townhouses, while the leisure district is full of theaters, clubs, and restaurants. I haven't been there in rotations. My old assistant, Clover, grew up there. Clover Bode was the darb of assistants; she really has the goods. It's difficult to find and keep laboratory assistants. The long hours. The large explosions.

Clover still works at my family's alchemy company. She now assists Steven Zozimos, a narcissistic ass of a chemist and physicist. His wife, Cora, is sweet and smart, though. From what I heard through the grapevine, Steven is currently on probation. He has to deliver on a few projects for the Tesla Space Exploratory Council, or he will be let go. Personally, I think the only reason he's still employed at HA is because Cora is talented. If and when I return to Fulcrum and HA, I wonder if I'll be able to snag Clover back. Steven lost his last assistant, Orin Needs, when he was charged with conspiracy, theft, and a bunch of other things for conspiring with Dr. Textrix, Dr. Carnot, and whats her name. Orin Needs will be lucky to see the light of turn for his part in what could have ended with my death.

I finish my sandwich. With my case in hand, I look for Jimmy the steward.

"Yes, Doctor?" he says.

"Where can I freshen up?" I hold up my case and jiggle it.

"Up the grand staircase, turn left, and down the hall to your right you will see the ladies' lounge." His voice still grates, but I'm getting used to it.

"Thank you, Jimmy." I hand him a couple of tokens. Since Tesla moved away from paper, slipping someone some cabbage has changed. I purchased tipping tokens to hand to the service staff so they could cash them in and add to their banking. "A little extra to make sure old grabby grandma doesn't steal my seat." I make sure the tip is generous.

Jimmy excitedly answers, "Oh my stars, yes sirree bob!" He pockets the tokens. "I will make sure your seat is ready for your return. And—let me bring you our famous dark raw cacao mousse topped with a passion-mango bavarois. It is our signature dessert."

"Sounds good to me, Jimmy." I smile.

I make my way up the grand staircase; I can't help but admire the luxurious decor of the airship. The walls are adorned with intricate patterns of gold ginkgo leaves and the floors are covered in plush carpeting. I turn left as instructed and make my way down the hall to the right. The door to the ladies' lounge is marked with a discreet sign, and as I enter, I am greeted with a room that is elegant and functional.

The room is filled with plush armchairs and sofas, upholstered in soft rose-gold velvet with gold trim. The walls are painted a soft pink and decorated with elegant paintings and mirrors. Crystal chandeliers hang from the ceiling.

There are several vanity stations set up around the room, each with a mirror, a stool, and a set of beauty supplies. There are also several private alcoves where ladies can freshen up in privacy. I make my way to one of the vanity stations and set down my case.

A lady dressed in a full-length drop-waist blush velvet robe with baby-pink fur collar, full over-long cuffs, and hem is seated beside me. The long V front reveals part of her sheer silver tulle dress. I cannot help but admire her ensemble. The well-dressed gal finishes powdering her nose and quietly excuses herself and leaves. I pull out my travel atomizer, which is filled with a deep spicy-scented eau de parfum—a gift sent over from Coco. It happens to be the one she was working on when I almost blew up her lab where it was being created. She sent a small note card with it:

Dear Zelda,

Good luck on your secret journey. I wish you could tell me where you are heading. I hope you find the answers to my dilemma there. Enclosed is the perfume you had a strange hand in creating. After your interference in the development of the scent via explosion and whiplash for my scientists, a new and wonderful scent came about. We have a working name for the new eau de parfum. I am considering calling it Zelda's Folly. The name sounds fitting.

Good luck, my friend. Safe travels. Return swiftly with a report.

Yours truly,

Coco

My lips part in a soft smile as I spritz my neck. Placing the atomizer down next to the case, I reach in and pull out the cold cream, rouge, and powder. Time to touch up the munitions. Placing a small dab of cream on each cheek, I massage the cool, light floral-and-powdery-scented cream into my skin. Air travel always seems to dry out my skin. I place the cream to the side and open the tube of rouge. A dab for each cheek. Rosy and dewy, perfect.

Placing the rouge back in the case, I look up to see a young mother leave one of the privies with her child. My attention moves back to the mirror and my powder. I can hear the door click open and shut as they leave. I take the small puff and freshen up the powder on my face. Dewy cheeks are fine, but a shiny nose is not. I pull out a little lip rouge and fix the bow on my kisser. All set.

I look down as I begin to tidy up my area. I hear the door again—a click open, a click shut. Then another sharp, short crisp *click*.

I feel something rush toward me. Before I can turn, my fur stole is pulled tightly around my neck, and I am jerked against the back of the seat. I grab at my stole. I cannot go out this way—death by fashion choice. I claw at the deep fur and gasp for air.

I try to fight back, but my attacker is strong and determined. I can hear the sound of my own gasping as I struggle to free myself. My vision starts to blur as I try to make noise and call for help, but my voice is barely a whisper. My strength is draining away. My efforts seem futile. I know I have to do something quickly before it's too late.

I use all my strength to push back, aiming for the attacker's face, to no avail. Through my tears, I see the atomizer. Grabbing at the bottle with the fingertips of one hand while the other is occupied with pulling the fur from my neck, I move the bottle close enough for me to grip.

I have one shot at this.

Using both hands, I aim the nozzle up above my head and hope against hope that my aim is good, or I am a deceased dame. I squeeze the bulb, spraying the oils and alcohol at my attacker. As the spray hits my assailant, they let out a surprised yelp. The goon's grip on my stole loosens, and I am finally able to break free. His eyes widen as he tries to wipe the spray off his face and out of his eyes.

He fumbles around, disoriented and confused, trying to regain his balance and composure. "What the hell was that?"

"It's called Zelda's Folly!" I dropped the bottle when I pulled the stole from my neck, so I need another weapon. My eyes dart to the cold cream still open on the counter.

"It stings!"

I grab the facial cream. "Who are you, and why are you trying to kill me?"

"You know who I am!"

"No, I don't," I insist.

"I tried following you, but you and your boyfriend wrecked my car and got away," he says.

"That was you?" My mind races, trying to figure out ways to incapacitate him and get to the door he locked and now guards blindly. "Also, he isn't my boyfriend."

"You could have fooled me. I've followed you around town trying to find out where she is hiding." His eyes are clearing up, and he takes a step in my direction.

"Your tin was a wreck long before we came around!"

"Now you insult me?"

"You just tried to bump me off, and you are crying about being insulted?" I take a step back. "Did you kill Lucy Marsh?"

His face twists in confusion. "Who is Lucy Marsh?"

"The girl you strangled."

"I didn't strangle anyone."

"You just tried to strangle me, ya goon." I take another step back.

He takes a step toward me. "That's different."

"You followed me a few turns ago and attacked Lucy by mistake." Reaching the counter, I place my hands behind my back.

"I only started following you the other turn when I found out you were looking for Ruth."

"How do you know I was looking for Ruth?"

"You told me."

"Did not."

"Did too."

"Did not."

"You told me in the elevator." He took a step closer. "Now that I know where she is, I don't need your interfering nose getting in my way."

"What elevator?" The open jar of cream is in my hand behind my back. I scoop out a bunch and look at my case, wishing it was closed. It would make a great weapon.

"At Coco Cosmetics. You asked me about Ruth." He seems almost disappointed I don't remember him.

I think for a moment. "You mean the security guard?"

"Yes! I'm the security guard John." His eyes are red, not just from the perfume but from anger as well.

"You're Ruth's stalker?" Now I can see why Ruth couldn't get any help from management. Now I really must speak with Coco about her security staff.

"I'm not a stalker! It's her family that is trying to keep her from me. You—you found her for me."

"A no."

"No?" He takes a step closer; he's only a little more than an arm's length away now.

"She said no, and you didn't listen. Her parents told you she said no, and you didn't listen. She went to management and complained. They told you no, and you ignored them and her. I'm telling you no. No means no."

I set the jar down and spread the lotion onto my other hand. I'm armed with a soft silky beauty product, and I am not afraid to use it.

His eyes widen to reveal flames of burning fury. Resentment toward me or anyone else that tells him no. He leaps toward me. I react quickly, smearing the cold cream into his eyes. He cries out in pain, momentarily blinded by the sudden onslaught. I take the opportunity to strike, landing a punch to his stomach. He doubles over, giving me a chance to run. Grabbing my open case, I whack him across the kisser, then make a dash for the locked door.

Knowing I only have a moment or two before he gets back on his feet, I struggle to unlock the door with my greased-up paws. I fumble with the latch, trying to turn it with slippery fingers. My hearts are pounding as I hear him getting closer. I try to wipe my hands on my dress, but it only makes them more slippery.

I have to act fast, so I use my elbow to push down the latch and turn the handle. The door finally opens, and I stumble out, falling onto my knees. Both of my stockings rip and run at the knees; I feel the burn as I slide along the carpet.

I cry out, "Futz!" I look up the hall. Not a soul in sight. I scramble to my feet, but two arms wrap around my waist. I fly off my feet and land on my side with a thud.

Chapter Thirty

I'm sprawled out on the carpet in the hall with the wind knocked out of me and that goon on top of me like a ton of bricks. "Get off, ya mug!"

"You hit me in the face."

I wiggle and worm, pushing on his head, wriggling out of his grasp. "You're attempting to bump me off!"

The delusional John responds, "You are all trying to keep me from Ruth."

"You are off your rocker," I mutter as I squiggle enough to get one foot free.

Greasy from trying to wipe the lotion from his face and eyes, his hands can't quite keep a grip on me. My free shoed foot contacts John's mug. The boob rolls back onto his ass, desperately holding on to my ankle.

I knock him again, and he falls on his back. *Thump.* His head hits the floor, and he is holding my shoe. Lucky for me, my foot is no longer in it. I hasten to my feet. John is still on the ground but between me and the passenger area of the airship. I look down the short hall in the other direction; several doors litter the walls.

I race to the first. Locked.

I dash to the next and pull at the handle. Nothing.

I dart farther down the hall, looking over my shoulder. Next door is a closet. That is a big no from me; I'm done with those.

Ruby's stalker is now on his feet, staggering toward me. I sprint to the door at the end of the hall, hoping it is accessible. The placard on the door reads *Exit*. I swing the door open to reveal metal stairs leading up with metal railings. I'm thinking this leads to the maintenance area of the ship. I hope I can find help among the crew. With one shoe on and one shoe off, I climb the cold metal stairs. A clomp and a soft pad echo off the stainless-steel steps.

The Empress airship is powered by a combination of a lifting gas, like helium, and heated air to provide lift and engines to provide propulsion. The gas is stored in large, lightweight bags within the body of the airship and is used to inflate the vessel. It also uses a combination of propellers and rudders to control its movement through the air. The propellers provide thrust to move the ship forward, while the rudders allow the ship to change direction. The pilot controls the airship's movement by adjusting the speed of the propellers and the position of the rudders.

Now, all this would be completely copacetic if I were still seated in the passenger area of the ship or even a crew-only area of the ship. However, finding myself on a gangway suspended above enormous clockwork gears and an electric propulsion engine with large bags of gas and heated air on either side, while being chased by a crazy person is not ideal but rather very dangerous.

I hear the clip-thud of heavy shoes coming toward me, and I turn to face my attacker. I look around; there is nothing I can use to defend myself. I'm done for.

"You should have stayed out of my way," the man growls, lunging at me.

I dodge to the side, narrowly avoiding his grasp. "You're delusional if you think I'm just going to let you hurt Ruth or anyone else," I retort, my hearts pounding with adrenaline.

He lunges at me again, but this time, I'm ready. I grab hold of his arm and twist it behind his back, causing him to curse. "Witch." He tries to break free, but I hold on tight, using all my strength to keep him in place.

"Stop trying to kill me," I yell.

He sneers at me. "You think you're so smart, but you're just a foolish broad. You'll never be able to stop me from being with Ruth."

"Did you just call me a broad?"

"Ruth belongs to me!"

"She's not property to be owned. She's a being with her own thoughts and feelings. She's made it clear she doesn't want anything to do with you." He thrashes wildly in my grip, but I hold on tight. I can feel the sweat and oil on my palms making my grip slippery. I know I can't hold on for much longer. "You think you're so tough, but you're just a weak-kneed sap."

"I'll show you who's weak, doll face." The man jumps backward, pinning me to the railing. He continues to arch his back, leaning further backward. "Looks like you're the one who's struggling, cupcake."

In a moment of desperation, I shove him with all my might and move from behind him, releasing his arm. The deranged sap stumbles backward, trips over the railing, and falls screaming into the gears below. The sound of metal grinding against bones and flesh fills the air, punctuated by an ear-piercing scream. The gears keep moving until there is silence.

I slump down on the cold gangway and sit there shaking.

Taking a quiet breath, I speak the spell for bravery that my sister gave me.

"Gaia grant me courage

and lend me strength.

Give to me true grit,

so that I may be brave."

I close my eyes and repeat the spell two more times.

Slowly rising from the suspended walkway, I brush off my torn garment, smooth my hair, and pull my shoulders back. I limp slowly back the way I entered. Once back in the hall, I retrieve my shoe and continue back to my seat.

I ignore the gasps and stares. I can hear the whispered comments. I keep trudging on as if all is as it should be. As I take my seat, I realize I lost my bag, which means my flask is missing in action.

"Ahem," a familiar tenor voice interrupts.

Slumping down, I say nothing, shoe still in my hand.

"Your overnight case, Doctor."

I look up and see a young lady in a steward uniform holding my case.

"Uh . . ." I sit up. "Thank you."

Jimmy continues. "Your stole and purse." He waves another steward over with my items.

I take the items and clutch them to my chest.

Jimmy waves another steward over. "Your dessert, Dr. Harcrow." He places the parfait glass on the table in front of me with a spoon and pure-white napkin.

"Jimmy . . ." I am left speechless.

"One more thing." He pulls from his pocket my flask. "I took the liberty of topping it off for you."

I open my purse to retrieve more tokens for him and the other stewards.

Jimmy puts up his hand to refuse. "No, thank you, Doctor. Just rest and enjoy your dessert. Also, another steward is going to come up with your luggage so you have an opportunity to change before we land."

"I should—"

"We've already informed the captain, and we will look into the security issues for our passengers on board."

I take a long swig from the flask and nod at Jimmy. Looking out the window, I see Aladar City on the horizon.

Then horror hits.

Not the fact that I almost died again.

Not that a man was crushed and mangled in the engine of the ship.

Not even the matter of all the questions I will face when the airship docks.

The thing I dread is the call I need to make to my sister, that I will have to bow out of babysitting because, like a nincompoop, I forgot. She is going to hate me.

My following visit to the ladies' lounge is uneventful. I have now changed into garments I had packed for my trip back to Capital City. I will have to buy a new outfit while in Aladar as my other outfit cannot be salvaged. I freshen up the munitions and brush out my cobalt-blue hair. With one last swig from my flask, I am ready to face the captain of the Empress and the Aladar City authorities.

I wait in my seat till the rest of the passengers disembark. The flour-loving Mrs. Gateson goes out of her way to walk past me and toss me the stink eye. I roll my eyes. Can this turn get any wackier?

"Dr. Harcrow?" A fine-looking man in a uniform covered in multicolored bars on his chest and gold fringe epaulettes addresses me. Tailored to fit perfectly, his uniform starts with a crisp, starched white shirt, a lapis-blue tie, and a matching double-breasted jacket made of a sturdy boiled wool. The jacket includes a row of pockets that hold maps and other navigational tools. The trousers, which match the jacket and tie, are tucked into polished black boots. The captain's blue peaked cap has a shiny black visor and sports a golden emblem with his rank.

I must say, overall, the uniform befits a leader of an airship crew.

"Captain," I say, looking up at the smooth-shaven, clean-cut man.

"Please accompany me to the gangplank." He holds out his arm.

Standing, I adjust my gloves and grab my case. "Of course." I link my arm with his and allow him to escort me off his ship.

"I apologize for any inconvenience you may have experienced aboard the Empress. We strive to deliver a pleasant and safe journey to all our passengers." He places his free hand over mine and pats it.

He is being overly kind. I can't understand why. It isn't like he was the cause of my attack. As we continue through the passageway toward the concourse, my curiosity gets the better of me. "Captain?"

"Sheppard," he says.

"Captain Sheppard, you are being too kind. A man fell into your engine. It would be remiss of me not to ask what type of damage that caused to the airship."

"Doctor, you were viciously assaulted by one of our passengers. It is far from your fault. Did you purposefully toss him over the side?"

"No. He fell backward."

"Well, there you go. Nothing to worry about. Our gears are strong and durable, and I am one of the premier pilots in Tesla. You couldn't be in safer hands. Granted, our crew has a bit of a gooey mess to clean up."

I cringe at the visual of torn flesh, shattered bones, and all that blood.

Captain Shepard continues. "Not to toot my own horn, I may be younger than most pilots, but I have more hours under my belt than some of our more seasoned pilots."

Glancing up at him, I have a strange feeling I might know where this is going. It isn't going to be about dinner, drinks, or sex, either. "Premier pilot?"

"If I may be bold?" His smile is encased on either side by deep dimples.

"You have my permission." I hold my breath and wait for it.

"The Space Exploratory Council is looking for pilots to man your ship to Biota. I'd like to throw my hat in the ring."

I scratch my head. "You've heard about the moon project?" I am in utter disbelief that the captain would think I had any pull, let alone make it sound as if it were my ship.

"I don't think there is anyone on Gaia who hasn't heard about the moon shot." He sounds like a kid excited about having dessert for dinner.

"I'm not in charge of who they choose," I say. "I'm sorry."

"But you can put in a good word for me." His eyes shine with hope.

"I guess I can. Sure." I really have no idea whether I can, but I'll say anything to get this awkward conversation to end.

"Thank you, Dr. Harcrow. I look forward to working with you."

"You're welcome."

He presents the gangplank with an outstretched hand. "This is where I leave you."

"Leave me?" I let go of his arm and stare down to the end of the platform.

"I leave you in good hands, I am sure." He gives a small salute, turns on his heels, and exits.

Staring at me from the observation deck is a group of well-dressed stiffs who have National Security Council written all over them. The one that appears to be in charge steps forward and holds out his hand. "This way, D r. Harcrow. We have a number of questions for you."

Slipping a piece of hair behind my ear, I gulp some air, hold my breath, and begin my descent down the ramp.

Chapter Thirty-One

The NSC agent stands waiting for me with an expression that reveals nothing. He's dressed in a suit of tweed in onyx, a color somewhere between gray and black. A silk tie in a matching color is tied precisely in a four-in-hand knot. The chain of a pocket watch is visible across his waistcoat. His long topcoat is open, revealing a large silver belt buckle and, attached to the waistband off to one side, an even shinier silver badge. A black fedora hat and dress shoes complete the outfit. He appears quite formal, professional, and serious. Very utilitarian.

Holding my chin up, I sway my hips as I stroll down the ramp to meet him.

I take the agent's hand and allow him to lead me toward the rooftop exit. Embossed with a raised and grooved geometric pattern, the nickel-finished doors of the elevator open, revealing two more well-dressed agents. This is becoming concerning.

I take a gander at the other mugs behind me and then at my escort. "How in Gaia are we all gonna squeeze into this elevator?" I plant myself in front of the elevator entrance. "I can hold the elevator for the next round."

The senior agent, who hasn't yet introduced himself, lets out a chuckle. "After you, Doctor." Shoving me into the elevator, he sends three of the other agents to cool their heels and invites one to join us for the ride. I give the two new operatives a once over. All the agents are dressed in the same rags. Regardless of their gender, the three agents in the elevator with me and the three waiting on the next one all have the same type of androgynous suit. Clunky, thick-soled black derby shoes, black woolen pants, a long black waistcoat with a badge pinned on the chest, a white shirt, black tie, leather shoulder holsters equipped with a weapon, and a black overcoat. It's more a uniform than a dress code.

The elevator dings, and the doors slide open, signaling the end of our ride. Surrounding me, my escorts walk me through the lobby, out through the double-wide glass doors, and into a nondescript vehicle. I slide into the back seat with the senior agent, and two of the agents hop into the front. We sit in absolute silence.

This is getting a bit creepy.

"Listen, can we do this later? Just drop me off at the Continental Hotel. We can catch up after dinner." I grab the handle to let myself out.

Crickets. Not a response or a sound. To top it off, the door doesn't open from the inside.

The auto starts and idles. Looking out the back window, I see the rest of the agents jump into a matching vehicle. Away we all go, down the main drag of Aladar City in the Financial District.

I try to initiate a conversation. "So, where are we headed?" When that doesn't get an answer, I ask another question. "What do I call you? Do you have a last name? How about a first name?" All I get is utter silence. "Okay, then I'll name you. I've got a couple of good ones I'd like to use." The names that cross my mind aren't exactly nice, but I give it a go. "Jeepers, let's see. How about Bas—"

"Bronn, Damon Bronn," the senior agent says, cutting me off.

"Okay, Bronn, Damon Bronn. Where in Gaia are you taking me? I'm on a tight schedule. I have to finish my business here so I can go back to Capital City so my sister can murder me."

"You can call me Agent Bronn. Your sister has been notified of your whereabouts, and she is fine. I found another babysitter, for which you can thank me later. Although I believe she may be angry with you in regards to something else. For that, Doctor, you are on your own."

"Jeepers," I say. "You still didn't answer my question on where you are taking me."

He doesn't answer, just stares straight ahead.

"How did you know I was supposed to babysit tonight?"

"It is my job to know."

"What else do you know?" I give him the side-eye.

He keeps his gaze straight ahead and speaks with no emotion. "Everything, Dr. Harcrow. Everything."

Under my breath, I sarcastically mutter, "Be careful, someone might think you're a hominid and not a replicant or android." Crossing my arms, I look out the window at the tall gleaming buildings jutting up into the sky.

"I'm all man, Doctor." A smirk appears on his face. "You can check if you want to."

I start to say something snarky but think better of it. Instead, I just glare out the window.

After a few more moments of pure uncomfortable silence, Agent Bronn says, "We are here."

The car pulls to the curb. The agent in the front passenger seat climbs out and opens the back door for us. She stands to the side with her hand on her weapon as we exit the automobile.

I stand looking up at my destination. The Continental, my hotel. He actually brought me here. I look at him, but his back is facing me. This Agent Bronn is a slick one. Was he always intending to bring me to the hotel?

All the agents have exited the vehicles. Two head in through the revolving door to the lobby. Two others have my belongings and are standing on either side of me. The last two bring up the rear. Agent Bronn leads the way. He insists on scooching through the revolving door with me. A little close for comfort.

The walls of the Continental are adorned with polished marble in shades of ochre and black. Large windows flood the lobby with natural light, highlighting the intricate geometric patterns etched into the marble.

The front desk is a beautiful piece of craftsmanship, made of rich, dark wood and inlaid with mother-of-pearl. The staff, dressed in starched malachite-colored uniforms with brass buttons, are ready to assist guests with any and every need.

To the left of the front desk, a grand staircase spirals upward, leading to the upper levels of the hotel. The banister is made of burnished brass and is adorned with scallop-shell patterns.

I look up at the lobby ceiling, where a beautiful sparkling chandelier hangs in the center, made of hundreds of glittering crystals that twinkle in the light. Live jazz music, played by a small ensemble on a raised stage in the corner of the room, drifts through the lobby.

One of the agents who preceded us into the lobby approaches us and speaks directly to her boss. "Sir, we have successfully checked Dr. Harcrow into her room. Agent B is surveying her room as we speak."

"Thank you, Agent A," Bronn replies.

"Doctor Harcrow is on the fifth floor, room 528. How should we proceed?"

I just stand there gawking, completely flummoxed as the NSC agents completely commandeer my visit.

"Dr. Harcrow," Bronn says, attempting to secure my attention.

"Huh?" I snap out of my daze.

"This way." He points toward the employee area. "We are taking the service elevator up to your rooms. Safer that way."

"Safer?" I repeat. "Why all the hubbub, bub?"

"Let's get you upstairs, and we will talk there."

The suite is grand and opulent, with rich fabrics and luxurious furnishings. The entryway opens up to a spacious living room, featuring a plush emerald-colored velvet sofa and armchairs arranged around a pink marble fireplace. I tour the suite, checking every corner.

The bedroom is just as palatial, with a dramatic king-size bed dressed in the finest linens and topped with a grand winged silver-gray hand-tufted headboard. A vanity table with a large oval beveled mirror and a comfortable reading chair sit in one corner of the room. The room also features a walk-in closet; I feel almost foolish with only my overnight valise and toiletries case.

The bathing room features bright-white marble floors and walls, a claw-foot soaking tub, and a separate shower. The fixtures are all made of polished brass. A separate water closet and bidet complete the room.

I make a mental note to take a long soak in the tub once these agents skedaddle. Dropping my cases on the bed, I join Agent Bronn and his minions in the living room. I plop down on the velvet couch. "Okay, why the special treatment?"

Agent Bronn takes a seat across from me on one of the chairs and folds his hands in his lap. "Can you recount for me your confrontation with your attacker?"

I scan the room for the other agents. Two are in the room with us. One stands at one of the double-hung windows, surveying the buildings across the way. The other stands with his back against the outer door. As for the other agents, I have no clue where they've gone.

I bring my attention back to Agent Bronn. "Yes, he confronted me in the ladies'."

"Go on."

I tuck my legs slightly under me and lean back onto the couch. "He came from behind and attempted to strangle me." I yawn.

"I realize you are exhausted from your ordeal; we will try to make this go quickly." His hands still clasped, he leans forward, resting his forearms on his thighs. "What did he use? Wire, rope, cord, ribbon?"

"Fur."

Bronn squints his piercing steel-blue eyes at me. "Fur?"

"Fur," I confirm.

The silver streak in his lamp-black hair reveals a little of his age, not unlike his next question. "Is that some type of slang?"

I slip a piece of hair behind my ear. "No. Just fur."

"Where did he get this so-called fur?" He makes air quotes with his fingers on the word *fur*.

My brow furrows, and I tilt my head. "From my shoulders."

"I'm not following."

I pick up the pace. "Crazy John grabbed my stole and tried to strangle me with it. I could have bought the farm, but I fought him off with perfume and cold cream."

"What?" He sits up straight and unclasps his hands, placing them on the armrests of the chair.

"Then he tackled me. I got away, and he chased after me."

"Continue."

I uncurl from the sofa and pace back and forth in front of the fireplace, giving an account of my harrowing experience. When I finish, I instantly search the mantel to see if a box of roll-ups came with this pricey suite. Lucky for me, it did. I place a gasper between my lips and try to spy a lighter. Bronn is quick to his feet, offering me light.

"Thank you," I say.

He places the lighter back in his pocket. "This agent—did he say anything?"

I take a drag. The smoke fills my lungs, and the dopamine hits my brain. "What agent?"

"The torpedo."

"Oh." I let out a small chuckle. "It was just a security guard."

"What security guard?"

"From Coco Cosmetics."

"Was he the bomber?"

"I don't think so. He was just an everyturn masher." I take another drag and sit back on the couch.

Agent Bronn scratched the back of his neck. "Why did a security guard from Coco Cosmetics follow you and try to kill you?"

"Wasn't his first attempt, either."

"I think I'm missing something," he says.

"The stalker's name is John."

"Your stalker?"

"No. Ruth's."

"Who is Ruth?"

"For someone who claims to know everything, you have no idea what I'm talking about."

"Obviously, we have our wires crossed," he says sheepishly.

Putting out the gasper in a glass ashtray, I explain the Ruth and John story. I purposely leave out Albert Slack and his role in the drama. No need for him to have reason to wade into my inquiries. Plus, I have no idea what Slack's possible early demise has to do with the explosion just yet.

Bronn seats himself next to me on the couch. He smells like a combination of musk, rosemary, sage, and oakmoss. And it is wonderful.

He leans towards me. "There hasn't been any move on you by Hyde agents?"

"Why would there be?"

He takes my hand in his, the touch of a second hand gently covering mine, creating a cocoon of warmth and protection. He is direct. "The race to Biota is heating up, Doctor. Your engine designs, as well as others', for the space vehicle are highly sought after."

"Since Textrix?" A shiver runs up my spine.

He tightens his grip, creating a comforting heat that first creeps into my hand, runs up my arm, and finally envelops my body. "More so now."

His warmth isn't enough protection against my own fears. I feel the blood drain from my face and confusion wash over it.

"You haven't spoken to your brother about it?" he asks.

"He hasn't said a word. No one in my family has."

"Your country needs you, Dr. Harcrow. Finish up whatever business you have here, and return to your lab."

I pull my hand from his and stand with defiance. "Excuse me?"

Agent Bronn rises from the couch. "You should communicate more with your family." He walks to the door, now flanked by his two agents. "You are very resourceful; you're going to need that going forward."

With that last sentence, he and his entourage leave.

My mouth hangs open. Obviously, they could care less about the crushed, mangled body that was once a delusional dope in the airship. Biota seems to be all that matters.

I make a mental note to call my brother, Ephron. After I take a long soak and eat a hearty dinner. Next turn, I'll visit Ruth.

Chapter Thirty-Two

The aroma of freshly steeped black tea fills the air, along with the sweet fragrance of freshly baked pastries and bread. I smile at the array of delicious items on the tray to choose from. I am grateful I thought to call down and have breakfast delivered to my suite. This way, I can lounge in my red polka-dot spider-silk pajamas and enjoy my feast in peace. I sip on the hot tea, appreciating a full breakfast with no Iron Maiden to whisk it away. The long soak I took last night left me relaxed, allowing me to get a solid night's sleep.

Now that I am rested and my stomach is being satisfied, I reflect back on my chat with my brother, Ephron. Ephron works for Harcrow Alchemy Inc. as CEO. He secures contracts from different councils and independent companies for an array of projects. He is my big brother, and I am closer to him than my other siblings.

Ephron is good at his job. Keeping a bunch of alchemists and tinkers in line is not an easy business. It is also why he probably has a private bottle of whiskey in his desk drawer.

Our conversation started out with the basic niceties: "Hiya, how you doing?" and "Everything is berries." The basic bull that warms up a difficult conversation to come. I nicely updated him on the current state of my affairs, leaving out Agent Bronn and his circus.

His response? Utter silence. I pushed him for the latest on the Tesla Space Exploratory Council Biota project, and I was met with more silence. My brother, my champion, is angry with me.

"I'm sorry. Once I finish with Coco, I'll head back," I promised.

Ephron told me not to hurry or bother. He was very matter-of-fact. He then hung up without even a goodbye.

I have a good stretch and rise from the sofa. Time to dress and put on the war paint for the interview with Ruth Cotter. I brought an afternoon dress in red that is simple yet elegant in design, with a dropped waist and loose, flowing skirt that falls just above my knees. The fabric is a lightweight crepe, which drapes beautifully and moves with every step I take. I accessorize it with a pair of stylish buckle shoes, also in red. The shoes have a low, chunky heel and a Mary Jane strap across the front.

Completing my outfit is a cloche hat in a matching shade of red. The hat has a low, close-fitting crown that hugs the head and a wide brim that curves down over the forehead, framing my face. A simple ribbon band encircles the base of the crown, tied in a neat bow at the side.

I take a twirl in front of the mirror. Picture perfect. The comfortable fit of the dress and practicality of the low heel make it perfect for traveling around town, visiting Ruth, and shopping for a new travel outfit, seeing as mine was so rudely destroyed by the now deceased masher.

Before I head out, I ring Mae, who answers after a long while. "Dar-ling."

"I was just about to hang up. What took you so long?"

Mae draws her *r* out even longer this time. "Darrr-ling, I still had my sleep mask on. There is a tap dance going on in my poor little head."

"Hangover?"

"A monster of one."

I give her my new hangover cure, complete with spell. "This will work," I say. "The tea is easy to make. Take a mug and fill it with water, steep chamomile and ginger for about five minutes. Sip slowly while saying the following spell:

"May the Universe hear my request,
so I can heal and rest.
Waves of healing wash over me.
Banish this hangover,
So I can dance once again.

"After you complete the spell and finish the tea, drink a full glass of coconut water."

I wait for Mae's reply.

Silence.

"Mae?" I yell into the mouthpiece.

"Ow!" she cries out. "Why are you screaming at me?"

"You weren't answering. I thought you fell asleep or something."

"I hear you. Tea, water, spell."

"Close enough."

"Where are you now?" Mae asks in a whisper.

"Aladar City, to talk to one of the suspects."

"Fill me in," she instructs. "Do not leave a single detail out."

I do just that. I even tell her about Agent Damon Bronn.

"He sounds dreamy," she says.

"That's what you got out of the whole story? That Bronn is a looker?"

"Well, isn't he?"

I can't lie. "Yes, he is."

"I did get more information about the goings-on over at Coco's. Hence, the hangover." Mae continues to fill me in on her night. "That Anne Sheridan is a real flapper. That gal can really cut a rug. She knows how to wriggle and shimmy—on and off the dance floor."

"How about details?" I request.

"She makes this cute little sound when—"

"Not those kinds of details. Details about the goings-on at Coco's. You know, the stuff Coco herself doesn't know. The scoop-boop-oop-a-doop."

"All right, darling, but I think my adventures on the town are more interesting."

"I'm sure they are. However, they are not going to help us solve this mystery and get me back to Fulcrum."

There is a small pause before Mae says, "You are finally returning?"

"Yes, I am returning." I let her in on the chat I had with Ephron last night. "He is really upset with me."

"It isn't you, Zelda. He is under a lot of pressure. Your father has been missing recently, which has caused a few clients to leave for the competitors." She clues me in on the happenings at H.A.

"I didn't know it was that bad. Oh, Mae, this is terrible." Tears form like tiny puddles in my eyes. Not enough to wipe away but plenty to blur my vision.

"Poppy is helping out at the moment by putting out a few fires. Settle this Coco business, and then I'll treat us to a lovely spa time to get you back on your feet."

"A spa retreat, Mae?" I ask. "I thought I needed to get back to Fulcrum pronto."

"Coco gave me the horrid details of your hair and skin. Monstrous. You just cannot reenter life looking haggard." Mae is overly dramatic. I can envision her waving her hands around frantically.

"We will see. Now, about Anne." I refocus the conversation.

"As you know, Anne worked in the typing pool. She started after the new office building was constructed. At first, everything was copacetic. Coco and what's his name."

I interject, "Piers."

Mae says, "Who?"

"Coco's husband, Piers."

Mae proceeds. "Coco and her husband seemed to be a team that couldn't be beat. However, she noticed after a few rotations that Piers seemed a bit moody. Always snapping at workers."

"Coco didn't do anything about it?" I ask.

"How should I know?" Mae sounds a bit short.

"I apologize for the interruption."

"As I was saying, he was Mr. Crabby Pants. Anne went on to say that he started not showing up to work. Juju took up the slack and managed the office."

"Really?" I shouldn't be surprised; Juju would do anything for Coco.

"One turn, according to Anne, Mr. Crabby Pants shows up with renewed energy and focus. Everything seems like it's back to normal." Mae clears her throat. "Then, out of the blue, the husband starts firing some of the secretarial pool and accountants in their respective departments. Anne says she was a bit nervous about being the next on the old chopping block. Just as quickly as he fired people, he hired new replacements."

"Let me guess, one being a Sally," I say.

"Now you're on the scent." Mae continues to spill the dirt. "Sally is continually paraded in front of Coco. You know Coco's appetite and taste; it was a no-brainer that something was going to occur eventually." She takes a breath. "Well, I guess things didn't progress fast enough for Sally. Or maybe it was Piers, I don't know. Piers moved Juju to being his executive assistant and put Sally with Coco."

"You make it sound like a sinister move."

"Anne didn't think anything of it at first, either. Till she witnessed a little hanky-panky going on in the file room."

"Between Coco and Sally?"

"Nope. Sally and Piers," says Mae. "They didn't see her, and she kept her mouth shut, fearing she'd lose her job. But Anne kept her eyes peeled after that."

"More instances?" I ask her.

"Yes, plenty more. Plus, the ins and outs of some of these new accountants."

"Coco didn't notice any of this?" I am appalled.

"Coco didn't, but she thinks Juju did."

"Why did she think that?" I press for more.

"Anne saw Juju talking with one of the junior accountants who had been with the company prior to the culling."

"Let me guess, Albert Slack."

"How did you guess?" Mae doesn't give me time to answer. "Juju seemed to start keeping tabs on Piers's comings and goings. Then, a few strings before the explosion, Juju went in and had a meeting with Coco behind closed doors. That was Anne's last turn at Coco Cosmetics, so she doesn't know much more than that."

"That is plenty." I am excited for this latest information. "Did Anne say how Juju or Coco was after the meeting?"

"Anne said Juju looked smug. Coco looked upset, and Sally appeared to have a slight smirk that she was seemingly trying to hide."

I gasp. "Sally was in the meeting?"

"She was. Anne thinks Juju doesn't know about Sally and Piers." Mae takes a pause, then asks, "Should we tell Coco?"

"Not yet, Mae. Let's find out if Sally is just a good-time gal or a cohort of Piers's."

"Does this information help?" Mae asks.

"I think so. I am interested in the meeting between Juju and Albert Slack."

Mae yawns. "Are you going to ask Juju about it?"

After the way Juju acted secretive around me, I don't think it would be a good plan. "I am going to ask Albert's sweetheart." I smile. "Ruth Cotter."

I hear Mae's yawn again through the receiver. I bid her goodbye and disconnect. Picking up the hotel-room handset, I call down for a ride.

"This is the address of my first destination." I handed over the piece of paper Nettie gave us with her aunt's address on it. Supposedly, Ruth is expecting me.

The ride is uneventful. The traffic is light due to excellent city planning. Aladar City is northwest of Capital City and a few kilometers from the northern shores of the continent of Tesla. Gaia is made up of several large land masses, most of which are their own countries. I am partial to Tesla, not just because it is home but because it has some of the most beautiful and diverse landscapes and hominids. Because of our desire to lead Gaia in technology and advancement in the sciences, Tesla recruits alchemists from all over. We have several species of hominids that call Tesla their home.

The hotels sit closer to the north shore, with the financial district to the south and the entertainment district to the east. The driver takes us through the financial district, with its bright, shiny towers that reach for the sky. He makes a slight turn as we head toward the city center. My driver navigates us through the roundabout and exits to the south, away from the entertainment district.

I gaze out the window and study the residential district. It starts with bland high-rise apartments with no character, then turns to modern-designed townhomes with rounded balconies and rooftop gardens. We drive on into an area full of multifamily homes, which is where we stop. Farther ahead are the single-family homes, and beyond that are the mansions where the elite citizens hang their hats and lay their heads.

The driver pulls up to my destination.

"Please wait here for my return," I say to the driver, before adding, "What is your name?"

"Chucky. No problem, your dough." He places the vehicle in park. I swing open the door and look out at the side-by-side duplex.

The two-family building allows the owner to live in one of the apartments and collect a decent amount renting out the other. The one-floor duplex is charming. Each side has a covered porch with a brick knee-wall designed for privacy. On the brick facade of each porch is the addresses in brass. Ruth's aunt's home is on the left. I rap on the front door and wait.

An older woman who reminds me of an older version of Nettie answers the door. She must be Ruth's aunt.

"Can I help you?" she greets me.

"Hiya, I'm here to see Ruth. I believe she is expecting me. I'm Dr. Zelda Harcrow."

The older woman turns her head and hollers, "Ruth, there is someone here for you."

A few moments pass before Ruth comes to the door. "Thank you, Aunt Becky. I've got it." She dismisses her and addresses me. "Nettie said you'd be coming. Let's take a seat on the porch." She exits and ushers me to the front porch.

"Thank you for seeing me."

"It's a beautiful turn out today. Being this far north, we don't get as many star-sunny turns, so sitting on the porch is a treat."

"It is a lovely turn." I agree, before jumping into questions. "Ruth, what can you tell me about your time at Coco Cosmetics?"

"At first, it was wonderful. The other factory line workers are so nice. Then—well, Nettie told you what happened." She pulls her handkerchief out of her sleeve and dabs her eyes.

"On that front, I have some good news. John will no longer be bothering you."

She lifts her chin and smiles, the corners of her mouth gently rising. Her eyes show a glimmer of hope. "I don't know what you did, but thank you! Now Albert and I can get married. Is Albert aware of the news? It's just, I haven't heard from him in turns. I hope he didn't get scared off by that creeper."

"About that . . ." Jeepers, I don't know where to begin.

"Oh. He's breaking up with me?" Rivers of tears flow from her eyes.

"No," I answer simply, not sure how I'm going to break to her the news of Albert's probable demise. I need a segue into how he may have bought the farm. *Keep it simple,* I tell myself. "Ruth—"

I'm cut off by her aunt, who comes out of the house and onto the porch with a pitcher of what appears to be some sort of punch. "I thought you gals might be thirsty." She sets the wooden tray down and picks up a glass and the pitcher. "Say when."

"When," I announce. "Thank you." I take the glass and a tiny sip of the sugary red concoction. It's quite tasty. "This is the berries."

"I'm glad you like it." She hands Ruth a glass. "Here you go, girl. You want a nip to add in?" She pulls a hip flask out of her apron and jiggles it back and forth.

I raise my eyebrows; this is my kind of aunt.

Ruth waves her hand and shakes her head, signaling her refusal.

"I'll leave you two to talk." The boozy Aunt Becky makes her exit, taking her flask with her.

I start again with my questions. "When was the last time you spoke to Albert?"

Ruth sniffs. "The turn of the explosion."

"Where was he before that?"

Ruth shifts in her heavy iron cantilever garden chair. "Here. After I skipped town, Albert followed a turn or so after. He only had a string off."

A string—that's eight turns. According to the records, he was marked present on the turn of the explosion. "Did Albert stay the whole string?"

"He received a phone call and said he had to travel back to Capital City for an important meeting," says Ruth.

"What turn was this?" I ask.

"The morning of the explosion. I kissed him goodbye, and he said he'd be back the next turn if he wasn't needed."

I scratch the back of my neck and ponder my next question. "Did he say who he was meeting? Juju, perhaps?"

She just shakes her head. Then the waterworks start, and she is bawling her eyes out.

"Ruth?" I stand and move to her side. Gently, I rub her back. "There, there." I realize I am a regular goof at this comforting business.

"Jeepers, he isn't coming back, is he?" she blubbers between sobs.

"I'm afraid not." I say this with confidence, even though the burned-to-a-crisp corpse hasn't been formally identified.

"W-w-what hap-p-pened?"

"The body found in the explosion was most likely Albert's." I continue to rub her back, failing at consoling her.

"Wait!" She stops mid-sob. "It might not be him?"

"It's a very slim chance it isn't. The evidence all points to Albert."

Ruth abruptly stands up. "Get out!"

"Ruth . . ."

"He could still be alive!" she yells at me.

"He would have come back, wouldn't he, Ruth?"

She collapses into the chair, wailing. "Noooo."

I squat in front of her. I need more answers from this hysterical doll. "Think. Did Albert tell you anything?"

"I-I-I don't know." Her face is a deep red and swollen from all the crying.

"Listen, Ruth, they are going to start blaming Albert for the explosion."

"Why?" she whines.

"Because one of Coco's new formulas showed up on Trade Island. They say he had an accomplice." I hate breaking this to her, but she needs to be prepared.

"They're going to blame me, aren't they?" Her voice trembles; she looks defeated.

"They may," I say.

"What do I do?" Her big eyes plead with me.

Standing, I walk to the porch steps. "Lay low for now. I put my card on the table; if you think of anything about Albert's mystery meeting, ring me up." I turn to leave, then stop and swing back around to face her. "It's up to me now to get to the bottom of this mystery."

Ruth buries her head in her hands and continues to sob. I hear Aunt Becky come out to the porch to collect her as I ankle back to the waiting auto.

Chapter Thirty-Three

I have had incredible luck in finding a new travel outfit. The shops in Aladar City are top notch. I found a lovely ensemble: palazzo pants and matching duster in cream and a spider-silk button-down blouse in a wavy pattern of blues, greens, and creams. In a hat shop, I found this marvelous felt wide-brimmed cloche hat with a band of blue and green to match the blouse. Since my shoes were ruined as well, I had the driver pop me up the next block to a snazzy shoe store. All that was left was a handbag, which I found to match the new shoes: a quilted leather purse.

Boxes and bags in hand, I ankle back to my driver. "Here you go, Chucky. Put those in the trunk." I hand off my purchases. "I'm finished."

"Aye, aye." Chucky the driver deposits my bags and hustles over to open the back door for me.

"Thank you." I slide in and gaze out the window as I wait for our departure. "Oh, my stars." I must be tired. I swear I just saw the Man in Black across the street. I blink several times, as if that would change the view. I still see him, and now he is walking away down the street. I panic for only a moment before an idea pops in my head. *This is one of the stupidest things I can do,* I think to myself.

As Chucky pulls out from the curb, I yell, "Stop!"

He slams on the brakes, and we both jerk forward.

"Take my stuff back to the hotel and have the porter leave it in my room." I open the auto's door. "I'm going to walk for a bit."

"How you gonna get back?"

"I'll find something. There will be a nice bonus in it for you."

"Your dough." He shrugs and leaves me behind.

I scurry across the street, keeping my eyes peeled for the Man in Black. He's sauntering down the sidewalk like he owns the joint, probably thinking I took off back to the hotel. How he sniffed me out in Aladar City, I don't know. I keep a few steps behind him, hoping he won't catch on. We pass a few stores, but he doesn't bat an eye. He must have a motorcar parked around the corner.

A sudden thought hits me: what if he ain't here for me? What if he's after Ruth to finish the job? I gotta warn her.

The sidewalks get more crowded, and I'm having a tough time keeping tabs on him. "Unicornfeathers!" I come to a halt. "I think I lost him." I spin around, checking left and right. "Maybe he's up ahead," I mutter to myself, hoping to get back on his tail.

I hustle through the throng of pedestrians, zigzagging through the crowd in search of the Man in Black. But the boob is nowhere in sight. I'm skirting past a few shops when suddenly a strong grip locks onto my arm and pulls me into the cover of a nearby doorway. I'm just about to let out a scream when a pair of lips mash onto mine. I jerk away, ready to fight, but it's only Agent Bronn.

I am livid. "What is the meaning—"

"I had to stop you from yelling out and giving away our position," he says.

"You think that kissing me is a good way to go about it?"

"I was thinking on my feet." A smile crosses his face.

"I don't think your feet have anything to do with it." I purse my lips and furrow my brow. "Why did you pull me aside, really? I was—"

"I know what you were doing. You were following a suspect."

"Then why did you stop me?"

"It is incredibly dangerous. Plus, you're crap at it." The smile fades from his mouth. "Go back to your hotel. Better yet, go back to Fulcrum."

"I'm not going anywhere just yet. I have a bomber to find. The bomber and the Man in Black may just be one and the same." I try to break free from his grip, but he just tightens his hold and shoves me farther back into the shadows of the doorway, blocking my escape. I roll my eyes.

"Leave this to the professionals. We have it covered."

"Oh, you do, do you?" I stick my chin out in defiance. "Now you've made me lose my suspect."

"He lost you first, Harcrow."

"What?" I stare at him in disbelief.

"He tagged you following him and hid behind a group of tourists. You walked right past him. Now he's following you." Bronn scans the street for any sign of the henchman.

"Oh," is all I can manage.

"Jeepers," Agent Bronn swears. Removing his fedora, he holds it up to conceal our faces and kisses me again.

The kiss is electrifying, and I feel it down into my toes. I also forget to be irritated. He is that good of a kisser.

He releases me from the kiss. "He passed by and didn't see you."

I find my irritation again. "If you ever try that again, it better come with a proposal."

He leans in as if he is going to kiss me again. His lips almost brush against mine. "Don't tempt me." Abruptly, he pulls away, places the fedora on his head, and with his viselike grip still on my arm, he pulls me out to the street curb, where a dark nondescript sedan has just pulled up. He shoves me in the back and leans in. "Agent P, take Dr. Harcrow back to her hotel. Make sure she gets to her room."

"You aren't coming?" I ask.

"Nope." Agent Bronn slams the door, and the auto peels out into traffic.

The drive back to the Continental is uneventful. Agent P insists on escorting me to my suite. Once inside, I kick off my shoes, shuffle over to the bed, and plop face down. I feel around for the chrome handset of the hotel phone and fumble it off its base.

"Operator," says a nasal voice through the receiver.

I roll over to stare at the ceiling. "Outside line, please."

An answer floats through the earpiece. "One moment."

Once I have an outside line, I ring up Ruth Cotter. Her Aunt Becky answers. "Hello." She sounds a bit soused.

"It's Dr. Harcrow. Is Ruth available?"

"She is resting. Your visit upset her."

"I am sorry about that. I just wanted to warn you both that there is a possibility that an extremely dangerous individual may be here looking for Ruth." I don't mince my words.

Aunt Becky seems to sober up fast. "What should we do?"

"If you have someplace you both could stay for a string or so on the down-low, that might be a good idea." I hate to scare them, but better safe than sorry.

"I think I have a good place. A friend has a holiday cottage farther west we can stay at."

"Can you give Ruth this list of names? I found them in Albert's things." I rattle off the names to Aunt Becky. "If Ruth thinks of anything that might help me, please have her ring me up anytime, morning, afternoon, or night."

I decide to stay in for dinner. It has been a long turn, plus I want to avoid the NSC agents spying on me. I place an order with room service for roasted boeuf with mashed tubers and gravy. I also order a bottle of their best vinum. Shuffling to the bathing room, I turn on the spigot to the soaking tub.

Relaxing in a tub filled with fragrant oils always helps me think. I ruminate over all the information I have gathered so far. I talk it through out loud. I let out a long sigh and mumble to myself, "I gotta figure this out.

"Maybe if I put a timeline of events together," I say. "First, the explosion." I shake my head. "No, that isn't first. Albert talks to Juju. Juju talks to Coco." I duck my head under the water and then resurface, splashing some of the fragrant oils out of the tub. "It starts before that, doesn't it?" I feel the story coming together. "Piers, Sally, Coco, Juju, Albert, mystery man, and the Man in Black. All the players."

I towel off and dress in my lounging pajamas and robe. I slip on my bedroom mules and retrieve my dinner from the room service attendant. I continue to work through the events that may have led up to the explosion and Albert's death.

I am halfway through the bottle of vinum when I push aside the half-eaten plate of dinner. Taking the bottle and my glass over to the sofa, I sit in front of the crackling fire.

Ideas are beginning to take shape. "Something happened to put Piers in a funk. Piers comes back with renewed energy and starts cleaning house. Why?" I take a gulp of the sweet, fruity fermented vinum. "He then replaces certain key people and brings in Sally. He can't get rid of Juju, because that would raise red flags." I jump up. "He makes her his assistant to control what she sees!"

I grab the bottle and pour another glass. Then I pace back and forth; I am on a roll. "Either Albert seeks Juju out or the other way around." I take a gulp of vinum. I must admit, I'm buzzed on alcohol, but that isn't stopping the wheels in my fantastic brain from turning. "They find something against Piers?" I take another sip. "Juju tells Coco. Did Sally tell Piers? Is that why Albert is dead?" I plop down on the couch and set my glass on the table. "That doesn't explain the break-in at Coco's or the joe that had a luncheon meetup with Piers." I sink into the cushions, my mind foggy from drink. "Then there is the Man in Black." My head falls into my hands. I am so tired; I must write this down.

The paper is soft, and the graphite pen glides silently along the surface. Making little bullet points, I write down the key players. The pen moves slowly across the paper as I put together a timeline. Now to connect the dots. I am starting to see a story unfold, but how do the mystery thief, the Man in Black, and the diner kid fit in? I scribble a few thoughts, close the book, take one last gulp of vinum, and stagger off to bed.

One would think that after the turn I've had, I would sleep like a dogacorn on a full stomach. Not tonight. I toss from one side to the other. Rolling to the side of the bed, I sit up and pour myself a glass of water from the bedside carafe. I am going to need help relaxing to fall asleep. Lucky for me, I brought along some valerian root. I down a dropperful of the herbal tincture and follow it with a glass of water. The valerian root reminds me of flowers. A palatable taste compared to many herbal remedies, which can be very bitter.

I close my eyes once more and slowly drift off, hoping for a dreamless sleep.

I find myself floating on a soft, fluffy cloud, surrounded by a dreamy, hazy blue sky. The air is cool and refreshing, and I feel weightless, as though I could float away.

Suddenly, I hear a loud, clanging noise. Looking around, I see a huge, metallic automaton robot approaching, its gears grinding and whirring as it stamps toward me. I try to fly away, but I'm too slow; the robot catches me and slams me to the ground.

As I struggle to get up, a sudden explosion shakes the very ground beneath me. A moon rocket flies overhead, leaving a trail of sparks and flames in its wake.

I hear a voice calling out to me and turn to see Coco in a sparkling evening gown, holding a tube of bright-red lipstick. "Hurry!" she cries. "We need to get to the launchpad before it's too late!"

I follow her, my heart racing with danger and excitement. As we run, she is replaced by my mother. She takes out a deck of tarot cards, shuffling them quickly and laying them out in a spread. She points to one card in particular: the moon.

"This is your destiny," my mother says. "You must be careful. Danger lies ahead."

With a jolt, I sit straight up. My pajamas are soaked in sweat. I must return to Capital City posthaste.

I pack my valise. I grab the outfit and hat I wore and stuff them in first. Next, I strip out of my damp pajamas and toss them in. I don't have time to be fussy and fold things nicely. With a quick snap of the latches, my valise is ready to roll. I throw on the new travel outfit I purchased yesterturn and quickly toss on the munitions. I stare at the red lipstick in my hand, remembering my dream, I shudder and toss it into the toiletry case. I heave the valise off the bed, take one last glance around the room, and hurry out the door, cases in hand, making a beeline for the next airship out of Aladar City.

As I step onto the rooftop airship concourse, the polished brass and stainless-steel gleam in the early-morning light, and the neon lights outlining the perimeter of the landing pad illuminate the entire area. The sounds of gears and hydraulics permeate the air as the engineers make last-minute adjustments to the engines and propellers.

I make my way to the passenger area; plush velvet chairs and chrome side tables decorate the space. I take a seat. The walls are covered in shimmering gold-and-silver mosaic tiles, making the small space seem much larger.

I glance out the large porthole windows and catch a glimpse of Aladar City's skyline. It's a breathtaking view.

As the airship lifts off the landing pad, I feel the gentle hum of the engines beneath me. Staring at the twinkling lights of the city below, the anticipation and apprehension of my return to Capital City sit in the bottom of my stomach like cement. Pulling out my hip flask, I take a few gulps to alleviate my anxiety and settle in for a hopefully uneventful trip.

I feel eyes upon me. Am I being followed again?

Chapter Thirty-Four

Followed or not, my trip back is uneventful. I cannot say the same for my arrival back at Ava's.

"What were you thinking?" Ava screams at me.

"What on Gaia are you in a tizzy about?"

Ava crosses her arms over her chest and narrows her eyes. "For crying out loud, lay off the crap. You are fully aware of what you did."

I hold up two fingers together. "By the stars, Ava, I swear I am clueless." I proceed to cross my hearts for an added punch in my sincerity.

"You taught Florence to fight!" Her hands fly to her hips, her eyes still narrowed like daggers.

"I taught her a couple of self-defense moves," I counter. "I told her it was just to defend herself."

"Self-defense!" she spits.

"Ava, what happened?"

"Your niece beat up a boy from school. I was called in to the academy by the headmistress. Flo and Eggs are both suspended for a turn."

I'm perplexed as to why Eggs would have been sent home as well. "Eggs?"

"I have no idea. The headmistress, Ms. Davenport, said they were being sent home for fighting. Supposedly, there is a zero-tolerance rule on violence. Eggs, Zelda. They sent Egbert home. This is serious."

"Did you ask them what happened?"

Ava's voice is calmer now. "All I got from Flo was that she had no choice."

"What did Eggs say?"

"Nothing. Absolutely nothing." Ava sighs. "He just keeps his arms crossed and his head down."

"Let me try to talk to them," I plead.

"You are going to do more than talk with them." Her voice is loud again.

"What do you mean?"

"I have to go back to the university. I have two more classes to teach. You, Zelda, are going to watch them." Ava grabs her jacket and purse.

"But—"

"You made the mess, Zelda. You clean it up." Ava ankles on over to the kitchen side hall to exit near the garage. She throws her head over her shoulder to add, "Oh, and don't try to pawn them off on Hazel. It isn't her job. Plus, the kids are scared of her." She leaves, slamming the door behind her.

"I'm scared of Hazel too," I call out after Ava.

I look over to see two beady eyes staring at me. Hazel, the terror of a maid, purses her lips and mumbles something under her breath. A shiver runs up and down my spine. I smile and wave at her, then dash up the stairs to find Eggs and Flo before she has a chance to give me the evil eye.

I sit with Flo on the edge of her bed as she excitedly tells me about the boy who was bullying Eggs at school. "Auntie Zelda, you won't believe what happened!" she exclaims, bouncing up and down on her bed. "This big bully has been picking on Eggs, calling him names and pushing him around. But I wasn't going to let him get away with that anymore!"

I raise an eyebrow, impressed by Flo's bravery. "What did you do?"

"He started on Eggs again on the playground." Flo grins mischievously. "I used the self-defense moves you taught me, Auntie Zelda. And let me tell you, they worked like a charm! I took that bully down and showed him who's boss."

I can't help but laugh at her enthusiasm. "I'm proud of you for standing up for your brother and defending yourself," I say, still chuckling.

"But get this," Flo continues, leaning in closer. "We all got sent home from school because of it! Can you believe that?"

I shake my head in disbelief. "That's not fair at all."

Flo nods in agreement, her face scrunching up in frustration. "Exactly! It's not like Eggs or I did anything wrong. But don't worry, Auntie Zelda. I'll make sure that bully never bothers us again."

I bring her up on my lap. "Did you tell your mom what happened?"

"Grown-ups don't listen."

"I'm listening."

Flo pats me on the cheek. "You're different."

I raise my eyebrows. "How so?"

"Momsy says you are irresponsible and think only about yourself, just like a child. So that's why you understand. You're just like me." Flo smiles and giggles.

My face falls at this knowledge of what my family thinks of me. "Jeepers," I whisper.

"Don't worry, Auntie Zelda." She kisses my cheek. "I still love you."

I wrap my arms around my niece and give her a squeeze. A small voice pipes up from the doorway. "Me too." Eggs sways back and forth.

I open up my arms, "Come here, you."

Eggs runs into my waiting arms and joins Flo and I in a hug. Nothing can beat this feeling right now.

I release my niece and nephew from my crushing hugs. "Listen, both of you." I move them to face me. "You must tell your parents what has been happening at school. The academy is supposed to be a safe environment for you to learn in. If you don't let the adults know what is happening, they can't help you fix the issue."

Flo balls her hand up into a tight fist and holds it up. "I have what will fix that bully. A knuckle sandwich right in the chops."

I cover her fist with my hand. "Jeepers, you're a regular pug, aren't you?" I lower her fist. "Self-defense should only be used as a last resort. It's always better to try to resolve conflicts peacefully if you can." I think that should earn me some points with my sister. Child, my ass.

Flo nods thoughtfully. "I know, Auntie Zelda. But sometimes, you have to do what you have to do."

I smile at her wisdom beyond her years. "You're absolutely right, Flo. And I'm proud of you for being brave and standing up for yourself and Eggs."

Eggs peeps, "Can we play Slides and Ladders now?"

"Ab-so-lute-ly!" I say. "Pull it out and set it up. I'm game."

I sit down on the floor as my niece and nephew set it up. "Okay, guys, let's get started!"

Flo spins the spinner. The arrow lands on four. "Woo-hoo!" she exclaims. "I'm moving up!"

Eggs giggles and spins a three. "Looks like I'm behind."

I spin and get a one. "Ugh, I'm off to a slow start."

As the game progresses, things take a strange turn. Flo lands on a square with a picture of a cicen fowl, and suddenly she starts clucking and bobbing her head like one. Eggs lands on a ladder and starts climbing, only to realize halfway up that he is wearing his pants on his head. I land on a square with a picture of a pie on it. "Mmm, I wish this game had actual pie," I say wistfully. I feel a wave of nausea before a plate of warm apple pie lands in my lap. "What is going on?" I ask, wishing I had envisioned ice cream on the side.

The clucky Flo spins again and reverts back to herself. "Phew, I hate when that happens."

"I don't remember this game being so interactive." I shove another bite of pie in my mouth.

With his pants back on where they belong, Eggs shrugs, spins the spinner, and moves his piece, avoiding ladders, slides, and a smashed cake.

When Flo lands on a slide, the books on her shelf come flying off and land on the floor. "Jeepers!" she swears.

"Flo," I reprimand, "watch your language, young lady. The two of us are in enough trouble already with your mom."

"Oops, sorry." She giggles.

"Ha-ha! Looks like you're going to have to work your way back up, Flo!" Eggs teases.

My spin grants me a slide down to practically the beginning, yielding me a pair of wet shoes. Slipping off a shoe, I turn it upside down, and water pours out. "This is one wild enchanted game."

The game continues to get crazier with every spin. More clucking, some mooing, a few sweets, more water, and ice cream.

Flo lands on another chute and groans. "Why do all the chutes hate me?" she complains as a cream pie appears from nowhere and smashes into her face.

Eggs lands on a ladder and climbs all the way to the top. "I'm the Slides and Ladders champion!" he shouts as he jumps up and down, waving his hands in the air. Suddenly, holographic fireworks explode over his head.

Flo and I both groan in defeat. "Looks like we've been defeated by the master of Slides and Ladders," I joke.

"Where did you get this game, kids?" I'm curious to know who developed all the special effects; it's pure genius.

"Grandpop gave it to us," Eggs says.

"He says it is special. Eggs and I are the only ones to have a Slides and Ladders game like this." Flo busies herself putting her books back on her shelves.

I knew it would have taken a remarkable genius to create it. I may be a bit miffed at Titus at the moment, but I can admit my father is a true genius. I wish I had that kind of talent.

Eggs and I help Flo put the game away and tidy her room. The doorbell rings. Once. Someone read the sign. The kids and I hear a commotion coming from downstairs, and a familiar voice echoes through the house.

My chin drops, and my eyebrows rise in disbelief. "It can't be."

Chapter Thirty-Five

"Mother!" I stand at the bottom of the stairs, utterly flabbergasted. "What are you doing here?"

Eggs and Flo push past me. "Grandma!" They squeal in delight as they wrap their little arms around my mother's legs.

"Oh, my precious pups," she says. I can hear the love in her voice. "Grandma brought a few trinkets with her; they're in my case." She looks up at me. "Don't just stand there; bring my cases in."

"And put them where?" I ask.

"In the guest room, of course."

"But I'm staying in the guest room." My voice is whiny and shrill. I can hear it, but I can't stop it. I am seemingly reverting to being a child in the presence of my mother.

Ave Harcrow-Galfry is from an extensive line of spiritualists, seeresses, and spellcasters. Magic runs deep in her veins. For a young-looking woman, she is not very modern. She doesn't approve of my complete independence and lack of husband. Mother also relies heavily on her Tarot deck to keep her abreast of the goings-on with her kids.

"I guess we will have to share," she says. "And make sure you pay the driver."

Shuffling to the door, I open it to find three full-size trunks, two cases, four hat boxes, and one toiletry case, as well as an old codger who must be at least one hundred rotations old with his hand out. My shoulders slump and I hang my head as I realize I'm going to be the only one hauling the luggage in.

Ave stays occupied with Flo and Eggs while I wrestle her luggage into the guest room. After taking a moment to catch my breath, I ring up my sister.

"What?" she demands.

"Ava, were you aware of a visitor coming to stay?"

"Besides you?"

"Besides me."

"Zelda . . ." Her voice rises an octave.

"Mother has just arrived," I say, ripping that bandage right off. No reason to beat around the bush.

"What?"

I pull the receiver away from my ear. I don't need to go deaf in one ear over this. "She just showed up."

"Did she say why?" Ava's voice has returned to normal.

"No," I say. "I don't think she wants to talk about it in front of the kids."

"Did she say how long she was staying?"

"She did not, though she appears to have brought her entire wardrobe. At least half of it, anyway."

"Jeepers, Zelda, what did you do?"

"Me? Why does it have to be my fault she's here? What about you?" I toss the blame right back at her.

"I'm almost finished with my last lecture. Let me pop back into the lecture hall and wrap it up, and then I'll race home." Ava sighs. "And Zelda . . ."

"Yes?"

"Do not let her read my cards." She abruptly hangs up on me.

Like I can make that happen. Mother has a mind of her own and is strong-willed. I guess I know where I get it from. It's hard to stop me once I clasp onto an idea. In fact, I have a few questions for Coco I need to ask. First, though, it's time to find out why the formidable Ave Harcrow has dropped in.

"The setup of this house makes zero sense. These modern designs are terrible. How are you to host dinner parties or even the modern cocktail parties they choose to have with these obstacles?" Ave continues to complain. "I mean, there is no flow to the house. And a garage off the kitchen; who in Gaia thought up that?" She shakes her head.

"Mother, I am sure Ava, Harvey, and the kids are very happy here." There is no time like the present, so I just straight-out ask, "Why the sudden and unexpected visit?"

"What do you mean, dear?" She gives Eggs a tickle, and he lets out a howl and a giggle.

"Ave Harcrow doesn't do anything without meticulous planning or at the very least calling ahead," I state.

"Not now, Zelda." She nods toward the kids.

I address my niece and nephew. "Should Grandma give you your presents now?" I widen my eyes and plaster a big smile across my face.

Flo and Eggs jump up and down like Presper jumping beans. "Oh, please, please, please, Grandma!" the kids yell in unison.

Mother narrows her eyes at me. "I know what you are trying to do Zelda."

My niece and nephew are still jumping around, begging for their gifts.

"You don't want to disappoint them, do you, Grandma?" I tease, knowing she'll give in and that the littles will run off with their new toys, leaving me to interrogate my mother.

She huffs. "Fine." The kids skip down the hall after her, heading for the guest room.

"Ahem."

Jerking forward, I grab my chest and turn to see Hazel standing with her hands on her hips and a scowl on her face. "You startled me," I say.

"I guess I am expected to get the room ready for Mystic Harcrow-Galfry?"

"Is that in your job description?" I smart back. I realize I may never get fed again if I talk to the Iron Maid this way, but sometimes I like living on the edge.

"With all that whooping and hollering from the offspring, I can't hear my stories on the VER anyhow. Might as well make your mother comfortable and get her a snack." Hazel dons her apron and grabs the sweeper from the closet.

"How come I don't get snacks!" I yell after her.

A corner of her mouth rises just a bit to form an evil smirk. Then she chuckles, before strolling down the hallway.

Cruel, just cruel.

Flashes of bright colors zoom past me and up the stairs. The giggles and screams that accompany the colors tell me that the kiddos have received their gifts from my mother and are happy as can be.

"I don't think I even got a thank-you," Ave says as she reenters the kitchen.

"Obviously, they loved what you brought them. I am sure you will get a ton of thank-yous later, along with a plethora of hugs and kisses."

"I made you a snack, Mystic Harcrow." Hazel sets a plate of cheese and fresh fruit on the table, then turns her head toward me. "This is not for you." Picking up her sweeper, she heads back to the guest room to finish cleaning.

"She doesn't seem to like you," my mother comments while taking a seat at the table. "What did you do?"

"Do?" I take the chair next to her. "I didn't do anything."

"Well, you must have done something." She pops a segment of citrus into her mouth.

"I exist. Is that enough?" I reach over to grab a piece of cheese off the plate. *Smack.* My hand jerks back from the sting. "Ow!"

"She said this was for me."

I gape at her. "Really?"

"I'm not having her mad at me. Really, Zelda, you have to learn to get along with other people better."

"Me?" I shake my head in disbelief. I can continue this crazy conversation, or I can take full advantage of this meager alone time I have with my mother. "So . . ." I fill my lungs with air and courage. "What happened?"

"What do you mean, what happened?" She takes a bite of the creamy cheese.

My mouth waters at the sight. Hazel really knows how to torture a gal. "Mother, you know what I mean. Why are you here? What happened? Where is father?"

"How do you know Titus left me?"

My eyes widen. "Left you? I thought he was missing or something. Not that he left you. Why would he leave?"

"He's been so secretive lately." Her voice is full of defeat and sadness.

I attempt comforting words. "He is always secretive about projects; you know that."

"It's more than the usual, Zelda. He disappears for turns on end. No, strings. He is gone for strings and strings. He won't tell anyone where he goes. I am at the end of my rope."

"What did he say?" I ask. "You did confront him, didn't you?"

"I made sure to read the cards first, of course."

"Obviously." I roll my eyes.

She tightens her lips as she inhales. "The cards never lie, Zelda."

"But you could misinterpret them." I place my hand over hers. "You shouldn't be reading your own cards. You know that."

She straightens up even more in the chair. "I read your father's cards," she states flatly.

"In this case, it may be the same thing."

My mother pulls her hand away and defiantly crosses her arms over her chest.

I close my eyes and take a moment to regroup my thoughts. I continue carefully. "What did the cards say?"

"Well," Mother begins, "the first card I pulled was the High Priestess. You well know that she represents hidden knowledge. It suggests that Titus is keeping secrets."

"Go on."

"The Moon I pulled next. The Moon card symbolizes illusions, deception, and hidden emotions. It indicates that there is something being concealed or obscured." Her eyes tear up. Like an illusionist performing a sleight of hand, she pulls a lace handkerchief from her sleeve to dab her eyes. "The Seven of Swords was up next. Deception, dishonesty, and secrecy. Need I say more?"

I can see her concern. The cards are not looking too favorable toward my father.

"Well, next up comes the Five of Cups." A wellspring of tears now flows. Between her sobs, she blubbers, "The Eight of Swords! He feels trapped, Zelda!"

My chair tumbles backward to the floor with a heavy clunk as I rush to her side. I wrap my arms around her. I suck at consoling others. I never know the right words to say. I've spent so much time in a lab that my people skills are nearly nonexistent at times. "Maybe he is keeping a secret about Biota."

"The Three of Swords, Zelda. The Three of Swords!" The distress in her voice can be heard between her sobs.

The Three of Swords can represent heartbreak or emotional pain when present in a spread about marital relationships. It's possible my father is lying about something. My heart is breaking, and I have no words to express my grief for my parents and the situation they find themselves in.

Luckily, just as I myself am ready to break down in tears, Ava comes home.

"What did you do, Zelda?" Ava's eyes narrow, and she clenches her fists at her sides.

"What? Wait! How come I'm to blame for everything?" I yell at her.

"If it weren't for you, they wouldn't be fighting!" she yells back.

"Me!"

"Ya, you!" Her finger points at me like a weapon.

"I'm not the one who kept everyone in the dark and put my daughter's life in jeopardy," I scream. "That was your beloved father." I am crying now. I feel an arm wrap around my waist, and warmth and familiar energy surround me. I bury my face in my mother's shoulder.

"Enough, Ava!" Mother is no longer crying. She's in mommy mode. "You girls shouldn't be fighting. This is all squarely on Titus's shoulders."

"I'm sorry, Zelda," Ava apologizes begrudgingly.

"Momsy, Momsy, Momsy!" The littles bound down the stairs and scamper into the kitchen. Eggs stands behind Flo, who speaks for them both. "Why are you and Auntie Zelda fighting? Is it because of us?"

"Oh no, baby. It was just a sisterly misunderstanding," Ava says. "Why don't the two of you finish playing upstairs. I'll call you down as soon as the grown-ups finish in the kitchen."

"Silly grown-ups!" Flo shakes her head, clasps Eggs's hand, and trots off to play.

Ava turns her chin to me and opens her mouth to lecture. "Do you—"

"Did you know," I say, cutting her off before she can finish, "that Eggs has been bullied every turn at that fancy school? Flo defended Eggs today. You should be proud of her, not punishing both of them."

"I had no idea," Ava whispers sheepishly. "Why didn't they say?"

"Better yet, why didn't that headmistress of yours inform you?" My back straightens, and I hold up my chin. "Those kids feel you wouldn't understand."

"Why wouldn't I understand?" Her hands fly up, her hands outstretched as if grasping for answers from the air.

"Because of me." I look toward our mother.

"Girls, why don't we sit down at the table. I don't think Ava has the full picture of what happened at H.A last rotation."

Not wanting to relive that harrowing time, I ask, "Mother, what about you and Father?"

She answers all teary eyed. "I'll fill you in afterward. I think Ava needs to hear your experience."

Chapter Thirty-Six

"I was a means to an end." I sniff back the new tears that are forming. "Father wanted to flush out the saboteurs and find the spies."

Ava sits across from me with her mouth gaping open. I can see the disbelief in her eyes. Like me, she's held our father on a pedestal. Yet Titus acts like a scatterbrained genius, with no regard for others. No regard for his children. He pushed Ava away because I showed more promise in alchemy. He left a business and political mess for my brother to clean up. What will he plague Phrennie with once she graduates from university?

"Why would he do such a thing?" Ava looks toward our mother for an answer.

Mother just hangs her head and shakes it back and forth.

"Without telling you?" Ava asks me.

"That's why everything went sideways. I had no idea of his plan, and I started snooping around."

Mother raises her head, lifting the handkerchief to wipe her nose. "But if you knew of his scheme, then it wouldn't have worked. Keeping you in the dark made it easier to flush out Carnot and Textrix."

"I wish now I hadn't removed myself so far from the family. I could have helped." Ava then asks, "Is this why he left?"

"I think he has someone else," says Mother.

"That, I still have a hard time believing," I say.

Ava nods in agreement with me. "What was his response when confronted?"

Mother quickly answers, "He accused me of having an affair."

My eyes widen, and I place the tips of my fingers firmly over my lips to keep from snickering.

"What!" she flails her arms wildly. "Is it so hard to believe another man might find me attractive?"

"Ahem." Ava clears her throat. "So who does he suppose you are having an affair with?"

"A.P. Griffin." Mother answers in such a matter-of-fact tone that my sister and I both burst into laughter. "Exactly what is so humorous about that?"

I venture a comment first. "Well—"

"I'll have you know, I was once quite the catch." She huffs.

"We are not saying you weren't," says Ava.

"You still are a catch," I add. "It's just . . . A.P.? Really?" I scratch my head and search for words that won't offend her. "A.P. is like family. You and he making whoopie seems a bit . . ." I can't seem to find the right word to finish the sentence.

Ava's face tells the tale that she just pictured our mother and A.P. cuddling. Her eyes go wide, along with her mouth. Then she squeezes her peepers shut and starts gagging. Honestly, I feel a bit of bile in my throat as well. No one wants to picture their parents having sex.

"For your information," Mother says, quite indignant now, "before Titus proposed, A.P. was courting me."

The kitchen becomes eerily quiet. If a pin dropped, it would sound like a clash of cymbals. I always wondered how my father was able to snag someone like my mother. Titus, the short, inattentive genius, scoring a beautiful, sophisticated, magical woman like my mother. But they have always adored each other. It's so perplexing, then, that either would think of cheating. There has to be another explanation.

Ava is the first to speak. "Have you read the cards since he left?"

"No. I am afraid to." Mother dabs the corner of each eye with her damp handkerchief.

My sister continues her questions. "What about a spell?" Ava shifts in her seat and leans toward Mother, placing a comforting hand on her arm. "Something for clarity or truth."

"Is that why he left?" I ask. "You did a truth spell?"

She nods with a sob.

Ava glances over at me. "Why would a truth spell make him leave?"

"Because that old man is hiding something. When deflecting didn't work, he knew she would perform some type of spell. What better way to keep a tight lip than to abscond till the spell wears off?"

"So he does have a cheap bit of calico on the side?" Her eyebrows rise, her jaw drops, and her face freezes.

I shake my head slowly back and forth, my brows furrowing. I stare at Ava and then my mother. Tilting my head slightly, I try to make sense of it. "I think something else is going on." How do I explain a gut feeling? My intuition is telling me, without evidence, that there is more to my father's actions. "Mother, I think you need to read those cards again. I don't think this has anything to do with your marriage."

"Are you seeing something?" Mother asks me.

Coming from an extensive line of seers and spiritualists, I can see why she would ask. "More like a feeling."

Ava says, "Zelda is right."

I almost fall out of my chair to hear her say I was right. Someone should write this down. It may never happen again.

"You need to read his cards again," Ava finishes.

"Here." A hand shoves itself under my nose. It is attached to a cranky housekeeper. "Found this under the bed. You should be more careful with your things."

I lean my head back to get a better view of the object. "My card case!" I thought I had lost it at Coco's, along with the little cloudlike substance. Suddenly, realization hits me like a ton of bricks. I jump from my seat and grab the card case. "It must be here!"

Hazel backs up and lifts the push-sweeper in front of her like a weapon to defend herself. "She is crazy, your sister."

"Not crazy! Where did you find this?" I shake the card case in front of Hazel's face.

"Zelda! Stop!" Ava yells at me. "You're scaring her." Ava rises to her feet.

Mother joins in. "What in the stars, Zelda, are you going on about?"

"The blue clue." I turn back to Hazel. "Where?"

Hazel is white with fright. "Under the bed."

I race to the bedroom and dive under the bed. My mother, Ava, and Hazel chase after me.

"Zelda, what in the stars are you looking for?" Ava bends over to see what I'm making a fuss about.

"This is all my fault!" Mother cries.

"How so?" Ava responds while watching me caress the carpet and dig into the pile.

"Clearly, the news about Titus has pushed her over the edge." Mother stands in the doorway, wringing her hands.

"I'm sure that isn't it." Ava straightens up, crosses her arms, and just stares at me wriggling on my stomach like a worm.

I chime in. "I found a unique substance in the aftermath of the explosion. I thought it was lost or stolen, but it must have tumbled out of my pocket when I tripped over the luggage."

"What is she talking about?" Mother asks Ava.

"I already swept under there," Hazel blurts out from behind Mother. "I am an exceptionally good cleaner. I take offense that you would think to find even a speck of dust under there."

"What? Ow!" I jerk my head up and hit the wooden bed slats. "Why didn't you start with that?" I wriggle myself out from under the bed. "Where?" I huff at Hazel.

Hazel stands frozen, mouth clenched and eyes bugging out.

I push Mother out of the way. "Zelda, what has gotten into you?" she scolds.

Grabbing Hazel's shoulders, I jerk her about her like a cocktail shaker. "Where is the dirt from the carpet?" I struggle the push-sweeper from her hands. "In here?" She grabs the handle, pulling the sweeper back.

Mother forces herself past us, zipping back to the kitchen.

Ava can't get past the Iron Maid and me wrestling. "Where are you going?"

Mother shouts back, "To read her cards, obviously."

I grip the handle of the carpet sweeper, my knuckles turning white. "Back off!"

Hazel stands her ground. "I ain't letting go."

Refusing to back down, I narrow my eyes at her. "Give it here before you get dusted."

She sneers, "You have a screw loose—make that multiple screws!"

I square my shoulders, ready to fight. "It's going to take more than a grouchy maid to snatch this sweeper from my grip."

She lunges at me like a chat on a mousacorn. We grapple, twisting and turning, each struggling for control of the carpet cleaner. The house fills with our shouts of insults and rebukes as we fight tooth and nail.

Finally, exhaustion sets in, and we collapse to the floor, breathless and completely disheveled. The push-sweeper lies between us, untouched.

Looking at me, she snatches the sweeper, hugging it to her once-starched, now-wrinkled apron, and shrieks, "In the bin."

My face red and pinched, I purse my lips. "Why didn't you just say that?" I don't wait for her to answer; instead, I scramble to my feet and hotfoot it toward the garbage.

"Now what are you doing?" Ava has her hands on her hips. All the shouting and commotion have brought both Flo and Eggs down.

I rummage through the bin, sifting through dust, grit, hair, food, and grossness. The stench fills my nostrils. I'm in search of a tiny piece of clear blue substance, a glimmering fragment that could hold the key to the explosion and Piers's sneaky behavior.

Flo tugs at Ava's dress. "What's wrong with Auntie Zelda?"

"I really don't know, baby." Ava hugs the children to her.

My fingers brush against slimy food scraps and crumpled paper, but I pay no mind. My peepers scan every discarded item for a sign of that elusive blue clue.

I hear Hazel's voice. "She is batty, and I am not cleaning up this mess. I'll be in the other room, watching my stories."

There, nestled among the dust and yesterturn's dinner scraps, I spot a glint of light. My hearts quicken as I carefully pluck it from its filthy surroundings. It's not big, but it holds a world of possibilities.

My sister catches her breath. "Jeepers."

Eggs whispers, "You shouldn't swear, Momsy."

I hold the tiny piece of enigmatic substance up to the sunstar's light, examining it closely. Its edges are smooth, and it seems weightless, yet it's solid in composition, from what I can determine. More than that, it is a potential clue in my search for the truth.

My mind races as I try to decipher the significance of this humble object. Is it broken from a larger piece, revealing a new material? I can't be certain yet, but I know I'm on to something.

"It's amazing," my sister says. "Wait, let me get something." She disappears farther into the house.

Eggs and Flo now stand on either side of me as I kneel in the strewn garbage, admiring the cloudlike substance.

"It's pretty," Flo says.

"Ah-huh," agrees Eggs.

"Here." Ava hands me a small metal case. "Took my capsules out of the pill box. It should be perfect for the material."

I nod. With renewed hope, I carefully place the blue clue in the small, protective container. It may be just a fragment, but it represents possibilities waiting to be discovered.

"I'll start the Areo. We need to get you and that bit of material to the university." Ava jumps into the maroon two-door automobile.

Standing up, I begin to brush the grime off my new pants. "Why the university?"

The Areo's electric engine whispers to life. "The university has a lab you can use. You're going to need to reverse engineer that thing to figure out what it is."

"Good point." I ankle over to the auto.

Flo chases me to the passenger door. "Can I come?"

"Fine." Ava calls over Eggs. "Come give Momsy a kiss and keep Grandma company.

Eggs gives Ava a peck on the cheek.

"Oh, and Eggs."

"Yes, Mommy?"

"Don't let Grandma read Mommy's cards."

Chapter Thirty-Seven

L ike Ethan's apartment complex, Tesla University is located in the older part of Capital City. Similarly, Tesla University buildings are remnants of a bygone time. The university existed long before steam and black carbon ruled Gaia. An elemental time. Granted, many of the monstrous stone-and-brick buildings have been retrofitted for more-modern forms of energy, but they still have an ancient feel to them.

Once, the prestigious university only taught those of certain groups: Hominids who could conjure thoughts and make them a reality. Those who could tell what would occur if certain paths were followed. Talented individuals who could create something from nothing using alchemy. It was a time before Nikola Tesla known as Dinas.

Now, the university, as well as our continent, has changed and grown along with its peoples, to a certain extent. Tesla University still caters to the magical but has expanded into other subject areas, such as the nonmagical forensic courses my sister teaches. It is the perfect place for me to experiment with the mysterious clue.

"I can't believe I've never been here," I say.

"You insisted on going to university on Trade Island," my sister responds.

"Well, this place seemed stodgy at the time, and Trade Island was working with newer ideas."

"Stodgy?" Ava gives me the side-eye as we walk through one of the main building's courtyards. "All your ancestors went here. Mother and Father went here. Both Ephron and I attended here."

I roll my eyes and mock under my breath, "Like I said, stodgy."

"What did you say?"

I sigh. "Nothing." Students are piling out of doorways. "Classes are over for the turn?"

"Yes. There are a few evening classes, but nothing that will interfere with our mission."

We're walking along one of the open-air corridors that run along the side of the building when I catch sight of the young man from the café. He appears to be chatting up some dish, flashing those pearly whites as he puts on the charm. He is leaning in to steal a kiss. He is going to either get slapped or—

"Auntie Zelda," Flo says, interrupting my thoughts, "what are you going to do with that clue?"

"I'm going to attempt to break down the clue to see what it is made from." My attention goes back to the roguish fella. I must have missed the action, because he now stands there alone. We should intercept him soon; then I can interrogate him about Piers.

"Won't that destroy the clue?" my niece asks, pulling my attention away from the young man.

"Maybe he's a student or a teacher?" I ponder out loud.

"Huh?"

My sister shakes her head and reassures Flo that the piece wouldn't be completely consumed in the experiment. "She'll only use a tiny sliver."

I quicken my pace.

"Zelda, you are walking too fast. Flo can't keep up."

"Sorry. It's just that the joe up there with the toothy grin . . ."

"What about him?" asks Ava.

"Do you know him?"

"I don't know everyone who attends here, Zelda."

"Yes,"—I point at the guy—"but do you know him?"

"I can't say I do. Why?"

"I saw him in a heavy conversation with Coco's husband the other turn. It didn't seem too friendly."

"Interesting."

Flo mimics her mom. "Interesting."

"It sure is, Flo," I agree.

Mr. Pearly Whites looks in our direction. His face falls, and he quickly turns and zigzags through the throng of students. He must have spotted me, but why would he run? He doesn't know who I am. At least, I don't think so.

Then I spy what spooked Mr. Pearly Whites.

"Zelda," Ava says, grabbing my attention. "Should we follow him?"

"No. We should proceed to the lab. Is there another path there?"

"Now you don't want to talk with him? I'm confused." My sister pushes me in the arm and points. "Turn here down this hall. We'll use the lecture-hall lab."

I take one more quick glance at what made Mr. Pearly Whites skedaddle: the Man in Black. I'm more interested in keeping my family safe and figuring out what this material is. Finding out how those two suspects relate to Piers and Coco Cosmetics can wait for now.

Ava and Flo lead me to large ancient metal doors. The two doors aren't shiny; instead, they're dull and show their history. Large rivets line the top and bottom of each door. Rings at least sixty centimeters in diameter are used to pull the heavy doors open. Towering to the ceiling, the entrance seems daunting.

"Help me with these, will you?" Ava says.

Together, we grab a door pull and yank at one of the monstrous entry doors. "Do you have to do this every time?" I complain.

"I can help." Flo grabs the ring and starts to tug.

I tug along with Flo. "Can't we just use magic?"

"The doors were made with magic woven into the metal," Ava explains. "Old alchemy at its finest. They're impervious to any spell to open them."

"Psychokinetics?" The door begins to slowly creep open with a moan of steel on steel.

"Nope. Never seen anyone open the doors with any type of magic. The caretakers open the doors every morning and close them for the turn after classes." Ava slides through the opening and pushes the door open from the inside. "There. We're in."

The lecture hall reminds me of a small colosseum. The amphitheater-style room has tiers of seating and long continuous counters that step down to a stage-style area. On the low platformed area sits a lectern and a large steel table. The industrial-style table has a setup that almost rivals my own lab at H.A. The apparatus will definitely suit my needs.

"Let's get started," I say.

"What do you need me to do?" Ava pushes up her sleeves and dons an apron. "Here." Ava hands an apron to Flo. "Give this to Auntie Zelda."

Flo skips over to me with a full-on grin. She is fired up to help. "Put this on," she says. "What else do you need?"

"Safety goggles," I instruct.

Flo skips off in search of goggles for us.

I retrieve my magnifying goggles from their case. Slipping them over my eyes, I begin flipping over lenses till I find the right magnification. "Ava, scalpel please."

"Don't you think that would be too large?" she asks.

"Maybe." I breathe out slowly as I extract the small blue clue from the pill box with tweezers.

"I can see if they have any fine steel wire." Ava rummages through a nearby cupboard.

Flo jumps up and down. "What can I do?"

"Hmm . . ." I ponder for a moment. "I know. Why don't you find paper and coloring utensils and take notes and draw pictures. You can do it from the front row there." I point to a bench and seat in the front.

Flo gives me a salute before running off to fulfill her task.

Ava assists me in extracting a tiny piece of the blue opaque material to use. The remaining bit I place back in the pill box with the tweezers. I hand Ava the pill box to pocket. Then I proceed with setting up the lab apparatuses.

The university has quite the setup. Every size beaker and test tube you could imagine. Top-of-the-line laser burners that would rival those I use in my lab back home. I adjust the tubing and fill glass containers with the different liquids I require for breaking down the mysterious substance.

"What is all this stuff going to do, Auntie Zelda?" Flo's little voice cuts through my quiet focus on the formidable task in front of me.

"I'm looking for the recipe that made the substance I found." I reply over the high-pitched squeak of a glass tube being pushed into a corked beaker.

"Like a cake?" asks Flo.

Ava brings a fire extinguisher over to me. "Just in case."

Ignoring my sister, I answer Flo. "Yes, like figuring out what is in a cake after it is made."

I start the laser burners and wait for things to start bubbling and popping. "So, Flo," I say, "what did you draw?"

Flo wriggles off her seat and skips over to us. "Here." She hands me a sheet of paper.

My jaw drops, and I shove the drawing at Ava.

Ava looks up from the colorful drawing. "What made you draw this?"

"It's what I saw."

"Saw where, sweetie?" Ava asks as she passes the drawing back to me.

"Up here." She points to her head.

"You imagined it?" I ask.

"No. I saw it."

I study the paper. The scene carefully crayoned onto the paper is a tad bit disturbing.

"You saw this?" I ask one more time.

Flo nods.

The picture appears to be of a man and a woman lying on the ground with X's where their eyes should be. An obelisk, colored red, lies next to them.

Ava squats down in front of her daughter. "Where is this?"

Flo just shrugs.

"Did you see this on one of the stories Hazel watches?" Ava asks.

The little girl just shook her head no.

I squat down to join my sister at Flo's level. "Tell me why you drew this?"

"It was either this or a scary man all dressed in black," replies Flo.

I swallow the lump forming in my throat. "Why didn't you draw the man in black?"

Flo sighs and giggles, patting me on the cheek. "Because I don't have any black crayons, silly."

"Obviously." I try to sound calm.

My sister gently grabs Flo's arm to regain her attention. "Who are these people you drew?"

She shrugs again. Through a big yawn, Flo says, "I'm hungry. Are we almost done?"

As Ava and I both rise, Ava says to me, "Listen, I'm going to take her home and get her fed and off to bed. I'll see what else I can find out about her apparent premonition."

"I understand," I say.

"Will you be okay on your own?"

"I should be. I'll holler when I'm done."

"Harvey or I will pick you up. Are you sure you'll be okay?"

"Don't worry. If I run into trouble and need assistance, I'll call on Hodge. He doesn't live too far from here."

Ava lifts her daughter into her arms. "Oof, you're getting to be a big girl."

Flo wraps her legs around her mommy's waist and snuggles her chin into the crook of Ava's neck. "Pretty soon, I'll be as tall as Auntie Zelda and you, Momsy."

I watch my sister carry my tired, hungry, and curious niece up the stairs, disappearing through the open door. I pivot around and study the apparatus on the long wooden tabletop. This isn't going to be easy without an assistant, but I'll have to manage. I step up on the platform and slide my safety goggles down over my eyes.

"Here goes nothing."

Chapter Thirty-Eight

I busy myself prepping the clue to be broken down. I now wish I had kept the pill box instead of giving it to Ava. If I blow this, I'll have destroyed the sample and won't be able to get another sample till later.

Ish kabibble.

A soft *clomp, clomp* descends toward me. "Ava?" I say without looking up from observing the liquids bubbling and popping from the heat of the lasers. "Did you forget something?" I jot down a few observations in a little notebook. "Glad you came back—"

The sounds of the shoes stop. Whipping around, I stand face to ugly mug with the Man in Black.

"Crap," I say under my breath.

"Aaaargh," he growls. As he lunges at me, arm outstretched, hands reaching for my neck, a deep guttural growl springs from his mouth. "Grrrr."

My body freezes in surprise. Is this how that sweet girl in the alley felt when he strangled her?

"Where is it?" he grunts.

His question is enough to snap me out of my petrifaction. Leaning back against the table, I reach for a beaker full of clear liquid. If I'm lucky, it's acidic. I yell, "In the beaker!"

He turns his head toward my reach. The liquid in the glass container seems to fly in slow motion toward his face, followed by the beaker. Liquid and glass reach his mug one right after the other. The beaker bounces off his schnoz and crashes into splinters on the stage.

He wipes his face and eyes with his hands. "Are you trying to drown me?"

Shit. It was water. The acid is on the other side of the table. Running around to the opposite side of the table, I look for an exit.

"Give it to me now, or I'll put you in the ground!"

"I can't. I already used it." I'm definitely not going to blab about my sister having the rest.

"Used it!" he grumbles. "Who did you give it to?"

"No one. It's in the test tube." I shift farther down the table as he creeps toward me.

The Man in Black stops dead and raises an eyebrow.

I study his face. His nose looks bigger than before. Cocking my head to one side, I squint. Yep, it's positively swelling from the hit it took from the beaker.

He scratches his forehead. "How big is the beaker?"

"How big is the what?" I ask. His nose keeps getting larger, and I can't stop staring at it.

"You said it was in a beaker." With a sudden burst, he runs around the table.

I escape to the other side. If I can stay on this side, I may be able to get to the exit and out of this jam. But I'll need a distraction.

"Your nose is huge," I say.

"That's not nice." He shuffles his feet along the floor, attempting to get closer to me. "You don't see me disparaging your facial features, do you?"

I move away to the opposite corner of the table. In this position, I may lose my straight shot to the only open exit. "It's swollen."

The Man in Black touches his overly bulbous nose and lets out a high-pitched shriek. "Ow!"

"Told you." I survey the table and alchemy apparatus. The experiment is ruined, there is no way to fix it, and I need to survive another turn to try again.

He breaks into another run, chasing me around the table. His shoes squeak as he immediately halts and changes direction.

I pivot, changing my gallop away from him. My hearts pound in my ears, fuzzing up my thinking.

He stops.

I stop.

"Where is the ledger?" he demands, panting.

I lean on the table to catch my breath and clear my head. There's a laser burner in front of me. My eyes dart from the burner to the liquid in the boiling flask above it. This is the worst idea ever. This may be extreme.

My eyes focus on my adversary. "What ledger?" My fingers move the dial on the burner. Then I move to my right. "I thought you were talking about something else." *Distract him,* I think. The pounding in my head slows down. "There is a second set of ledgers. Why would I have them?" I turn the dial on another laser burner to high.

"Lay off the crap. You went to that Slack kid's place. You must have it." He doesn't move.

I look at the risers of tables and benches on the side of the lecture hall. I'd have to get at least five rows up to come out of this unscathed. I might have seconds at the most. "You killed Albert Slack when he didn't give you the ledger?"

"I didn't bump him off. He had already bought the farm when I found him. I thought the explosion might have taken care of it." He leans both meaty hands on the table edge, leaning in. "But it wasn't there, was it?"

"You set the explosion to destroy the ledger?"

"Did I say I set the explosion?"

"You didn't set the explosion?" My peepers zero in on one of the flasks; it's bubbling and burping. I don't have much time left.

"I retrieved the package and skedaddled before the place went kablooey."

"How did you—"

A pop and a squeak interrupt me.

The Man in Black starts. "What was—"

"Nothing. You said"—I move a little more to my right—"you know who set the bomb?"

"Of course I do. That's why I didn't take the entire satchel, just the paper. I'm no sap. I'm too smart to be fooled like some dumb mug."

That, I think, is up for debate. I shift to the left, hoping he'll assume I'm going to make a break for it.

"Hey," he yells. "Stop stalling. Give me the ledger." Pushing off the table, he runs toward the left end of the table.

It worked! The chemicals are both popping and bubbling over now. Time for me to hit the deck. I run as fast as my feet can carry me. Taking two steps at a time, I reach the second riser. The Man in Black is hot on my heels.

A rumble and a *POW* echo through the hall. A high-pitched scream pierces my ears. Is that from the Man in Black or from the explosion. I turn my head to glance behind me. The first explosion slowed my pursuer down by knocking him off his feet and flat on his ass.

The next explosion is coming, and I'm not up far enough yet. Crap.

A series of loud bangs, one right after another, cause me to flinch. I stop, turn, and glimpse the mug chasing me. He is getting back on his feet. Peering over his head, I see the final flask.

Time's up.

I dive under the table.

KABOOM!

The weight of the tables crushes my ribs. I wasn't far enough away from the last blast.

My eyes burn from the fumes.

I can barely breathe.

Through the ringing in my ears, I can hear the creak of the long wooden counters used as desks above me.

They shift.

The last thing I see is the tabletop falling toward my head.

Chapter Thirty-Nine

"I think she's coming around," I hear my mother say. She sounds a bit fragile; she must be worried. Now I'm worried.

"She destroyed an entire lecture hall. Hundreds of rotations of history gone in one irresponsible explosion." Ava sounds normal, so I must be all right.

"She is lucky to be alive," Mother says.

"Zelda is going to wish she were dead once I get through with her." Ava's voice sounds sharper than usual. I am definitely going to be hunky-dory.

Mother quiets her down. "Now, Ava, you don't know whether this is her fault. Wait till she can explain what happened. This kind of stuff would happen to Titus all the time."

"Father blowing up laboratories left and right doesn't ease my mind or help in any way."

I'm not sure I want to open my eyes and face my sister's wrath. But I'll need to face her sooner rather than later. Deliberately, I flutter my eyes open.

"There she is," my mother sings. "How are you feeling?"

"How is she feeling? She should feel like crap! She just damaged a lecture hall and possibly my career with it. How is she feeling, my—ugh!" Ava stamps over to the corner and violently crosses her arms over her chest.

"There, there, Zelda, don't try to sit up yet; you're probably going to be a bit sore." Mother fluffs my pillow.

I can hear Ava grumbling under her breath. She is definitely teed off. I feel bad about the explosion, and I hope Ava doesn't get fired for my actions, but all I can think is, *Where is the Man in Black?*

"Did the explosion get him? Is he dead or just hurt?" My throat is dry, my voice hoarse.

"He who, honey? You were by yourself." Mother caresses my forehead. Turning her head, she addresses Ava, who's still skulking in the corner. "She must have been hit on the head a lot harder than we first thought."

I grab my mother's arm. "No, he was there—that's why—is he dead?" Like my thoughts, my words tumble out in fragments.

My sister pushes herself away from the wall and ankles over to my bedside. "Who are you talking about, Zelda?"

"The bozo, the muscle, the murderer, the man dressed all in black." With my throat still sandpaper, my voice is just a whisper.

"Jeepers, Zelda, what happened?" I've obviously piqued Ava's curiosity.

"Darling girl, Zelda is still a little fragile," my mother insists. "We should let her be. You can interrogate her later."

I move my attention to my sister. "Get Ethan," I tell her.

"I will," she answers. "But I need to know more—"

Mother interrupts us. "Not now, girls. Zelda's been out for two turns. She needs her rest."

Two turns? Jeepers. What in the stars? I've been out for two turns? "Where am I?" At last, I have a bit of sense in my head to try to gather information about my surroundings. What I find only makes me panic.

The room I'm in appears to be stark white, with no pictures on the walls. All it contains is the bed I'm in and an obviously uncomfortable chair against one wall. There is no medical equipment, no tray table, nothing that would specify where I am. Jinkies, if my mother and sister weren't here, this place would give me the heebie-jeebies.

"Calm down," Ava says. "You're at the clinic here at the university. We have a fine working staff of healers.

"Now, tell me about the man."

"Really?" Mother interrupts. "You two have to do this now?"

I struggle to sit up. Mother anchors me as I use her to pull myself into a seated position. Rubbing my temple, I attempt to ease the pounding. Feeling farther up my head, my hand stops on rough layered fabric. I look to my mother.

She answers my unspoken question. "You had a nasty bump and a considerably sized gash on your scalp down to your forehead. Sadly, it's going to leave a nasty scar."

Ava drags her wireless out of her handbag and dials. "Ethan," she says into the mouthpiece, "drop everything and come over to the university's health center." There's a short pause. Ava nods. "Yes, she is awake. She said there was someone in the lecture hall with her." Another short pause before she speaks again. "Right. Are you sure?" The next pause is a little longer. "Okay, see you soon." Ava shuts the wireless off and shoves it back in her bag.

"Is he coming?" I ask.

"Yes. We'll wait for him, and then you can tell us about the mysterious stranger and why you blew up the hall." Ava moves her attention to our mother. "Let's get some lunch and let Zelda rest while we wait for Ethan."

I must admit, I am still a bit out of it, and resting sounds pretty copacetic right now. "You both go. I'll just rest my eyes."

———⟫●⟪———

A FEW HOURS LATER—THOUGH it only feels like moments to me—I'm reclining in my clinic bed surrounded by my mother; my sister; her husband, Harvey, who sits on the Tesla Health and Safety Council; and Ethan Hodge, forensic specialist and my friend.

Ethan takes my sister's place at the head of the bed, gripping my hand. "How are you feeling?"

"I'm sore all over, and my head hurts. Did you find any evidence of the Man in Black?"

Ethan squeezes my hand. "Is he the one who was following us after we left Birdtown?"

"That was Ruth's stalker, one of the security guards at Coco Cosmetics. He took a header down into some nasty gears; he's no longer a worry."

"Then who is the man in black?"

"The Man in Black is the one who strangled that poor girl Lucy Marsh in the alley."

My brother-in-law pipes up. "What was he looking for? Why did he attack you?"

"It appears there's a second set of ledgers that were stolen, and he's looking for them."

"Do you know who he works for?" asks Harvey.

"My guess? He works for Coco's husband, Piers Astuce."

"You're not sure?" my sister asks.

"I have no proof, but I would bet my life that he works for Piers." I press my fingers to my temple, hoping to ease the current banging in my head.

"What about these ledgers?" asks Ethan.

"From what I can surmise, it's a second set of ledgers from the cosmetics company."

"And now Piers wants them back," Ethan says.

"And he thinks I have them."

"Well," Ava says, "then who is the young man you wanted to speak with before we went to the lecture hall?"

"I saw him having an argument with Piers, and then the Man in Black followed him." I could use something for the pain.

"That was the turn we went for lunch," says Ethan.

"What have you pieced together so far?" Ava asks.

"To be honest, I don't know. Everything is so jumbled up in my head right now."

Standing at the head of the bed, Mother strokes my hair and orders everyone out. "She needs her rest. We can all talk about this later."

I tug on my mother's sleeve. "Mother, I need to talk to Ava."

Ava exchanges places with Ethan. "What is it?"

"You need to get the rest of the clue out of Capital City. It's important. It has something to do with Coco, Piers, and the explosion. I just don't know how yet." I lean back into my pillow. I am tired. I just can't stop now.

"How would that be related to the ledgers, the man in black, and the young guy?" she asks.

"I don't know. I do know it's all mushed up in my head. I can almost see it." I close my eyes against the pounding.

My mother gives everyone the bum's rush. "Enough. Everyone out. Shoo, shoo, shoo. Let her rest, and we can talk more later."

As everyone files out of the room, Ava turns to me. "Zelda, I love you; you are my sister. But you're not going to be able to stay at the house. I have to protect the kids. We don't know what the man is capable of."

"Piers or the Man in Black?"

"Either," she says.

"I understand. I'll see about getting a room somewhere downtown. I'm so sorry, Ava, about all of this."

"I don't think it could have been helped in my opinion. To be honest, Zelda, it seems like trouble just follows you wherever you go lately."

After the door closes behind my sister, I reach under my pillow and grab my wireless, which Ethan was kind enough to bury underneath my pillow when my mother wasn't looking. Mother is convinced I need lots of rest and I should not be disturbed in any shape or form. I think a lot more dreadful things are going to happen if I don't start trying to make sense of this mess now.

First thing I do is call Mae.

She answers on the first ring. "Darling."

"Hello, Mae."

"Ava called me. How are you doing? She said you blew up the university. I mean, really, Zelda, a whole university? I'm not even sure whether that's possible."

"Mae, I did not blow up an entire university. Just inside one room."

There is a bit of silence before Mae speaks again. "Then why would she tell me you blew everything up?"

"I don't think she meant I blew everything up, as in buildings. I think she might have meant just that room and her job at the university."

"Oh, Zelda darling. She must be furious with you."

"Yes and no," I say.

"Oh?"

I let out a small sigh and wish again for painkillers. "She realizes I may not have had much of a choice as I was trying to save my own skin. On the other hand, I'm sure she wishes with all her hearts that I could have found a way other than blowing everything to smithereens."

"I thought you just said you didn't blow everything to smithereens?" Mae says dryly.

"Only the area I was in was blown to smithereens." I rub my forehead and move the conversation on to the purpose of my call. "Mae, I need you to do me another favor."

"Darling." Which means *of course* in Mae's head.

"I mean, I hope you can help me do a little digging while I'm laid up."

"Darling, it's what I live for."

"Funny," I say, not laughing.

"I am. Now tell me, what is this digging I am to do?"

"I need you to use your powers of persuasion on DSI Flynn."

Silence.

"Mae?" I hope I didn't lose her.

Mae finally pipes up. "Who is DSI Flynn?"

"He's Inspector Greyson's DSI," I say quietly.

"Why?" she asks.

"I want you to see if there's anything on Coco's new assistant, Sally."

"The one Piers is poking?" she says rudely.

"And Coco," I add.

"Sally is a bit of a vamp, ain't she?"

"She is something or other. Not sure what."

"How come you're not asking the local Legere Legalis or that copper you've been hanging with?" asks Mae.

"You mean, Ethan Hodge?"

"That's the one," she says.

"It would put his job in jeopardy. No one knows he's been helping me."

"What is her name?" Mae asks.

"Sally Renis," I say.

"My middle name is Discretion, darling."

Chapter Forty

"Mae, I'll call you back." I close up the wireless and properly greet an unexpected guest. "Inspector Zex, to what do I owe this visit." I try to sound chipper and welcoming. My voice betrays me with false syrupy sweetness.

"Dr. Harcrow." Her greeting is stiff and curt. Her stare digs into me with equal tart. "I have a few questions for you."

"Indeed," I say.

She stands straight as an arrow in her black tailored suit and stiffly starched white button-up dress shirt. Her lips are blood red, and her skin is as pale as ever. I wonder if she ever wears a different shade of lip rouge; maybe then she wouldn't look like she's ready to tear a person's throat out at any given moment.

"Dr. Harcrow, can you please give your account of the explosion in the Flamel Auditorium." This time, she doesn't bring out her notebook. She nods to the barely visible constable standing slightly behind her and to the side.

I adjust myself in the clinic bed, sitting further up. "It was an accident."

The constable seems diminutive beside the stature of the inspector. Her umber hair is cut short, close to the scalp. I can't see her eyes with her head dipped low and her shoulders shrugged up. I wonder if that's due to working with the intolerable inspector or just bad posture. She holds a notepad up close to her face, and a pencil wiggles back and forth as she takes notes for her rigid boss.

"An accident?" Zex repeats.

"I'm an alchemist. These things happen." I don't come out and tell her about my would-be assassin because then she would just try to stop me from investigating further.

"Tell me about the man dressed in black. I am told he was attempting to accost you." The inspector clasps her arms behind her back and lifts her chin.

"The explosion was just an accident. I wasn't paying attention."

"Lay off the crap. I have a masher out there who has already killed one person that we know of—Lucy Marsh, who was dressed suspiciously like you. Remember her?" The veins in Zex's neck start protruding, and she raises her voice. "Now you are supposedly attacked by the same perpetrator. The truth, Dr. Harcrow!"

"I wish I could tell you what you want to hear."

"You are a well-renowned alchemist; by all accounts, you are quite talented. You can see why I find your story weak." A wide grin engulfs my face, and she clears her throat, narrowing her eyes. "Why are you smiling?"

"You said I was talented."

"My stars, woman, this is no joke."

"Alchemy never is."

Inspector Zex's arms are now at her sides, fists clenched. "We are not through, not by a long shot." She waves her constable out the door and proceeds to follow.

"Inspector," I call after her, "if there was someone in the lecture hall with me, he would have to be made of some pretty sturdy stuff to survive that explosion. And . . . he would be hired muscle."

Inspector Zex nods. "I see."

"As to who hired him, there is no proof. Nothing to connect him to his employer."

"I hope you know what you are doing." Zex turns to exit, stops, then turns back to me. "You're dangerous, Dr. Zelda Harcrow. Dangerous to yourself and those around you. I can't wait till I see the back of you." With that last sentence hanging in the air like a noose, Zex leaves, closing the door behind her.

My next visitor is the healer. Thank the stars! My head is playing like an out-of-tune percussion band between my ears.

The healer looks to be about twenty rotations, a baby face with full, round cheeks, a golden complexion, and neatly coiffed hair. "I have some pain relief for you," he says.

"You are my favorite person right now," I coo.

His chubby fingers present me a small cup with two capsules. "It's the good stuff."

"Now you're on the trolley." Without hesitation, I dump the capsules into my mouth. With the glass of water the healer hands me, I wash down the medicine. "Thank you," I say as I hand him the empty glass.

"I'll be right back to change your bandages. Don't go anywhere." The healer chuckles at his own joke.

As he leaves, the wireless rings.

"Hello?"

"Darling."

It's Mae.

"Mae, sorry I didn't ring you right back. My head is pounding."

"I hope they give you something stronger than feverfew," she says.

"The healer gave me some of the hard stuff. I hope to be drifting away soon."

"You are going to be blotto any moment." Mae laughs.

"Mae, I appreciate you helping me. You are my best friend." I am now beginning to feel the effects of the dope.

"Darling, don't you get all soupy on me. You'll make me blubber all over." I can hear a faint sniff on the other end of the wireless.

The healer rolls in a tray filled with gauze bandages, tape, scissors, and other paraphernalia. "Sorry to interrupt, but we need to change your dressing before you head off to la-la land."

"I have to go. Love you, Mae."

"Love you too. Heal up fast."

A click and dead air. I close my wireless and nestle it back under the pillows.

"There now," the healer says as he puts down the last bit of tape to secure the bandage that encircles my very sore skull. "Lie back, and let's get you comfortable."

I can feel the dope doing its thing. My eyelids refuse to stay open. My limbs are like lead. My breathing begins to slow. I hear the high-pitched squeaks of the healers cart diminish as everything fades to black.

———————◉———————

I'M NOT SURE HOW LONG I've been out. With no windows, it's difficult to say if it's turn or night. On the upside, I feel a bit well-rested, and I'm ready to blow this joint.

I'm not up exceedingly long before Ava slides into my room with Ethan in tow.

"Oh, good, you're up," says Ava.

Ethan just smiles and waves. I think he might be a little frightened of my sister. She can seem a bit grouchy at times.

"Do you think I could get out of here today?"

Ava examines my bandages. "I can't see why not."

"I'll go get one of the healers," Ethan offers. He slips out of the room.

"I'm surprised Mother's not with you," I tell Ava.

"Mother's watching the little ones. Zelda, once you're settled, she'll come by. On another note, I had the blue cloud substance delivered by secure carrier to our brother over at H.A. Efron says he'll put Dr. Ravenscroft on it."

"Good. If anyone can help determine the substance, it'll be Olga." Dr. Olga Ravenscroft is a short, pudgy prudent woman—a clever alchemist who leads with her head. She is a long-trusted employee of H.A.

Ethan reenters, bringing with him one of the healers. This time, I have a tall, lanky young woman. All the healers seem to be noticeably young. I'm beginning to wonder if I'm being treated by students. I have yet to see anyone older than me, and I haven't seen that many rotations.

The healer, Kashi, says, "Well, Dr Harcrow, how are you feeling today?"

"I'm feeling much better, and I'm ready to blow this pop stand."

"Not so fast. Let's take a look at that head wound." Kashi unwinds the bandages from my head and removes a few pieces of gauze. Getting up close, she examines the gash, which has been neatly glued up. "It looks like it's healing fine, and you most likely don't need the full bandage anymore. You're going to want to keep the wound clean and dry. It's going to leave a scar, a noticeable one, but there are many potions—as I'm sure you know, being an alchemist—that you can use to minimize any deep scarring. Magic can only do so much."

"Thank you, healer." Then I add, "I can be released now?"

"Let's hit the brakes for a minute." Kashi pulls out a small pen with a pinpoint light at one end and flicks it back and forth in front of my peepers.

I know what she's looking for. She needs to make sure I no longer have a concussion. "Well, healer, is everything jake?"

She nods. "I don't have a problem releasing you today."

Excellent! I start pulling back the covers and swinging my legs over the side of the bed.

"Not so fast." She stops me. I don't have a problem releasing you, but you must at least be under supervision for the next turn. After that, if you exhibit no problems, you are free to resume all activities."

"Aw, that's balled up," I whine as I throw a look over to my sister Ava, who has in no uncertain terms told me I could no longer stay with her. Which is understandable. Someone has tried to kill me three times, and I'm no closer to finding out what Piers is up to. I don't want to put Flo or Eggs in any danger.

Ava steps forward. "Why don't you call Coco? I'm sure she's got more than enough room in that massive mansion of hers to put you up for a night, and she has servants."

"That sounds like a really clever idea," Ethan adds. "Plus, you might be able to get more information by being on the inside."

The corners of my mouth lift, and I give a small chuckle. "I like the way you two think."

With wireless in hand, I dial up Coco. "Hi, it's Zelda."

"I heard what happened. How are you feeling?"

"I am doing so much better, Coco."

"I am so glad to hear that. I feel responsible."

"This is not your doing."

"Don't try to spare my feelings. I know it's true. And on top of that, all that beautiful work we did on your hair and your nails literally went up in smoke."

Leave it to Coco to worry about my appearance. Then a small thought occurs to me. What does my hair look like, and will I need a wig?

"Coco, I have a favor. They'll let me out of the health clinic if I have a place to stay, not by myself, at least for one turn."

"Zelda, are you sure you should be leaving the clinic if they don't want you to be alone?"

"Healer said I was fit as a fiddle and in a turn be ready to play."

"Stay with me. I have more than enough room, and maybe we can do something with your hair while you're here."

"I so appreciate this, Coco."

"I have to work late, though, and it's the servants' turn off. They won't be back till later this evening.".

"If it's too much trouble—"

"No, not at all," Coco interrupts. "I'm just saying, as long as you don't mind being at the mansion with just Sally till I get home or the servants come in."

"No problem whatsoever. You said Sally's there. She's not at the office with you?"

"She said she wasn't feeling very well today, so I went ahead and sent her to the house. I'll try to call ahead and let her know you're coming."

"You are a darb of a friend, Coco. Thank you so much." I give a thumbs-up to my sister and to Ethan, letting them know that all is well and I've got a place to stay.

"One last thing," says Coco. "If you can, go in through the servants' entrance, just in case I can't get hold of Sally by the time you get there. Let yourself in, and make yourself at home."

"Thank you again, Coco, I so appreciate this. I'll see you tonight." I hang up the wireless and turn my attention to Ethan and my sister. "We're all set. I'm just going to need a ride over to Coco's."

Ethan raises his hand. "I can drive you over; I still have the sedan."

"That would be the berries, Ethan."

"I'll bring the auto around out front." He gives my shoulder a gentle pat and leaves the room.

"I'll let Mother know where you'll be staying. She'll probably want to come up tonight, if you can handle that."

"It'll be better for her to see me now. She'll worry less."

"True," Ava says, "especially considering she read your cards again."

"You're joking."

Ava lets out a laugh and a snort. "Nope."

I brace myself by clenching the bed sheets. "Rip that bandage right off. Let me have it."

"Without going through card by card, I'll just summarize."

"Well, don't keep me wound in the sheets. Out with it."

"The cards say you need to watch out for someone hidden in the shadows that will cause great unintentional harm."

"Is she saying we have another player in this drama?"

"That's basically what she read."

"Is this harm toward me?"

"She didn't say."

"Well, that's very unhelpful." I hop off the bed.

"It's possible her reading is a bit off with all this drama between her and Father."

"Have we heard from him yet?" I both want to know and don't want to know, all at the same time.

"Not a peep," says Ava.

"I cannot believe he's ditching Mother. He adores her. It's so unlike him to just skip out like this."

"He is being inconsiderate, to say the least. I've asked Harvey to put out some feelers to see if something more is going on. And I talked to Efron."

"What did he have to say?"

Ava starts helping me out of the clinic gown. "Efron said he tried to question A.P. about Titus."

"And?" I button up the silky blouse Mother packed in an overnight case for me.

"A.P. is giving Ephron the runaround."

"I thought A.P. was just as perplexed by Titus's behavior as we were?"

Ava helps me on with a pair of wide-legged slacks. "That's what Efron thought. Now he thinks A.P. knows more than he's saying. I don't know if it's something he's learned recently or if A. P. has known the whole time."

"You don't think anything has happened to Father, do you?" I slip on one shoe, then the other.

"Honestly, Zelda, I don't know. Tonight, I'll try a location spell. We can go from there and decide what is next."

"Sounds like a plan," I say. "Ava? I'm worried."

Ava puts her arms around me gently. "I know. So am I."

Chapter Forty-One

"I have news." Ethan starts up the electric engine of the borrowed sedan. "I hope it's good news," I say. "I could really use some just about now."

"Not sure you would categorize it as good news per se. More like neutral news." He pulls away from the curb. "Maybe it is good news. I mean, it at least answers one of the questions we have."

"Stop chewing gum and out with it already." I huff a little in frustration.

"Sorry. Yes, the body found in the explosion is—"

"Albert Slack."

Ethan touches the tip of his nose with his finger and nods.

I close my eyes and take a cleansing breath. I need to calm my racing thoughts and focus my brain cells.

"Are you okay?" Ethan takes a hand off the wheel and places it on my shoulder. He soon returns his hand to the steering wheel and concentrates on the road in front of him. "What are you thinking?"

"Just trying to put the pieces together." I suck in another breath. "The pieces I have, at least." I blow out the breath, along with all the tension I've been holding between my shoulder blades. My head is beginning to ache again.

"What are you missing, and what do you have?"

I look out the passenger window and gaze at the scenery crawling by. We are now out of the city and entering Countryside. It won't be long before we arrive at Coco's mansion. I angle my head toward Ethan.

"I found a list of names at Albert's place. I gave the list to Ruth's aunt. I'm waiting to hear back from Ruth whether she recognizes any of them." I shift around in the seat, trying to find a more comfortable position. My bruises have bruises. "I asked Mae to gather some information on Coco's assistant, Sally. Did I tell you there's some hanky-panky going on between her and Piers?"

Ethan gasps. "I thought she and Coco . . ."

"She is. They are."

"I could have run her name for you," he says. "I can help. Just ask."

"I can't risk you getting in trouble or alerting Detective Zex."

He huffs. "I'm a big boy. I can take care of myself." His normally easy-going demeanor is replaced by scowl.

"I know you can, but if anything goes wrong, my sister will hang me."

"Your sister is hard-boiled." His face relaxes, the sulky expression disappearing, replaced with a gentle smile.

As Ethan drives on, I steer the conversation back to the mystery I'm trying to solve. "Maybe the little bit of evidence you were able to work with can help me. Here is what I do know."

"There is something else I need to tell you," he says before I can continue.

"That sounds ominous."

Ethan takes a moment to clear his throat. "NSC came today to confiscate the rest of the evidence from the explosion. They also took the evidence from the Lucy Marsh case."

"I figured they would be have taken everything sooner rather than later. I have the blue clue in safe hands, so I'm not concerned about losing that evidence to NSC. The Marsh thing, though, is surprising."

My head is playing eight to the bar in my head. I pop a couple of feverfew capsules in my mouth and swallow them dry. Then I retrieve my flask from my bag and wiggle it back and forth. Not a sloshing sound to be found. My throat isn't the only thing that's dry.

"There's more." His voice goes up an octave on the last word.

"More?" My curiosity is piqued. "And . . . ?"

"And I spotted your father getting into one of the NSC motors that accompanied the truck."

I gasp. "Titus?"

Ethan just nods.

"Are you sure?"

"I don't think he knows I saw him."

His concentration stays on the driving. Mine, however, just flew out the window. How is my father, Titus Harcrow, involved with the explosion? Better yet, how long has he been chummy with the National Security Council.

I take another deep breath and blow it out with all my might. A shiver tingles up and down my spine. My body trembles. "Pull over."

"What? Why?" He brings the borrowed sedan to a stop on the berm.

"I need a drink." My body shakes with trepidation.

"After your head injury, I don't think that's a good idea."

I raise my voice. "Screw that."

"Glove box."

"Huh?"

"Open the glove box."

The latch makes a sharp screech then a click as I turn the knob, opening the glove box. "You've been holding out on me, Ethan!" I seize the dull metal hip flask from the compartment.

"Share," he states firmly.

"You betcha. Ethan, you are a good egg," I reply enthusiastically.

I take the first swig and pass the hooch to my companion.

"Let's forget about my father for the moment." I wait for my turn at the fountain.

A belch erupts from Ethan's stomach, and he hands me the flask. "Your turn."

"Thanks." I take another belt, wiping the strong brown liquor from my lips with the back of my hand. "Let's go over what we know."

"I think I should take notes," says Ethan.

I knock back another belt before handing off the flask. I've got an edge now; the buzz is definitely an improvement over the pounding. "What I've surmised so far is the following: The body was Albert's. The explosion was meant for someone else." I take another hit from the flask. "The bomb was in the satchel."

Ethan interrupts. "How do you know where the bomb was planted?"

"Oops, I forgot to tell you. Although in my defense, I was concussed." I rub the back of my neck, close my eyes, and recount my conversation with the torpedo in the Flamel Auditorium.

He grabs my hand and gives it a gentle squeeze. "I'm happy you got the information. The way it came to you, not so much." Ethan releases my hand and continues to put graphite to paper, jotting down all the details.

I go on with my thoughts. "Albert was there to meet someone other than the assassin. The man dressed in black arrived after Albert's death."

Ethan put down his notepad. "Who was Albert meeting and why? Was the bomb planted to take out the assassin or his employer?"

I let out a sigh. "Do we have one event or two?"

"These are some great questions, Zelda."

"None of which we have answers for."

"What should we do next?" says Ethan.

"Honestly, I'm not sure." I think that last swig muddled my brain. I'm going to have to start sticking to noodle water.

"What about that guy in the diner?"

"I have one better. What about the break-in at Coco's house?"

"If you could learn what was taken while you're staying at her place, that could help."

"I don't believe Piers is going to be a good sport and take me into his confidence. Now, drive on. I have some sleuthing to do."

Ethan shifts the motor into drive and pulls out onto the paved country road.

"When we arrive, use the employee and delivery entrance."

"Is there a reason?"

"Coco asked if I would enter through the back. Seems it's the servants' turn off and only Sally will be there."

"Might be an opportunity to interrogate her."

"I'd feel more confident giving her the third degree after I've spoken to Mae," I say.

"Go in with answers and see if she lies?"

"Precisely, then when I've caught her in the lies, I might get her to confess about Piers and what he is up to."

We pass the first driveway and enter the second, marked for employees and deliveries.

"We have arrived," Ethan says.

The entrance is a bit longer than the main drive. The driveway the employees use is masked from the front of the mansion by lines of purposely planted large conifer trees. The trees were obviously chosen because they don't lose their leaves with the change of seasons. Therefore, no matter what time of Gaia's rotation it is, no one would ever notice the comings and goings of the servants or delivery people. We can, however, catch glimpses of the front entrance as we make the turn to the rear of the residence.

"I thought you said Coco was working late."

"She is."

"Isn't that her car out front?"

I crane my neck to see. "I can't tell. Maybe it's Sally's."

"Well, at least you won't be alone."

"I'll be fine. I really am feeling better. No need to worry."

Ethan comes to a stop in front of the employees' door. "You want me to come in with you?"

"You better get back to work. I can manage." I lean over and give him a peck on the cheek. "Thank you for driving me."

Ethan's face turns a pale red that makes his eyes look bluer and his hair look whiter. He turns to face me. "Zelda?"

"Yes?"

He plants one straight on my kisser. An awkward silent moment passes like an eternity. Not sure how to respond, I pull back and slip out the passenger door with my overnight case. I wave goodbye as I enter through the door off the kitchen.

"Jeepers," I whisper. I'm going to have to deal with that sooner rather than later. For this moment, though, I need to find Sally.

I call out. My voice echoes through the hall. The place is so large, you probably couldn't hear a herd of stampeding, trumpeting unicorns run through. I set my things down and begin my hunt for Sally.

I pop my head into each of the first-floor rooms. No Sally.

Coco said Sally wasn't feeling well. She could be upstairs, resting. I ankle over to the main stairs in the hall and begin my ascent.

The stairs curve up to the second floor. As I approach the upstairs landing, I hear some strange grunting noises coming from the room that serves as Piers's home study.

My body tenses up. Each muscle becomes more rigid with every step I take. A sense of dread rises up my neck to my cheeks like suffocating tendrils. It takes all my willpower to continue my climb. My stomach flips upside down. I can hardly breathe. I won't call out; I can't call out. My voice is trapped inside me. I creep closer and closer to the door. Being as quiet as a mousacorn, I drop to my hands and knees and crawl to the closed study door.

I reach for the handle.

I gently press down, avoiding the click most latches make.

I push the door open, just a crack.

Only a crack. Just enough for me to see.

Just enough not to be seen.

Angling my head to the side, I peer through the crack in the door with one eye.

What the . . . ?

Chapter Forty-Two

I grimace, squeezing my eyes shut. My brow furrows, and I gag at the scene inside Piers's office. Delicately, I close the door and release the handle. That was not what I was expecting in any way, shape, or form.

There inside the study was Sally, bent over the oversize dark-grained desk, naked as a jaybird, leisurely filing her nails while Piers grunted and thumped away, playing hide the salami in her chassis. His pants lay around his ankles, and his cheeks (the ones on his face) were flushed red.

It was something I did not need to see.

A simple yet audible snicker emerges, and I slam my hand over my mouth, hoping I wasn't heard.

No such luck.

"What was that?" Sally asks beyond the closed door.

"What was what?" Piers responds.

"I think I heard someone," she says.

"Just close your head and stand still." Piers begins to grunt again.

That was a close call. Gathering myself together, I position myself to make a stealthy exit downstairs. I'll make enough racket once I'm down there that'll they believe I just arrived.

A new thought rises in my brain. How am I going to tell Coco? It was different when Anne Sheridan relayed the story, but now I've witnessed the no-pants dance myself.

On my hands and knees, I start the crawl.

"I swear, Piers Daddy, I heard something," Sally coos in a baby voice.

"Fine," he grumbles. "I'll go check, but when I come back, ya better be willing to play my flute till the music runs out."

"Aw, Daddy, you know how I dislike blowing the wet noodle."

I gag a little at the unfortunate visual of that sentence.

Swack. The hard slap of flesh on flesh sings through the closed door. Piers must have hit Sally pretty hard.

I know I really need to hotfoot it out of there, but jeepers, this conversation is loony, and I can't seem to pull away.

"I'm sorry, Piers Daddy," Sally cries. "I know how much you like living the good life. We can do that together." Her voice shifts back to a high-pitched baby sound. "In fact, Daddy, I'll let you do that thing to me you're always wanting to do."

Piers's voice is still filled with venom. "I can't wait to leave this place. Have my own money."

I crawl closer to the door and lean in to hear more.

"Piers baby, I did everything you asked. You promised me we'd be living high on the hog together. I did all that spying for you. I keep Coco satisfied beyond measure so you could get Juju out. You promised."

"I know, baby. I'm sorry." His voice softens. "I'm just frustrated. That stupid kid stole my copy of the formula he created. Now those thugs want their money back, and the formula."

"What happens if they don't get it?" she says.

"My life won't be worth much. But don't worry, I've got a plan."

Crap. This doesn't sound good. Should I stay here and eavesdrop or skedaddle and hope I can figure out his next move before he can act on his nefarious plan, whatever it is?

"Aw, Daddy. I'll make you feel better. Here, take this, and I'll get into position."

I move back away from the study door. They must have forgotten about the noise I made. I'll keep with my original idea of pretending I just arrived. I crawl backward on my hands and knees, attempting not to make a peep.

My foot inadvertently brushes something. I whip my head around in time to see a floor vase teetering on its base. Crap! I edge back on my feet and reach for the vase. *Thud.* The vase plops onto the low-pile carpet.

I freeze.

I listen.

I hope they didn't hear that over Sally's small screams.

Piers stops laughing.

Chapter Forty-Three

I scramble to the vase, putting it back in its upright position. Knowing it's going to take Piers a moment to pull up his trousers, I begin looking for an escape. It would take too long to get down the stairs, so I begin to look for an alternative.

Piers's study sits at the corner where the hall turns. One option is to run down the long hall and hope I find an open door behind which I can hide, but that would leave me with the problem of how to get out later without being seen or having to explain how I got there.

Another option is to go down the shorter hallway toward the back of the house. The shorter hallway has three doors and a window at the end. I know one door leads to the rooftop because that's how I was brought down after the break-in. Another door leads to the servants' back staircase—a staircase the employees use to move between floors without disrupting their employers. The third door is a mystery, and the window is out. Hanging outside this house once was enough for me.

I only hope I can find the door that leads to the back stairs.

Through the closed study door, I can make out Piers, with Sally in tow, stumbling and swearing. I need to act fast. Hustling down the short hallway, I face two possibilities. Knowing that the last door on the right leads to the roof, I am left with the opposing door on the left or the door before the roof access on the right.

The door to the office is swung with such force that I can hear the door handle smack the wall. No more time to waste. I pull open the door on my right, hoping I made the correct choice.

Jeepers! Another closet!

With no time to sprint across the hall, I unhappily enter the closet and close the door softly behind me.

The walk-in linen closet has built-in drawers along its base and cupboard shelves that climb to the ceiling. If Piers opens the door, he's going to see me and the jig will be up. Opening one of the cupboards, I push aside a stack of

261

sheets and hoist myself up. I fold into a ball, and with one hand, close the cupboard, leaving me in a closet within a closet.

After this, I don't wanna see the inside of a closet for an exceedingly long time.

Piers and Sally must have gone down the other hallway first. I can hear doors opening and slamming shut; it's just a matter of time before they check in here.

"By Gaia, I swear I heard something," Piers grumbles.

"There ain't nobody here, Daddy."

"You were just yammering earlier that you thought someone was up here."

"Ow!" Sally cries out.

"Talk to me like that again, and I'll twist the other one," says Piers.

Sally answers in a seductive tone. "Promise?"

"You are so naughty." Piers chuckles. "Come here, you."

"Oh, Daddy, don't stop."

There is a slam against the outer closet door and some distinct groaning. I want to groan too, but in complete disgust. These two are way too much.

"Come on, baby, Daddy has something he wants to give you."

It's quiet for a moment. They must be moving away from the door and back down to the study and their kinky little games. I slowly push open the cupboard where I am held up. Poking my head out, I listen for any movement.

"Daddy, you forgot to check the closet," Sally says to Piers.

The door handle jiggles, and the door glides open.

I grab the cupboard door and close it upon myself again. I squeeze shut my eyes and hold a breath of air.

Click.

I open one eye. A bit of light seeps through a corner of the cabinet in which I'm tucked away.

"Nothing," says Piers. Click, and the light disappears.

I wait.

No voices.

Nothing.

Opening the cupboard once more, I peek out.

The light is out, and the door is closed.

I gingerly lower myself out of the cupboard and tiptoe to the door. I lean my ear against the wooden door and listen.

When I hear nothing, I push the lever of the door handle down slowly to release the catch with as little sound as possible. Popping my head out, I peer down the hall for signs of the two sadistic lovers. The coast is clear. I freeze as I listen for any rumblings coming from the office. Other than a few loud expletives from Sally and a couple of sinister cackles from Piers, there's nothing to keep me from blowing this pop stand.

One foot in front of the other, I creep to the door across the hall. The polished silver-colored metal door handle makes no sound as I pull on it to reveal my escape route.

Locked.

"What?" I whisper under my breath. Who locks the staff's back stairs?

I stop and look toward the study. Who locks the staff's stairs? Piers does. That way, no one can come up and catch him with that cheap bit of calico named Sally. Change of plans, then. Somehow, some way, I am going to have to sneak down those front stairs. I shake my head in frustration. What else could possibly go wrong?

Taking my time, I purposely take a step, then freeze and listen. It may take me longer to get down the stairs this way, but there will also be less chance of my getting caught. My foot moves forward and softly crunches down on the soft carpet with barely a sound.

A click-shuffle-click sound rises to greet my ears. Piers is still having his fun with Sally; the moans and groans are still loud enough for me to hear through the shut study door. So did someone else enter the house? I strain my ears to listen for another footstep. I'm at the corner of the hall, and the stairs lie in front of me.

Almost home free.

"Get dressed. The old ball and chain will be headed home soon." The study door creaks open, and Piers's voice is no longer muffled by the closed door. "And clean yourself up. She is probably going to want to play with the kitty when she gets home."

I lie flat against the wall in hopes he doesn't become aware of my presence.

"What about my present?" Sally pleads.

"What present?" Piers's voice becomes more muffled.

Sally whines in a baby voice, "You promised."

"That I did," he says.

Their voices become more distant. They must have gone farther into the study, but the door is still open. I look back down the hall. The roof or the window?

I tiptoe to the end of the hall. By the stars, hopefully the latch doesn't make a lot of noise when I pull on it. I slide the latch, and it clicks. I freeze.

Then I let out a sigh.

With my hand, I gently push open the window. I look out and down. There is a ledge. This is not a promising idea. I climb over the sill and straddle it, grateful that Mother packed a pantsuit for me.

Now standing on the ledge outside the house, I decide my next move. Inching myself along the ledge away from the open window, I pull my wireless out of my pocket.

"Hello," says the voice on the other end.

"I need you to come and get me," I say.

"I don't understand."

"Ethan, you need to turn around and come back to the house and get me."

"But I'm almost back to the city."

"I'm begging you. It is imperative."

"Okay, but one question."

"Sure, if you step on it and get here as fast as you can."

"Why are you whispering?" he asks.

"Long story short, Piers and Sally are doing the nasty, there was a closet and a locked staircase, so I need you to come to the back of the house and get me down." The fingers of my free hand try to dig into the stucco for imagined security from falling.

"None of that makes sense," says Ethan.

"I'll fill you in when you get here." My voice is shaking. "Hurry."

"On my way to you now."

Through the open window, a ruckus inside makes itself known. "Oh, crap," I whisper.

"Zelda, what happened?" Ethan shouts through the receiver.

Bringing the wireless down to my chest to mute Ethan's pleas for a response, I listen. I hear a scream and a groan. Something being knocked over and more groaning and moaning.

Putting the phone back up to my ear, I say, "It's nothing."

"Nothing?"

"Just Piers and Sally again, only this time, they left the door open."

"Ew," Ethan exclaims.

"You got that right. And I have to listen to it."

"Hang tight." Ethan disconnects.

Even though the noisy duo has quieted down, I ease farther away from the window and farther down the back side of the house. At some point, I am going to run out of ledge. I glance to the outside corner of the house and find a possible solution to my current situation. A white wooden trellis filled with climbing turquoise roses reaches up beyond the first floor. If I shimmy over to the trellis, I can use it as a ladder, climb down, grab my bag, and wait for Ethan. The only hurdles are a few windows between me and my way down to the ground.

Balancing precariously on the second-floor ledge of Coco's mansion, I realize this escape plan might have been better in theory than in practice. The late-afternoon sun casts elongated shadows, turning the elegant facade into a theater of absurdity. I peer over; the climbing roses seem much farther away now than they did from the open window.

Regretting my decision to exit out the window, I now teeter on the ledge, the tips of my shoes overhanging the stucco ledge. With an exaggerated gulp, I inch sideways, pretending I'm a circus performer, not someone who's about to break both legs in a fall.

With a sigh of relief, I finally reach the trellis adorned with Coco's turquoise climbing roses. The delicate scent of roses surrounds me as I transfer my weight onto the trellis. As I start climbing down, my foot snags among the trellis and roses. I quickly find myself dangling, suspended upside down halfway to the ground like a comically inept acrobat. The roses' thorny tendrils entangle not only the trellis but also my escape plan. I dangle between the trellis and the ground, contemplating for the umpteenth million time the poor life choices that led me to once again hang upside down outside Coco's home.

I can make out the crunch of tires on the gravel below me. I hope it's Ethan and not one of the many staff that are employed here.

"Zelda!" Ethan yells up at me. "What are you doing?"

"Keep your voice down. I don't want anyone to hear you." I wriggle in an attempt to grab the trellis with my hands, and my foot begins to slip. As my foot dislodges, I let out an undignified yelp. Just in the nick of time, Ethan appears below me, his eyes wide with disbelief. Ever the loyal friend, Ethan races to the rescue, positioning himself directly beneath me, arms outstretched. My rapid descent aligns perfectly with Ethan's heroic attempt to break my fall, and I suddenly find myself draped over his outstretched arms, his face buried in my chest.

Ethan tries to say something, but his voice is stifled by my cleavage.

"What? I can't understand what you're trying to say."

I feel his chin move up and down against my breastbone as he mumbles something again.

"Huh?" Lifting myself off him, I roll over onto my back. "Sorry about that."

Ethan gasps for air, his eyes wide as he takes a moment to collect himself. "I was just trying to ask if you were okay," he finally manages, a mix of concern and amusement in his eyes.

"Besides the fact that I completely fail at escape plans, I'm perfectly fine."

Ethan snickers. "You sure know how to make an entrance, Zelda."

"You mean exit," I say. "I'm just glad you're a good catch."

"You think I'm a good catch?" He props himself up on his elbow.

My face reddens a little. "You know what I mean."

Ethan flashes a lopsided smile. "Glad I could be of service. Now let's blow this pop stand."

Chapter Forty-Four

"Jeepers." I punch my leg. "I forgot my case."

"Do you want to go back to collect it?" asks Ethan.

"No. Just take me to Coco's office. It's more imperative that I talk with her before she leaves for home." I slip a piece of hair behind my ear. With a long sigh, I close my eyes, lean into the seat, and cross my arms.

"Talk to me, Zelda. What's wrong?" Ethan continues to keep both hands on the wheel as he steers the tin slowly off the back drive and onto the country road.

"It's just a feeling." I feel the pull of the automobile as it accelerates, gently pushing me deeper into the tin's passenger seat.

"What do you mean?"

"I just sense something is wrong. Or maybe I'm just missing something."

The rhythmic purr of the engine and the gentle sway of the car lull me toward sleep. Filtered sunlight warms my eyelids. The electric vehicle's subtle vibrations offer a comforting massage, and for a fleeting moment, the feeling that something is amiss melts away.

Abruptly, the tin swerves with a jolt that catapults me out of my rest. Panic tightens its grip as my eyes fly open and I grasp the dashboard. The squeal of tires blend with the thundering beat of my hearts.

Straightening out the sedan, Ethan pulls to the side of the road. "Are you all right?"

"What in the stars was that?"

Ethan is still gripping the steering wheel, knuckles white. "A tin came speeding toward us and drifted into our lane. Almost ran us off the road."

"Did you see who was driving?" I roll my shoulders and stretch my neck in an attempt to relieve the tension from that near miss.

Ethan rubs the back of his neck. "I guess we better get back on the road."

Reaching over with one hand, I massage his back between the shoulder blades. I can feel the tension in his muscles melt away, and the corners of his mouth turn up slightly. Closing his eyes, he rests his head on his hands, which still clench the steering wheel. Gently, I place my other hand over one of his.

Ethan looks up at me. "It's never a dull moment when you're around, is it?"

I pull back. "You mean dangerous."

Facing me, he retrieves one of my hands from my lap, clasping it between his. His eyes stare straight into me. "I owe you so much."

"Ethan, you don't owe me anything. We're jake."

"Yes, I do." He squeezes my hand, sending the warmth of his sweetness and gratitude through my veins. "My career is because of you. The doors that have been opened to me are because of you and your family."

My head slumps with the knowledge that he's only helping me out of obligation and the crush that comes along with it. I've used him poorly. I've taken advantage of him and used him. I guess I'm more like my father than I acknowledged. My sister is right; I'm not very self-aware, and I don't think about how my actions affect others.

Ethan releases his grasp and, with a finger, lifts my chin.

"I am so sorry," I tell him. "I've been so focused on me and this case, I never took into consideration—"

In a flash, his lips are on mine. It's a fleeting moment, a tender connection that sparks warmth within me.

"I make my own decisions. I choose to help you." He leans in again, and our lips meet. His touch is featherlight, a brush of intimacy that leaves a trace of sweetness in the air. Straightening up, he shifts the sedan into gear and judiciously pulls back out onto the road.

I should really say something. Instead, I gaze out the window at the ever-moving scenery.

I'm startled by the buzzing of my wireless. Now what? "Hello?"

"Zelda!" cries a frantic voice over the airwaves and into my ear to mesh with the dull ache of my head.

"Mother, what's wrong? What happened?" I don't let her get a word in edgewise. "Is Ava all right? The kids? Did something happen to the kids?"

"Thank Gaia you're alive," she says when she finally gets a sentence in.

"I'm fine. Where are you?"

"Oh, Zelda, it's all so horrifying. I'm glad you're not toast too."

"For crying out loud, Mother, you're all balled up." I swivel to face Ethan. He glances at me, and I shrug. "Tell me, are you safe? Where are you, and what is going on."

"I came to check on you."

"Check on me where? Mother, where are you?"

"I'm at Coco's, of course."

"You're at Coco's?" I am hoping she didn't get an eyeful or earful of Piers and his vamp.

"Yes, that's what I said, and there's blood everywhere."

My eyes widen. "I think I'm missing something. Whose blood, Mother? Yours?"

"By the stars, no. It's someone else's."

"What someone?"

"I can't tell; it's a mess. Blood and brains all over that awful patterned carpet. Coco really should hire a decorator."

"I'm turning around, and I'm coming straight there. Don't do anything or touch anything, okay?"

"You need to hurry. I'm feeling very faint." Mother's voice cracks a little.

I nod at Ethan. "Turn it around and step on it. We're going back."

It doesn't take long for us to reach Coco's. This time, Ethan drives up the main driveway. There sits my sister's Areo. Ethan and I exit the sedan, and the echo of our hurried steps reverberates against the smooth marble stairs, announcing our presence. The large front door stands wide open. I slide Ethan a look of concern.

Ethan blocks my entrance with an outstretched arm. Ever the copper, he halts me in my tracks, a human barricade of authority and concern as he meets my eye with a firm gaze that silently conveys to proceed with caution.

My wireless buzzes out a startling ring. Ethan nods to me to answer. "Hello," I whisper.

"Zelda, is that you at the front door?" Mother whispers back.

"It's us. We're coming in now." My heels don't touch the ground as I sprint to the grand staircase.

I look up to see my mother clinging to the rail, slowly descending toward us.

We meet.

I embrace her. She holds tightly on to me.

"Oh, it is so hideous," she says, her voice shaky with stress.

Pulling back, I introduce Ethan. "Mother, this is Ethan Hodge, my friend."

Ethan holds out his hand. "How do you do . . . ?"

"Mystic Harcrow-Galfry," I respond, presenting my mother.

She shakes his hand. "You can call me Ave. Mystic Harcrow-Galfry is so formal."

"Yes, ma'am." Ethan shifts his attention up the stairs. "What happened?"

Chapter Forty-Five

E than strides toward the open study door, his gaze deciphering the room's interior. His body shudders involuntarily, and he leans against the doorframe, gripping it firmly. My eyes fixate on him, goose bumps spreading over my arms.

He inhales deeply and makes a visible effort to regain his composure. His spine straightens with purpose. With his copper training engaged, Ethan begins to take control of the scene.

"Mystic—I mean Ave, please call up the Legere Legalis."

Then he addresses me. "Zelda, when you were here earlier, did you see anyone else?"

"Why?" Curious and determined, I lift my chin, square my shoulders, and move to the study door.

"Zelda, trust me, you don't want to see this."

"Move aside, Ethan," My voice reveals a hint of impatience. My eyes narrow, silently demanding compliance.

Ethan closes his eyes, shakes his head, and relents, stepping aside to grant me access to the study. With a deep breath, I lean over the threshold.

There on the carpet, in pools of thick crimson liquid, lie Piers and his cohort, Sally. Their faces are almost unrecognizable.

My hand flies up to cover my mouth, but I am determined to hold it together. The walls and ceiling are splattered with gray matter and blood. I close my eyes and turn my head away from the gruesome scene. I can feel the bile rising in my throat.

I jump as I become aware of Ethan's unexpected presence behind me.

His hands gently rest on my shoulders. "Let's move back into the hall." The touch is grounding, a silent reassurance amid the horror.

The wail of sirens is, at first, barely audible, distant. With each passing moment, the sound intensifies, seeping into the very walls of the building. The sirens creep in like an unwanted nuisance. My mother, Ethan, and I brace ourselves for what we all know will come next.

271

A familiar voice rises from the great hall. "I want uniforms at each entrance. I also want a sweep of the entire first floor. See something, tag it and make a note. Do not touch anything."

I roll my eyes and let out a grunt of disappointment. Inspector Zex—of course it would have to be her. I wonder silently if she's the only inspector on the whole Legere Legalis force.

Inspector Zex's voice is now louder. "DCI Miller, take some uniforms and search the second floor. Secure any exits." She now stands at the top landing. She looks straight at us without acknowledging our presence. She continues to bark out orders. "DSI Snoggs, you're with me."

"Yes, ma'am," says an obviously wet-behind-the-ears DSI.

Zex shoots her a look.

DSI Snoggs stutters, "I-I mean Inspector." She pulls out a notepad and a writing utensil that shows a nervous pattern of teeth marks at its end.

Zex strides over to my mother and me and stands straight as an arrow in front of us in her overly starched shirt and neatly pressed suit. Her head turns sharply to Ethan, who stands guard at the study entrance. "Hmm." Clasping her hands behind her back, she turns her attention back to us. "Exactly what happened here?"

"We don't know," I blurt out.

Zex looks my mother up and down. "Who is this?"

"This is Mystic Harcrow-Galfry. My mother."

"Ahem." Mother clears her throat and raises an eyebrow at me.

I let out a small sigh. "Mother, this is Inspector Zex."

She nods at me, then turns her attention to the inspector. "It is nice to meet you."

Zex just grunts and nods.

"I am sure you are going to want to know how I came across the bodies," Mother says.

"Every detail would be appreciated."

I lean in. "Well, I'm supposed to—"

My mother puts her hand up to shush me. "Zelda dear, I know you mean well, but please, dear, I can speak for myself."

Inspector Zex gives me the stink eye. Her voice, though, softens toward my mother.

"Please go on, Mystic."

"Thank you, Inspector Zex." Mother places her hand to her hearts and tilts her head. "This has been all so much."

"Just take your time." The inspector reaches out and lightly pats my mother's arm.

My jaw drops. I get disdain from Zex, and in just a few sentences, my mother gets empathy?

The inspector continues, "I must say, I really admire the way you kept your birth surname after you married."

"Thank you. Most in my family keep their maiden name. We adopt our partners' surnames and place them before our own. This new modern thing of giving up your family name when you marry is very strange. Call me old-fashioned."

The inspector's body seems less rigid.

"You, ma'am, are not old-fashioned," says the inspector.

"Thank you. You know, you really take charge of a scene. I can tell you are going places. You should let me read your cards sometime."

"Mother," I grumble.

Zex shoots me the stink eye again before reengaging my mother. "I would be honored."

I roll my eyes.

"Please start from the beginning," the inspector says, moving the conversation back to the crime scene.

Mother pulls back her shoulders and takes a deep breath. "My eldest daughter had her former student drive Zelda here, where I was to meet her and get her settled in."

Zex glances over at Ethan, faces my mother, and nods for her to continue.

"Well, I got here first."

Did my mother just lie?

"You arrived first," Zex repeats.

"Yes. The front door was open. I entered and began calling out for someone. I looked around briefly and then came upstairs. Saw the opened door . . ." My mother shivers. I am unsure if that was for real or just for effect.

"When did FCI Hodge and your daughter arrive?" Zex questions.

I raise my brow and tilt my head toward Mother. I'd like to hear this story too.

"As I said, I saw—I saw—I—" She puts her hand to her mouth and lets out a small whimper.

My stars, that woman can put on a performance.

"Ma'am, it'll be okay. Did you see anyone else besides the deceased?" The inspector reaches out yet again and pats my mother's arm.

Before Mother can answer, one of the DCIs who is coordinating downstairs jogs up and whispers something to the inspector. "I see," is all she says in response.

"Is everything okay, Inspector Zex?" asks Mother.

"What do you know about a suitcase in the staff hallway downstairs?"

Jeepers. My mother doesn't know about my left-behind suitcase. We are in a load of manure now.

"My suitcase," I blurt out.

Mother shoots me a *be quiet* look. I clamp my mouth shut.

"Yours? I thought your mother got here first. You couldn't have come in the back. The Legere vehicle is out front. Care to explain?"

Mother smiles. "Oh, I left it there."

"You left her suitcase?"

"Yes. That's why I was meeting her here. To bring her an overnight bag and get her settled in." Mother smiles sweetly again. "With all this going on, I completely forgot where I left it."

The inspector nods. She's bought it.

"As for Dr. Harcrow and FCI Hodge?"

Mother clears her throat with a soft *ahem*. "After I found . . . the bodies, I called Zelda, and then I called the Legere."

"You called your daughter first?"

"Of course. I wasn't sure if she was lying in a ditch somewhere. Really, what is the world coming to?"

Zex just nods.

Mother continues to weave her story. "I heard them come through the front, they came up, Ethan Hodge secured the study, and we waited till you arrived."

Inspector Zex stares at me. "Did you touch anything?"

I am taken aback a bit; however, with my current track record, I can see her point. "No. I didn't go into the study."

"Take your mother back to your sister's. She has been through a shock." Zex pivots abruptly and ankles over to Ethan with DSI Snoggs in tow. "FCI Hodge, what have we got here?"

Tugging at Mother's hand, I pull her toward the stairs. "Let's blow this joint before any more questions are asked," I whisper.

"Good idea." Mother gallops alongside me down the grand staircase.

"What about my suitcase?" I ask.

"Leave it for now."

"Mother?"

"Yes?"

"I think we should drive to Coco Cosmetics and talk with Coco. I don't think she should hear about what happened here from strangers."

"I'm on the trolley with that."

We climb into Ava's Areo and creep down the driveway. Once on the main road, I gun it, speeding toward Capital City's industrial area. I wonder how Coco is going to take the news.

Chapter Forty-Six

Mother and I exchange looks. Coco Cosmetics definitely has the most inept security ever.

"I'm sorry, ma'am. I'm not sure how to reach her," says the security guard behind the desk.

"Maybe try calling her office, sport?" I say.

"Oh!" The baby-faced kid smiles and vigorously nods. Picking up the receiver, he punches a button. "Yes. Hello, I have visitors for Coco Charden-e."

My eyes widen. The kid can't even pronounce the name of the person he works for.

The sap nods at the phone and says, "Yes." He hangs up and looks at me, then at my mother. "She's not in there."

I lean on the counter. "Did you ask where she was?"

"Was I supposed to?"

I sigh. "I think so."

"Do you want me to call up there again?"

"Jeepers, now you're on the trolley!" I look at my mother, who has a stiff grimace on her face. I think she just might bust a gut holding in that laugh.

He picks up the receiver once more, punches the button, and waits. "Do you know where Coco Chardon-e is?" Once again, he mispronounces the name of the owner of the company. He looks up at me. "They say she might be in one of the laboratories."

"Did they say which one, by chance?"

"Should I have asked?"

I pinch the bridge of my nose with my thumb and forefinger and squeeze my eyes shut. I'm not sure if my oncoming headache has to do with the lump on my head or the lump behind the desk.

"Come on, Mother. Let's go find Coco."

"Wait! Wait!" says the young, inexperienced security guard. "You can't go there."

"Beat it, kid." I wave off the goof and grab Mother's elbow. I pull her along as I ankle straight out the back to the old building.

It takes no time at all to find Coco; she is alone, studiously working in one of the lower labs. Sitting on a stool in front of a sterilized rectangular stainless-steel table, she is hunched over with two small beakers. One is filled with a clear, syrupy liquid, and the other with a thin amber liquid. Coco is taking dropperful after dropperful of the clear liquid and expelling it into the amber liquid, changing its viscosity. After each dropperful, she stirs the amber liquid with a glass stirrer, stopping to take notes after each addition.

Her concentration is so deep, she doesn't hear us enter the room. I turn to my mother. "I hate to disturb her when she's creating. I know what can happen when someone interrupts an alchemist. It's never good."

Gently smiling, Mother brings her right hand up to her chest. With her palm facing her, she gracefully swishes her hand out toward Coco, turning her palm up.

Coco raises her head. "I didn't see you there." She stands up and removes the goggles from her head, placing them on the table.

My mother's gifts always amaze me.

"Sorry to disturb you, Coco," I say.

"Ish kabibble." Coco walks around the table to greet us. "How are you feeling, and what have you done to your hair?" She gives me a gentle squeeze. "I thought I was to meet you at my place. Ave, it's wonderful to see you." She embraces my mother.

"Other than a few bumps and bruises, I'm doing all right."

"Coco dear, we have some news," says Mother.

"Did you find who blew up the upstairs laboratory? I hope Piers didn't have anything to do with it. It would just break my heart if he did."

"That's not exactly what this is about," I say.

Coco wrinkles her forehead, completely perplexed.

Mother places a hand on Coco's forearm. "Maybe we should all sit down."

I concur. "Good idea."

"You two are beginning to worry me." Coco's body trembles as she takes a seat at the end of one of the long stainless-steel tables.

I'm not sure where to start. This is a delicate conversation that I am not prepared to begin.

As I pull the stool up to sit next to Coco, the legs of the metal stool scrape against the cement floor, producing a sharp, grating sound that cuts through the air and puts me further on edge. Putting her hand on my knee, my mother sends a calming energy to wash over me. Now calmer, I know I can begin the story, but I believe the more difficult part would be better told by my mother.

"It seems Piers wasn't exactly truthful," I begin. "I don't believe he started out to hurt you. From what I can tell, he got involved with some unknown group that was a bit dangerous." I continue to fill her in on the few details I know. Her face twists in shock when I tell her about Sally's role in the deception. She goes pale, and then a crimson flush of embarrassment colors her cheeks.

"Did they steal the lipstick formula? Were they responsible for the explosion?" Coco's voice cracks, and a lonely tear travels down her cheek.

"I'm still waiting for some information. Honestly, I don't think they were responsible for the explosion. Coco, the lipstick formula is safe and has nothing to do with any of this. It was just a ruse to help cover up Piers and Sally's deception," I say.

"You keep saying 'was.' What aren't you telling me?' She straightens her spine, steeling herself for more sour news to come her way.

This is where I might be a coward or a good friend. I yield the rest of the sordid story to my mother.

Mother gently presses her hand to Coco's. "My dear, I am so sorry to have to tell you what I found at your beautiful home today." Mother proceeds to inform Coco of Piers's and Sally's demise—leaving out some of the more gruesome details.

Coco sits in disbelief. No bawling her eyes out. Just utter silence.

"Mother, I think she's in shock."

"It seems so. Do you have a flask or something?" she asks me.

"I'm tapped out. Dry as the desert. How about you?"

"Really, Zelda." Mother makes a tsk sound with her teeth.

I open my mouth to make a smart-alecky remark; however, a commotion behind us interrupts.

A voice that reminds me of nails on a slate board bellows out, "Coco Charden, don't move. You are being taken into custody to answer questions about the untimely demise of Piers Astuce and Sally Renis." Inspector Zex charges over with two of the DCIs from earlier to take custody of Coco.

"Hold up!" I yell. "What on Gaia is going on?"

Inspector Zex gets up in my face. "I thought I told you, Harcrow, to take your mother home."

I move in until our noses are almost touching. The tension in the room is palpable.

My mother intervenes. "Zelda, let the inspector do her job. I'm sure she has evidence to support her suspicions."

"Thank you, Mystic Harcrow-Galfry, I do. The weapon used to pummel the victims—a marble desk obelisk—was found on the floor of Miss Charden's roadster."

I puff out my chest. "Anyone could have placed it there."

"Her car was spotted racing from the scene," Zex states.

"Oh, yay?"

"Your friend, FCI Ethan Hodge, identified the vehicle as the one that almost drove you off the road." Zex smirks.

I take a step back. Then I stare at Coco, my head cocked to the side. "Coco?"

Coco wakes from her daze. "I swear, Zelda, I didn't do this. I was here working in the lab all afternoon."

The inspector steps around me to question Coco. "Do you have a witness? Anyone to verify you were here during the time of the attack?"

Coco shakes her head and buries her face in her hands. She begins to cry. "I swear I didn't hurt them."

Zex signals to her DCIs to escort Coco out.

Coco looks back at me, crying. "What do I do?"

"Do not say anything. I'll find your legal department and get them to meet you at the station." I choose to believe my friend. I cannot fathom her bashing anyone's head in.

Mother and I stand in silence in the empty lab for what seems like an eternity.

I break that silence. "Good job getting out of the inspector what the evidence was."

"Thank you." She straightens her skirt and adjusts her hat. "After we get her legal team rounded up, I think we need to get back to your sister's and put our heads together. You are going to need some help on this, Zelda."

"Mother?"

"Hmm?" she acknowledges.

"How bad is my hair from the explosion?"

"Just keep your hat on, dear, and people will barely notice."

Chapter Forty-Seven

We sit around the dining room table, finishing up what I would call a delectable meal. For all of Hazel's faults, she is one heck of a cook.

Setting her white linen napkin down over her plate, my sister stands up. "I think we should retire to the kitchen table for tea and a much-needed discussion, while Hazel tidies up."

The legs of Harvey's chair scrape softly along the floor as he moves away from the table, the shuffling sound serving as a reminder that the meal has ended. Following Harvey and my sister, my mother and I place our napkins on the table and head to the kitchen.

Teacups and saucers are laid out, as well as a small jug of milk, a jar of honey, and a dish of sour citrus fruits.

As I wait for Hazel to pour our tea, I ring up Mae.

"Darling," she answers.

"It's Zelda. Any news?"

"On what?"

"I asked if you could get more information on Sally Renis."

"Oh, that," Mae says.

"We have some new unexpected circumstances." I give her the lowdown on recent events.

"Darling, you're pulling my leg."

"On the level, Mae."

"This is no good."

"I'm behind the eight ball on this one, Mae. I need all the information you can give me on Sally Renis."

Hazel brings over the pot and pours the tea out into our cups. By the time she gets to me, the small pot is empty. "I'll make more," she says.

I relay all that Mae found out from her latest conquest, DSI Flynn.

"According to Mae, that broad was a regular gold digger, a chippy, if you know what I'm saying. And her name isn't Sally Renis."

"Tell us more," says my mother.

"That little cheap bit of calico had a number of aliases. She has a rap sheet longer than my arm." I watch as my family enjoys their evening beverage. I still sit with an empty cup.

"Did he dig up anything on her with Piers, Coco's husband?" Ava asks.

"Sally, as we know her, liked to latch onto rich men and drain them dry. Her acquaintances—or known associates, as the Legere refers to them—told him that she hooked up with some fella who had an opportunity land in his lap that spelled big moolah."

"Did they say to whom he was selling?" Harvey motions to Hazel that he needs a refill.

I hold up my cup too. "Only thing they knew was that once they got their hands on it, they were going to sell it to the highest bidder in the Underground Market."

"I'll talk to my contacts in the NSC, see if there's been any chatter," says Harvey.

Ava starts into the discussion with some news of her own. "I found your pretty boy. His name is Jack Foxx. He's a self-proclaimed playboy. Thinks he's the chat's meow. He hangs out at that new club downtown called The Pink Note. Also, he's a bit of a braggart. Rumor has it, he claims he created something that is going to make him rich."

"Do you think the substance I found is what he created, and Piers was looking to sell?"

"Possibly," Ava says. "Tomorrow, we can find him up at the university and ask him some questions." Ava holds her cup up for Hazel to fill.

Hazel also fills my mother's cup. It's finally my turn, but just as Hazel is about to fill mine, she stops dead. "Did the university boy kill the man and his mistress?"

I wiggle my cup for attention.

"I wish I'd paid more attention to Flo's drawing," says Ava.

Hazel ankles over to Harvey for another tea refill. I look inside my cup. Still bone dry.

Mother's voice goes up a notch as she pridefully remarks, "Flo has the sight? Oh, how wonderful!"

Ava calms her down. "I don't want Flo to know her picture came true. She's too young to understand how it works, and she may blame herself."

Mother looks like a deflated balloon. "I guess so."

"Hazel, top my mother's cup off, please."

Hazel complies. Here is my chance. I hold up my cup, and Hazel comes over to fill it.

"Sorry, it's empty again," Hazel says.

"Can you make another pot?" I plead.

She looks at her wristwatch. "No. It's time for me to go home." Trotting over to the sink, she places the pot on the counter, takes off her apron, and disappears.

I slump back in my chair. No noodle water, and my flask is juiceless. I listen to the three share their ideas on who killed Piers and Sally. Was it Mr. Pearly Whites, the Man in Black, an unknown person Piers owed money to, or maybe Coco really did do it out of revenge?

"I wish Titus wasn't hiding," Mother says. "We could really use his brainpower. Plus, I miss him."

"He isn't missing," I blurt out.

The chatter ends, and everyone stares at me with their mouths open.

I remain in my slumped position. "He's not missing or hiding or whatever you want to call it. Ethan saw him with the NSC agents who removed the evidence from the Coco Cosmetics explosion and the Lucy Marsh homicide."

"He must be looking for the blue substance," Ava surmises. "He doesn't know you had some and I sent the rest to H.A."

"If that's true, it's his own fault. Acting all cagey," Mother grumbles, her annoyance apparent. With a sharp exhale, she slams her teacup down, the porcelain emitting a loud *clink* as it hits the table. "I'll have some strong words for him when I see him," she announces, her tone full of irritation.

Harvey excuses himself from the kitchen table with a quiet, "I need to make a quick call." With a scrape of his chair against the tiled floor, he rises, his footsteps heavy as he makes his way to the sliding glass doors leading out to the patio. The door slides open with a soft whoosh, allowing a rush of cool air to blow into the room. A sense of tension lingers in the air, a silent nod to the issue of Father hanging over us.

"It's getting late," I say. "Time for me to head over to the hotel."

"Harvey booked you into the Ominus Capital Hotel downtown." Ava rises and collects the teacups from the table, taking a brief moment to examine Mother's for cracks. As she grabs mine, she asks, "Why didn't you have tea?"

I push my chair back from the table. "Because your housekeeper hates me."

"Don't be ridiculous."

Mother keeps the peace by smartly changing the subject. "Think about trimming up your hair. It's a bit singed in a few places."

The acrid smell has followed me all turn. I touch my brittle hair and frown.

"It'll be fine." Mother gives me a warm hug goodbye and retires down the hall to the guest room I once occupied.

Chapter Forty-Eight

P lush carpet cushions my steps as I enter my room. No suite this time, just a room with an en suite bathing room. A large, comfortable bed with crisp linens and a plush duvet is the centerpiece of the room. The chaise lounging couch that sits under the double-hung window is sumptuous, upholstered in rich sapphire-blue velvet, inviting me to relax and unwind. A crystal chandelier hanging in the center of the room casts a warm glow. The Ominus Capital Hotel is very elegant.

I unpack a few pieces from my trunks and take my toiletry case into the bathing room. Mother is right; I need to do something with my hair. Especially if I'm going to do something goofy like tracking down Mr. Pearly Whites, a.k.a. Jack Foxx, at The Pink Note tonight.

I'm certainly not waiting till tomorrow.

With the crispy ends of my hair trimmed and my war paint on, it's time to pick out a killer outfit. I choose an above-the-knee flowy chiffon dropped-waist number. Complete with cream-colored feathers on the hem and silver beads in a scalloped pattern on the bodice. To camouflage the dressing on my forehead, I don a pearl-and-beaded circlet. The shoes I choose are gold leather printed with polychrome floral sprays, with a tall heel, narrow waist, and splayed foot that are easy to cut a rug in. I give myself a once-over in front of the full-length mirror. This kid thinks he's a gift, so I'd better look the part of a good-time gal. I grab my compact dance purse and take the lift down to my waiting taxi.

The Pink Note is the hottest and newest club in Capital City, and is filled with patrons of all backgrounds coming together to enjoy a night of revelry and escape. Everyone has their glad rags on. The joint is jumping, and the booze is flowing. Tonight, it features a live jazz band sharing their energetic music with the crowded dance floor.

I keep an eye out for my mark as I shimmy my way to the bar for a little libation. I order myself a Monkey Gland. It's a delicious cocktail composed of gin, orange juice, grenadine, and my favorite, absinthe. All served in a martini glass. A weird name, but a tasty drink.

Turns out, I don't find him. He finds me.

"Let me get that." He flashes me his pearly whites.

I turn my head sideways. "Huh."

"Is that a yes on the drink?" Jack asks.

"Turn your head sideways."

"Okay?" Jack moves his head to the side, touching his ear to his shoulder.

"No, the other way."

He shrugs and moves his head.

"It's you!" I can't believe I didn't notice it before.

"It's me."

"You nearly killed me on that roof."

He smiles. "You wanna dance?"

"You're asking me to dance?"

"Yes."

"Fine." I slam back my drink, banging the martini glass down on the bar. Grabbing Mr. Pearly Whites Jack's arm, I drag him to the dance floor.

The cake-eater is a regular floor-flusher. He has all the moves. The musicians begin playing "The Varsity Drag." It has a lively tempo and catchy melody, making it a favorite for dancing the Hop Bottom to.

When the song ends, I motion to him for another round.

I order another Monkey Gland, and he orders a Gimlet. I decide to ask a direct question. "What did you take from Piers's study?"

"Something that belonged to me." He knocks back his Gimlet and orders another.

Usually, I would keep up with a companion, but I need a clear head tonight. I just sip my drink. "He must have been furious."

"He was mad at me way before that."

"Why?" I wave over the bartender and hold up two fingers. "Did you do something else?"

The bartender brings over our drinks. I encourage Jack to drink faster.

"Do you know he tried to have me killed?"

I act as if I'm shocked by the revelation. "Seriously?"

"But I tricked them. Unfortunately, he got to the formula first." The liquor is starting to loosen Mr. Pearly Whites' tongue.

"Formula?" I bat my eyelashes. "What kind of formula?"

"I wanna dance some more." He wrenches my arm and drags me out to the dance floor. The band is now playing a Foxtrot. Jack is a smudger; you couldn't get a piece of paper between us.

I step on his foot. "Oops, sorry. Must have had one too many."

He limps back toward the bar but stops dead in his tracks.

I see what he sees.

"Come on, let's blow." I pull on his jacket. "Out the back."

The metal door bangs against the brick as I fling open the door. I snag Jack's hand and make a dash for the back alley. The torpedo, dressed head to toe in black, is hot on our heels.

I scan our surroundings for an easy escape and something I can use as a weapon.

"You don't want to go there again," I warn him, adrenaline coursing through my veins.

The man in black sneers. "You cheated."

"How did I cheat?"

"You tried to polish me off in that explosion. You two make quite the team, always trying to take me down," he accuses.

I look at Jack. "So you're the one who set the bomb at Coco Cosmetics."

"He was supposed to take the satchel with him," Jack says. "He wasn't supposed to leave it behind."

The Man in Black growls menacingly and lunges toward me, but I swiftly sidestep, narrowly avoiding his grasp. Seizing the opportunity, I leap onto our attacker's back, gripping him tightly as he thrashes wildly, attempting to shake me off. "Why are you trying to kill us? Piers is dead; it's over!" I shout.

Jack readies himself to strike, pulling his arm back for a knuckle sandwich. However, his aim is off, and the blow misses the target.

The assassin manages to pry my arms from around his neck, causing me to tumble to the ground.

I feel nauseous, and my head starts to spin. I see the boot of the torpedo hovering over my head.

Jack lands a solid punch to the man's kidney, eliciting a pained scream.

I roll out of the way before his boot can make contact with my skull. Lightning starts shooting around us.

"What's that?" yells Jack. Distracted by the flashes of light, Jack doesn't block the blow the Man in Black delivers to his chin, laying him out on the concrete cold.

Struggling to stand, I witness a swirling tunnel materializing before me.

"What on Gaia is that?" Piers's henchman demands, panic-stricken.

"It's a portal." I realize the dreadful situation we're now in. "And I think I know who wants Jack's formula."

I snag a nearby lid from a trash can. "You'd better get something to fight with," I instruct the assassin.

The Man in Black grabs another trash lid.

"We've come to collect what's ours," says a shadowy figure as he exits the portal.

Another figure emerges behind him. Standing before me are two agents of Hyde. The agents are dressed in steel-gray one-piece uniforms. They look more like garbage men than agents. The two burly Hyde agents make a move toward the unconscious Jack.

"This is bunk; I'm no sap." The Man in Black dumps his lid and hightails it out of the alley and into the city.

"Coward!" I scream after the man who has now tried three times to send me to the big sleep.

I take a stand in front of Jack. I can't let Hyde get that formula. But without Jack or the torpedo, I'm toast. "Go back where you came from!" My voice is shaky and weak.

"Look who we have here," says the first agent. "All dolled up and ready for her trip. Dr. Zelda Harcrow."

The second agent chimes in. "We've got a twofer."

They both laugh.

I need to think.

But there's no time.

There's no spell.

There's no help.

I'm in trouble.

Chapter Forty-Nine

The enemy agents come charging toward me, and instinctively, I hurl the lid I'm holding in their direction. It connects with a solid thud, striking the second agent square in the throat. He staggers back, clutching his neck with both hands as he struggles to breathe.

Turning to his pal, the first agent grimaces and says to me, "You're out of ammunition, Doctor."

Summoning every ounce of determination, I muster a burst of energy fueled by sheer terror. With a swift motion, I extend my hand, channeling my focus into manipulating the forces of physics. I visualize removing the friction between Gaia and the agents, while simultaneously harnessing the power of the air molecules around me. With great effort, I push forward, propelling both enemy agents back through the portal.

The portal is still open, releasing bolts of electricity and wild wind. Panic sets in as I realize I have no idea how to close someone else's portal. Kneeling beside Jack, who remains unconscious, I frantically shake his shoulders.

"Come on, Jack, wake up! We're running out of time." Desperation creeps into my voice as I slap his cheek, hoping to jolt him back to consciousness. But he remains motionless, unresponsive. With a deep breath, I steel myself, preparing to deliver another sharp slap.

Before I can strike, I feel a close presence near me. Something familiar.

The portal suddenly closes.

Thinking I see a figure duck around the corner, I rise to my feet. "Father?"

Jack finally comes to. "Hey, what happened?" He rubs his jaw.

"Long story. Let's go back to my place so we can put some ice on that chin." I help Jack to his feet and support him as he staggers to the street. "Must have been my imagination."

"What's your imagination?"

"Nothing. More like wishful thinking." Raising my hand, I hail a taxi.

The drive to the hotel is quiet. Time enough to formulate a plan. I need to know more about Jack and Piers's partnership and the plan to sell the formula to Hyde.

I settle Jack on the chaise lounge with a towel full of ice. Patting the cushion, he wiggles his eyebrows at me. "Why don't you take a seat next to me."

I smile, turn my head, and roll my eyes so hard, they almost fall out of my head. This cake-eater is too much. "I'll be right there. Let me get into something more comfortable." Escaping to the bathing room, I frantically jumble through my things for items to perform a spell and prepare a sweet little mickey to slip Mr. Jack Foxx.

I cut a piece of parchment to resemble a figure. Using makeup, I add features. On the parchment, I write *Jack Foxx*. Anointing a small white candle with thyme and primrose oil, I place it on top of the paper figure and light it. I focus and speak the following spell three times.

"I summon forth the truth, hidden deep within,
To reveal the secrets of Jack Foxx,
Illuminate the darkness, bring hidden truths to light.
As this flame burns, so, too, shall honesty arise,
From Jack Foxx's lips, no more deceitful guise.
May the words he speaks be pure and true,
Unveiling secrets hidden from my view.
By the power of this spell, I command and decree,
Let truth be spoken, for all to see."

I neatly tuck the sedative packet in my stocking garter. Then I strip down to my skivvies, embroidered silk tap pants and bra. Slipping on a shimmering silver velvet robe with batwing dolman sleeves and a fur collar, I make my entrance.

"Va-va-voom, baby," Jack howls.

"Glad you like."

"Come over here, sweetheart, and I'll show you how much I like." He swings his legs off the chaise lounge and sits on my bed.

The buzzer for the room sounds. *Saved by the bell,* I think to myself. "Looks like our libations have arrived."

A young gal pushes in the wheeled bar cart. The chrome bar cart contains everything you'd need to concoct a decent cocktail. An ice bucket with tongs, a shaker, bitters, an array of garnishes, and best of all, whiskey. Handing the gal a token for a tip, I escort her out. Time to make the drinks. I take my time. I need more time for that candle to burn down. With my back to Jack, I prepare our drinks. His with a little something extra in it.

"Here you go."

"Thanks, baby." He attempts to drain the glass.

"Hey, take it easy. That's some top-notch giggle water." I stop him from downing the whole thing. I need him to only take sips. If he drinks it too fast, there won't be enough time for me to get the information I need.

"I hear you." He winks at me. "How about a little smooch?"

"I'll check you later." I move my glass between him and my lips. "How about you tell me all about you and Piers."

"That dope and his doll tried to scam me out of a lot of moolah." Jeff starts to waffle a bit.

"Steady now. How were they going to scam you?"

"Gave me a place to develop my idea, told me he could get me a position with a big alchemy company. He had pull, he said. With his help, we could both be rolling in the dough." Jack took another sip of his drink. "Can I have that kiss now?" He puckers up.

"What happened next?"

"He tried to do me in." He starts to make kissy sounds at me.

"Tell me more."

"I rigged an explosive and put it in a satchel with the formula and a sample of the product. The guy who attacked us was supposed to take the whole thing to Piers. Instead, the dope only took the parchment with the formula on it." He giggles, then abruptly stops. "Why am I telling you all this? What did you do to me?"

I'm about out of time. "Jack, tell me about Hyde."

"I want to cuddle and pet you." His voice is slurring now. "I don't know anything. Can I see what's under your robe?"

"Sure." I stand up, unhook the front of the robe, pull it open, revealing my lingerie. "Tell me why you killed Piers and Sally."

"You're beautiful." In the same breath, he adds, "I didn't kill them. I got my formula back. I didn't need to kill them." He lunges toward me and passes out before he even reaches me.

Fastening my robe, I ankle over to the hotel phone. "Outside line, please."

In a few moments, I'm connected to a number in Fulcrum.

"You said to call if I needed assistance," I say.

"It's good to hear your voice," says Inspector Chance Greyson. His voice is deep and calm. I wish I didn't miss him.

"Can you contact someone at the NSC to come to my hotel? I have a blossoming alchemist here who has come to the attention of Hyde."

Knowing it won't take long for the NSC agents to arrive, I clean up the spell and change into street clothes. The room door buzzer sounds just as I'm exiting the bathing room. Looking over, I make sure Jack is still passed out on the floor.

"Who is it?"

"NSC Agent Q, Dr. Harcrow," calls a feminine voice through the wooden door.

I open the door to the agent, granting her access to my room. "He's over there."

"I'm here to secure the room." Agent Q moves around the room, inspecting every corner and crevice. Then the agent opens the door to the hall. "All set, sir."

Several other agents enter, followed by my new friend, Agent Damon Bronn, and his bluer-than-blue eyes. "Agent Bronn, I'm surprised to see you. I thought you worked in Aladar City."

"I go wherever I'm needed, and it seems I'm needed here by you. What did you give this poor slob?" Bronn proceeds to check on Jack Foxx's condition.

"Just a truth spell, and I sipped him a mickey."

"So, Hyde is interested in this bozo?"

"It appears so." I give him no details of my confrontation with Hyde agents. "The torpedo Piers hired told me."

Agent Bronn points to Jack. "He can corroborate that?"

Knowing Jack wasn't a witness to the events in the alley, I feel comfortable smudging the truth a bit. "He was out cold for some of it."

"And the torpedo?"

"He got away."

"Convenient." He turns his attention to his agents. "Get him on the bed, and let's wake him up."

"Can't you just remove him? It's been an extraordinarily long turn, and I'm exhausted."

"We are going to need your room for the rest of the night and morning." He takes my coat out of the closet and hands it to me, along with my purse.

"Are you serious?" I'm livid. "Where am I supposed to go?"

He takes me by the arm and leads me to the door. "You are a very ingenious woman, Doctor. I am positive you will figure it out."

Agent Bronn walks me down the hall and to the lift. With a ding, the doors slide open, and he escorts me inside. "I don't concede to this commandeering of my room."

"I know." Agent Bronn pulls me in and plants one right on my kisser. "Good job, kid." He turns and walks away as the doors close on me.

Standing in the lobby, I try to figure out my next move. I'm without clothes or even a toothbrush, let alone a place to lay my head. Making a decision, I ankle over to the garage and start up my Zenith.

I have one option open.

Chapter Fifty

"That is quite a story, Zelda." Ethan embraces me and then holds me out at arm's length, giving me a once-over. "Are you sure you're not hurt?"

"I think I've done enough damage to my body already. I don't think I can do any more. I'm just tired." I yawn before asking, "Are you sure you don't mind me staying here?"

"I don't mind in the least; you should know that." Letting go of my arms, he slides his hands down to hold mine. "Follow me. I'll lend you some pajamas for you to wear. I'm sure you don't want to sleep in your clothes."

I follow Ethan into his bedroom and wait as he rifles through his wardrobe for something I can wear.

"This should work. Might be a little big." He hands me a two-piece Larimar-colored cotton-pongee pajama set.

"Thanks." I take the set into his bathing room to change.

"Zelda, I'm going to make up the couch so you can have my bed."

I holler back through the door as I roll up the sleeves of the oversize pajamas. "Ethan, I can't take your bed. I can sleep on the couch."

"Absolutely not. My house, my rules."

"If you insist." I really don't want to sleep on the couch; a nice soft bed sounds fantastic.

As I emerge from the bathing room, my ears catch a sudden clamor from the main living area. Pausing, I strain to listen.

The shatter of glass. A muffled grunt.

"Ethan! What's happening out there?"

As a loud bang reverberates through the walls, I sprint into the main living area, just in time to witness Ethan assuming a defensive stance, his face marred by cuts, likely from the shattered glass of the now demolished coffee table. To my right, the Man in Black struggles to his feet, using the wall for support, before he lunges at Ethan, wrapping his arms around Ethan's waist and forcing him back onto the couch. Ethan retaliates, raining blows down on his assailant's back with his fists.

This wakes up the sleeping bird housed on Ethan's tiki bar.

"Ethan!" I scream.

"I'm a witness, I'm a witness—awk, awk, awk," squawks the nameless horned parrot.

"Run, Zelda!" Ethan yells as he takes punches to the face.

I could run, but I can't leave Ethan in this mess that I have brought to his door. Leaping over what is left of the coffee table and pushing the upended chair out of my way, I make sure my weight is evenly distributed between my slightly bent legs, and then I send my foot flying sideways into the Man in Black's backside, forcing him to his knees on the floor.

"You bi—"

Ethan interrupts the Man in Black's swearing with a right hook to the jaw.

The rude bird squawks at the torpedo. "Shut up, stupid! Shut up, stupid!"

I look at the bird. "It's about time you got something right."

The crude bird screeches at me. "You're a looker—awk. Hot-tot-tot—awk." He lets out a shrill whistle, rocking back and forth on his perch. "I'm a pretty bird, I'm a pretty bird."

Our adversary lies among the broken glass, clutching my ankle and pulling it toward him. I lose my balance and fall flat, kicking at the Man in Black's face in an attempt to free myself. Ethan's eye is swelling shut, making it difficult for him to see. He slides off the couch and lands on his knees, exhaustion evident in his slumped body. With a burst of strength, he slams his fist into the torpedo's belly. The Man in Black recoils and releases my foot.

I scramble to the other side of the bar, using the counter for leverage to pull myself up. Ethan remains slumped against the couch, conscious but immobile. The Man in Black crawls toward the bar, inching closer with each agonizing movement.

The horned parrot ruffles his bright-peridot feathers, screeching and rocking frantically on his perch.

"Why are you here?" I scream at the Man in Black.

"Revenge."

"Revenge for what?" Grabbing a martini glass, I hurl it in his direction. It crashes next to him, breaking into a million pieces.

"For my employer." He pushes himself up onto his hands and knees.

I throw another glass; this one hits his shoulder and bounces off. "I thought Piers was your employer." I need something heavier.

"He was till you killed him." The torpedo is standing now. His face is swollen and bruised, his knuckles red with blood.

I pick up a heavy lead-glass decanter and hurl it at him. He deflects it with his arm, sending it flying into the wall, where it explodes on impact. "I didn't kill Piers, and neither did Coco," I assert. I pitch an orange at him.

"Stop throwing things at me," he says, his voice determined.

"Stop trying to kill me." I pick up the heavy glass ice bucket and heave it at him. He steps to the side, dodging it, and continues to move toward me. I grab whatever I can and chuck it at him, but it barely slows him down. Glancing from the ice pick in my hand to the Man in Black, I flip the pick so I'm holding the sharp pointed end. With it raised above my shoulder, I fling it with all my might.

The naughty bird screams.

The Man in Black stops dead in his tracks, the ice pick protruding from his forehead. My hand flies to my mouth as I catch my breath. "Oh my stars," I gasp. He's still standing, still alive. I motion to my forehead and then to his. He reaches for the pick handle, and I shake my head. "I wouldn't pull that out if I were you." A shiver of dread tap-dances up and down my spine, causing me to scrunch up my shoulders and shake.

"You!" he bellows. He takes a menacing step forward, one hand reaching for me while the other pulls the ice pick from his skull.

At first, blood oozes from the wound, but then the thick, gooey fluid loses its viscosity. His eyes widen in shock and disbelief as the hole in his head begins to spurt bright-scarlet blood. His face turns ghostly pale as all the life drains from him. With a final, feeble attempt, he drops to his knees, then pitches forward toward the bar, collapsing on his side on the now-drenched carpet.

I can't move. I'm glued in place by the surrealness of it all.

"I'm a witness, I'm a witness—awk, awk, awk. You're a looker, I'm a pretty bird." The idiot bird catapults me back into the here and now. It continues to chatter away as I rush over to Ethan.

"Ethan, we need to get you to a healer."

"I think I may have broken a rib or two." He attempts to smile at me. He's missing a tooth.

"Let me help you up." I jump as loud noises come from the apartment's front door. "What now?"

The door creaks and groans in protest as it's forced open, the hinges straining against the pressure. The latch gives way with a sharp crack and a rush of air as the door swings wide open.

A voice shouts out orders in a very shrill but commanding tone. Inspector Zex, shock gun drawn, bounds into the apartment, along with a half dozen or so coppers, including her DSI Snoggs.

Holding Ethan up as tears cascade down my cheeks, I blubber to one of the coppers to get Ethan to a healer pronto. The confusion around me is overwhelming. Inspector Zex orders me to sit on the couch and wait while she secures transport for Ethan.

"You could have gotten him killed. In fact, you both could have bought the farm. I warned you. You are lucky I don't arrest you." Her eyes shoot daggers at me.

"I know. I know." I sob into my hands.

"If you weren't who you are, I'd put you in a hole so deep, no one would ever find you. But you have some pretty important people looking out for you." Zex signals DSI Snoggs to her side. "Take notes, Snoggs." Zex holsters her shock gun and rocks back on her heels. "Now, Dr. Harcrow, I want a play-by-play of what happened here tonight and why you are in Ethan's pajamas."

I sense a bit of jealousy in her voice. I can't relay to her all that transpired before I arrived at Ethan's, but I refer her to Agent Bronn, which seems to calm her down and allow her to accept me donning her crush's nightwear.

The Legere Legalis takes away the body of the assassin, and I finish answering all of the inspector's questions.

As she's exiting the apartment, the inspector turns to me. "Your friend Charden is still on the hook for her husband's murder. Nothing you've done disproves that."

I say nothing.

She looks at the cage with the now-quiet parrot. "He still has this thing?"

The horned parrot hollers, "I'm a witness, I'm a witness—awk, awk, awk."

"Not anymore, you creepy bird. The fakeloo artist copped a plea, so we don't need the jingle-headed bird."

DSI Snoggs clears her throat to get the inspector's attention. "Your transport is waiting, Inspector Zex."

The rude bird whistles. "Zex needs sex, Zex needs sex, hot-tot—"

Faster than a blink of an eye, Inspector Zex draws her weapon and fries the poor bird. The obnoxious bird falls to the bottom of the cage. "Let's breeze, Snoggs." Zex disappears out the door.

"For crying out loud!" I sprint over to the cage. "You really bought the big one this time." My voice cracks. "I know I shouldn't shed a tear, but it's your own doing, running your beak like that."

"Shut up, stupid; shut up, stupid—awk, awk." The now-featherless bird pops up onto his tiny bird feet and shakes his head.

"Unbelievable."

Chapter Fifty-One

"I come bearing gifts," I call out. "Where is Mother?"

"She is at Coco Cosmetics doing what you should be doing." Ava points to the covered cage. "What is that?"

"It's a pet for the kids." I cock my head to the side. "What do you mean, what I should be doing?"

"She is trying to find an alibi for Coco." She crosses her arms over her chest. "I don't want a pet."

"But he needs help."

Eggs and Flo come racing downstairs. "Auntie Zelda, your back."

"I stopped by to give you something special."

"No," my sister says, attempting to put her foot down.

"Look." I lift off the sheet to reveal a naked horned parrot wearing a cut-out sock as an outfit to keep it warm. Its little horn now sits a little more crooked on its head.

Ava gasps. "What on Gaia happened to that?"

My niece and nephew jump for joy.

"What is its name?" Flo asks.

"Can I name him?" Eggs pleads.

"He doesn't have a name," I answer. "Yes, you can name him."

"You mean her," Ava says, correcting me.

"Her?" I lift the cage to get a better view. "How can you tell?"

"Trust me, it's a girl."

Eggs jumps up and tugs at his mommy's skirt. "I want to name her Penny."

"I'm a pretty bird, I'm a pretty bird—awk, awk, awk," Penny squeaks.

Flo folds her hands. "Please, Momsy, can we keep it? Please?"

"Please?" Eggs joins Flo in trying to convince Ava to keep the bird.

"I'll think about it. Why don't you get some peas out of the fridge and feed it."

"Yay!" the kids whoop it up.

"Take Penny upstairs."

Each holding one side of the cage, the little tykes climb the stairs.

Ava puts her hands on her hips. "What happened last night?"

"I have a feeling you already know," I say.

Ava makes us tea.

"Where's the Iron Maiden?"

"It's her turn off. You had a message from a Ruth; she tried your wireless, but you didn't answer. She said the names were a list of guests for her wedding."

"Doesn't matter anymore," I say.

Ava and I proceed to have a civilized conversation. I tell her of my going toe to toe with the agents from Hyde and that I believe Father was nearby and closed the portal. She isn't surprised.

My wireless buzzes for my attention. "Sorry," I apologize to Ava as I answer the call.

I put my hand over the mouthpiece. "It's Mother," I say to Ava.

"Zelda, guess what I did?"

"I'm here with Ava. What's your news?"

"I found a witness who saw Coco working in the lab during the time Piers and the vamp were murdered."

"Who was it?"

"One of her alchemists. They came in to get some pipettes. Coco was so deep in concentration, she never realized they came and went!"

"Mother, you are the chat's meow."

"You got that right!" she says through her laughter. "Listen, I'm driving with Coco now. We're headed back to her place to get a few things and meet up with Juju there. I don't think it's healthy for her to stay at that house right now."

"I couldn't agree more." I hang up and fill Ava in on the conversation. "Looks like happy endings all around for Coco. We solved the explosion, and she was cleared of murder."

"I talked with Doctor Ravenscroft today about the cloudlike substance we sent her," Ava says.

"What's the verdict?"

"She said it's mostly air."

"That can't be." I'm in total disbelief.

"It's made up of some sort of polymer strands. She'll tell us more as she investigates further."

I rub my chin. "I wonder what type of applications you can use it for." I rise from the table. "Ava, I'm going to head over to Coco's and meet up with Mother." I suddenly have a thought.

"Zelda," Ava starts. "I have a bad feeling."

"Me too." I sit back down.

Ava's eyes go wide. "Who drove Coco's car?"

My stomach flips. "Who left the murder weapon in the car?"

Ava stands up abruptly, her chair tipping over and crashing to the ground. "Who has access to Coco's house?"

"Juju," I whisper.

"Mother saw her in the cards."

"Ava, Mother and Coco are on their way to meet Juju now." My body tenses up, and my eyes widen as I raise my hand to cover my mouth. How did I miss it? Too many players.

"Get on that contraption of yours and get over to Coco's now," Ava screams at me. "I'll call Inspector Zex. Hurry!"

I push the Zenith to her max. The wind rips at my face, trailing my scarf straight behind me. I can only hope Mother foresees the danger she's about to face.

Pulling up to the front marble steps, I lay my bike down and race inside the mansion. I can hear Juju screaming angrily through her sobs. They're in Piers's office. I sprint through the grand hall to the stairs. Taking two at a time, I reach the top landing and dash to the study, where I see Juju holding a long kitchen knife to Coco's throat.

My mother is pleading with Juju to let Coco go, but her please are falling on deaf ears.

Juju spots me. "In here now!"

I comply.

Mother hangs on to me tightly.

Coco is frozen in terror as Juju holds the knife to her throat.

I try to talk to Juju. "I spoke with Ruth Cotter. She wants to know what happened to her fiancé, Albert."

Her voice falters, and she stops yelling. "I'm sorry about that."

"Did you—"

"By the stars, no."

In a soft, calm voice, Mother says, "Tell us what happened, Juju."

Juju sucks in a breath. "We were to meet so he could hand over the books Piers had cooked up, along with the actual real ledgers. I was late."

"Go on." I take a step toward Coco and Juju.

"Stay where you are," Juju screams. "Don't come any closer."

I put my palms up. "I'll stay right here. Just tell me about Albert."

"He must have been seen by that monster of a security guard."

"You mean John?"

"Yes, him. I was about to walk into the old laboratory when I saw John strangle Albert. The guard was so angry. I was scared, so I hid in the hall. When the guard realized he had done Albert in, he panicked and scurried out of the room. When the coast was clear, I went in and grabbed the ledgers from the floor, where they had been scattered. Then I left."

"You didn't tell anyone? You just left him lying there?"

"When I got back home, I heard on the VER about the explosion. I didn't know who to trust. I didn't know if that security guard was on Piers's payroll."

I pull my mother behind me to protect her. I know I need to disarm Juju somehow without getting Coco hurt.

"I love Coco," Juju sobs. "Piers was draining the company dry. It's going to go belly up."

Coco lets out a moan of agony—the kind of sound you'd hear from a wounded animal.

"When you came to town and started nosing around, I mustered up the courage to confront Piers."

"You came to the house," I say.

Juju sobs and nods.

"What happened?"

"He was bopping that vamp, Sally. I just saw red. He set things up so Sally could dig her claws into Coco. He took my Coco away from me."

The knife tip digs slightly into Coco's neck, drawing blood. Coco whimpers.

Oblivious to the pain she's inflicting, Juju continues. "I just picked up the statue and hit them, over and over again. I didn't mean for Coco to be blamed. I just ran. I forgot I took the statue with me. I've been holed up in a dive motel in Bunkertown."

"So, you decided to come clean," I say. "That's good. I'm sure the Legere Legalis will understand when you tell them."

"There's nothing left for me. My life has been Coco Cosmetics. I lived and breathed that company." Juju is bawling now.

"You're hurting Coco. Why don't you let her go?" I plead with Juju, looking for some way to distract her.

"She has nothing left either."

Coco's eyes open wide, and she whimpers a small "No."

I've been keeping Juju engaged in conversation, searching for that single moment to intervene before she carries out her grim intentions on Coco, then herself. Out of the corner of my eye, I catch a glimpse of Mother making her move. She deftly snatches up a small glass sphere from the desk beside her.

I give her a subtle nod.

Swiftly, Mother launches the sphere. It zips through the air, narrowly missing Juju's head. Instinctively, Juju flinches, her attention diverted for that crucial second. Seizing the opportunity, Coco wrenches her hand free, pulling the blade away from her neck, and falls to the floor.

Without missing a beat, Inspector Zex springs into action, her body propelled forward as she tackles Juju to the ground with a determined force.

Zex secures Juju and hands her off to DSI Snoggs. "You finally did something right, Doctor," she says, throwing me a sideways compliment. "You should stop by and see Ethan at the clinic."

"I think maybe it's best I don't just yet. Maybe you can go in my stead."

Inspector Zex's hard-lined mouth softens to a gentle smile. "Maybe I will," she says as she exits with her collar.

I sit down next to Coco in the parlor. "What are your plans now?"

"First thing I'm going to do is to dump this heap. I'll use the credits to keep the company afloat till the new lipstick comes out. I may have to lay off some people, but eventually, we'll thrive once more. I just can't believe I was so taken in by Piers."

I place my hand on her shoulder.

"It doesn't matter, does it. The damage is already done. So many lives ruined," she says.

Mother pipes in. "Coco, you should let me read your cards. I can help guide you."

"You won't have time." Father stands in the doorway of the parlor, a massive bouquet of apology flowers in his arms.

As Mother walks over to him, I catch my breath, unsure what will happen next.

"I should be extremely cross with you, Titus."

"As you should be." He clears his throat. "I am sorry I've been unbearable lately."

"So why will I not have time to advise Coco?" she asks him.

"You know that little resort island off the coast of Baekland?"

"The one I've been going on about?"

My father smiles and hands her the flowers.

"You are forgiven, this time. Don't ever disappear on me again, Titus Harcrow."

Father gazes at me. "Are you ready to forgive me yet?"

"I'm working on it." I wonder what his connection to the NSC is and if that's why he dropped off the face of Gaia.

"That is the most I can hope for." He scratches his goatee. "Oh, I think I saw Mae out front flirting with some copper,"

"Mae? What is she doing here?" I run past my parents as they start canoodling out in the hall. "Mae Griffin!"

"Dar-ling!" Mae embraces me. "I hear everything is all copacetic now."

"Yes. All the *i*'s are dotted, and all the *t*'s are crossed. And this time, I didn't fall, I didn't panic, and I did it all sober."

"I am proud of you, darling. I booked reservations at that new spa out west." A small growl emanates from her large shoulder bag.

"You brought the mutt?"

"I can't leave Pip behind." Another growl and yip emerge from the bag, along with a bulge-eyed head.

"That dogacorn hates me."

"Don't be silly." Mae hooks arms with me, and we chat about our plans as we stroll inside.

About the Author

Lisa Hogan is a writer, artist, and photographer living an inspired life in Texas. She loves fast talking racy movies from the 20's and the 30's. She is a mystery addict, a Sci-fi and fantasy geek. She writes what she loves to read and watch. She loves to travel with her family and play in her garden.

Instagram @lisaj.hogan

Email author@lisajhoganbooks.com

Facebook @lisajhoganauthor

Read more at www.lisajhoganbooks.com.

www.ingramcontent.com/pod-product-compliance
Lightning Source LLC
Chambersburg PA
CBHW051519260626
47170CB00003B/684